DIVERTED

COAST GUARD RECON BOOK 1

LORI MATTHEWS

ABOUT THE BOOK

Nick Taggert was injured on his last assignment for the Coast Guard. Now, too hurt to go back to his former position and not wounded enough to be benched, he's assigned as the new Coast Guard team leader in…Panama. They're there as part of a drug interdiction unit, but really, they're Team RECON. Recon as in reconstructed. Each of the four men is like him; a Humpty Dumpty. Except they were trying to put themselves back together so they could do what they loved best, kicking ass and taking names.

Dr. Carolina Alvarez had moved on from research and was working for Doctors Without Borders. A chance meeting with her old boss set her on a dangerous mission to deliver much-needed medicine to South America. Her failure would mean the sure extinction of a tribe clinging to their ancient ways.

Nick should have realized from the instant Carolina walked back into his life things would not go according to plan. But harbored resentment still clouded his vision. Now they were on the trail of the missing vaccine, and the assignment just turned deadly

Diverted

This one is for my friends, many of whom made this book possible, all of whom make my life better in immeasurable ways. Thank you from the bottom of my Prosecco glass.

ACKNOWLEDGMENTS

The idea for this book started with a phone call to a friend familiar with the shipping world. Parvez Mansuri patiently answered my questions and supplied my writer's brain with the fodder it needed to get the juices flowing. He supplied many interesting details that helped not only with this book, but with books to come in this series. Joseph D'Elia (Lieutenant, USCG) similarly answered all of my questions about the Coast Guard and was very encouraging when I told him I was taking what he told me and putting my own spin on it. I couldn't have created Team RECON without his help. Dr. Jie D'Elia also happily supplied me with her pharmaceutical knowledge and helped me to understand the science behind diseases and vaccines. Without these people this story would not have happened. I am truly grateful to them for sharing their knowledge and being so patient under my barrage of questioning. Any mistakes are my own.

My deepest gratitude also goes out to my editors, Dana Isaacson, Corinne DeMaagd and Heidi Senesac for making me appear much more coherent than I actually am; my cover artist, Llewellen Designs for making my story come alive: my virtual assistant who is a social media guru and all round dynamo, Susan Poirier. My personal cheer squad which I could not survive without: Janna MacGregor, Suzanne Burke, Stacey Wilk and Kimberley Ash. My mother and my sisters who told me to dream big. My husband and my children who make my hair turn gray but also make me laugh.

And to you, the reader. Your emails and posts mean the world to me. The fact that you read my stories is the greatest gift ever. Thank you.

PROLOGUE

February 9th, 2021

Alejandro Garcia glanced at his watch and seethed. He abhorred tardiness, and the man was late. Stirring his coffee, he watched people stroll by the cafe window. He, unlike most of the world, hated Paris, especially in January. The cold invaded his bones, and gray skies hung heavy overhead. Even the Eiffel Tower looked dirty and dingy in the falling mist.

Garcia sighed. He found the French to be tedious. They thought too highly of themselves, and their lack of work ethic astounded him. The constant rioting about trivial things illustrated a society too pampered to be taken seriously. He had no idea why the French government tolerated such behavior.

He rechecked his timepiece and took a sip from his cup. However, they did serve excellent coffee, and for that, he was willing to forgive quite a bit.

A black car pulled up to the curb. The driver came around and opened the door. A tall distinguished-looking gentleman emerged. "Finally," Garcia mumbled as his ten o'clock appointment entered the café twenty minutes late.

Edward Langston approached the table, hand outstretched. "Sorry, I'm late. Ran into a traffic snarl. Protesters wouldn't let the car past."

Garcia stood and shook hands. "Of course. Please." He gestured toward the opposite chair. "May I get you something? Coffee perhaps?" It galled him to play host to this American, but it was a small price to pay for the benefits this man could provide to Garcia's country.

"I'm fine. Can't stay long." The men sat. "Look." Langston leaned forward. "Our agreement… I must say I have some misgivings."

Garcia ground his teeth. Langston couldn't back out now. Not when Garcia was so close to sealing his country's future on the world stage. "You don't want to run a live test of your experiment?"

"Of course, we want to run the test," Langston said. "Don't be stupid. I want to make sure you understand the risk you're taking. None of this can come out. Ever."

Garcia nodded. "Agreed. It would be bad for all of us and, yes, we understand the risk. Your mosquitoes will save millions of lives and change the world. We want to provide you with the opportunity to prove their efficacy. Many of our population are affected by mosquito-borne diseases; it is perfectly logical for you to test your theory in our country. As to the other part, that will remain a secret, I can assure you."

Langston hesitated before giving a curt nod. "We have a deal."

"When will the testing begin?"

Langston frowned. "Our people should be in place at the end of March, maybe slightly later. By the summer, we should know if it's working or not."

Garcia nodded again. "Good. The sooner, the better. No delays."

"Obviously," Langston snarled. "I'll be in touch when we're ready to go."

"Everything will be ready to proceed." Garcia forced a smile.

"Make sure it is. This is very important. To both sides."

Garcia's jaw ached. The American's attitude was insufferable. "It will be smooth on my end, I can assure you."

Langston studied him for a minute. "You're sure your boss is on board with this?"

"You need not worry, Mr. Langston. As I said, things will flow smoothly on my end." Garcia curled his hand around the coffee cup and squeezed. He would prefer if the cup were Langston's neck, but that was not in the cards. At least not yet. He reminded himself there must be sacrifice to achieve success. His day would come.

"Fine." Langston stood up, and Garcia rose with him. "I'll be in touch," Langston stated, then turned and exited the cafe. He got into his car and drove off.

Garcia returned to his seat and signaled the waiter, who brought another piping-hot coffee.

Americans. Another group Garcia hated. Not so different from the French. Always thinking they knew better and possessed the upper hand. Not this time. This time, Garcia had the advantage, and things were just as they should be.

CHAPTER ONE

"Bring him over here, Muhammed!" Dr. Carolina Alvarez pointed to the now empty table along the wall of the tent in the makeshift hospital. Two local men half carried half dragged the unconscious man between them over to Carolina and put him face down in front of her. The sound of sporadic gunfire erupted, but everyone in the tent ignored it.

"We found him washed up on the beach," stated Muhammed, the taller of the two. "We didn't want to just leave him there. It would not be right."

Carolina gave him a brief smile as Gabe, a nurse, came over and helped her move the injured soldier onto the table. The man was dressed in military fatigues so helping him could be risky for Muhammed and his son, but they were good people. They put politics and religion aside to help someone in need. Carolina had seen that a lot in Yemen. What the world was told about the Yemenese, and the truth of the matter wasn't even close. Of course, she'd found that was the way of it in most of the countries she'd worked in.

Doctors Without Borders only went to places in need, and most of those countries had political problems.

"Thanks for rescuing him, Muhammed. Do you know where he got shot?" Muhammed and his son Ahmed both shook their heads. The son was the spitting image of the father. It was like seeing double.

"He's not shot." Ahmed turned and mumbled something to his father in Arabic and then said, "Stabbed. In the back." It was hard to hear him over the din of voices in the tent.

Carolina helped Gabe turn the man onto his side. "Take his vitals," she said as she leaned over to see the injured man's back.

Muhammed cleared his throat. "We go now."

Carolina nodded. "*Shukran*, Muhammed," she said, trying to thank him in his own language but he was gone. Probably good he wasn't there to hear her butcher it.

There was a lot of blood soaking into the man's shirt. She peeled it back to reveal a long, deep gash that went right across the man's back from his right shoulder to his left hip. "Jesus. He was hacked, not stabbed." She peered closer at the wound. It was ugly and it was going to take a lot of work to fix. She cursed silently. A slash like this needed a plastic surgeon in a real hospital not a general surgeon in a make-shift hospital tent. She'd do what she could, but it wasn't going to be pretty. "Colin, I'm going to need your help!" Carolina didn't even look up as she yelled for the other doctor. "Gabe, how are his vitals?"

"They suck," he stated. "His pulse is weak and his pressure is low. His breathing is shallow."

"Hang a unit of blood and then grab the portable X-ray. I need to see if his ribs are broken."

Gabe quickly hooked the man up to the IV and then skirted the table and moved to the other end of the room.

"Colin?" Carolina called again as she noticed a birthmark

on the man's right shoulder. It looked sort of like a four-leaf clover. Another flurry of gunfire sounded, drowning out Colin's answer. Just then the flap of the tent was pushed open wider, and a new group of injured were brought in.

"You're on your own," Colin called. "I'll take the new ones."

"Shit," Carolina mumbled. "Let's hope your birthmark is a sign you're lucky." *You're going to need it.*

Gabe came back with the portable X-ray and set it up. He quickly took pictures of the man's torso. After a brief pause, he consulted the tablet on the machine's stand. "Look like four broken ribs."

"That's not good. Okay, let's get his wound cleaned and stitch it up. But first we need to see if any of his organs were damaged either by the hacking or from the broken ribs." She leaned closer. "It looks like it missed his spine completely. This guy is lucky as hell. Half an inch more, and his spine would have been severed."

She heard a grunt and straightened, looking down at her patient's face. The lines on the exposed side of his face were etched into his skin and his eyes were open. They were a very distinctive shade of blue. Like the sky on a cold day in winter. "Hey, can you tell me your name?"

He remained silent, staring at her.

"Do you know where you are?"

He watched her but said nothing.

"Okay, well then, whoever you are. We're going to take care of you. I'm going to give you something for the pain, and then I'm going to stitch you up. You were very lucky."

He raised an eyebrow. "Lucky. Sure." He closed his eyes again.

CHAPTER TWO

Six months later

"You know, Carolina..." said her stepmother as she pointed toward the bowl of green beans on the table. Carolina swore silently and handed her stepmother the bowl of green beans. It was coming. It was always coming from her stepmother. Honey Alvarez loved to lecture, and as a biology professor that was beneficial but specifically Honey loved to lecture her stepdaughter about how Carolina had not lived up to Honey's expectations.

"I'm still not sure why you are wasting your time and talent in your current job when you could be doing so much more."

What? What the hell was this? Honey had found a brand-new angle. Now she wasn't doing enough? "More? I work with Médecins Sans Frontières in hotspots all around the world. How could I 'do more'?"

"I know that you help people in need and Doctors Without Borders is a worthwhile organization, but you could be helping a greater number rather than just the handful you see every day." Honey set the green beans back down on the table. "Carrots please," she demanded.

"Handful..." Carolina couldn't believe what she was hearing. Her father, Ricardo Alvarez, handed her the carrots to hand to Honey. Sunday dinner at its finest. Never complete without Honey pointing out Carolina's shortcomings. It had been this way her entire childhood. She had thought things would change when she became an adult and joined Médecins Sans Frontières but she'd been dead wrong. It didn't change. The nitpicking had only gotten more brutal

Carolina balled her left hand into a fist. "I see more than a handful of people per day. I am providing healthcare to people who would otherwise not have any. I am making a real difference. I help save people's lives!"

Honey swallowed her carrots. "Yes, yes, but look at you. You're underpaid and overwhelmed. You're obviously exhausted, and you look dreadful. This is aging you tremendously. You look forty not thirty-five."

Carolina's mouth dropped open. Did Honey really just say she was old? What the fucking hell was wrong with this woman? She turned to her father, but he had his head down and was busy eating. Heat crawled up her cheeks, and her heart hammered in her chest. She spoke through clenched teeth, "And what would you have me do, Honey? Get a job in an ER here in New York?"

Honey shook her head, sending a ripple through her sleek blond bob. Her big blue eyes looked scornful. "No. That's a complete waste of your talents. You have a gift, Carolina. Your intelligence is a gift and shouldn't be squandered. You need to go back into research."

And here it was. The crux of the matter. She should have seen it coming. Honey had been devastated when Carolina left her job as a cancer researcher and joined MSF.

Carolina glanced at her watch. They'd only made it five

minutes into dinner. That had to be a record of some kind. Usually, Honey had to build up to it, feign warmth and do the usual small talk about her work and her dad's work, and then when Carolina mentioned her own work, Honey would harrumph.

Launching into the lecture five minutes into dinner, ten minutes into Carolina's visit, was a new low for Honey. Carolina's eyes narrowed as she looked at her stepmother. Something was up. There had to be for Honey to skip the niceties that she so prided herself on performing.

"What's going on?" Carolina turned and looked at her father at the other end of the table. "Dad?"

He sat there silently, his brown eyes looking blank. He smiled slightly at his daughter but remained quiet. His dark brown hair lay flat to his head, and his shoulders seemed more slumped than Carolina remembered. He looked old somehow. Older than he normally did. His blue button-down and khaki pants were a little large on him. Was he eating enough?

"Dad?" she asked again.

He smiled. "There's nothing going on, sweetheart. Your stepmother is just concerned for you. For your career."

"My career is fine."

"It is most certainly not fine," Honey snarled. Her fork smacked against the plate with a vehemence that matched her outburst, making Carolina jump. Honey made a show of carefully placing the utensil on her plate. "Carolina, you need to stop wasting time and go back to what you are good at. You need to beg Javier for your job back. You belong in research. You were going to *cure cancer*! How can you give that up?"

Carolina's shoulders sagged. Back to this again. "No, Honey, I was *not* going to cure cancer, and neither was Javier. We were making strides, but the project was never going to work. We needed to rethink everything and…" There was too much water under that bridge with Javier. Her former mentor had treated her horribly in the end, but she wasn't about to get into all that. Honey would just take Javier's side, and her father would stay silent and give her that small smile he always used.

"And I don't want my job back. It's been over two years. You really need to let this go. I like helping those who really need it. I enjoy my job. You need to respect my decisions."

"Your decisions are foolhardy and stupid. You are thirty-five. You should be over this rebelliousness by now."

"Rebelliousness? That's what you think this is?" Heat flooded Carolina's cheeks again. Her fingers tightened on her fork. It was the same argument over and over. She'd listened to Honey when she was a child. She'd tried to please her, but there was just no making Honey happy, at least not for Carolina. She turned to her father. Surely, he would support her in this. She was his only daughter. He met her gaze and then looked down at his plate.

"Dad, do you think I'm being *rebellious*?" Acid dripped off the word.

He locked gazes with her and then sighed. "I think you should listen to what Honey has to say."

It was as if someone stuck her with a pin, and she deflated like a balloon. All the anger drained, and she was left with a big, empty void of loneliness. It was her father's fall-back line. He always deferred to Honey when it came to Carolina. She stared at her plate and blinked back her emotions. Just once, she wanted him to back her up. Just once.

She placed her fork on the table. She couldn't eat anything else. Her belly had soured with the knowledge that she was once again on her own. Carolina didn't bother to look at Honey. Her self-satisfied smile would be in place and seeing the smug expression would only make Carolina feel worse.

"As I was saying, it's time to get serious again. You were building a great reputation that you destroyed, but if you go back to the lab, you can pick up where you left off. You can call it a bit of burnout, but now you're back and ready to throw yourself into the project again. I spoke with Javier—"

Carolina's head shot up. "You spoke to Javier?". He'd been positively abusive when she left, and for Honey to actually speak to him again was a betrayal of monstrous proportions.

"Well, no," she admitted with reluctance. "I bumped into him at NYU. He was there to do a guest lecture. I admit I would have called him if I'd known he'd be so open to your return."

"My return…" Carolina couldn't believe what she was hearing. She quickly glanced at her father, but he refused to meet her eyes and just continued to eat.

"Yes!" Honey's eyes lit up. "He said he would be absolutely thrilled for you to come back. He is sorry you left, and he actually admitted you were the best assistant he ever had. Oh, Carolina, it's wonderful news. You can get your place back and get your career on track again. Now, unfortunately, you have been away for a long time, and there will be a few new, younger colleagues who you will have to compete with in order to gain back your reputation, but I feel sure if you put in extra hours…"

Carolina blocked out the sound of Honey's voice. She was shaking all over. She dropped her fork and curled both hands into fists. *How could she?* How could Honey *betray* her like that? How could her father sit by and do *nothing*? Javier had been a hard taskmaster and showed her no leniency. He had made her work long hours and then refused to listen when she pointed out that his theories weren't working. He'd *thrown* things at her when she finally got up the courage to quit!

She'd had enough. Placing her palms on the table, she pushed her chair back from the table, interrupting Honey mid-stream, and announced she was leaving.

Honey's mouth dropped open, and then her eyes narrowed. "Sit back down," she said with ice in her voice.

Carolina looked at her father one last time, but he only gave her that sad look of his. She turned to Honey. "Yeah, I don't think so." She walked out of the dining room, down the hall, and grabbed her coat from the foyer. She was out the door in seconds.

Forty-five minutes later, back in the city, Carolina leaned against the subway door and yawned. The train ride in from New Jersey had been a slow one and the motion of the train had made her sleepy. The switch to the subway hadn't helped either. Her subway car's air conditioning wasn't working, and the excessive heat in combination with the stale air was making it hard to keep her eyes open. At least she managed to get the spot by the door. She could lean on the doors without having to lean over anyone who was seated and be crushed against all those holding the poles in the middle.

She ran a hand under her dark brown ponytail, lifting it off the back of her neck in hopes of having some sort of cooling effect. Her naturally curly hair frizzed in the summer heat and humidity, so wearing it in a ponytail was one of the only ways to tame it.

She yawned again. The stuffiness of the subway car lulled her, and the smell of sweaty bodies filled her nostrils. She was gagging to get home and stand under a cold shower. Her anger had long since burned itself out, leaving only hollowness in its wake.

She should have known Honey would eventually speak to Javier and then ambush her. It was a classic Honey move. Really, when she thought about it, she was surprised it hadn't happened sooner. After all, it had been over three years since she'd left research to work with Médecins Sans Frontières. Something most parents would be proud of. Not hers.

The subway jolted to a halt, and the usual crush of people pushed by Carolina to exit the train. A second later, she was jostled again as people pushed their way on. Ah, life in New York City. There was always a million people doing whatever she was doing. She'd become quite used to it, but there were times when coming home to New York City didn't seem all that restful.

What she needed was a peaceful, tropical vacation. She still had a few weeks before she was due to go back on duty with MSF. Maybe she would book a real vacation. Honey was right about one thing, as much as it pained Carolina to admit it. She was exhausted and needed a break but going back to work with Javier Florez was not possible.

Memories flooded her mind. It would have been much better had she not gone into research, but she'd been so desperate to feel that her father and her stepmother were proud of her. They were both professors, so research seemed like a good choice.

And then she'd met Javier during her last year of med school. He'd been so convincing. They were going to beat the odds together, he'd said. Who the hell was she to think she could cure cancer? That auspicious goal had been just another of Javier's pie-in-the-sky ideas. He had needed a top-notch assistant who could keep up with him, and that's what Carolina had been.

Until her need to help people finally won out. Not that

research wasn't helping people, but she needed to witness the correlation. She needed to be there, in person and hands-on, to heal people. That one-on-one interaction was the thing that gave her the most joy but it had taken her years to realize it. Years of still not pleasing Honey or gaining her father's love. She would never get those years back, but at least now she was doing something she loved, even if she was feeling burnt out.

She leaned against the subway door as it rattled down the track. If she was honest, it hadn't been all bad working for Javier. He'd taken her in and made her a part of his family in the beginning. For the first five years, he'd been a father figure to her, advising her and offering her warmth that had never come from her own father. He'd even taken her back to his home country, Ecuador.

She went with his whole family. It had been a wonderful experience. She'd gotten to see, from a distance of course, the Tarchuarani people that Javier had spoken so highly of. Imagine in the twenty-first century there was still a group of people native to the rainforest, that eschewed all modern-day conveniences and almost all interaction with other groups so they could live as their ancestors had for centuries. It had been the most amazing experience, and Carolina had been happy.

So happy in fact that she finally got up the courage to point out to Javier that the theory behind the research they were doing was wrong. The results showed again and again that his cocktail was not going to cure cancer no matter what delivery method they used.

Javier had screamed at her, yelling that she was an idiot and what did she know? She was just a baby when it came to research. How dare *she* question *him*? That's when she knew she had to get out. Research was dead to her. She'd been working at it to please others, not herself.

She sighed heavily as the express train rocked on its tracks. Her stop was next. Her stomach growled. Now that she had calmed down, she was hungry. She glanced at her watch. Eight forty-five. She would grab some Chinese food on the way back to her place. It wouldn't be too busy at this time. Most of the dinner crowd would be gone.

The screech of metal on metal told her she was approaching her stop. She moved forward to the opposite doors and waited. The train rolled to a stop, and the doors opened. She exited the train, buffeted by the rush of bodies leaving as she left, and put a bit of hustle into her step. She wanted to get her Chinese and get home to have that shower.

Carolina moved up the long escalator slowly. A steady tide of people rushed past her on the left, running up the long steep escalator. She was always afraid of falling down this set, so she stood still and firmly gripped the handrail.

She stepped off the escalator at the top and started moving toward her exit. A hand reached out and grabbed her arm. She swung around suddenly, fist clenched. She was so startled she dropped her arm. "Javier? What the fuck?"

"Carolina. I am so happy I ran into you." Javier Florez stood there smiling in front of her like a demon summoned from the depths of her mind.

She stared at her former mentor, shock coursing through her body. What the hell was he doing at her subway stop? "Did Honey call you or something?" Would her stepmother stoop that low?

Yes, she would.

"What?" Javier looked confused, disheveled actually, which was weird. Javier normally dressed in khakis and a neatly pressed button-down. Not a hair out of place. Today, he had on khakis, but they were wrinkled and so was his white shirt. It looked like he'd slept in his clothing.

Carolina pulled her arm out of his grip. "I'm not interested in coming back, no matter what Honey said."

Javier blinked and grabbed her arm again then pulled her over in front of the stairs that were set between the two escalators, so they were out of the way of the people exiting. "Yes, I bumped into Honey, and she mentioned you were home and would like to get back into research, but that's not why I'm here. I don't care about that, Carolina." He glanced over his shoulder and then turned back to her. "I mean, I wish you would come back, but now is not the moment to discuss it. Look, I don't have much time. Seeing Honey yesterday brought you to mind, and I need a favor. I dropped the information off at your apartment. I need you to do something for me. You are the only one who can." He darted a furtive look around the subway station again.

Carolina swallowed. This was not the Javier she knew. The disheveled nature of his clothing, his wild eyes, the constant looking over his shoulder... Had the stress finally gotten to him? Did he finally realize his theory on how to cure cancer wouldn't work? Did he have a psychotic break?

"Carolina, I know I must look a mess, and I'm probably scaring you, but—" He looked around and then moved closer. "I'm being followed. I did a stupid thing, and now they are after me. My ego finally got the better of me...just as you predicted." He smiled and, for a moment, Carolina saw the old Javier, the father figure she'd looked up to.

"I—"

Javier cut her off. "I need you to take a vaccine I made down to Ecuador. The Tarchuarani are dying, and they need this vaccine. I can't make the trip. I'm being watched." He locked eyes with her. "I need you to do this, Carolina. It will be the single most important thing you are ever likely to do. You can save an entire group of people. They need you." He squeezed her arm as if to emphasize the point.

Carolina blinked and tried to gather her thoughts. Javier wasn't making any sense. Another subway train had just arrived, and people were starting up the stairs toward them. Javier noticed and pulled on her arm to move her over out of the way. They were standing next to the down escalator now.

"I dropped something off at your apartment. It will explain everything in detail." He glanced over his shoulder again. "I must go before they find me. I will call you in a few days." He let go of her arm and stepped back. "Please, Carolina." His eyes pleaded with her.

"Javier—" A group of people made it to the top of the stairs and moved between them. A man with a Yankee's baseball hat pulled low over his face appeared at the top of the stairs. He was wearing workout gear and had a large gym bag hooked over his right shoulder. He glanced at Carolina, and their eyes locked. His were a cold ice blue. Fear danced across her skin. He turned away and swung the bag hard, hitting Javier on his right side, knocking him off balance.

Javier teetered at the top of the escalator trying to keep his footing, his arms windmilling, but it was too late, and he tumbled headfirst down the escalator. Carolina watched in horror as he bounced, his arms and legs flailing the whole way down.

Someone screamed, jarring Carolina out of her stupor. She glanced around quickly, but the guy with the gym bag was gone. Carolina flew down the stairs to find a battered Javier crumpled at the bottom. She hit the emergency stop button, and the escalator ground to a halt.

Javier was face-up but lying in a heap. There was no doubt in her mind that he'd sustained multiple fractures, and from the odd angle of his neck, he was quite possibly dead. She knelt down and immediately checked for a pulse. Finding one, she assessed his injuries as she dialed nine-one-one.

When the operator came on the line, she explained the situation and that she was a doctor and recited a litany of his potential injuries.

The emergency operator assured her help was on the way.

"Javier, can you hear me?" She frantically looked around. There was a crowd gathering and some MTA workers were coming down the stairs.

Javier groaned, and his eyelids fluttered.

"Javier, open your eyes."

She ran her hands over his limbs and then down over his ribs. She gingerly prodded his neck. "Javier, open your eyes," she said again. He had several broken bones in his arms and legs, and she was willing to bet a few broken ribs. He seemed to be having problems breathing. She hoped it wasn't a punctured lung or worse, a broken neck.

"Javier!"

His eyelids flickered and then opened. "Carolina…" His voice was soft, labored.

"Javier, I need you to stay with me. Help is on the way."

The MTA workers arrived next to her. "What happened?" a short, balding man asked. The name tag on his blue MTA shirt that stuck to him in the heat was Hal.

An elderly woman who was part of the gathered crowd said, "He fell down the escalator."

Another voice said, "I think he was pushed."

Javier's eyes flickered open. "Carolina…I need your help… Tar…"

"I'm here, Javier. Help is on the way. You need to hang on." She checked his pulse. Rapid and irregular. Not good.

"Carolina…

"Don't try to speak, Javier. Save your energy."

"Carolina…listen. Package…you…help…save them."

"Javier, just hang on."

The MTA employee said, "You need to step back, miss. An ambulance is on the way."

"I'm a doctor."

Hal looked to the top of the escalator and swallowed. "He fell all the way down that?" His eyebrows reached his hairline.

The elderly woman nodded.

He looked at Javier. "That's not good."

To say the least. Carolina tried to rouse Javier again, but he'd passed out. A few seconds later, two EMS people came around from behind the stairs. They must have come down in the elevator. They were pushing a gurney. They immediately came over and started working on Javier. Carolina filled them in on his current situation and her fears about his injuries. "Broken ribs, possible lung puncture on the left side. Definite head and neck trauma. The left leg is broken, and the left shoulder is dislocated."

They listened while they worked to stabilize him. A minute later, after putting him on a backboard and securing his neck, they lifted him and put him on the gurney. They pushed him back toward the elevator. Carolina started to follow behind them when someone touched her arm.

"Sorry, ma'am, but I need a statement from you." There were two uniformed police officers standing beside her.

Carolina stopped. She hadn't even seen the two officers arrive. "Oh…of course."

"Did you see what happened?"

"Yes. I—"

"Let's start with your name and address."

Carolina took a deep breath. She was torn. She wanted to go with her old boss, see that he was treated properly, but she knew she had to answer the officers' questions. She let out the breath she'd been holding. "My name is Dr. Carolina Alvarez." She gave them her address.

"So tell us what happened." The cop had his pen poised above his notebook.

"Someone pushed Javier down the escalator."

"Pushed? Wait, you know the guy?" the first officer asked.

Carolina hesitated. This was about to get more complicated. "Yes. He's my former boss."

"Were you meeting him here?"

"What? No. I was on my way home and we…bumped into one another."

The cop's eyes narrowed. "When did you leave the job with this Javier…?"

"Florez," Carolina supplied. "About three years ago."

The cop made a note on his pad. "Did you part on good terms?"

She bit her lip. "Look, I would really like to see if he's okay. Is all this necessary? I am sure there're cameras that caught the whole thing. Why don't you check those out?" She had no intention of revisiting what happened between her and Javier with the officer. It would just muddy the waters.

"So not on good terms then?" The cop made another notation in his notebook. He turned to his partner and said something that was too quiet for Carolina to hear. The second cop nodded and went up the stairs.

Carolina sighed. "I would like to go now."

"Just a few more questions. Tell us more about the fall. You said someone pushed your former boss. Do you know who?"

Carolina swallowed. Those ice-blue eyes would haunt her. "There was a guy wearing a Yankees baseball cap pulled low over his face. He had on workout gear. A navy T-shirt and gray shorts. He had a black duffle bag over his right shoulder. He came up the stairs, and Javier and I were standing near the down escalator. The guy reached the top of the stairs and swung his duffle bag, so it hit Javier and knocked him off balance. Javier tumbled down the escalator."

"So the guy in the workout gear hit Florez with the gym bag, knocking him down the escalator?"

"Yes," Carolina nodded.

"Could it have been an accident?"

She shook her head. "No. No way. It was deliberate."

The cop made a notation in his book. "Then where did he go? The guy with the gym bag?"

"I don't know. I was too concerned about Javier to notice." It was the truth. The guy was gone when she'd looked around. "But maybe someone else saw him."

The cop turned to the MTA worker. "Did you see this guy with the duffle bag?"

The station employee shook his head. "Nope. I was dealing with some unhappy customers when someone banged on the glass and told me a guy had done a header down the escalator. I came down here, and that's when I saw this one leaning over the dead guy on the escalator."

"He's not dead," Carolina snapped.

"Sorry. The injured guy. I'm shocked the guy's not dead. That's a hell of a fall."

The cop turned back to Carolina. "You're sure you saw someone hit him?"

She nodded. "Someone else saw it, too." She turned to the MTA guy. "I heard them tell you that they saw Javier get pushed."

The cop turned to the MTA guy. "Is that true?"

"Well"—the man scratched his beard— "someone did say that, but...it was a big crowd and I'm not sure who it was."

"So you didn't get a look?"

"No."

The cop sighed and turned back to Carolina. "Can you give me a more detailed description of the guy?"

Well"—she paused— "I don't really know. He turned in a hurry. I just got a quick impression of him. Tall, powerfully built." For some reason, she didn't mention that he'd looked directly at her. Could she remember his face? She couldn't picture it. Just his ice-cold eyes. She shivered. The man had scared her even before he'd pushed Javier. Did that mean that all the stuff Javier had said about someone following him was true?

She gave the cop a once-over. He was younger than her, probably late twenties, but he already had an air of disillusionment and bitterness. He didn't seem like he was overly impressed with the situation. She had the feeling he thought she was a bit of a hysterical female. If she told him that Javier said people were following him and that he was in trouble, she was sure he would totally dismiss her.

"Hair color?"

"No idea."

"Eye color?"

She paused then shook her head. Telling the cop about the man's ice-blue eyes would only serve to make her seem more overly emotional. Besides, how much of the population had blue eyes? It wasn't going to narrow down the search.

The cop tried one more time. "Any distinguishing marks?"

Again, she shook her head.

The cop closed his notebook. "Wait here." He moved a few feet away and spoke into his radio.

Carolina sighed. Exhaustion settled on her shoulders like a heavy blanket. She needed to check on Javier and then she needed food and sleep. This was all way too much to take on an empty stomach with little sleep.

"Okay, Miss—"

Carolina cut the cop off. "Doctor."

"Doctor," he said with a smirk, "you're free to go."

"Thank you." Carolina immediately walked over to the stairs and started up. Even though she was a runner, she was winded when she got to the top. The MTA guy wasn't wrong. It was a long way from the top to the bottom, and Javier had crashed down most of it. She would call the hospital when she got back to her place and check on him, but she was worried.

Javier had looked a bit…overwrought, to put it mildly. But what if he was telling the truth? She looked at the spot where Javier had been standing before he fell down the escalator. No. Not fell. He was pushed. He was definitely pushed. Javier was not lying. He was in trouble. A shiver ran down her spine. The man with the ice-blue eyes knew exactly what Carolina looked like.

CHAPTER THREE

Carolina called the hospital and was told Javier was in critical condition. They weren't sure if he was going to survive the night. His head injury was worse than she feared. He was currently in a coma. Should she go over there and offer her support? No. There was nothing she could do, and she didn't want to get drawn into conversations about what exactly had happened. Plus, it wasn't like she was close to Javier and his family anymore. He'd seen to that.

Instead, she stopped for Chinese and then headed home. She'd lost her appetite again, but she knew she needed to eat, otherwise she'd wake up at four a.m. starving, and there was nothing in her fridge.

A wall of heat had hit her as she exited the subway station and had stayed with her through her food stop and all the way home. She welcomed the coolness of the air-conditioned lobby of her building. It was now close to eleven, and all she wanted to do was eat quickly, grab a shower, and go to sleep.

Lenny, the doorman, called out to her. "Dr. Alvarez?" He

was wearing his uniform with his name stitched on the pocket and looking a little worse for wear. The heat was getting to everyone.

"Hi, Lenny. How are you?"

"Good. How are you?" He didn't wait for an answer. "A package came for you earlier tonight."

Her heart skipped a beat. In all the drama, she'd forgotten what Javier had said about dropping off a package for her. "Thanks." She took the yellow padded envelope that Lenny offered. Her name was written across the front in Javier's chicken-scratch handwriting. There was no mistaking the distinctive scrawl.

"Are you okay, Dr. Alvarez?"

"Wha-What? Oh, yes, Lenny. Fine." She gave him a hasty smile and buzzed off toward the elevators. She caught one just as the doors were about to close and rode the whole way up to her floor with two elderly women and their dogs. She recognized the ladies as being from the floor above hers. They met every night in the lobby and took their dogs outside to do their business on the tree just outside of the building. Then they turned around and came right back in again. Safety in numbers. She didn't blame them one bit.

Carolina unlocked her door and entered her apartment. Then she turned and closed the door quickly, making doubly sure she locked it. She threw the envelope on the coffee table not able to hold it any longer.

She went over and started to put the kettle on, but then abruptly slammed the kettle down and walked over and grabbed a wine glass instead. This situation called for a drink if ever one did.

Carolina retrieved a bottle from the fridge and poured herself a glass of Sauvignon Blanc. She headed to the sofa, sat, and tried to focus on the view out her window. She'd bought the apartment about fifteen years ago with a small inheritance from her mother. The city had changed around her and now her building was considered high-end. The apartment was worth three times what she paid for it or more. It was the view of the Hudson River that convinced her to buy the place and it usually soothed her thoughts, but not now. Her mind raced. She glanced down at the envelope on the coffee table in front of her. She didn't trust Javier. Carolina swore as she put down her wine glass and grabbed the envelope. "Javier, what the hell have you gotten me mixed up in?"

She tore the flap of the envelope and upended it. A USB stick fell out into her hand. She glanced into the envelope, but the flash drive had been the only thing inside. Carolina leaned back on the sofa and studied the memory card. Finally, she reached over and pulled her laptop out of her bag and set it on the coffee table in front of her. She hit the power button and took a sip of wine as she waited for the laptop to boot up. Dread filled her belly. Ice-blue eyes haunted her along with the distinctive *thunk* of Javier's body hitting the escalator steps.

The home screen showed on her laptop, so she plugged in the thumb drive. A second later, she opened the drive. It contained several files. Carolina clicked on the first one. It was an image of a shipping document for a cargo of some kind going from New York to Ecuador.

She opened the next file. A formula of some sort—the vaccine Javier had mentioned. He called it Florevir. Carolina's eyebrows went up. Since when was Javier involved in making vaccines? But she wasn't remotely surprised he'd named it after himself. His ego was just short of legendary.

There were a few other files, but the last one was a video file, so she skipped right to that one. She opened the file, and

Javier's face filled the screen. He looked frazzled and old. Like he'd aged twenty years in the last week. He had dark circles under his eyes, and his gray hair stood up in tufts. She grabbed her wine, leaned forward, and pressed play.

"Carolina," Javier said, then stopped and stared blankly at the screen. He blinked. "Sorry. Where was I? Right. First off, I am truly sorry for my behavior. I can see now what a complete idiot I made of myself when you left. Like an adult-sized child. Please do forgive me." He smiled, and in that second, she saw the old Javier. But then his face changed again. The smile disappeared and he looked tired, scared.

"Regardless of your forgiveness, I need you to do me this favor. It is not really for me. It's for the Tarchuarani. Do you remember them? You came to see them with us that one summer. They are dying, and no one will help. I am aware of how crazy that sounds, and right now, you must be thinking I have become a doddering old fool or something."

Carolina took a sip of wine. "You don't know the half of it," she murmured.

On screen, Javier shook his head. "I haven't lost my mind. I can assure you. I am more lucid and saner now than I have ever been."

He paused again and stared at something off-screen. A second later, he started speaking. "I don't have time to tell you all the details, but the short version is this. A friend who is still in contact with the Tarchuarani tribe noticed some of them were sick. He asked questions and discovered the Tarchuarani have started dying in alarming numbers. There aren't many of the tribe left to begin with, so this concerned him greatly.

"Guillermo, my friend, asked to see the dead, but that's not allowed. Instead, the chief gave him a detailed description. They all had the same symptoms. These include red welts and weakness, coughing, shortness of breath. Guillermo happened to be in the village when one of the members passed. He was jaundiced, and by the looks of things, Guillermo thought the cause of death could be multiple organ failure.

Javier stopped again and took a sip of water. "Guillermo wondered if a new disease emerged from the Amazon, but soon realized no one outside of the tribe had become ill. Guillermo himself has been in the village and contracted no symptoms. Upon further discussion with the leader of the Tarchuarani, he discovered a possible source. The pharmaceutical company Biodome Technologies is doing some experiments in the area with mosquitoes.

"The Tarchuarani developed a sort of immunity to mosquitoes over the years and rarely are even bitten. The chief of the tribe said the mosquitoes have changed. They are biting the Tarchuarani continuously. Guillermo spoke to the scientists performing the experiments, and they admitted Biodome Technologies genetically modified some mosquitoes and released them in the area. They are working on a project to stop mosquitoes from spreading diseases.

"As you know, any genetically modified mosquitoes will be more robust than the normal ones, but they also carry different viruses. The one these mosquitoes carry is called the Hestiavirus, harmless to ninety-nine percent of the population. The thing is, Carolina, because of a genetic mutation, the vast majority of the Tarchuarani are susceptible to the virus. Their bodies cannot fight it off. The virus slowly shuts down their organs, and they die.

"Now, I did the research, and I created a vaccine, Florevir." Here he paused for a second and his eyes lit up. "Carolina all that work we did on a cancer vaccine, it paid off. Florevir is a therapeutic vaccine. It didn't work for cancer, but it works for the Hestiavirus. All of our research was not a waste. It's amazing. I can't wait to show you in the lab—well, you don't need the details now, but I used an older vaccine as a base and created something that not only prevents the disease from taking hold but cures those who are infected." He'd lifted his fist to his mouth, as if overcome by the idea of his success.

Carolina hit pause. Javier did it? He really created a therapeutic vaccine? If it was true, it was amazing. Companies all over the world were working on therapeutics for cancer. Creating one even for this new disease or virus was a major breakthrough. She hit play again.

"I sent a few doses to Guillermo, and they were successful. We don't have time for an all-out study and the required trials that we would usually do. The Tarchuarani will be dead by the time that comes to fruition. I'm not sure how long it will last. I feel the vaccine might end up being a yearly shot," he waved a hand, "but that's an issue for down the road. I manufactured many more doses, but they need to be delivered." Javier looked away from the screen again. There were some muffled sounds, and then he came back.

"Carolina, I made a mistake." He smiled weakly. "You know how much it pains me to say those words."

She took another sip of wine. She did. Javier hated to be wrong and outright refused to admit it most of the time.

The smile vanished again. "I called the head scientist at Biodome and told them I knew what they were doing with their mosquito testing and that the tests were killing people. That was a serious error on my part. I thought they didn't know and would appreciate being told, but as I say, I was wrong. Things have changed since I started making noise. Some of my funding dried up. I was also dropped from some boards and asked not to present at certain conferences. I was...accosted one night and told if I were to persist in this manner, bad things would happen to my family and me." Javier swallowed.

"I…cannot risk my family."

He couldn't take a chance his family might get hurt but what about her? Her life wasn't as valuable? She snorted. *Typical Javier.*

"I know I am being watched. I took an enormous risk getting this video to you. I cannot take the vaccine to Ecuador myself. I am convinced I won't make it. But you, Carolina, you can make the trip and take the vaccine to Ecuador. I need your help to save the Tarchuarani.

"Everything you need to make the trip is on this memory card. I had a grad student who works in my lab book passage for one person on a freighter that leaves in two days. I have a contact onboard named Dewey Figueroa. He's the in-law of a family I know in Ecuador. He will help with everything. I know there's not much time, but people are dying. Please, Carolina, be careful. Some powerful people do not want this information known. They *will* come after you if they find out. Stay safe…and thank you."

The screen went dark, and Carolina shuddered as a coldness settled in her chest. She sat back on the sofa. What a strange story. Javier looked demented. She wanted to dismiss Javier as ill or suffering from senility, but after what she saw in the subway, it was hard to discount what he was saying. Javier had actually created a vaccine. This had to be real.

A memory of the Tarchuarani rose in her mind. They were a beautiful, strong people. She hadn't been allowed to interact with them, but their pride and strength came through with every step they took and the effort they spent living the exact way the many generations before them had. Just seeing them had touched her in a way nothing else had. She still had dreams about them. The thought of losing the whole tribe was devastating. That couldn't be allowed to happen.

She leaned forward again and typed in the name of the

tribe. Her screen filled with articles by *National Geographic* about the tribe and its history. Nothing jumped out at her until she found a short Spanish language article on the second page. It was from three weeks ago. Unfortunately, her Spanish was poor. Since her stepmother didn't speak it, her father hadn't bothered to make Carolina learn it. She could understand a bit if people spoke slowly. Even then, it was mostly medical terminology. She certainly didn't use it in everyday life, and what she'd learned was Puerto Rican Spanish not Ecuadorian Spanish. There were differences.

She used the search engine's app and translated the article. It noted an unusually high number of deaths for the tribe. Doctors were investigating, so people *were* paying attention. But were they the right people, and were they doing anything about it?

She wished she could speak with Javier. She had so many questions. Or maybe... She opened the other documents on the drive. There, a phone number for Guillermo. She grabbed her cell and started to dial but stopped. What if everything was true, and they really were tracking Javier? Were they following Guillermo, too? Would they know about him? She put her phone back down. Did she take the chance and call Guillermo or not?

Carolina snorted. "This is ridiculous!" She hopped off the sofa and headed to the kitchen for more wine. She couldn't believe she was actually entertaining the idea that any of this was real. Typical Javier, just assuming she would run headlong into danger to do this for him. He hadn't changed at all. He knew her weakness, her desire to help people so well, and used it against her to get his way. He had done it countless times when she worked for him. It had topped the list of the many reasons why she'd left.

She needed to walk away from this. She had a job where people depended on her. Where they needed her and where she made a difference. That's what mattered, wasn't it?

But she was burnt out. She'd just gotten back from a stint in Ethiopia and, before that, she'd been in Yemen. The idea of a well-stocked lab with running water and electricity and a comfy chair did have its appeal, the small voice in the back of her brain reminded her. A quick trip to Ecuador for Javier, and she could have all of that again. No. She didn't want that. She wouldn't work for Javier.

She told the voice to shut up. She was not traipsing off to Ecuador on Javier's say-so. She wasn't a young, naive, fresh-faced doctor anymore. She was a grown woman capable of making her own decisions.

She stared across the room at her laptop. If the Tarchuarani were dying...

She set her glass on the counter and then glanced at her watch. Ecuador was only one hour behind New York. So 10:30 local time. Not too late to call considering the circumstances. She snatched up her purse and headed out the door, locking it behind her. The bodega around the corner sold burner phones. She couldn't believe she was considering doing this, but *what if* scenarios kept playing out in her mind. Damn Javier. He knew she would never be able to let this go.

Carolina rode the elevator down with more dog walkers and exited the lobby in a hurry. Ten minutes later, she arrived back in her apartment with a burner phone in her purse. She hoped that the movies and TV were correct that burner phones couldn't be traced. Carolina took the phone out of the packaging and plugged it in. Then she sat back down on the sofa and watched the video again.

Carolina finished the video a second time and took a huge slug of wine. Her hand shook as it hovered over the phone on the coffee table in front of her. Should she do this?

Maybe she was losing her mind. She took a deep breath—only one way to find out. Carolina grabbed the phone and dialed the number Javier had provided for Guillermo.

The phone rang and rang. She almost hung up when a voice answered, "*Sí*?"

Shit. "Um, yes, I would like to speak to Guillermo?"

There was a muffled sound, and someone else got on the line. "Hello?" The word was said with a thick Spanish accent.

"Hello, yes, I would like to speak to Guillermo."

"Sí. This is Guillermo."

"Ah, Guillermo, my name is Carolina Alvarez. I'm a friend of Javier Florez."

"What's in the scientist?"

Carolina frowned. "What?"

"What is in the scientist?" Guillermo asked again.

What the hell? She started to hang up when a thought hit her—the beer stein on the shelf behind Javier's desk. The handle was a cartoon man wearing a white lab coat. Javier called it his scientist mug. She took a deep breath. "A baby tooth from his oldest child, a paper clip from his dissertation, and a purple rock from the day he met his wife."

"It is good to speak with you. Javier said you would call. I...was not so sure. He told me about your fight. Women, they hold grudges, no?"

"No. Not always." She already didn't like how this conversation was going. "Look, Javier sent me the stuff, but can you fill in the details?"

"If you have the stuff, you have the details. The travel plans are all there. Where you should be, who you should speak with. It should be easy to follow."

She gritted her teeth. "I understand the travel plans, but what I want are details about what is going on."

"Javier did not tell you?"

"He sent me a short video that leaves me with more questions than answers, and I can't ask him currently."

"Why?" Guillermo sounded guarded.

"Javier is in the Intensive Care Unit of a local hospital. He…fell down an escalator in the subway station. He has a fractured skull and a small brain bleed. He's in a coma."

"*Dios mío.* Carolina, it is not safe for us to talk. You must do as Javier instructed. Write down this email address."

Carolina dutifully grabbed a pen and made the requisite note.

"Do not call me again on this number. Email me from a new email, and I will send you a new number when I have it. Get rid of that phone. Get another one. We'll talk again soon."

"I just bought this phone. It's disposable!"

"It doesn't matter. They'll have the number if they bugged my phone. Get rid of it and get another."

"Wait, Guillermo!"

"We must not stay on—"

"Is what Javier is saying true? Is the danger real? Are the Tarchuarani going to be extinct?"

There was a slight hesitation, and then Guillermo said, "*Si*, God help us. It is real." The line went dead.

Carolina stared at the phone in her hand and then quickly dropped it onto the sofa beside her. What the hell had she just done? Javier had gotten her involved in his mess again. Carolina grabbed the phone and got up from the sofa. She took the sim card out of the phone, grabbed a boot from the closet, and then crushed the small piece of plastic under the heel.

She went out onto her balcony and threw it as far as she could. She took the cell phone apart and broke each section into smaller pieces, and then threw those off her balcony as well, watching them fall into the bushes below. She went back inside and sat down on her sofa.

She reached for her wine with a shaking hand. Carolina knew she should ignore the video and the call with Guillermo. She didn't owe Javier anything. She should just forget everything. Go on vacation like she'd been thinking earlier. It would all be okay. For her.

But not for the Tarchuarani that were dying in Ecuador. For them, tomorrow might not come.

CHAPTER FOUR

Nick Taggert stretched his arms above his head and cursed. Pain ripped down his back. The weights he'd been lifting clanged on the floor when he gave into the pain and immediately dropped them. The whole floor vibrated. That would teach him to do extra sets of lifts. He was pushing his body too hard, and his back was on fire. Maybe it was time to listen. He glanced at the floor. There were cracks in the tile and not just where the weights had fallen.

He grabbed his towel off the workout bench and threaded his way through the makeshift gym while wiping the dripping sweat off his head and neck. He caught a glimpse of his reflection in the window. The scar on his back still looked pretty angry but the redness was fading. His shamrock birthmark remained untouched. Lucky. That's what the doctor had said. He was lucky to be alive. Somedays it didn't feel like it.

He rubbed his dark brown hair with the towel, blotting the sweat before it trickled into his eyes. Panama in the summer was brutally hot and humid. Add to that their current headquarters, an old warehouse that didn't have much in the way of air conditioning or solid internal walls, and the whole thing was one soupy mess. The floor shook slightly under his feet as he moved. Not the best feeling in the world.

The old army ads popped into his brain. *Join the army, see the world.* Well, he'd joined the Coast Guard thinking he would be patrolling the coast of the United States. He'd had no idea that the USCG actually worked all over the world. They maintained a presence on all seven continents much of the time.

Of course not all of the places were vacation hot spots. Panama was not top on his list of places to see. Not that there was anything wrong with Panama per se. It was a nice country with friendly people, which was good since they'd been stationed here for about six months and had done nothing but drink and get to know the locals. Panama was corrupt in all kinds of ways which made life a bit difficult. It wasn't like they weren't doing their jobs, but there wasn't a whole lot for them to do.

There was, sadly, a lot of corruption and drug activity, which was how he and his team ended up there in the first place. The Coast Guard was responsible for drug interdiction. Just a fancy way of saying "go spend time in the jungle and stop the inflow of drugs to the US." Like that was even a real possibility.

Nick walked around the temporary wall that separated the temporary gym from the workspace and went over to a six-foot folding plastic table that was pushed up against the wall. The workspace was really a series of long tables in a warehouse sectioned off from the other areas. The sound carried, and the ceiling was thirty feet up. He grabbed a bottle of water from the small apartment fridge that was sitting on the table and turned around, studying his men as he drank deeply.

The workroom was laid out with three rows of tables with an aisle down the middle and a row of tables running down the side wall. Each table had a chair in front of it and a laptop on it for a total of nine stations. Along the back was a series of metal storage cabinets. "Hey, Tag, how was your workout?" Axel Cantor asked from behind his computer that was set on the left table in the first row.

"Fine. And thanks for checking on me, by the way. I know you felt the floor vibrate in here."

Axe grinned. "Finn and I didn't hear any yelling, so we figured you didn't drop through to the ground floor. And since you were silent, you were either fine or dead. We couldn't help either way."

Nick shook his head. "Nice. When was the last time you worked out?"

Axe looked to be in great shape but, it was hard to know for sure. He didn't exercise with anyone else. Nick guessed it was because, in this heat, Axe would have to take off his long-sleeved shirt, and he didn't want anyone to see his burn scars.

"I did a full workout early this morning."

Nick nodded and took another gulp of water. "Anything come in?"

Axe shook his head. "Nothing but the usual requests for information updates. I already did the requisite paperwork and sent off the list of recent activity, which is bupkes. It's so hot even the cartels are taking time off."

"Bupkes? Is that the formal name?" Finn Walsh asked from his spot one row over and two tables back. He was folding a small piece of paper multiple times.

Axe grinned. "Yes, as a matter of fact, it is."

"Thought so," Finn replied. His doctor had told him to take up some hobby to relax. Finn apparently decided origami would work. Currently, he was working his way through all the animals found in zoos. The whole collection was on display on the table beside him.

"Where are Elias and Cain?" Nick already had a good idea, but he hoped he was wrong. Both Axe and Finn looked up at Nick but remained silent. "Fuck," Nick mumbled. "I'm going to grab a shower and then head over to collect them." Again.

"Do you need some help?" Axe asked.

Nick hesitated. Getting Elias and Cain out of the underground gambling den where they liked to hang out was sometimes tricky. "Yeah, maybe. Let me think about it but be ready to go."

Ten minutes later, after a cool shower and a change of clothes, Nick stuck his head in the door to the work area. "Let's go."

Axe and Finn got up and followed him down the hall to the stairwell and down to the ground floor. They were walking toward one of their SUVs when the end door of the warehouse went up and another of their SUVs rolled in and came to a stop about twenty feet away. Elias Mason was driving, and Cain Maddox was asleep in the passenger seat.

Elias parked the vehicle and got out. He stretched his long jean-clad legs and grinned. "Sorry, Tag. Long night at the tables, but it was a good one." He flicked his curly dark hair out of his equally dark eyes and scratched his beard. His gray T-shirt was loose yet, his muscles were visible underneath. "I definitely need a shower, and then breakfast is on me."

Nick wasn't amused. "Upstairs now," he ground out.

Elias's face slowly lost its smile, and he started walking toward the stairs.

The limp wasn't too obvious, but Nick knew by the set of Elias's jaw that the leg was killing him. He was in serious pain. Sitting all night at the poker tables would guarantee that. "Take the elevator. That's an order."

Elias grunted but switched directions slightly and made for the freight elevator. He lifted the gate with a bang and got in. Then he slammed the gate down and jabbed the button hard. He slowly disappeared from sight.

"Cain!" Nick roared.

Cain opened his eyes and blinked. He straightened up and got out of the SUV. "Taggert," he said as he closed the door. He was wearing black combat pants and a black T-shirt that emphasized his bulging muscles. The top of his black hair was pulled back in a man bun, and his startlingly green eyes had a guarded look.

Cain always looked dangerous, if not downright deadly. At least that's what he'd been told by several of the ladies at the bar where they all hung out. Nick gritted his teeth. To him, Cain just looked like shit. There were dark circles around Cain's eyes and lines around his mouth. Nick would bet Cain hadn't had more than a couple hours sleep in the last few nights. "You have to stop going with Elias. You need sleep."

Cain walked over to the group. "If I don't go with him, he'll go anyway, and being there without backup is insane."

And that was the truth of it. Nick cursed. "Upstairs. Now. All of you."

The guys turned and made for the stairwell. Nick watched them go. The problem wasn't Elias or Cain or any of them. The problem was they were bored off their asses. Even he was struggling. Rear Admiral Lower Half George Bertrand had inherited the group of them. Injured and not quite ready to go back to their respective special operations groups, he'd stuck them down in Panama to work "drug interdiction," but really it was to sit on the bench and heal.

It was all good in theory. Take the top guys and give

them extra time to get their shit together. The Coast Guard invested millions in training Nick and the rest of his new so-called team. They didn't want to lose all that if they didn't have to.

Bertrand had said as much when he'd called Nick into his office about seven months ago. "I have a problem. I've got five of you hotshot operators that are in need of more downtime to get back to operating shape, but the top brass doesn't want you all sitting around behind desks. Apparently, you all get into serious trouble when you're not…engaged in your normal duties. The brass does not want any more incidents like having their top tier operators being arrested in a bar brawl.

"So, you are being sent to Panama to work drug interdiction." Nick's neutral expression must have slipped because Bertrand immediately held up his hand to stop any complaint. "I know, drug interdiction is not your usual bailiwick, but it is now. At least until your back is fully healed and you can return to your unit."

Nick ground his teeth. "Permission to speak freely Sir."

Bertrand nodded.

"Maritime Security and Safety Teams aren't remotely like drug interdiction. I don't know anything about drugs. We deal with terrorists and port security. We—"

"I know what MSST does, Master Chief."

Fuck. He'd pissed the old man off.

"Drug interdiction is not so different from what you do on MSST. Drugs or terrorists, they all come through the coast and the ports. You know what to do to stop them. This isn't up for debate. Now, you're going to be team lead. You'll have four other guys with you. Two from MSRT, another MSST guy and one TACLET. They'll all meet you down in Panama. You leave tomorrow. Good luck and for god's sake, don't let them get out of control. I'm counting on you." That was six months ago. And it was getting harder and harder to keep them all in line.

Nick's phone rang. It was Artie Johnson from Alcohol Tobacco and Firearms. Jesus, finally something to do. "Taggert," he barked into the phone.

Ten minutes later, he walked into the workroom area. The guys were all seated at their respective tables, trying hard to look like they actually cared about what he was going to say. He had to admit he'd been worried about how this was going to work out when Bertrand had told him that he would be in charge.

Cain and Elias were Maritime Security Response Team guys, the Coast Guard equivalent of Navy SEALs. Finn was MSST like him and Axe was part of the Tactical Law Enforcement Team. Anyone of them could have challenged him and given him a rough go but they all had settled in as best they could. He understood that their behavior wasn't so much a reflection on him as it was on their situation. He appreciated that they called him "Tag," instead of Master Chief and included him in their revelry. He was one of the guys but when push came to shove, he was the top guy. The buck stopped with him.

Nick stood at the front of the room. "Look, I know this sucks. You guys have all done a great job of making friends and cultivating contacts, but now you're bored. You can only do so much small talk and drink so much beer."

"We're still good on the beer," Axe said with a grin.

Nick smiled briefly. "However, we're all down here for a reason besides doing drug interdiction. Bertrand wants us to get better so we can get back into the action. We have to work on that as well."

"But how do we do that while we're down here sitting on our asses doing nothing?" Finn's frustration came through, and Nick knew he was only voicing what they were all feeling.

Nick might be their boss, but he was also one of them. "It's hard, I know. I struggle, too, but we have to maintain a low profile and keep working on tracking the drugs that are being shipped to the US. Being backup for the DEA occasionally is fine, but really we're here to just track shipments and heal, emphasis on the healing part."

Elias growled, "We're all fine. Bertrand can kiss my—"

"Don't push it, Elias. We all have to find creative ways to keep our skills sharp without getting into trouble." He met each man's gaze until finally it landed on Elias. He glared at him. "And that does not include gambling all night in an underground club."

"I was establishing my cover and making important contacts in the underworld."

"I think you managed that the first ten times you went. Enough." He met their gazes once more. "You guys need to clean up your act and maybe your appearance. If Bertrand sees your long hair Cain, he's going to lose his shit."

Nick shifted his weight to relieve the pressure in his back. "On another note, Johnson just called. He wants help for another river run up into the jungle." The guys all sat up straighter at this news.

"Are we all going?" Axe asked.

"Fuck ya, let's do this. I haven't had a good jungle run in months." Elias grinned.

Nick frowned. "No. He only wants two guys. It's Finn and my turn according to the rotation. Axe, I need you to be our overwatch from here. I don't trust Johnson's guys to fully have our backs. Follow our GPS signals on the monitors and stay in contact via earbuds. They're still in the planning stages and want our input. It's going to take a bit of time, but we'll need you by the end of the week."

"What about me and Cain?" Elias demanded.

Nick pointed at him. "Right now, you two are going to grab some sleep, and you're going to do it here so Axe can keep an eye on you. I want you both rested and ready to go when we get back." He turned to Axe. "Shoot them if they try to leave."

"Roger that." Axe grinned again.

"When Finn and I get back, we're all going to go on a training mission, so I want you all in top form. Finn, gear up. We leave in twenty minutes." Nick turned and left the room. He had no idea what the hell he would do for a training mission, but he would have to think of something. None of them were any good at sitting around. They were all highly trained men used to being in the fight, and sitting on the sidelines was killing them, physically and mentally. They might not be ready for the main event, but if he didn't find something for them to do soon, they were all likely to implode.

CHAPTER FIVE

Carolina leaned over the ship's rail and stared at the cranes moving on the dock below. A sweltering Panamanian sun and intense humidity stuck her khaki shirt and faded cargo pants to her body like a second skin.

Her stomach churned over her current situation. What she wouldn't give to be back in New York, sitting in a café with her best friend, discussing Amira's plans to open a new clinic in Morocco. Carolina was used to being uncomfortable in her environment, but this situation felt like there was a dark cloud hanging over it. In truth, she'd felt safer in Yemen than she did right now.

The smell of salt water mixed with exhaust from the machinery on the dock filled her nose and mouth. To get rid of the taste, she took a swig of water from her bottle. She had been standing on the ship's deck for only fifteen minutes, and she already desperately needed to take a shower.

"Yours will come off shortly," Dewey Figueroa said as he walked toward her along the deck of the ship.

"Hey, Dewey." She smiled as her contact joined her at the railing. He wasn't tall, only a few inches more than her five feet five inches. He had a lean build, and his calloused hands indicated he did some kind of manual labor. His faded green T-shirt and ripped work pants had seen better days. His warm brown eyes and friendly smile were true indicators of his Ecuadorian heritage. He'd been kind to her since the first moment they'd met on the dock in New York a week ago.

"Thank you, Dewey."

"For what?"

"For getting me this far. You took good care of me on the ship, as you promised."

"My pleasure, Carolina." He touched her on the arm. "I know you're nervous. Don't worry. I'll make sure you are safe through the next bit as well. Javier is a family friend. I wouldn't want to let him down."

The crane picked up a container three away from hers. She'd kept close tabs on her red container since the moment they'd loaded it on the ship back in New York. Lives depended on its contents. She wasn't sure why Javier had paid for the whole container. The vaccine was made into a powder and packed as single doses in small vials. The whole lot was less than a standard pallet, but Javier had packed the syringes in the same pallet to fill it. The saline needed to reconstitute the vaccine once she arrived in Ecuador was only two pallets, so they didn't need the whole container space, but she assumed Javier didn't want too many eyes on it. Sharing a container would have meant it was less of a secret.

"Tell me why we have to leave this ship at this end of the canal. Wouldn't it make more sense to take the ship through the canal and offload the cargo on the other end if we need to switch ships?"

Dewey glanced around. "Please don't ask questions like that quite so loudly or out in public."

She blinked and tried once again to re-frame her thinking. When she was posted overseas, she knew to avoid asking too many questions but then there were people around that she knew and trusted. Except for Dewey, she was all on her own here. She hated not having a better understanding of the whole picture. It put her at a distinct disadvantage. Knowing who to speak to and what to say was always key in dangerous situations. It made her queasy that she only had Dewey to rely on. *Thank God for him.*

"You're in a time crunch," he explained. "That's why we get off here. If we stay on this ship and go through the canal, the process takes longer and costs more. If we leave and drive to the other coast, we can meet the other ship and get underway to Ecuador a day earlier with a lot less hassle from customs."

She studied his face, but he gave off nothing to indicate he was lying. Still, it seemed odd.

Dewey sighed. "Carolina, we're trying to move your cargo through with as little fuss as possible. Javier said he wanted the drugs through quickly and quietly. This is how we accomplish that. Please don't ask any questions. They could lead to difficulties for all of us." Dewey stared at her, making his meaning clear.

Once the cargo was unloaded, it would be put on a truck and driven across the country and then put back on another ship and sailed down to Ecuador. People moved cargo this way all the time or, at least, so Dewey said. It saved a lot of time and money. Major shippers had been doing it for years. What they were doing wasn't technically illegal, but it was certainly unorthodox, and that made her nervous.

The paperwork she had for the cargo would probably raise a lot of red flags under normal circumstances. She wasn't sure what kind of deal Javier and Dewey cooked up, but Dewey seemed confident they would get the cargo through customs with no problems. That part probably *was* illegal.

She nodded. Dewey was right. The fewer questions asked, the better. She had no interest in spending time in jail for trying to smuggle drugs through the Panama Canal. She wasn't entirely sure about the legality of taking the vaccine through Panama, but it certainly would attract attention.

The memory of Javier lying at the bottom of the escalator came to mind, and she shuddered. Attention was a bad thing. It had Javier hanging on to life by the merest of threads.

But if taking the container off the ship and driving it across Panama was the best way to proceed, she needed to accept that and move on.

Carolina held her breath as the crane picked up her container. Dewey nudged her arm and gestured toward the gangplank. She reached down, grabbed her duffle bag, and followed Dewey off the ship.

As they weaved their way along the dock, she lost sight of the red container. Dewey better know what the hell he was doing. If she lost the vaccine, people would die, and she wouldn't be able to live with herself if that happened. Since her mother's death in a car accident when she was just a baby, she'd made it her mission in life to beat death at its own game. Delivering the vaccine was just another round in that war.

They walked up a couple of steps, entered a makeshift building, and came to a stop in front of the customs counter. The uniformed official assessed her, Dewey, and then the paperwork Dewey had handed him. He spoke to Dewey in Spanish. Carolina tried to follow along, but they conversed too quickly for her to keep up. She only caught a word or two here and there. She wanted to ask Dewey what the customs agent said, but after their last conversation, she thought it would be better to keep her mouth shut.

She took in her surroundings: a modular building, not

unlike a container itself. The windows at the rear had air conditioning units blocking their lower half, dimming the interior. A bare bulb in the ceiling added light, but the room remained relatively dark. The AC units weren't pumping out much cool air. Carolina wiped sweat off her forehead with her rolled-up sleeve.

The counter divided the building in half. The front part was for people declaring their cargo, and the back half was for customs employees. Two agents sat in the back behind desks while two other desks remained empty.

The place smelled like stale sweat with a bit of burnt coffee thrown in, courtesy of the coffeemaker on a small table in the corner. She looked up and noticed a camera in the back corner of the room and glanced over her shoulder to confirm there was one in the front corner, too, above the door. She turned back and focused on the Panamanian officials at the counter.

The conversation between Dewey and the officer went back and forth for a minute or two. Dewey leaned across the desk to point out something on one of the customs forms the officer was holding. The officer nodded.

If Carolina had blinked, she would have missed the exchange; they were that smooth. Dewey had dropped an envelope on the counter, and the customs officer scooped it up and tucked the envelope up his sleeve. The exchange was over in seconds, and the men's bodies had blocked the cameras. *Not their first rodeo.*

Did Javier know Dewey was good at this sort of thing? Family friend or not, Dewey was a smooth operator and just the sort of guy needed in this situation.

The customs officer took the paper back over to his desk, stamped it, and returned to the counter. Handing the paper to Carolina, he said in clear, crisp English, "Have a nice day."

"Um, you too," Carolina mumbled before she followed

Dewey out of the office. So the customs guy spoke English. She should have guessed as much. *Note to self, things are not always as they appear.* She would do well to remember that. The learning curve for this experience was super steep, and something told her she was going to need to up her game if she was going to survive.

Dewey glanced at her and laughed. "Most people here speak perfect English."

"Good to know." Glancing around, she asked, "Where's the container?"

"It's already been loaded on a truck. The driver is waiting for us."

"I thought we just got through customs. How could they have loaded it already?"

Dewey picked up his pace. "That's for show and so they can get paid. They would have told us earlier if they were going to yank the cargo."

They weaved their way back down the dock through towering rows of corrugated metal boxes. At the end of the line, there was a row of trucks waiting for their new loads. Carolina searched around until she spotted it. "Zero, one, eight, five. There! That's the container." She pointed to a truck on the far side of the dock.

Dewey nodded, and they walked over and banged on the driver's side door. The driver stuck his head out the window. He had long black hair tied in a ponytail and a full, shaggy black beard. His arm was covered in tattoos, and his face looked weathered and downright dirty. The driver grunted something and waved at Dewey. Dewey waved back and gave the man a smile. The man smiled in return, and Carolina instantly wished he hadn't. His teeth were black and rotting. Dewey started around the other side of the truck, and she reluctantly followed.

Dewey opened the passenger door and nodded at

Carolina. When she hesitated, he smiled in encouragement. "Don't worry. José's a friend. I know he looks scary, but he won't hurt you."

She frowned at him but didn't move. Did she want to do this? The sharp jab in her belly said no, but she didn't have much choice. If she didn't get in the truck, the Florevir vaccine couldn't get to its destination. Her belly cramped again, but she climbed into the cab of the truck anyway.

José gave her the once-over. He had piercing blue eyes, which sadly lingered on her chest. She glared at him, but he didn't care. She sat on the bench seat and slid to the middle, right beside José. Dewey climbed up and sat next to her. He exchanged more words with the driver, they performed some sort of handshake right in front of her, and then Dewey settled back into the seat.

Carolina did her absolute best not to touch the driver. His dirty jeans and formerly white tank top had definitely seen better days. She sent up a silent prayer of thanks that the windows were open because he stunk like body odor mixed with spicy food.

José reached down, grabbed the gearshift, and slammed it into gear. His arm hit her leg. They started rolling down the dock toward the exit. He hit her leg again when he shifted a second time.

Carolina glanced at him. "How long will the drive to the coast take?"

The driver grumbled, "About an hour and a half." His thick accent made him difficult to understand.

She hazarded another glance at the driver. He appeared taller than Dewey, although she couldn't tell for sure. He seemed to be all-around bigger than Dewey, too, but not fat. He suddenly glanced her way, and their gazes met. Carolina again noted the blueness of his eyes—disconcerting because they were so different from the rest of him. At least he wasn't stoned. Of course, he could be using drops to keep the whites of his eyes clear, but he didn't seem the type to bother with subterfuge.

When he shot her a smile, she almost gagged. The rank odor of this man on top of his rotting teeth were enough to make her feel queasy. She closed her eyes and cursed Javier for putting her in this situation. She was even angrier with herself for letting it happen.

They'd left the port city and were now traveling along a busy motorway. The traffic was heavier than she'd expected with quite a few other trucks on the road. It really could have been any highway in the southern United States. Palm trees and brightly colored flowers lined the highway but it was the occasional monkey in the trees that reminded her she wasn't back home but here in Panama.

At least the drive would be quick. The clamminess of her skin reminded her she hadn't had a real shower in…a while, and the rest of her wanted to feel safe. She'd lost her peace of mind some time ago after viewing the video from Javier. Out of all the war zones and developing nations she had worked in, she never felt as alone as she did at this moment. This wasn't like working for Doctors Without Borders. The fear that niggled the back of her neck didn't come from worry over being shot at, but from knowing there really was no backup to help her if things went bad.

She had been determined but terrified when she'd met Dewey on the dock in New York. Javier had left directions on when and where to meet the man, and from that point on, Dewey had taken her under his wing. The trip down hadn't been so bad. Her cabin had been basic but adequate, but she had to walk down the hall to a bathroom that she shared with the crew, which had made her a bit nervous. She always showered as quickly as she could—not that everyone hadn't been nice to her. Maybe "nice" was too strong a word. They'd been distant but polite.

She shifted her weight as José hit her leg again with the gearshift. She glanced at her watch. Halfway there. The tropical foliage gave way to small towns as they drove, and then it was like the forest gobbled them up again and it was just a sea of green with bursts of color out of the window. She gritted her teeth. She could do this. They would get to the other side of Panama, then board another ship. In a couple of days, all of this would be over.

She tried to relax her shoulder muscles and concentrate on the wonderful colors flying past. It really would have been a lovely drive if she'd been there on vacation. Instead, unease lurked in the pit of her stomach.

The truck suddenly turned hard to the right, and she fell against José, then back toward Dewey. "What's going on?"

"We have to leave the highway here and be checked," said Dewey, indicating a turn-off ahead where Carolina saw a bunch of trucks lined up on the narrow side road. It wasn't a wide exit. Just a one lane affair that disappeared around the curve with jungle encroaching on the right.

"Okay. How long will that take?"

Dewey smiled. "Not long for us."

"Why?"

"Because we're not being checked." The other trucks had rolled to a stop in a line that led to a weighing station, but José took another right turn that had been hidden by the curve and kept going down a narrow two-lane road surrounded by lush vegetation on either side. They appeared to be driving away from civilization and into the unknown.

Her heart stuttered in her chest, as if she needed any further indication this wasn't good. "Where are we going?"

"We can't be searched, so we're going to take a back road

the rest of the way. Don't worry. We'll be fine." Dewey smiled at her. Usually his smile reassured her, but not this time. Panic crawled its way slowly up her chest to her throat. Her instincts screamed this was all wrong. The road narrowed further, and its painted lines disappeared.

"Dewey, we should go back." She clenched her hands together in her lap until her knuckles were white.

"No. This is fine. I told you before. José is a friend. We'll be fine."

She glanced at the driver, but he stared out at the road ahead. "Be that as it may, I'd like to go back to the highway." She swallowed hard and tried to remain calm. She trusted her instincts, and they were screaming at her to get out of there.

Dewey patted her arm. "The highway would mean being caught for sure. You don't want to be caught. Trust me. Everything is okay."

Her palms were slick with sweat. "No, Dewey. I really would like to go back to the highway. I'm willing to risk being caught. I can explain everything." And even if she couldn't, speaking with the authorities was better than dying in a ditch somewhere in the remotest regions of Panama. "Please, let's go back to the highway."

She silently cursed Javier. She should have just delivered the Florevir to Dewey and had him bring it all the way to Ecuador, the hell with Javier. But she knew why Javier wanted her there. Guillermo needed help reconstituting the vaccine and administering it, but he also needed a doctor on hand in case something went wrong when the Tarchuarani received the Florevir. She was well versed in emergency medicine and familiar with side effects from her former work in research. Who better than her to recognize if things were going south?

Dewey's phone went off. He glanced at the screen, then

his watch. He texted something and put his phone back in his pocket.

"What's going on?" Cold sweat trickled down her back as the hair on her arms stood up.

Dewey smiled at her again. "Nothing. Just my wife."

"Dewey, I want to go back. Now." Her tone left no room for argument.

Dewey lifted his hands as if to appease her. "Fine. We'll go back. We can turn around after the next big bend, okay?"

Carolina nodded. They drove in silence for a minute or two before a large curve in the road appeared. As they rounded the bend, they saw a black pickup truck ahead, blocking the road. Two men stood in front of the vehicle, cradling machine guns.

"Dewey?" Fear made her voice squeak.

Dewey frowned and blinked a couple of times. Uncertainty crossed his features.

Her stomach sank as their truck screeched to a stop. She glanced at José, looking for help, but he impassively stared straight ahead.

She turned again to Dewey. He glanced at her and licked his lips. "It's okay. No problem. We'll deal with it."

The two gun-wielding men walked toward their truck but then stopped about thirty feet out. The shorter of the two wore a red bandana around his neck and a pair of old cargo shorts. He pointed his large machine gun at the windshield of the truck. Carolina held her breath. If she got shot and left for dead on the side of a dirt road in Panama, her stepmother would never let her hear the end of it.

The gunman motioned Dewey out of the truck. The other one, who wore a stained, gray T-shirt and had a bushy beard shot through with gray, yelled something Carolina couldn't hear, but José put his hands up. Her heart slammed at her ribcage as she did the same. She couldn't wrap her brain around the scene playing out in front of her. This couldn't be happening.

Dewey slowly opened the door and climbed out of the cab. He closed the door, and Carolina lost sight of him until he was in front of the truck with his hands up, about twenty feet from the men. They motioned for him to halt, then said something that had him nodding.

"What are they saying?" she asked José.

He shrugged. "Something about the drugs."

The man with the red bandana moved closer to Dewey. They seemed to be having a friendly chat now, and Dewey dropped his hands. Carolina tried to marshal her body's response. Her hands, which were still in the air, shook violently, but she couldn't make them stop. Her throat closed, causing her to breathe unevenly. Working for MDF had led her into all kinds of difficult situations, but she'd always had backup. This was a whole new level of stress. She had no readily available coping strategies for this surreal scene.

The gunmen relaxed. Dewey, who'd seemed worried before, suddenly appeared almost jovial. Was it relief that made him suddenly happy? The gunman next to Dewey smiled. They were sharing a joke. Carolina had a sinking feeling the joke was on her.

The chatty gunman's phone went off. He answered, said a couple of words, and hung up. He stepped back and motioned her and José out of the truck. Carolina slid to the right side of the truck and got out. When her feet hit the ground, her knees buckled, but she caught the door and pulled herself back to a standing position.

She stumbled around the front of the truck, her knees still wobbly, and came to a stop about ten feet behind Dewey.

He turned and smiled at her. "You're okay, Carolina.

These men will not hurt you." She wanted to believe him, but her instincts said otherwise.

"Unfortunately," Dewey continued, "they will be taking the drugs."

"But you have to convince these men not to take the drugs. Lives depend on it."

He grinned. "I am truly sorry, Carolina. You seem like a nice lady, but did you really think you could travel with a shipment of illegal drugs and not be hijacked?"

When she stepped forward, the tall, bearded gunman swung his weapon around and pointed it at her. She stopped. Her heart pounded in her chest. "Dewey, these drugs—they aren't what you think."

"Do you know what I think? I think they are an experimental drug. Designer drugs are all the rage these days. No doubt these will fetch a lot of money. I know you were bringing them down here to test them on us, but now we'll ship them back to test them on you. And we'll make a lot of money doing it."

"But, Dewey, what about Javier? I thought you two were friends."

He shrugged. "We are. But the money I will make from this deal will buy me new friends."

"But—"

"Shut up," said the bandana-wearer. Now he, too, was pointing his gun at Carolina.

She looked behind her where José stood leaning against the front of the truck with his hands up like he was just along for the ride, and he found this all really boring. The tall gunman pointed at him and shouted, "Keys."

José tossed him the keys.

The shorter guy used his gun and gestured for Carolina to move farther away. She stepped back. Dewey walked toward her side of the truck. She couldn't let them go without trying one more time. "Dewey, these drugs—"

"Enough!" A hard man replaced the guy she'd thought was a friend. "Move away and be thankful we haven't killed you...or worse." His lips curled into a sneer, and he leered at her. She took an involuntary step back.

Dewey and the bandana guy climbed up and into the truck. Dewey threw Carolina's bag out the window. "There. Be happy you got that much."

The bearded gunman got in the vehicle that had been blocking the road and drove off. The truck started to roll. Carolina wanted to scream at the top of her lungs, but her throat had completely closed up. Her heart lurched as if it were on the brink of stopping. The Tarchuarani were going to die because she couldn't get the vaccine to them. Their blood would be on her hands. Her belly dropped to her knees as she watched the truck disappear down the road.

It took a full thirty seconds after the truck disappeared for her lungs to be able to function again, and she drew in a deep, staggering breath. Turning, she jumped at the sight of José standing directly across from her on the other side of the narrow road. She'd forgotten about him. *Oh, fuck.*

For maybe the second time in her entire life, she was paralyzed by fear. The first time had been when Javier, her mentor and supposed advocate, started throwing beakers at the wall over her head and cursing at her. Now she was alone in the wilds of Panama with a man she knew nothing about. Why didn't it surprise her that Javier was involved in this horrible situation, too?

She stared at the driver. "What is the fastest way back to civilization?"

José nodded back in the direction they'd come. Carolina stooped and picked up her duffle bag. Her hands shook as they closed around the straps, and it took her a few seconds to get her breathing calmed down enough so she wasn't gasping for breath. Straightening, she put the bag across her body and started walking toward help.

Carolina heard a sound and looked behind her. In José's hand was a big shiny black gun, and it was pointed directly at her.

CHAPTER SIX

He'd been shocked to see Dr. Carolina Alvarez walk out of the Panamanian customs area with Dewey. What's the expression? Of all the gin joints in all the world, here was the doctor who had made a mess of his back and was now smuggling drugs. He'd always thought if he ever saw her again, he'd just shoot her but this...this was so much better.

Despite the gun in his hand, Nick smiled at the woman looking at him wide-eyed. She had no clue who he was. Then he remembered his disguise, which included rotten teeth.

"Are you fucking for real?" Carolina yelled at him. "*Now* you bring out your gun?"

Nick lowered the gun and shrugged. "A Glock against a couple of machine guns is not a fair fight. Plus, they didn't shoot."

"Wait! Where's your accent, José? You had a thick accent before." She'd gone pale.

He smiled again. This was going to be fun. "So many things in Panama are not what they seem. Anyway, why don't you take a seat on the side of the road? My people will be here in a minute."

"Who are your people? And can they help me get my shipment back?"

Nick laughed. "No, they cannot." The audacity of this woman blew his mind. "Your shipment is long gone."

Carolina's hands balled into fists. "Someone must be able to help me. The police even. I have to have those drugs back."

This drug-smuggling doctor wanted the police to help her? Nick shook his head. She was either incredibly stupid, which he knew from their previous interactions wasn't true, or she thought all the cops down here were as crooked as she was. If that were the case, this pretty smuggler would be in for a rude surprise when meeting his pal, Captain Martinez of the SENAFRONT, the local border police, who was as honest as the day was long. "No one is going to help you, so just take a seat and wait for my people."

"I'm going back to that weighing station," she declared. She turned and started walking down the road.

Exhaustion hit Nick like a wave. He'd just come back from being backup for a DEA raid that had taken a week to plan and execute. He'd already been up for twenty-four hours when Dewey called asking for help on this little adventure. Nick needed food, a hot shower, and sleep, not necessarily in that order. The fake beard itched like crazy, and the stuff on his teeth tasted horrible. This woman had been part of the incident that screwed up his whole life, and she didn't even remember him. He had no fucks left to give. Nick raised the gun and fired, the bullet hitting the dusty road about two feet in front of the crazy bitch.

"Jesus fucking Christ!" she shouted. "Have you lost your mind?"

"Sit the fuck down!" Nick roared back. He was done being nice.

Her mouth opened, then she snapped it shut. She slowly

eased her duffle bag to the ground and sat down on the road beside it, all the while staring at him with hatred in her eyes.

Big deal. The feeling was mutual. He just wanted this to be over so he could go back to Colón and sleep. He didn't need the flood of memories seeing her had brought. The time in the makeshift hospital with her. The agony of his wound. He had spent the last year trying to forget all of it. His back was reminder enough.

Two minutes later, the sound of engines reached his ears and then, within seconds, two SUVs rounded the curve and halted in front of them. Carolina hopped to her feet, but he waved her back down.

Finn was in the passenger seat of the first black SUV. He already had the window down and a gun pointed at Carolina. Behind the wheel, Axe put down the window. "Jesus, Tag, you look like hell."

"Thanks. What took you so long? I thought you were going to back me up. If things had turned to shit, I'd have been a dead man."

"We ran into a traffic jam." Axe shook his blond head. "I told you this setup would be hard to do." He adjusted his sleeves so that they covered his arms to his wrists.

"Wasn't like I had a choice," said Nick. "Dewey and his people were calling the shots. Anyway, mission accomplished. Let's get her loaded in and back to the office. I want this sorted out ASAP. I'm supposed to be on vacation this week." He walked around the front of the SUV to the passenger side. "Stand and place both hands out in front of you."

Carolina looked up at him. "What?"

"You heard me."

"I don't understand," she said as she stood. "Are you arresting me?"

"Now you're getting the picture." Could she really be so dense? No, not dense, incredulous that this was happening to her. He smiled as he pulled out a zip tie and secured her wrists in front of her. Then he marched her to the blue SUV, where he opened the tailgate and helped her up. He pushed her down onto one of the benches that ran along the sides of the vehicle. Elias came from the front of the vehicle and hopped up into the back, sitting down opposite of her.

"Tag, man, you stink. I'm glad I'm riding back here."

"Yeah, well, it's part of my earthy charm. See you at the office," Nick said as he hopped down from the back of the truck and closed the tailgate. He knocked on the roof, letting Cain know he was good to go.

Then he went over and climbed into the black SUV. Axe and Finn both turned to look at him. He settled in the soft seat and dropped his window. "You guys might want to put your windows down. I haven't showered in a while."

An hour later, the two vehicles pulled into a large warehouse in Colón. The gates rolled closed after the black SUV, and the men disembarked.

Nick hopped out. "Elias, take her up to interrogation. Let her stew for a bit while I grab a shower and some food. I'll take the first run at her in an hour or so. She seems like a bit of a cream puff, so it shouldn't take long until she starts talking."

"Will do, Tag. Hey, Axe, it's your turn to clean the SUVs. Add a pile of air fresheners, too—like industrial strength. Taggert stunk it up."

"Ha, ha," Nick said as he crossed the floor to the freight elevator. Within ten minutes, he stood under the hot spray of a shower, letting the warmth work its magic. He scrubbed every inch of his body twice over and did the same with his hair. He'd thrown the beard in the trash before he entered the shower and now, he rubbed his face to get rid of the adhesive and used extra shampoo to get rid of the goo that had held his fake ponytail in place.

Usually, he grew his own beard before he did any kind of undercover gig, but Dewey had called him out of the blue yesterday. Something had happened to the regular guy and, at the last minute, he needed a stand-in. He had been slowly building a good rapport with Dewey over the last few months. He hung out at a bar Dewey frequented and sometimes bought him beers which would hopefully lead to more contacts in the drug trade. Dewey knew him as a down on his luck American who spoke a little Spanish since his mom was Puerto Rican. His cover was as a day laborer and sometime delivery driver.

Nick let the warm water hit between his shoulder blades. Even now, his muscles hadn't relaxed from the morning's adventures, as if they knew something bad was still coming.

An off-kilter vibe had him going back over the events of the morning. Something felt wrong, like a pebble or a splinter. It was irritating him. And then seeing Dr. Alvarez had totally thrown him.

Dewey's call had set off alarm bells. Usually, his team knew if some new drug was coming through town. Even if they didn't find out on their own, the DEA would give them a heads-up. The fact that the drugs came from the United States was also weird but he was trying to build a rapport with Dewey so he wasn't really in a position to turn down the job and they certainly wanted knowledge of any new drug that was coming on the market because it would only be a matter of time before it showed up all over the U.S.

He stood under the spray a little longer than he normally would. Ever since the machete attack in Yemen, his muscles bunched up differently as if they had little spurs on them that got all tangled up. Alvarez had said that might happen. She'd warned him that recovery could be long and painful. The broken ribs would be the worst she'd said but she was wrong. The worst was his back just not feeling like it once did. He was never sure that he could function at one hundred percent because his back didn't feel normal. *Someone hacked your back with a machete. Normal is in your rearview mirror.* US Coast Guard Master Chief Nick Taggert would absolutely never be the same.

His mind automatically turned away from those dark thoughts to Dr. Alvarez. How did someone go from being a Doctors Without Borders doctor to smuggling drugs? It was opposite ends of the spectrum. She'd fucked up his back so maybe her luck had run out and she'd been fired.

Alvarez was something else. Call the police to help her find her drugs? He grinned. He'd love to see Captain Martinez's face when she suggested that he help recover her stolen drugs.

Still, there weren't many women at the top end of the drug trade, and they usually didn't look like her. Alvarez was more refined and a damn sight better looking with dark curly hair and chocolate brown eyes.

He remembered those brown eyes filled with worry and empathy when she spoke to him about his injuries. She sat with him for hours those first few days in Yemen. The softness of her voice, her touch. He'd seen those eyes in his dreams many times. They'd kept him going while he was in intense pain. But that was before he realized that she'd screwed his career with her care for his injuries. The Coast Guard doctor said the way she'd stitched up his back meant he had a lot of unnecessary scar tissue which was why his back felt jacked up all the time. He didn't trust it, and if he didn't trust it then how could those around him trust that he could do his job properly? He ground his teeth. He still sometimes saw those brown eyes in his dreams.

Nick got out of the shower and toweled off. He pulled jeans and a navy T-shirt out of his locker. It felt good to put on clean clothes. It was gonna feel even better to put food in his empty stomach, but best of all would be when he could finally lay his head on a pillow and stay in bed for at least twelve hours.

He made his way from the locker room down the narrow hallway to the kitchen. "Finn, whatcha got cooking?" The enticing scent of spiced meat and oregano hit him, and his mouth watered.

"Heated up some leftover meatballs for sandwiches." Finn handed Nick a large plate. "All the fixings are on the table."

Nick grabbed the plate and a roll and sat down at the table. Within minutes, his plate was clean. He debated having seconds, but he needed to be sharp to question Little Miss Sunshine in there. Who knew what tale she would tell? If he overate, he was afraid he'd fall asleep and miss it.

He got up from the table, put his dishes in the dishwasher, and poured himself a cup of black coffee. He left the kitchen and walked into the warehouse's primary office area. It was cordoned off from the rest of the space by temporary office partitions.

Axe was sitting at his makeshift desk. "You ready?" Nick called.

"Sure thing, Tag," Axe responded. "Let's go get this cream puff to confess all her sins. Fifty bucks says she tells all in thirty minutes."

"She'd better," Nick replied. "I've got a ticket to Boston, and I don't want to be hung up with this mess one minute longer than necessary."

CHAPTER SEVEN

The DEA—at least that's who she thought they were— shouldn't be arresting her at all. Taking Florevir across the country wasn't illegal as far as she knew, and it wasn't like the vaccine was staying in Panama. It was supposed to be on its way to Ecuador. People moved cargo like this all the time. Or so Dewey had said. Shit. Maybe it was illegal. But it was for an excellent cause. She almost laughed out loud. That was the lamest excuse ever. She could just see herself saying to the judge, "But your Honor, it was for a good cause," as she was being hauled out of the courtroom on the way to a Panamanian jail. Her palms broke out in a sweat.

The first man entering the room was blond, muscular, and about six feet tall. His pale blue eyes focused on Carolina with laser precision as he sat down on the left side of the table across from her. He'd been the driver of the first SUV that had pulled up after Dewey hijacked the truck. She had a good memory for faces. She wanted to be able to complain about how they'd treated her to their bosses.

The second man, a few inches over six feet tall with brown hair and blue eyes, looked familiar.

Carolina sat up straighter in her chair. "I want to call my lawyer." The interminable wait had played havoc with her nerves, stretching them to a near breaking point. She had tried to rein in her impatience, but that was a losing battle. She was not a patient person. It was one of her biggest faults.

"You've mistaken us for someone who cares what you want," the dark-haired man said as he took the seat on the right across the table from her.

Her lungs froze in her chest as recognition set in. José! But not just José. She remembered those eyes. "Nick Taggert."

Her heart gave a mighty thump. She hadn't seen him since some men in American military uniforms had come and removed him from her care in Yemen. He'd been in bad shape still, and she didn't want them to take him without her knowing where or what medical assistance he would be offered. She didn't have a choice, though. They'd made that abundantly clear.

Her shoulders relaxed as a flame of hope burned in her chest. Maybe things weren't so bad as she imagined. Surely Nick would help her as she helped him. She tried to reach out but, the cuffs stopped her. "How are you?" She gave him the once over. He looked better, which was not hard since the last time she'd seen him, he'd been suffering from massive blood loss and had an infected wound. The anguish in his eyes back then had scarred her soul. She never wanted to see that kind of pain again.

Nick remained silent.

Cleaned up and beardless, he was quite attractive with those piercing blue eyes that exuded intelligence and a strong jaw that would make cover models jealous. He looked much improved and he sure as hell smelled better too.

Carolina smiled at him. "You look much better. How's your back?"

His eyes were chips of ice, and the rest of his face was inscrutable.

Her belly twisted. Why was he being so cold? "What are you doing here? What does the US military have to do with this?" She frowned. Maybe they could help her get the drugs back. But then hope died in her chest. Nick had been there at the hijacking and had done nothing to stop Dewey and his cohorts from getting away. She had no clue what was going on. The Tarchuarani were going to die because Nick had not intervened. She curled her hands into fists, as much to get the blood circulating as from frustration. "How could you?"

Nick glanced up from reading the paperwork in his hands. "How could I what?"

"Let them take my cargo!"

He shook his head and went back to reading the papers.

She had no idea what his problem with her was, but it would have to wait. "We don't have time for this," she said between clenched teeth. "They're getting away with the drugs. I need that shipment back. I want a lawyer."

"Junkies will always find another way to get high. There's always more product out there. If you're worried about family members, then start talking, and maybe we can help. Who is your supplier?" Nick demanded.

"My supplier? What?" What the hell was he talking about?

The blond guy asked, "Why were you bringing the drugs *down* the coast?"

"Down the coast?" What were they going on about? Seeing Nick Taggert here in Panama had totally thrown her off, and now she was having a hard time following what they were asking.

The blond tried again. "Are you here to test them out? Easier to use people down here as guinea pigs?"

"I don't… You've got it all wrong." Carolina sighed, frustration oozing from every pore.

The blond man frowned. "So if we've got everything wrong, why don't you tell us and set the record straight?"

Carolina took a moment to gather her thoughts. The hope that burst into life when she'd seen her former patient had died a quick death. He had no interest in helping her, that much was obvious. She chewed her lip.

Javier had been explicit that she was not to talk to anyone except the people on a list he gave her. Dewey had been one of those people—and look how that had turned out? Still, should she trust these men? Could she trust Nick? Surely, the fact that she saved his life counted for something. All those hours she'd spent with him must have meant something. At least, they did for her, and she'd thought for him, but maybe not.

Panama had certainly lived up to its reputation as being corrupt as far as she could tell. First, the customs guy and then Dewey, who was even some sort of relative of Javier's. If he'd had no issue selling her out, would these men remotely care? But they were American military, or at least Nick was. Maybe he switched to work for the DEA or something. Either way, they must work for the American government in some capacity. They had to be trustworthy, didn't they?

Then there was the fact that Javier had spoken to Biodome Technologies, the company that created the mosquito trials, and he'd ended up in the hospital in a coma. Javier had told people about the Tarchuarani being ill and the vaccine for them, but someone had pushed him down the escalator.

Nick glared at her. "Let's start at the beginning. For the record, what's your name? And what are you doing here?"

"I want my phone call. I want a lawyer."

The blond smiled. "We're not cops, so we don't play by

those rules. We'll turn you over to local cops later if you don't cooperate. I'm not altogether sure that's what you want. Local prisons aren't nice."

"You're not cops but you're American military or DEA, right?"

The blond shook his head. "Nope."

She turned to Nick. "But American soldiers came and got you in Yemen."

His eyes flashed, but he remained silent. His partner glanced at him but also stayed mute.

"Who *are* you?" she pleaded with Nick, but his gaze remained cold as ice. Fear snaked its way through her body. Maybe Nick had gone rogue and was now part of a drug cartel or something.

"It doesn't matter who we are. Answer our questions, and we might let you go," Nick growled.

Carolina's stomach rolled. These men stood between her and freedom. She couldn't fathom why Nick wouldn't help her. She'd always thought they'd had a connection. As a matter of fact, she had thought at the time, they might have...what? Hooked up? She'd thought they would hook up somehow. She'd fantasized that he would come and find her once he healed, and they would spend some time getting to know one another better, in every sense of the word. Stupid fantasy. Obviously, she'd totally misjudged the situation.

Regardless of the past, she needed to get out of here, if only to tell Guillermo the Florevir was gone. She needed help, and it wouldn't come from Javier, who quite possibly would never wake up again. Damn him.

She took a deep breath. What she truly wanted to do was to reach across the table and strangle Nick for not stepping in and saving the shipment, but she needed to let her anger go if she was going to convince him and his partners—whoever they were—of her legitimacy. Worst of all, she needed their help.

She glared at Nick. "As you already know, my name is Dr. Carolina Alvarez. I am from New York. I am…was bringing a shipment of medicine to Ecuador for the Tarchuarani people."

"Who are the Tarchuarani people, and why do they need these drugs? " the blond man asked.

She laced her fingers together and took a deep breath. "First, the shipment doesn't contain illegal drugs, at least not the kind that can get you high. The drug is a vaccine called Florevir."

The blond man glanced over at his partner, and they both looked back at her. "Say that again. A vaccine?" He folded his arms across his chest.

"Yes. The Tarchuarani are an indigenous tribe that lives in the Ecuadorian Amazon. There're only a few hundred of them left to begin with, and now they are dying. It's complicated, but they need this vaccine, or they will *all* die—and this tribe of people will cease to exist. We will lose part of the human race forever."

Nick's eyes narrowed. "If your story is true, wouldn't the whole world know about it?"

She swallowed. It was a good question; one she couldn't exactly answer. Javier had provided no insight, and Guillermo wouldn't say too much on the phone. She'd only spoken with him three times, and each time he would help her with what she needed at that exact moment and nothing else.

"The situation is complicated and, to be honest, I don't understand everything myself, but what I am telling you is true. And yes, before you ask, I do realize how crazy I sound."

The blond spoke up. "If you know it sounds crazy, then

why expect us to believe you? We're not stupid. It doesn't take a scientist to know how vaccines work, especially in this day and age. If these people, the Tarchuarani are already sick, then a vaccine isn't going to help them."

"It's a therapeutic as well as a prophylactic vaccine, meaning it triggers the body to produce antibodies and immune cells that can fight the virus already present in the body *and* prevent it from future infections. These types of vaccines are relatively new. We, that is scientists," she amended, "have been working on creating them for about the last twenty years. There's one for a certain type of cancer that's in use but in truth, it's not all that effective. This is actually a huge breakthrough for the scientific community. This could lead to all kinds of new therapeutics being developed. It's a big step forward in the vaccine development world."

She took a deep breath. "And I expect you to believe me because it's the truth." What else could she say? It *was* the truth, and it did sound crazy, even to her own ears. Why the hell had she gotten involved in this mess? If she could go back now and do it all again, would she still come? Images of the Tarchuarani ran through her head. They were such a strong, beautiful people. Their loss would be devastating. Yes, she would do it all again. No question.

"You created some new wonder drug that's so groundbreaking it will save a whole tribe from extinction and no one in the world knows about it." The blond snorted. "Seriously, what are the drugs for? Is this some new designer drug that someone down here bought from you?" the blond demanded again.

"I didn't create it and it's not a designer drug. You cannot become high using this no matter how it's administered. I don't think you will even be vaccinated if you snorted it."

Nick cocked his head. "I thought vaccines were liquid. This is powder."

Her heart lurched in her chest. "How do you know that?"

"I checked them out when you were in customs."

She cursed softly and then said a silent prayer that none of the vials were contaminated. Javier had not produced a lot of the vaccine.

"You don't ship a vaccine in liquid form if at all avoidable. As a liquid, the vaccine would need to be kept at specific temperatures. A powder is more stable and easier to ship. We reconstitute them once they arrive at the location." She stared at Nick, willing him to believe her.

"You can see where this sounds crazy, right? If this tribe is as sick as you say, why isn't it on the news? Why isn't the pharmaceutical company or whoever made it screaming from the rooftops so they can be heroes in the press for saving this tribe and making such an amazing scientific breakthrough?" Nick shook his head. "Nice story, but it's got more holes than a sieve. Tell us the truth. It will go a lot smoother for you."

"I *am* telling you the truth," she said through gritted teeth. "The tribe is dying. Javier Florez manufactured the vaccine. He's a world-renowned doctor that specializes in medical research. He's been working on creating a therapeutic vaccine to fight kidney cancer for years. He has a personal connection to the tribe, so when he was told about the illness the Tarchuarani are facing, he used his current research and created a vaccine he called Florevir to fight a virus called Hestiavirus. He would be here himself, but he's currently in the ICU at New York Hospital. Someone pushed him down the subway escalator because he made this vaccine. Someone doesn't want Florevir to be given to the

Tarchuarani. Check it out for yourself if you don't believe me."

She had nothing to lose so she might as well tell the whole truth. Maybe if she could convince these men of the threat, then she had a chance.

Nick studied her and leaned forward in the chair. "We'll go check out your story, but you better hope it's real because if I find out this is all one big lie, I'll be back in here, and I won't be so friendly next time."

Her heart raced at the threat, but she remained silent. She had nothing to add that would make the situation any better. Nick seemed to hate her for some unknown reason, but there was nothing she could do about it at the moment. She said a silent prayer as she watched the men get up and leave the room. She was in serious trouble and had no one to turn to for help.

"Javier, please, please, please wake up," she whispered to herself.

Axe grunted and ran a hand through his blond hair. "How does she know your name?"

"Long story." Nick didn't want to talk about it, but he was going to have to at some point.

Axe grunted. "What do you think of *her* story? You seem to know her a bit. Is she telling the truth?"

"I think it's sounds like a pile of bullshit." Nick walked down the hallway and went through the doorway into the office space. "We let her stew for a while and see if she comes up with a better story." He walked over and sat down at his desk.

Did he really think it was bullshit? From anyone else, absolutely, but from Carolina, no. Fuck. He wanted it to be bullshit. He wanted her to be lying so he could pass her off to one of the locals and she could spend time in a Panamanian prison, but chances were good there was at least some truth to her story whether he liked it or not.

"So you're not going to check out what she said?" Axe leaned his butt on the edge of the table.

"I didn't say that. I'll poke around and see what I come up with. Why? Do you believe her?" Nick wasn't so sure he trusted his own judgment about anything to do with Carolina Alvarez.

Axe shrugged. "There's a couple of things about her story that make it seem more plausible than most."

"What stands out to you?" Nick leaned his chair back on two legs.

"Hey, Axe, Tag. How'd it go with the lady drug smuggler?" Finn asked as he strode into the room.

"We were just discussing it," said Nick. "Axe was about to tell me why he believes her bullshit story that the drugs are a vaccine she's trying to get to Ecuador to save a dying tribe that no one's heard about."

Finn whistled as he came over and leaned on the table opposite Nick and Axel. "Really? That's a new one. You believe her, Axe?"

"I don't know if *believe* is the right word. Some of Dr. Alvarez's story rings true, and I have questions."

Finn raised his eyebrows. "Like what?"

Axe grimaced. "Like, why was she bringing drugs down from the U.S.? The flow of drugs is always north, *to* the U.S. It makes no sense. It won't be illegal in the U.S. at this point. Why not keep it up there and sell as much of it as you can before the government hacks get around to outlawing it?

"And if it was some major new drug on the market," Axe said, warming to his subject, "wouldn't she have brought security? No one is stupid enough to travel with an illegal drug shipment without security. No one. I don't care where you're from or if it's your first time. She doesn't strike me as stupid."

Finn tilted his head. "You know, there is one thing that bothered me about this from the start." He turned to Nick. "You said Dewey acted cagey about who he was working with. He's usually more talkative about stuff, isn't he?"

Nick nodded. "It's true. He likes to brag and preen but normally deals in only smaller quantities. This is a huge score for him. Delivering a new designer drug would make him a bigger player instead of a small-time hood. Might even get him a bigger cut of the profits. I'm guessing that whoever is behind the hijacking has to be one of the big boys. Probably one of the cartels, or it could be the FARC."

"You think it's the *Fuerzas Armadas Revolucionarias de Colombia*?" Axe said. "That would be a bit out of the ordinary for them. They usually don't get involved in anything new. They like to stick to the safe stuff, meaning cocaine. How would Dewey hook up with them?"

Nick rocked his chair forward so all four feet rested on the floor and then rocked it back again. "A better question is…if the drugs are narcotics, then how did Dewey find out about them, and how did he become the middleman? And how did he know Dr. Alvarez didn't have a buyer already lined up? Dewey is wily as a fox and has an extreme sense of self-preservation. He wouldn't be ripping off one of the big boys to give to someone else." He rubbed his face. It made less and less sense that the drugs were street drugs. Alvarez was most likely telling the truth. "I didn't ask Dewey enough questions when I had the chance, I guess."

Finn snorted. "When did you have the chance? The two-minute phone call when he offered you the job or the forty-five minutes you were in the truck with him and the pretty doc? There was no chance for you to find out anything else.

We were damn lucky you could pull something together in our limited time frame."

Nick frowned. "Maybe that should have been another red flag. Dewey set the deal up in a hurry. Usually these are set up months in advance. I got the impression he didn't have more than a couple of weeks' notice for the whole thing, and when he called me from the ship, he was in a panic. His usual guy was down and out with some sort of stomach bug. He was desperate."

Another thought came to Nick. "It could also be why Dewey was pretty uncertain when we were hijacked. I had a distinct feeling he wasn't comfortable with the men with the guns. If he is trying to move up and play with the big boys, he would have a lot riding on this.

"Also, I had a minute before they came out from customs, and I checked out the shipment. They didn't even try to disguise it. It was just sitting there all wrapped up on the pallet. It didn't look like anything I'd seen before either. It was packaged differently than cocaine or heroin."

Finn cocked his head. "So, do you think it's a possibility that Dr. Alvarez is telling the truth, Nick?"

His gut was telling him that, as much as he hated the idea, she was telling the truth. Still…"There's a lot of missing information. Her story has major holes. Why would such an operation be carried out in secret? And could a single man create a vaccine in record time to help these people?"

He put his chair down again. "Finn, do me a favor. Check to see if local law enforcement or any of our counterparts have heard anything about the shipment. Dig deep. We didn't have time to do any background before I had to meet Dewey. See if any one of the known players is talking. Try to find out who the original buyer was that Alvarez would've been selling to if this is a street drug."

"Will do, boss." He went over and dropped down at his workspace.

"Axe, dig into the good doctor's background and the guy she mentioned: Javier Florez. Find out whatever you can on him."

Axel nodded. He stood and walked to his desk.

Nick turned to face his computer screen. It was time for him to see if he could uncover anything on the Tarchuarani. He glanced at his watch. He needed sleep. His hopes of Dr. Alvarez quickly giving them the info they wanted had fled in the interrogation room. Now his dreams of vacation were vanishing as well.

CHAPTER EIGHT

Three hours later after a brief nap, Nick walked into the workroom. At his desk, he hit his mouse and made his screen come alive. He logged in again: no new mail. "How's it going?" he asked as he swiveled in his chair to look at Finn and Axe. "Either of you making any progress?"

"Some. You want to hear it now?" Finn got up, poured a cup of black coffee, and brought the mug over to his boss.

Nick took a sip of coffee. "Sure. Why not? Has anyone checked on Dr. Alvarez?"

Finn nodded. "I checked on her a few times. Gave her a snack. Escorted her to the bathroom. She's grumpy but fine."

Nick nodded. "Axe, you find out anything?"

Axe nodded. "Sure. I'm always happy to share." He came over and sat down behind Cain's table. "Where are Elias and Cain?" he asked as he pulled down the sleeve of his T-shirt to cover his burn scars.

Finn leaned his butt against the same table and rotated his shoulder a couple of times. He wore his hair long these days and was always brushing it out of his eyes.

Nick swiveled his seat sideways to see them both head on. As team leader, part of his job was to keep up with his team's physical and mental health. Finn's shoulder was stiff by the looks of things, and Axe was still self-conscious about his burns. Elias still limped from his gunshot wound. Cain was always pissed off, and Nick's back was stiff and still hurt. Report respectfully submitted. If only. Bertrand would never let him get away with a report like that. He always wanted details.

Nick sighed. "They're out getting supplies. Groceries and other necessities." He indicated the lockers where they stored all of their weapons and equipment. They needed some new binoculars and mosquito repellent. They lost both during their latest raid with the DEA. "So, who wants to go first?"

"I'll go," Finn said. "Nick, while you were getting your beauty sleep—"

Axe cackled. "Three hours isn't beauty sleep. A beauty nap, maybe, and if you ask me, he needs at least another twenty-four hours to be even passable. Beautiful is a long way off."

Nick threw a balled-up piece of paper at Axe. "Thanks. I'll remember that next time you've worked long hours and need a nap."

"As I was saying." Finn cleared his throat and shot a glare at Axe. "No one heard a damn thing about this shipment until Dewey called you in as a driver. Local law enforcement doesn't have a clue, and the members of the alphabet soup down here are completely in the dark. The shipment isn't on anyone's radar. I asked about any chatter on new designer drugs, and they said it's been crickets lately. Everybody is just doing the usual thing."

Nick pushed his chair back on two legs. "So, what are you thinking?"

"Wait, there's more. Or should I say less?"

"What do you mean?" Axe doodled on a pad of paper on Cain's desk.

Finn cocked an eyebrow. "There is no buyer."

"You mean you haven't found one yet," Nick corrected.

Finn shook his head. "No. I mean, there isn't one. None of the usual players were in on the deal. The local DEA guys are hearing all sorts of chatter now that word has gone out about the shipment. The big boys are all pissed about missing out on this new drug.

Nick frowned. "So how did Dewey know about the shipment? That's question one for the good doctor. What about you, Axe? Tell us about the doc and her pal."

Nick sighed to himself. He really didn't want to know anything more about Carolina Alvarez. She already haunted his dreams. He had a feeling that knowing more about her would only make it harder to hate her.

Axe dropped the pen he'd been doodling with and sat up straighter in his chair. "Carolina Roma Alvarez was born in Connecticut thirty-five years ago. She is the only daughter of Ricardo and Maria Alvarez. Maria died in a car accident shortly after Carolina was born, and Ricardo went on to marry Dr. Honey Winthrop. Carolina did very well in school, excelling in the sciences and graduating from high school at the top of her class. She attended Yale for her undergraduate degree in Biology, then went on to attend Harvard Medical School. She did her residen—"

"Cut to the chase on this one. I have a feeling you could go on for another twenty minutes about her many accomplishments." Nick faked a yawn. "You're putting me to sleep." He didn't need to hear how smart and successful Carolina was. She'd screwed up his back. That's all he needed to know.

"Fair enough. The important thing to note is she stayed at the top of her class all the way through, and she focused her studies on the research aspect of medicine—specifically, cancer research, which is where she met Javier Florez. She worked for him for a couple of years and then, seemingly out of the blue, made a major shift by joining Doctors Without Borders. She's worked in some pretty rough spots." Axe paused and glanced at Nick, giving him the chance to comment, but Nick wasn't biting. He had no interest in sharing what had happened in Yemen. Axe continued. "And her colleagues have nothing but high praise for her."

"Do we know why she made the shift?" Finn finished his origami elephant and set it next to the giraffe on his table.

Axe shook his head. "No, but I can tell you Javier Florez was totally pissed off when she left. Rumor has it he had some kind of tantrum when she told him she was leaving. Like he threw shit and screamed like a son of a bitch at the good doc."

"How in the hell did you find that out?" Nick asked.

Axe grinned. "My incredible wit and charm translates down the phone line almost as well as it does in person."

Finn snorted. "Uh-huh. Sure."

"They were working together at New York University, so I called and found a chatty assistant. She said Carolina shocked everyone when she left—abandoning not just her job with Florez, but research altogether. Many people thought her and Dr. Florez's combined brainpower and skill put them as top contenders in finding a cure for cancer."

"So Alvarez was on the road to cure cancer, and she up and quit to become a trauma doctor?" Finn raised his eyebrows. "That makes no sense."

"Agreed," said Nick. "Any hint of an affair between the two, or sexual misconduct?" His gut churned at the thought of some guy laying his hands on Carolina. Shit. He needed to get his head straight. *She's the bad guy, remember?* He needed to hold on to that thought and let go of any fantasy he might have had about bedding her.

Axe shook his head. "Not a whiff. Javier Florez is more than twenty years older than she is—not that the age difference matters—but he is also married to a much younger woman who dotes on him. The assistant I spoke to said the whole thing struck her and others as super weird, and even Florez appeared to be unclear on why Alvarez quit.

"Florez, by the way, is definitely capable of creating a vaccine. The assistant said it would be possible to create a vaccine in a short period if another vaccine could be modified."

Nick took another sip of coffee. "So, if the materials were available, Javier Florez could quite possibly have created a vaccine to treat an illness in a short amount of time."

"Yes," Axe confirmed. "What about you, Nick? What did you find out?"

"There *is* a group of people in Ecuador called the Tarchuarani. They live in the Amazon, and they avoid any contact with the outside world. They are a small tribe, only a few hundred. I searched extensively, but only found one article that was relevant, stating these people are indeed getting sick. It was a tiny newspaper from the local area by where the Tarchuarani live. It confirmed Alvarez's story. The Tarchuarani are dying off. At the current rate of fatality, it won't take long before they are extinct."

Finn doodled again. "I don't get it. Why isn't it all over the news?"

"My question exactly. I called the reporter who wrote the story—Tony Something. His editor said he's away at the moment but cited an insider as the source for the article. I'm going to try to find the source. And I called the Ministry of Public Health in Ecuador to see what they say about the Tarchuarani. I'm waiting to hear back from both."

Finn looked at his boss. "So, what do you think? Is Dr. Alvarez a quack, or is she telling the truth?"

Nick sipped his coffee. That was the million-dollar question, one he didn't have an answer for. Yet.

CHAPTER NINE

Nick stared at his laptop then rubbed his face with his hands.

He was dropping the ball on this operation, and he knew it. He was distracted by Alvarez. He'd been off his game since the moment he'd seen her at the port. He needed to put his personal feelings aside and focus on facts.

The truth was he believed Alvarez, but her story did have holes. She was holding something back. He needed to go in there and get it out of her, but he was too unsettled. Too tired, too pissed off to work cleanly. And he was out of practice.

These days, his drug interdiction role meant mostly sitting behind a desk. He'd been pushing the rules by doing undercover work whenever he possibly could. Sitting around drinking beer with the guys had been fun for the first few months but, after a year, it got old. These men were highly trained, highly skilled members of law enforcement. The sitting around was killing them a lot faster than any of their injuries.

He missed running through jungles, rappelling down

from helicopters, boarding hostile ships, and taking on the cartels. At these thoughts, his back twinged as a reminder: *before is over.* He was benched. His back stiffened up way too easily for him to function at the required hundred and ten percent that his MSST team needed from him.

He leaned back in his chair. The last twelve hours—hell, the last week—had left him exhausted and drained. It was more than a lack of sleep. It was a lack of a life. He hadn't had a real vacation in more months than he could count, and he sure as hell wasn't going now.

Or maybe he was getting old at thirty-eight, and burnout was catching up with him. The reasons didn't matter. Exhaustion was now a constant companion, and if he didn't do something soon, it would be joined by its old friend, depression. And then he'd really be in trouble.

Nick ran a hand through his hair. If he accepted Alvarez's story that it really was a vaccine and not a designer drug, then no matter which group of assholes had it, once they found out it was just a vaccine, they'd be out for blood. They'd need someone to blame for the cockup; killing Dewey wouldn't be enough. To send a message, they'd want to take out anyone involved—no matter how small their role, which meant hunting down Nick's alter ego, the smelly José. No one would be allowed to screw with them and live. It was going to get ugly. The last thing he needed was to have one of the cartels looking for José. It would jeopardize his team. "Fuck."

"What's wrong, boss?" Axe asked.

Nick opened his mouth, but his phone rang. It was his cover identity line. Working on drug interdiction in Panama made them a target. They were given cover IDs as businessmen with a small import/export business. Some of the local law enforcement knew who they really were, but Nick and the team were very choosey about who they told. Their lives might depend on it. Nick always adhered to protocol and used his cover ID whenever making any calls to outside sources. Better to limit the damage as much as he could. He picked up the receiver and said, "Peter James."

"*Señor James, mi nombre es Oscar Gómez. Soy el asistente de Alejandro García. Usted llamó con preguntas sobre los Tarchuarani y su enfermedad.*"

Nick paused. His Spanish was okay but for important stuff, he needed it to be in English so he didn't miss anything. "*Lo siento. Mi español no es tan bueno. ¿Habla usted Inglés?*"

"Yes, I speak English. Mr. James, my name is Oscar Lopez. I am the assistant to Alejandro Garcia. You called with questions about the Tarchuarani and their illness."

Nick was caught off guard. Alejandro Garcia was the right-hand man of the President of Ecuador. Why would his assistant be calling? "*Si, Señor* Lopez. Thank you for returning my call."

Lopez continued in heavily accented English. "Mr. Garcia wanted me to thank you for your interest in the Tarchuarani people and reassure you he is aware of the issue and is working with local doctors to treat the tribe. He is wondering, however, why this is of interest to a shipping businessman in Panama?"

"Mr. Lopez, after reading an article on the illness and its effect on the Tarchuarani people in one of your small local papers, I heard a rumor that medicine might be needed to treat the illness and I wanted to offer my services. My company's expertise is in shipping items to and from the United States."

"What type of medicines are you referring to?" Lopez sounded worried.

"Ah, well, if they need a treatment drug or a vaccine of some sort." Nick waited a beat to see how Lopez would react then added, "We would be happy to work with you to bring it to Ecuador."

Lopez's voice went up an octave. "Vaccine? What makes you think we need a vaccine? Who else have you spoken to?"

The strong reaction took Nick by surprise. He'd obviously hit some kind of panic button. "I haven't spoken to anyone, Mr. Lopez. My assistant pointed out the article to me, and I wanted to be first in line to offer my services in case you needed help obtaining medicine or supplies from the United States. You know, the early bird gets the worm. Our rates are reasonable, and our American connections are vast. I am sure we can acquire whatever is needed and deliver it to you in record time."

"We don't need anything, Mr. James. Thank you." The line went dead.

Nick stared at the phone in his hand a moment, then hung up the handset.

"Who was that?" Finn inquired and then took a bite of an apple.

"Oscar Lopez. He's the assistant to Alejandro Garcia." He sat back in his chair. "Now, why would one of the top advisors to the Ecuadorian President have his assistant call me back when I called the public health office and spoke to a minor clerk?"

Finn shrugged. "He wouldn't. Your call shouldn't have rung alarm bells that high up."

Nick frowned. "Agreed. Finn, find me a picture of Oscar Lopez and a recording of his voice so we can be sure the caller was him," he said as he stood up.

"Axe, check the tracker I put on the shipment now. It's been almost eight hours. Let's see where it is and find out who actually took it. We may need to go and pick it up."

Axe shook his computer mouse. "So you believe her?"

Nick shrugged and then walked over to the fridge. He

pulled out another bottle of water. He didn't want to commit even though his reluctance had more to do with their shared history than the facts of the situation. "Still not sure, but that phone call made me curious enough to want to check her story out further." His phone rang again, and he walked back over to his table. He glanced at the screen and grimaced. His boss. He let the call go to voicemail. Bertrand would want answers, and he didn't have any. Yet. It was time to play hard-ball with the good doctor. She knew a lot more than she was saying, and there was no place Nick hated more than being in the dark.

CHAPTER TEN

Lopez's hands shook, and he wiped them on a tissue as he entered Garcia's office. Alejandro Garcia smiled. He liked Lopez being terrified of him. His last assistant had made a serious mistake, and the following day he didn't show up for work. Rumor had it Alejandro had had him killed for his error. Alejandro didn't disabuse anyone of the notion. Rumors were occasionally true.

Lopez swallowed hard as he stood on the other side of his boss's desk. The office was dark except for the ambient light from the windows and a small desk lamp. Garcia preferred the darkness. Too much light gave him a headache.

"*Señor, hice la llamada telefónica como solicitó.*"

Alejandro Garcia leaned over his desk, so his face was partially lit by the lamp. He knew he resembled a devil at that moment, which was precisely why he did it.

Lopez shuddered.

"Speak English. You need the practice," Garcia barked.

"Yes, *Señor*—Sir." Lopez's voice shook. "I called Peter James as you requested."

"So what did you find out?"

"The call was from some businessman looking to make money. He wanted us to hire him if we need to bring anything in from the U.S. Another greedy American. He saw the article and wanted to be the first to offer his services. That is all."

"I see. Fine then. You may go for the evening but stay close to your phone in case anything...develops."

"Yes, sir." Lopez gave a small bow and backed out of the room as quickly as possible and closed the door after him.

Garcia leaned back in his chair. One small article in a tiny newspaper. That's all it took to cause a problem. His jaw hardened. His people were still searching for the reporter. He'd gone to ground, but when they found him, they would find out the name of the source. The reporter would talk, or he would die. This project was too far along to stop now. He couldn't have more people finding out about it. Not just yet. Not while there was still time to save the Tarchuarani. They needed to be dead, and that needed to happen soon.

Now he had to worry about some businessman in Panama. Was it an innocent inquiry? He would have his people check into it further. He would lose sleep over this. He curled his hands into fists. Without sacrifice, there was no success. He could sleep when the Tarchuarani were no more. They were a sacrifice for him to achieve his biggest success.

He got up and smoothed out his clothing. He was going to dinner with the President, and the man would want a progress report. Garcia would keep this to himself for now. *El Presidente* was still upset about the creation of the vaccine. At least Garcia could report they had successfully hijacked it, so the vaccine wasn't a problem any longer. Langston's people had taken care of that. For once, Langston had done something useful. Garcia stepped around his desk and headed out of his office. It would be a good night. His President would be happy with the news Garcia had everything under control.

CHAPTER ELEVEN

"So let's start again, Dr. Alvarez. Tell me from the beginning exactly how you got here and don't leave anything out. The devil is in the details," Nick said.

Carolina bit her tongue. It was late. She was tired and hungry. Patience was hard to come by. She drew in a deep breath and launched into her story.

"I worked with Dr. Javier Florez at NYU in the medical research department. We were out of touch for a few years after we didn't part on the best of terms." *Understatement of the century*. Her palms still got sweaty at the memory of Javier throwing beakers over her head at the wall behind her. She swallowed hard, and her heart did a little stutter in her chest. The sound of shattering glass still made her jump.

"Anyway, he…we bumped into one another one day last week." Was it really only last week? It felt like she'd been at this for months. "He told me what was going on with the Tarchuarani. At first, I wasn't sure what he wanted me to do. He said he didn't have time to explain it all at that moment, but he would get me details.

"Javier claimed there were people after him, so he

couldn't risk taking the vaccine to Ecuador. He hoped I could get it there safely. He said I was one of the only people he could trust, and he was scared. Terrified, actually. He was convinced he was being followed. Apparently, he was right. He was pushed down the escalator at the Seventy-Second Street subway station in New York. It's one of the longest staircases in the city. I'm surprised he is still alive."

"Wait. So, this Javier guy, your former boss—was he your lover? Did he have something over you?"

"God no! *Yuk!*" She bit her lip. "Javier is more like a father to me. When I worked for him, I was close with both him and his wife. They sort of adopted me and took care of me. I used to have dinner at their house all the time. Javier's father was an anthropologist for the Universidad San Francisco de Quito, and one of the few people who ever had contact with the Tarchuarani.

"Javier used to go with him when he was studying these people. Javier and his wife took me to their home in Ecuador, and I got to meet his father and see the Tarchuarani in their village. I wasn't allowed to approach them or anything since they shun the modern world and don't wish to be exposed to it any more than absolutely necessary. Javier's father built up a rapport with them over many, many years. My visit was brief but fascinating. They have an incredibly vibrant culture. It was amazing. These people are so—"

"Amazing?" Nick supplied and snorted.

"Yes!" She struggled to make this man understand. "They have chosen to stay true to their roots and their traditional way of life. Do you know how rare that is, or the level of commitment and belief that requires? It's truly astounding and should be revered. Their loss would be catastrophic to humankind.

"Anyway, Javier provided details for me as to how to ship

the vaccine and who to speak to. It was all going well until ... Dewey double-crossed me."

A knock sounded at the door. "Come," Nick called out.

The blond guy from earlier walked in. "Boss, we got confirmation," he said as he sat down.

Nick nodded.

"Who are you people?" she blurted out.

Nick studied her. "That's not important at the moment."

The blond man nodded at her. "Dr. Alvarez, we've confirmed your story as far as we can. Javier Florez was working on something in his lab in New York, and his assistant knew it had something to do with Ecuador because she heard him mention it during telephone conversations. She doesn't speak Spanish, so there's no guarantee she heard correctly. Florez didn't share details.

"The lab assistant also confirmed Florez had purchased a large amount of an older vaccine that had been used to treat a variant of malaria, but she didn't know anything else. She asked Florez what it was for, but he refused to explain. He said he needed the old vaccine for research. Currently, he is still in the ICU at NYU Hospital. There are signs he might come around, but no one is saying one way or another at this point."

Carolina's belly churned. Did these men believe her?

The blond man continued. "We cannot confirm that Dr. Florez was assaulted at the subway station. The NYPD responding to the call that day said they thought it was accidental. The video we were given is inconclusive. The man with the bag might have hit Florez intentionally or by accident.

"So, we're left with no real facts other than Florez worked on something he kept secret. That something may or may not have to do with Ecuador. He is in a coma in the hospital."

Nick pointed to the blond man. "My friend here confirmed Dewey did receive calls from someone in Ecuador. He has a sister-in-law from there, so that may not be unusual. We did request Florez's phone records. Normally, this takes a while, and we would have to sort through a lot of red tape, but we got help from an unexpected source.

"The FBI was already investigating Florez, and when we ran his name up the flagpole, it pinged with them. An agent named Floyd called and asked about our interest. When we explained, they offered that Florez had been in touch with someone in Ecuador. Several people, in fact. The FBI are interested to find out who Florez was in contact with and why. They would like to speak to you."

A cold sweat broke out on her back. This was all so out of control. Now the FBI were involved. Was that good or bad? She had no idea. She certainly didn't want to give up Guillermo's name. He was the only contact she had left. If they arrested him, then the Tarchuarani would never get the vaccine.

Of course, he could be a part of Dewey's double-cross, but she'd bet against it. After all, Guillermo knew Florevir wouldn't make anyone high, so why would he work with Dewey? But if Guillermo wanted money, he might be willing to see if Dewey could sell the drugs before anyone found out they were useless as recreational drugs.

She dismissed that idea. Guillermo was too cautious and concerned about getting the vaccine to the Tarchuarani. Giving up Guillermo's name wasn't an option. She would do her best to continue to protect him. If Javier told her the truth, then Guillermo was the only one who could get the Florevir to the Tarchuarani, but did she believe Javier? She had no answer to that question at the moment.

The two men were studying her, gauging her reaction.

"Why are the FBI investigating Javier?" she asked.

Nick leaned back in his chair. "Isn't that interesting? Of everything I said, including the FBI wanting to speak to you, you choose to ask about Florez. Why is that?"

Carolina remained silent.

Nick cocked his head. "As I am sure you are aware, *Doctor*, when you place big orders for things like vaccines and other types of drugs from the national stockpile, it gets flagged by all kinds of government agencies. Florez ordering a bunch of a long-dead vaccine no one was using resulted in certain officials asking questions. That's how the FBI got involved."

She let out a pent-up breath. "So they were worried about what *Javier* was doing?"

Nick nodded. "And now they're worried about you."

Jesus. That was all she needed. As it was, Nick wasn't her biggest fan. The FBI asking questions would really frig things up. "Well, I'm not in the country, so that must worry them less."

"Not really. They're sending an agent down, arriving tomorrow morning. They are really very eager to speak with you."

The room spun a bit, and she spread her feet farther apart to keep her balance. The FBI were coming to question her. Her heart slammed against her ribs. This was all so out of control.

While they all sat around discussing irrelevant issues, the Tarchuarani were dying. Javier had been right on the money when he'd said any government agency involvement in the vaccine shipment would be fatal.

"Bring her water and some fruit or something," Nick instructed, and the blond man left the room. "You looked like you might pass out."

She nodded and licked her dry lips. "I'm sorry. I just need some food."

Nick nodded. He left the room, spoke to someone outside, then came back and took his seat again. A minute later, the blond man returned and placed a bottle of water and an apple in front of her. She opened the bottle and drank half. The apple was harder to consume with the cuffs on, but she managed. It was delicious since she was dehydrated and starving.

"So what happens now?" Carolina asked, setting the demolished apple core on the table.

"We're tracking the shipment and intend to bring it back here to check it out. You're going to sit tight, and we'll see what happens."

"What do you mean, tracking the shipment? You can do that? Who are you guys? Who *do* you work for?"

The blond man looked at Nick and, at his slight nod, turned back to Carolina and grinned. "The United States Coast Guard."

Carolina frowned. "The Coast Guard? You expect me to believe that?" Her frown turned into a glare. "If you don't want to say, fine, keep your secret, but don't tell me lies."

"He's not lying," Nick growled. "We work for a special operations unit of the United States Coast Guard."

She blinked. "Seriously?"

"Yes, seriously," Nick growled.

Carolina locked eyes with him. "Have you always worked for the Coast Guard?"

He gave her a curt nod.

Well, that explained why no other members of the military she'd treated in Yemen or Ethiopia had ever heard of him. And she had asked every single one of them back when she thought she and Nick might…connect. "Why would the U.S. Coast Guard be stationed in Panama? Aren't you supposed to be out on a ship somewhere along the coast of the United States?"

The blond man smiled. "One of the roles of the Coast Guard is drug interdiction. We work all over the world to stop the flow of drugs into the US. We're under the radar about it so most people don't know, but we do far more than just save you from your sinking sailboat."

She leaned forward in her chair. "What about the shipment? How are you going to track it?"

Nick smirked. "I stuck a GPS tracker in with the drugs when I checked them at the port. We've been following it the whole time."

Carolina swore as her shoulders sagged. The relief was so profound she found herself tearing up. "Thank you, God." Looking up at Nick's steady gaze made her blink rapidly. She was not about to shed tears in front of this man.

He glanced at his partner, and the two stood up. "Do you need to use the facilities again?"

She nodded.

Nick indicated his partner with his chin. "This is Chief Petty Officer Axel Cantor. He will take you, and then he'll take you to a cell for the night. I'm afraid it's the only accommodation we can offer you. If the drug is a vaccine, then there's no interest from us, but the locals may have a different idea. You took the vaccine off the ship and ran it through customs at top speed. I'm thinking there was a payoff. They may want to talk to you about that. But first, the FBI wants to chat with you in the morning."

She stood up. "Can you let me know when the shipment is back in your custody?"

Nick nodded. "Sure." He turned and left.

Axel gestured for her to exit the room as well. Another man stood in the hallway. He was large and muscular with the top of his dark hair tied back in a man bun. She followed him to the restrooms with Axel following behind her. The new guy stopped outside the door and turned to her. "Please don't try anything. It will be a waste of time, and chances are excellent you will be seriously injured."

Carolina looked up at him and nodded. He hadn't said it to intimidate her. He was just making a point, and she believed him wholeheartedly. He undid her cuffs, and she stepped inside the restroom. It was a regular bathroom with a toilet, a shower, and a sink. She'd love to take a shower but settled for using the facilities, then washing her hands and face.

When she walked back into the hallway, the dark-haired man put her cuffs on again and led her to a holding cell. It didn't have bars, but rather it was a room with four white walls, no windows, and a steel door. There was a cot with a mattress and blanket. She stepped inside and turned around. The man removed her cuffs. "Get some sleep, Doc. You're gonna need it."

He closed and locked the door behind him. The overhead light went out, leaving her in complete darkness. Carolina felt her way over to the cot and sat down hard. The mattress hadn't appeared stained or anything, but she was still skeeved out.

How in the hell had she gotten here? Carolina was going to have to speak to the FBI the next day, and she couldn't decide the best course of action, whether or not to tell them about Guillermo. Damn Javier. His message had been clear: No governmental agencies, whether from the US or Panama, should be involved. Well, she'd already accidentally gotten one agency involved. The Coast Guard had nabbed her in the wilds of Panama. *Jesus.* Of all the groups she thought she'd have to watch out for, the US Coast Guard didn't rank in the top five hundred.

She lay down on the mattress and blinked back tears. It had been a long day. Her muscles ached and her head pounded. Her stomach rumbled but she was too stressed to even think about asking for more food. She hadn't slept well since she left New York. She was still reeling from Dewey's betrayal. Overwhelmed didn't adequately describe it. When she and Dewey had arrived this morning, she had no idea what had been in store for her. She wished she knew at the time. Her body clock was telling her it had to be at least midnight.

She was relieved they were tracking the shipment. That meant they could get the vaccine back from Dewey and his cohorts. She pictured Nick out in the night somewhere, chasing her cargo. Would reclaiming the vaccine involve a gunfight or some sort of wild and crazy operation? Like the one that had gotten him hurt. She certainly hoped not. She wouldn't be able to forgive herself if something happened to Nick. He may hate her guts, but she didn't feel the same. To her, he was still the man on her operating table that had needed help, which she so willingly had given.

Carolina shivered. She reached down and found the blanket, spreading it out over her as best she could. It smelled like fabric softener, which made her feel slightly better.

How the hell was she going to get out of this mess? The mere thought of her parents hearing the news of her stint in a Central American jail was enough to make her never want to go home again. She could already see her father's disapproving face. Honey was never going to let her live it down and, somehow, no matter what part Honey played in the whole thing, it would all be Carolina's doing.

CHAPTER TWELVE

N ick shifted his weight to one foot and peered around the base of the tree. He was hidden in the jungle about twenty feet from the fence line of a FARC (*Fuerzas Armadas Revolucionarias de Colombia*) stronghold. They called themselves a revolutionary army, but they smuggled cocaine and other drugs. Nick ground his molars. They claimed it was only to fund their revolution. *Allegedly.* Who knew what the truth was with FARC, but they were always involved in bad shit, no matter what they claimed.

He glanced down at the screen he was keeping hidden with his hand so it didn't light up the darkness around him. Tracking the vaccine here had been the easy part, but also a surprise. This wasn't a typical FARC type of thing. Nick hoped they weren't planning some big attack that they needed cash to make happen. That would make his life more difficult.

The tracker was still holding steady at this location. He studied the compound. There were five buildings he could see, only two emitting light. The rest were dark on the inside, only lit by the exterior lights of the compound. They were all made of corrugated metal with some windows roughly cut in. Some of the windowpanes were broken, but most were intact. The largest building was in the middle of the compound. The other smaller structures were spread out around it. No guards were visible. No noise. Nothing. Even though it was one fifteen in the morning, there should have been some kind movement. He touched his earpiece. "Anyone got eyes on any guards? Any signs of life?"

"No," Axe responded.

"No movement," Finn agreed.

"Nothing, boss," said Elias.

"Cain?"

"Zero movement. No visual on anything human," Cain replied.

A bead of sweat trickled down Nick's neck. He'd expected armed guards everywhere around the compound. Conversations and noise should be coming from the open windows on the building on the other side of the fence. The security lights broke up the darkness but showed no humans. Only bugs danced around the bulbs.

This was a cartel stronghold. The GPS tracker said the vaccine was here. But the normally bustling compound appeared empty. Not a good sign. Ever. He searched his field of vision for any indication of life. Nothing. Could it be a setup, with heavily armed cartel members hidden and waiting? All of the hairs on the back of his neck were standing up. Something was very wrong.

Taking a deep breath, he relaxed and let his senses take in everything around him. The night was still. The scent of flowers mixed with surrounding greenery filled his nose. Crickets and other bugs were chirping and buzzing, but no human voices reached his ears. He could taste moisture in the air as the inky darkness settled around him. He knew in his gut they were the only ones there. Not good.

Actually, Nick's team shouldn't be there either. Bertrand would have a shit fit if he'd known they were out on this kind of op with their injuries. The DEA stuff they were doing was supposed to be minor, and it generally was. Bertrand would not sign off on something like this, which is precisely why Nick didn't tell him. Better to beg forgiveness than ask permission. The part Bertrand didn't get was every member of his team were top level operators, the best the Coast Guard had to offer. On paper, it was great for them to rest but, in actual fact, it meant they were losing their skills while they were losing their minds. They didn't do well sitting around. They had all been billeted out to one part of the military or another. A couple with the SEALs, a couple with the Rangers, and he'd been doing some work with the Marines when he'd gotten injured. And now they had all been dispatched to Panama to heal—whatever the hell that meant.

They were a ragtag bunch, Team RECON as they called themselves. Recon as in reconstructed. A bunch of Humpty Dumpties, except they were trying to put *themselves* back together so they could go back to what they loved best, kicking ass and taking names.

Nick should have called Bertrand the moment they'd realized Dr. Alvarez was telling the truth about the vaccine. The whole mess would've been handed off to the locals. But he'd promised the guys some sort of training exercise to keep up their skills. It seemed like a good idea at the time. Now that they were here, he had his doubts. It was bad. He knew it in his bones but it was too late to stop. The team's blood was up and they were happy to be in the hunt. Taking this away from them would be cruel no matter what his bones were telling him.

"Go!" Nick got up and moved surreptitiously through the undergrowth. He reached the fence in seconds and grabbed his cutters, but the fence already had a cut in the chain link. *Fuck*.

"We are late to the party," he transmitted to the others. "I repeat, we are not the first to arrive."

A series of squawks sounded in his ear, his team acknowledging the message. He'd called in extra bodies from the local US military training base. These soldiers had support roles since they were just learning jungle combat. He hadn't been keen to have a bunch of green kids with him, but this type of op wasn't in his job description, so backup choices were limited.

He slipped through the cut in the fence and stayed crouched low while running to the structure. He hugged the wall as he moved down to the end of the building. A quick peek told him it was clear. He rounded the corner, gun ready. But he was confident no one was there—alive anyway.

Could they all have tried the new drug and died from it? His gut churned. In that case, Dr. Alvarez would be in a world of trouble. Bringing a new drug into Panama that caused its users to die after one dose would be a death sentence for her. The Panamanian government would hold her up as an example of how the U.S. blames everyone else for their drug issue, but now there was proof that the drug problem came from within.

He stayed low until he came to a window. He popped his head up for a quick peek, but the room was empty. When movement registered in the corner of his eye, he swung around, but it was Elias entering a shed across the compound.

Finn's voice sounded in his earbud. "Boss man, I think you'd better come see this. I'm in the largest building."

"Roger that." He made his way over to the large structure. The corrugated steel walls had seen better days. He came around the edge of the door and saw Finn standing, looking at something. Nick moved to take a closer look and froze. All the air whooshed out of his lungs as his mind tried to take in the sight.

In front of him was a mountain of bodies heaped one on top of another.

He closed his eyes and opened them again, refocusing on the horrific scene. Men had been thrown in a heap, arms and legs everywhere as if it were garbage day and someone had taken out the trash. His brain fought to make sense of something so incongruous. He attempted to count the number of men in the pile, but his eyes couldn't focus long enough to separate each arm and leg and decipher who it was attached to.

The copper scent of blood and the foul stench of excrement filled his nose, burning all the way to his gut. The poor bastards' bowels had let go after they'd died. The odor was just starting, meaning they hadn't been dead long. In just a few hours, the reek of death would be horrendous. Buzzing flies were already swarming the mound. With the jungle heat, decomposition wouldn't take long to begin in earnest.

Repulsed, Nick had to force himself to look more carefully. The dead men all appeared to have been shot. He met Finn's stunned gaze. Neither man said a word. Calls of "Clear!" sounded in Nick's earbud. Every man eventually made their way to where Nick and Finn stood until all five were staring silently at the nightmarish sight.

Finn cleared his throat. "Do you think any one of them could be alive? Should we be checking?"

Nick shook his head. "Most have body and head shots. My guess is whoever rounded them up made sure these men were dead with a shot to the head."

"Jesus." Elias shook his head. "This is beyond anything we've seen. Even for the most depraved cartel kingpin, there's no need to do something like this. Ever."

Nick realized that the commander of the backup men was approaching their position. He stepped out of the warehouse and headed him off. "Wallace, take your guys and go. We got this."

Wallace frowned. He tried to look beyond Nick, but Nick shifted his weight, and Axe came to stand beside him, blocking Wallace's view.

"You sure, Master Chief? We can provide backup in case anyone else shows up to the party."

"No, we're good. Thanks for the help."

Wallace shrugged and nodded. "Yes, sir. Anytime." He turned and called out to his men. They assembled in the middle of the compound, then headed out the gate and back to their vehicles. Nick and Axe stayed in position until they'd gone.

"No need to have news of this massacre go any further than necessary—at least for the time being. Once word gets out, it will be all over Panama in minutes." Not to mention D.C. Nick's boss was going to have his ass for being involved in this mess. Nick walked back to the doorway and asked, "Does anyone see the tracking device?"

The team did a quick search of the building but came up empty.

"You know what that means, don't you?" Axe's voice was laced with dread.

Nick nodded. "Our GPS is under the pile of bodies. These twisted bastards led us here."

Elias leaned on the wall by the door. "What the hell are we going to do now?"

"And where's the vaccine?" Cain added.

"Good questions," Nick acknowledged. "For now, let's call in the Border cops. This is going to fall to them since it involved a FARC compound. Axe, reach out to Captain Martinez. We'll let him deal with it."

Axe frowned. "Okay, but what do I tell him?"

"How about a version of the truth: intel about a new drug led us here, and this is what we found."

Finn snorted. "Martinez is not going to like that. He'll go apeshit."

Elias nodded. "Oh, yeah. He already hates us. This won't help."

Nick didn't see they had much of a choice. "Martinez will have to live with it because it's the truth. More or less. As we are mere guests of the Panamanian government, this matter is most definitely outside of our purview." He nodded at Axe. "Make the call. The rest of you, look around and see if there's anything left behind that might give us a clue as to who is behind this or where they went. You got twenty minutes. I want this done before Martinez shows up."

He watched his men fan out around the camp. They were all professionals, but this was beyond anything they'd dealt with before. After this was done, he'd have to keep an eye on all of them. Make sure they coped okay. Hell, he had to find a way to cope himself. "What a fucking nightmare," he mumbled as he left the warehouse, surveying the compound from the central open space.

Axe joined him. "This is bound to start a turf war. I mean, one or two guys go down in a firefight, sure, but the systematic killing of every man in this compound is a declaration of war. This is a FARC compound. Only the big boys would take them on, so this isn't the work of any local gang. It has to be either the Sinaloa or Juarez cartels—or the Zetas. But I can't see any of them coming into the Darien Gap and taking the compound. It would be an all-out war."

Nick nodded. "It's overkill. The cartels are bad, and the Zetas are even worse, but no one does this kind of shit. There is a bigger picture here that we're not seeing. Yet." Nick called out, "Finn!"

The operative came jogging over. "Yes, boss man."

"Did anyone you talked to say anything about any new dealers in town or any new players on the board?"

Finn shook his head. "Crickets. There's nothing going on at the moment. As a matter of fact, my black-market sources say it's been quiet."

"Quiet how?" he asked.

"A downturn in volume that worries them. And there's been a few other odd things going on. The Zetas are busy with problems up north, and the FARC have had a rash of bad luck with their shipments—one shipment got lost over the side of a mountain in Columbia, that type of thing—but nothing in the wind is raising alarm bells." He narrowed his eyes. "Why? What are you thinking?"

Nick gestured back toward the building with the bodies. "What message is being sent? And who is it being sent to?"

Nick pulled out his cell and hit a couple of buttons. From his phone, he heard ringing, but there was a corresponding ringing coming from the piles of corpses within the warehouse. He turned around, and the knots in his gut tightened. He walked to the doorway and ended the call.

Hitting redial, he said, "See if you can find Dewey. I'm calling his phone."

Axe and Finn went inside and started the grim search for the ringing. "Maybe it's just Dewey's phone," Axe said, ever the optimist.

Finn shook his head and pointed with his gun. "No. It's Dewey."

Nick joined them. "Where?"

"Sorry, boss," Finn said and pointed again.

Halfway down the mound, an arm stuck out. Recognizing Dewey's tattoo, Nick squatted down for a better look. From the lower angle, he saw Dewey's head. His eyes were still open, an expression of shock frozen on his face.

"Fuck." Nick stood up and signaled to his men to leave the building. "We don't need to be messing up their crime scene."

"Axe, how long 'til Martinez is on site?" Nick asked.

"He's seven minutes out," said Finn.

Cain and Elias came back to stand with the rest of them. "What's the plan, boss man?" Elias asked.

"We stay 'til Martinez gets here then we hightail it back to HQ. I left Dr. Alvarez at HQ being guarded by a few foot soldiers. A sudden cold chill ran down his spine. "I'd thought about security in terms of her trying to break out. I didn't consider that someone might try to break in and harm her."

Axe shifted his weight to his right foot and spat into the dirt. "Do you think someone'd want to kidnap or kill her?"

Unease filled Nick's chest. What if the tracker was a trick to lure them to the site so whoever killed the men could find Carolina? "On second thought, Finn and I will wait for Martinez. Axe, you head back to HQ with Elias and Cain and make sure it's secure. I have a bad feeling and don't want to take any chances. We'll be right behind you. I want check-ins at ten-minute intervals."

The guys nodded, and Axe, Elias, and Cain jogged across the compound and left through the main gate. They had parked the SUVs in the trees just out of sight around the bend in the road. He called the guys back at the warehouse, and everything was fine. He warned them to be on their toes. The feeling of unease was growing.

When the sound of the approaching vehicles reached them, Nick and Finn moved, taking cover behind the warehouse. Being careful was second nature to them, and after seeing the results of a bloodbath, neither wanted to be out in the open in case the men responsible were coming back. He took a quick look around the corner and saw Martinez and his men approaching in a fleet of powerful SUVs of

SENAFRONT vehicles. The National Border Services were here. This was their mess to clean up now.

Nick and Finn walked out to meet them. The lead SUV had barely rolled to a stop when Captain Juan Pablo Martinez hopped out and moved to stand in front of them.

"Taggert, what's this mess your man spoke about?" Martinez demanded. Juan Pablo was a tall man but reed thin. His black hair was slicked back. His olive complexion had turned a deeper shade since Nick had last seen him. He must be spending more time at the beach with his family or his mistress. He was a lucky man with two beach houses.

"You're going to want to check out that building." Nick indicated over his shoulder. He'd told Axe to be deliberately vague on the phone. People were always listening here in Panama.

Martinez signaled to one of his men. The man jogged over to the warehouse and stopped dead as soon as he hit the open doorway. He paused, then bent over and threw up. Martinez swore under his breath and marched over to the warehouse entrance.

Finn raised an eyebrow, silently asking Nick if they should warn Martinez. Nick gave a small negative shake of his head.

Martinez got to the doorway and halted. His body stiffened. His hands curled into fists. When he turned back around, a pang of guilt hit Nick. Martinez's face had lost its impressive tan. He looked like he needed to puke like his officer. Instead, he walked back over to Nick and said, "What the fuck happened here?"

Nick shook his head. "I really wish I knew. The place was silent and deserted when we got here."

Martinez, as if driven by the horror of what he'd just seen, started pacing. He couldn't stay still. "You know this is a FARC compound?"

Nick shrugged. "Really? I had no idea."

He glanced at Nick and seemed to realize he'd spoken out loud. He promptly shut his mouth and stomped away, taking out a cell and making a call.

In a quiet voice, Nick said to Finn, "Go and back the SUV up to the gate. Be prepared for a quick getaway. If Martinez gets a bug up his ass, he could hold us up for hours, and we don't have time to spare."

Finn nodded and broke off from the group, started across the compound as Martinez finished his call.

"Additional manpower is on the way along with several forensic teams." He wiped sweat from his brow. "This is pure evil."

Nick wholeheartedly agreed but kept his mouth shut.

Martinez started barking orders, and his men scattered in all directions. He turned back to Nick. "Okay, Taggert, walk me through how you came to be here again. In detail, this time."

Nick obliged, giving him the truth but with limited details. He completely left out the part about him being the driver of the truck transporting the missing drug shipment and that Dr. Alvarez was back at HQ. He didn't want to bring up the vaccine. He needed time to figure out this fiasco without Martinez mucking it up.

"I will need a written statement from you," said Martinez.

"Of course," said Nick. Paperwork was supposed to be filled out for every interaction between his team and the locals, but neither side usually bothered. But this mess signaled a shitstorm to follow. All the i's needed to be dotted and the t's crossed. "I'll get something to you first thing in the morning," Nick told him.

Martinez gave him a curt nod. "We'll be in touch if we have questions."

Nick turned to go, but stopped and said, "Good luck, Martinez." He didn't bother adding the *you're gonna need it* part. It was implied.

Martinez opened his mouth, but his cell went off, and he just waved Nick away, taking the call.

Nick jogged across the compound and got into the idling SUV with Finn at the wheel. The vehicle took off almost before he pulled the door shut. He leaned back in the seat and closed his eyes, but the horror of what he'd just witnessed was not easily erased. The three hours of sleep he'd managed to carve out that afternoon weren't nearly enough, but they were all he was going to get for a while. This whole op had been a clusterfuck from the start with Dewey's surprise summons. A feeling deep in his bones confirmed it was about to get much worse.

CHAPTER THIRTEEN

A loud thump sounded startled Carolina awake.

Then…silence. Goosebumps rose on her arms. Her heart tapped out a rapid beat against her rib cage. She listened, but there were no more sounds. She didn't know how long she had been asleep. It might have been the whole night, but from the level of fatigue she was feeling, she guessed it couldn't be more than two or three hours. All those years in med school, and more recently with Doctors Without Borders, had trained her body to keep track of time.

She closed her eyes. A few more hours of sleep would be good…

The silence was shattered by gunfire. Carolina shot off the bed and stood ready in the middle of the room. She'd kept on her clothing and shoes so she could be ready for something like this. Except there was nowhere for her to go and nothing she could use as a weapon. The room was pitch-black. She couldn't even see her hand in front of her face.

More gunfire erupted, sounding closer. Her heart rate soared. Gunfire had become part of her existence when she was at work in places like Yemen, so she recognized it right away, but there she had the support of the other medical staff and usually some sort of security setup. She was all alone here.

After another thump, there was the sound of a key turning in the lock. Carolina's heart slammed in her chest and her breath came in gasps.

The door opened, and light flooded in. Carolina raised a hand to block the harsh brightness. A man she'd never seen before entered. He wasn't quite as tall as Nick but still a large man. His dark hair was curly, and he was dressed in camo gear and a bulletproof vest. He was holding a large automatic weapon, but she had no clue what kind. He looked like he could be a local Panamanian, but maybe not. Maybe more Mediterranean, which meant he could be from a whole host of countries. *Was he a friend or foe?*

"Dr. Alvarez. I'm Chief Petty Officer Elias Mason, one of Taggert's team. You need to come with me." The sound of gunfire was louder. Definitely inside the building.

"What's going on? Where's Nick?" She blinked rapidly as her eyes adjusted to the light.

"You need to move now." He pointed toward the door with his gun.

Carolina stepped out into the hallway and found that the man who had led her to the restroom earlier in the day was waiting there, wearing the same outfit as his teammate. He looked even scarier now than he did then.

His green eyes followed her every move. It reminded her of a cat waiting to pounce. "You need to do everything we say. Do not hesitate to follow our instructions. If you deviate from this, you will be killed. Do you understand?" he growled.

She nodded as she heard her grandmother's voice in her head. *"Carolina, that's the type you don't want to meet in a dark alley."*

Nan, you have no idea. Carolina took a deep breath and tried to wrangle her thoughts as she followed Green Eyes down the hallway. Elias was behind her. There was yet another burst of gunfire and some yelling. They moved quickly down the hallway and into the workspace. The blond guy who had interrogated her earlier was there with Nick, and they were filling bags with guns and other equipment from the cabinets along the back wall.

"Here." Nick threw a bag at Elias. "Cain, eyes on the door. Not sure how much longer Wallace's recruits and Finn can hold these guys off down there." Green Eyes was named Cain, Carolina noted. Both men followed Nick's instructions, leaving her standing by herself in the middle of the room.

"What's going on? Who is shooting?" she demanded.

Nick glanced up at her and went back to packing. "The tracker was a trap as well as a message. Whoever has the vaccine wanted to see who was watching the Florevir shipment, and they followed one of us back here. Someone out there wants everyone who knows about the Florevir dead." He looked directly at her, and their gazes locked. His eyes were ice cold. "Or maybe they just want you dead."

A shiver went across her skin, and Carolina swallowed hard. "So you don't have the Florevir?" A volley of gunfire sounded, and the floor next to her exploded. She screamed and turned away as she was showered with debris.

"Go stand in the corner of the outside wall," Nick barked. He pointed to the corner of the room. "The steel beams in the flooring and frame will stop the bullets." He turned to Cain and nodded. Cain left the room. More gunfire. Much closer this time. Whoever was shooting was definitely getting nearer. Maybe on the stairs.

Carolina's heart hammered against her rib cage. Her shoulder hurt where a large chunk of the floor had hit her. She gasped for breath. She'd never been this close to being shot. Not in Ethiopia. Not in Yemen. Adrenaline spiked in her system and made the world seem like it was moving in slow motion.

Nick stuffed one last gun into a large duffle bag and zipped it up. "I'll take Alvarez with me. Axe, you finish packing as much as you can. Elias, I want you to rig the place."

Elias looked up at Nick. "You want me to blow it?"

"Yeah, we don't have time to grab all the equipment, and we can't leave the computers behind for anyone to find. Pack as many laptops as you can and blow the rest."

"You got it." Elias stood and made his way to the last cabinet and started pulling out all kinds of equipment.

The radio that was beside Nick on the table came to life. "More enemies incoming."

Nick grabbed the radio. "Roger that, Finn. We're pulling out with a bang. Can you hold them off for a few minutes?"

"Will do," the voice said again.

"Cain," Nick called. Cain's head popped back around the corner several seconds later. "I'm taking Alvarez with me. Axe is packing up the important stuff and Elias is rigging the place to blow. Go back up Finn and those soldiers, but when Elias says he's ready, get your asses out of here. We'll all meet up at the rendezvous point at oh five hundred."

Cain nodded and left the room again. Nick grabbed a couple of large duffle bags and walked over to Carolina. "Stay close behind me and don't deviate, otherwise you won't make it. We don't have time to fuck around."

Carolina nodded. She had no plans to screw up any kind of escape. The gunfire was increasing. She wanted to be as far from here as possible. "Where are we going?" she asked.

Nick ignored her and handed her a bag. It was heavier than she'd expected. He'd made it seem very light the way he was holding it. She slung the pack over her shoulders and grabbed the duffel he'd put at her feet.

Nick took off across the room and down the hallway, and she followed. They turned into the kitchen area in front of the fridge. *Was he stopping for snacks?* When he yanked out the massive fridge, there was a large hole in the wall behind it.

"Go," Nick commanded.

Suppressing any hesitation at the surrealness of it all, she carried her bags through the hole and onto a landing as the sounds of more shouting and a rapid burst of gunfire filtered through the building. She descended the stairs into darkness. The only light was from the hole behind her. She stopped on the stairs to wait for Nick, who threw the other bags through the hole and onto the landing, then came through after. He pulled the fridge back in place.

The stairs were pitch-black. Her heart slammed into her rib cage, and a cold sweat broke out on her back. She leaned against the wall but immediately regretted it. Cold and damp penetrated her thin shirt.

She heard a click, and the beam of a flashlight appeared on the stairs. Nick handed it to her. "Hold this." She did as she was told, but her hand trembled slightly, causing the light to vibrate. She rested the light against her thigh to keep its beam steady.

Nick loaded up the gear, then grabbed the light from her. He pushed past her, which jammed her hard against the wall, scraping her back on the cement. But she didn't say a word. It wasn't the time. He pounded down the stairs at breakneck speed. She went after him as quickly as she could, but not as sure-footed. The weight of the bags was throwing her off balance. She wanted to curse and ask him to slow down but knew he wouldn't.

"Doc, you've got to move faster," he said from in front. "We don't have much time. You need to haul ass."

She cursed silently as he hit the bottom of the stairs a few seconds before she did and took off at a jog. When she stepped off the last stair, it took her a second to adjust her load and take off after him. The floor was uneven, but she was used to that from running on New York City sidewalks. Even with the awkward burden of the bags, she easily caught up to Nick. *So there.*

But she wasn't used to running with extra weight and knew she was going to have to do some major stretching after this or her back would seize up. Assuming she survived, of course. A nervous giggle fought to free itself from her chest. Laughing in front of Nick would not help if she wanted him to take her seriously. Obviously, he had doubts about her, and she needed his help to get the Florevir back and down to Ecuador.

Nick halted suddenly in front of her, and she crashed into him. He was solid as a rock wall.

He grunted. "You okay?" He turned and shone the flashlight in her direction.

"Fine," she said. "I can keep up." And she could, too, as long as they weren't going to run twenty miles like this.

Nick turned back, and his flashlight lit up another long stairwell. This one went up. He started taking the stairs two at a time. *Oh, brother.*

She put her head down and started up, taking the stairs one at a time but at a respectable clip. It was like a nighttime stadium workout. *Yup, except for the gunfire and the cement walls that smelled like mold.* Thankfully, the gunfire had disappeared. However, she was sure she saw something alarmingly big and furry skitter across the step in front of her. She ignored it. She did not want to know what lived in the tunnel.

She stopped suddenly when Nick turned the flashlight off. The darkness was complete. She shivered and waited a beat, then whispered, "What's going on?" She heard Nick shifting his bags around, but he said nothing.

"Nick?" Panic clawed its way up her chest. Her throat was starting to close over. She never thought of herself as afraid of the dark, but she'd never been in a situation like this before. "Nick?" she whispered again.

"It's okay, Carolina," he spoke softly. He was perfectly calm, not even winded. "I'm just making sure no one's outside this door."

After what seemed like an eternity, he shifted the stuff again.

"Are you ready to move?" he asked.

"Yes." She stood up straight and tried to loosen up her shoulders despite the load.

Nick pushed the door open. The fluorescent lights made her blink.

"Carolina, move now." Nick's voice was controlled, but she sensed the urgency.

She dropped her hand and looked down at the stairs. She came up the last few steps like that, then stepped through a door. They were in a parking garage.

Nick started across the cement flooring, and she followed. His head swiveled from side to side, so she did the same, though not sure what she should be looking for. She figured she'd know if she saw it.

He stopped at the trunk of an old dusty black Jeep parked halfway up the ramp. He opened the back and dumped inside all the gear he'd been carrying. He motioned for her to do the same. Nick closed the back and then hopped in the driver's side. Once she was in the passenger seat, he leaned over and flipped her visor down, then he reached behind her seat and handed her a hat. It was olive-colored with a wide brim. "Put this on and keep your face angled down."

"Who am I hiding from?" she asked while doing as she was told.

"Everyone. There are cameras around, and I don't want anyone to be able to identify you if we can avoid it." He pulled a ball cap out of the glove box and put it on his head, then pulled out a Glock. He tucked it under his thigh on the seat. "Just in case," he said.

In case of what? she wanted to ask, but better he concentrated on getting them out of there, though where they were going, she had no idea. Was he worried whoever was shooting at them back there would find them?

She tried to temporarily suppress the burning need to know everything that was going on. She was used to being the one giving orders. This sitting back and doing what she was told rubbed her the wrong way. It was contrary to her nature. She linked her fingers together in her lap and tried to think calming thoughts, but none came to her. Meditation wasn't her thing. All that came into her head was Javier falling down the escalator, and that wasn't helpful at all.

They pulled out of the parking garage and drove down the street. He seemed to be moving toward the city center. The streets were getting wider, and the stores were changing from industrial business to corner stores and mom and pop shops. Nothing was open since it was the middle of the night, but there was an occasional person on the street.

A huge explosion rocked the Jeep. She whirled around to look behind them. There was a fireball shooting up into the sky. She looked at Nick. "Was that the warehouse?"

"Yes."

Her heart hammered in her chest. She struggled to breathe. "Oh, my God! Did everyone get out okay?"

He shrugged. "I assume so."

"But…what if they didn't?"

"Then they didn't." He stayed focused on the road.

She was aghast. "But they're your men. Aren't you worried? Can't you contact them and see if they're okay?"

"No. We'll meet up in a couple of hours. Everyone will follow protocol."

"But why blow it all up? I mean, couldn't they just leave like we did?"

"No. We didn't have time to destroy all of the hard drives and equipment, so the best thing to do is blow the place. All of the intel we've gathered on various cartels, gangs, and other groups is on those hard drives, as well as emails from our commanding officers and other classified information. We didn't have time to pack it all so blowing it was the only choice. We can't leave anything behind that the cartels could use against us. There's information about our DEA contacts on there. We can't jeopardize their lives as well as our own."

She licked her lips, and her hands shook as she brushed her hair back out of her face. Her fingers were dirty, and she looked for a place to wipe them off but realized her clothes weren't much better. Her khaki shirt was smudged with grime and her cargo pants had a stain of some unknown origin. Maybe from the tunnel? She didn't really want to think about it.

Outside her window, the shops looked more polished. Bigger buildings with fancier stores. Lots of places to grab coffee or eat. Like the downtown of every major city. In a few hours, it would open up like normal, but her world was far from normal. Sirens sounded in the distance. People were dead, and buildings were blowing up. She prayed she wasn't next.

Her thoughts were flitting from one thing to the next. Suddenly she turned to Nick. "The vaccine!" She couldn't believe she forgot about it. "Where is it?"

His razor-sharp gaze met hers. "We ran into…a problem."

"A problem? Does that mean you don't know where the vaccine is?" As she studied his face, her heart sank.

"Yes. It's been moved. Whoever took the shipment found our GPS tracker and left it behind. Like I said, it was a trap."

She gritted her teeth. "Who has it then? Do you know where they've taken it?" The Tarchuarani could be dead in a month or two—an entire people and culture wiped off the face of the earth.

Nick stared out the windshield. "We're not sure, but we're following up on several leads."

"That's bullshit, and you and I both know it. How about telling me the truth?"

"You want the truth?" Nick swerved the Jeep to the curb and screeched to a halt. He leaned across the center console of the Jeep, so their faces were inches apart. "We got to the compound where your vaccine was supposed to be, and we found a stack, a literal pile, of bodies—all of them shot. Buried beneath them was our tracker so we'd be sure to find those men. Any idea why someone would do that?"

Carolina was stunned. She closed her eyes and said a quick prayer for all the dead people. She hadn't gone to church in years, but after dealing with ill and mistreated people for the last few years, she needed to believe in something greater than humankind. She opened her eyes. How could a vaccine cause so much death? "I've told you everything I know. I'm so sorry these men lost their lives, but more are going to die if we don't find that vaccine." She shook her head. "Does this…type of thing happen often down here? I mean, is…a stack of corpses someone's signature, like a specific cartel or group?"

Nick's jaw muscle pulsated. "This *type of thing* has never happened down here. This is not a local gang or cartel *thing*.

It's a new experience, lady, and it seems like an awful big coincidence that it happened right when you got to town. So why don't you tell me again about this vaccine. Who wants it? Who knows about it?"

Carolina did her best to keep her temper in check. She counted to ten and then said a Hail Mary or two, but it was no good.

"Answer me damnit!" Nick roared.

Emotion bubbled beneath the surface like magma working its way up through the earth's crust. Fatigue rolled over her. "I told you everything. Javier asked for my help. I agreed. He gave me the information, and I followed his instructions. I'd love some answers, too, but since he's still in the ICU and in a coma, we're shit out of luck." She glared at him as she took another breath. "What are you doing to find the Florevir?"

Nick stared at her. "You're not getting it. Whoever put the tracker under all those bodies did it because they knew someone would come for the vaccine. My guess is they thought it would be you. They want you. That's what happened back at the warehouse. Those men were coming for you. So you better start talking. I want it all. The whole story. Your life, and now the lives of my people, all depend on it."

Carolina's hands shook. Numbing fear rolled over her entire body. Javier falling down the escalator played in slow motion in her mind. Someone wanted that to be her. Some unknown person out there actively wanted her dead. This whole trip was a giant mistake. She thought she could save the Tarchuarani on her own, like some hero in an action film. Stupid. And now she might pay for her stupidity with her life. She closed her eyes and bit her lip. She fought the urge to puke.

Nick put the Jeep in gear and rolled away from the curb.

"You said that Javier was in ICU, and you couldn't ask him questions, so how did he give you the instructions that you were following to get here?"

She didn't want to tell him about the USB drive because then he'd know the rest of the plan. On the other hand, without the vaccine, there was no plan. And someone was trying to kill her. "He sent me a USB stick."

"What do you mean he sent it to you?"

"He left it in an envelope with my doorman."

Nick glanced her way and then back out through the windshield. "What's on the drive? Do you have it with you?"

She shook her head. "There was a video of instructions and the documentation I would need. I memorized everything on the stick and hid it in my apartment. Javier was adamant that I didn't tell anyone what was going on. He said he was in trouble, and there were people who wanted the vaccine. He didn't tell me why."

"Dr. Javier Florez told you all of this, you memorized the information, but didn't bring it with you?"

"That's right." Carolina felt the weight and hostility behind Nick's glare. She had to convince him she was telling the truth. "You must have looked through all my stuff. I don't have the USB stick here. It's back in my apartment in New York."

Nick tapped his fingers on the steering wheel. "Did you put it in a safe? Not that it would matter."

"What does that mean?"

"Someone wanted to stop Javier and pushed him down the escalator, and now they came for you. We can assume they have the USB stick unless there's some other way for them to know your plan. Who doesn't want you to take the vaccine to the Tarchuarani?"

"That seems like an awful big leap. Maybe it was a drug war thing that got the men killed down here. We don't know for sure they want me. Maybe they want you and your team dead. And what Panamanian has the resources to break into my New York apartment?"

"Maybe the same ones who pushed Dr. Florez down an escalator?" Nick reached across her and opened the glove box. "Here," he said, handing her a cell phone. "I want you to check your messages at your apartment and on your cell."

Carolina sighed. She started to put her phone to her ear, but Nick reached out and stopped her. "What now?" she asked.

"Put it on speaker," he demanded.

He still didn't trust her. "Okay." She dialed the number and went through the steps to access her voicemail. She had five new messages. She hit the button. The Jeep filled with a reminder from her dry cleaner that her clothing was ready, and did she want to come pick it up? The next message was her neighbor telling her to stop banging around so much. Carolina frowned as her belly knotted. She wasn't there. *Who was making noise in her apartment?*

The last few calls were from her doorman. "Hi, Dr. Alvarez. The men are here to install your new garbage disposal. You didn't mention you were getting work done. We usually require prior notice, so I need your authorization to let them into your apartment. Call me back." Then he listed the number. The next message was more of the same from her doorman.

"Did you order a garbage disposal?" Nick asked.

She shook her head. "I don't like garbage disposals." The knots that had started in her belly now traveled to her shoulders. Her whole body tensed, and she broke out in a cold sweat.

"Call your doorman and ask him to go up to your apartment and check on it."

She glanced at her watch. "They're an hour ahead of us. It's three in the morning in Manhattan."

"Yes." He stared at her.

Her heartbeat ticked up a notch, but she made the call.

A groggy voice answered. "Weston Towers."

"Hi, Lenny, how are you? It's Dr. Alvarez in Six-B."

"Dr. Alvarez? Ah, I'm fine. How are you? It's kind of late to call. Is everything alright?"

"Yes. I'm out of town and just got your messages."

Nick frowned at her. But what was she supposed to say, calling at this hour? She didn't want the doorman to think she was a nutjob who called in the middle of the night to check on her apartment. She'd have to tip him extra at Christmas. "The thing is, Lenny, I didn't order a garbage disposal. Can you possibly go up and look at my place? I'm a little concerned." *Another understatement.*

"I'm confused, Dr. Alvarez. These guys had all the correct paperwork with them. They showed me the work order that you'd signed and paid. I swear, I'd never have let them in if they didn't have that."

'I know that, Lenny. I think it's all a big mistake. At worst, I have a new garbage disposal. No worries. I would just appreciate it if you could check on my apartment for me."

"Um, well, I'm here by myself since it's so late. You know I usually do the day shift, but Dan needed the night off for something, so we switched. Let me get Brian from maintenance to cover the desk. I'll call you back. Can I reach you on this number?"

She glanced at Nick, who nodded. "Yes, this number is fine. Thanks, Lenny," she said before ending the call. "Someone broke into my place."

Nick nodded. "And they were professionals. This isn't someone off the street."

She wiped her palms on her cargo pants and wondered if she was going to be sick. The phone rang, and she jumped. She glanced at Nick, and he nodded. She answered the call and put it on speaker.

"Dr. Alvarez, it's Lenny. I'm opening your door now."

"Okay, thanks." There were a few muffled sounds, and then the familiar squeak of her hinges sounded over the phone.

"Holy shit!" Lenny said. "Oh, my God."

"What's going on?" she asked, trying to keep her voice calm, but she already knew what he was going to say.

"I'm so sorry, Dr. Alvarez. Your place… It's trashed. It looks like a bomb went off in here." Lenny's words tumbled over one another. "I need to call the police. But they had the right paperwork. I swear they did! I followed the rules!" The pitch of his voice was rising with every word.

"Lenny, I know you did. It's okay. None of this is your fault. Absolutely none of it, okay? I will make sure management knows this as well," Carolina said in her best patient-in-a-crisis voice. "Before you call the police, I need you to go over to the plant by the balcony, the one with the pot that's a face." She'd gone with her best friend, Amira, to one of those paint-your-own pottery places and found this huge pot with a funny face on it. They'd had a great time painting the pot. Then Amira had bought her a hardy fern to put in it.

"I probably shouldn't go into your place. The police won't like it."

She sighed inwardly. "It's okay. I just need to know something. Can you go to that plant?"

"Um…okay."

There were muffled sounds, and then he was back. "Okay, I have the plant."

"There should be a baggie hidden in the pot, covered by dirt. Is it still there?"

"Um, the plant isn't in the pot. It's on the floor. There's dirt everywhere. The pot is broken."

Carolina's gaze met Nick's. She shook her head. "Okay, Lenny, thanks so much for checking. Why don't you lock up again and call the police? You can give them this number if they want to speak to me."

"Yes, ma'am."

"Lenny, don't tell them about me asking you to check the pot. What's missing isn't important. It was of sentimental value, and I just don't want to have to explain it all to the police."

Lenny hesitated briefly. "I won't say anything."

"Thank you. I really appreciate it."

"Dr. Alvarez, I am so sorry about all this."

"Me, too. Don't worry, though, it's not your fault. We'll talk again later."

She ended the call and stared blankly at the scenery they were whizzing past. They had the USB stick. "Those men really were after me. All those people died because of me."

Nick glanced at her. "Yes, you're the target but those men died because someone somewhere doesn't want the Tarchuarani to survive."

Carolina swallowed hard. They had all the information Javier had given her. They'd hijacked the vaccine and killed many men for it. Who were *they*?

CHAPTER FOURTEEN

Nick ran a hand through his hair and then put it back on the steering wheel. He stole a glance at Carolina. She still had dust in her hair from the flooring debris. *Jesus*. His heart had almost stopped when the floor had exploded around her. A few inches to the left, and she would have been dead.

Last week he'd have thought that's what he wanted, but seeing her terrified and almost killed... It didn't bear thinking about. He might blame her for his back, but he didn't want her dead. He wanted her far away from here. From danger. From him.

All those hours she'd spent with him in Yemen, talking about life, family, the things they had in common. They both loved to travel and explore new places. They liked hiking and biking and swimming.

He hadn't reached out when he first got back to the United States, but he'd thought he would find her *after* he'd healed and ask her out. He wanted to be one hundred percent before they reconnected. It bothered him that she'd seen him only at his weakest. He wanted to be healthy when they reconnected. He wanted to take her for a hike and then a barbecue or something. He'd had plans for them. Camping under the stars. He'd dreamed of her often. Right up until the doctor in California told him what a mess his back was, and he may never regain all the feeling in it. She still haunted his dreams, only now they were nightmares.

He tightened his grip on the steering wheel. "We have to figure out who wants you dead. Who doesn't want the vaccine to get to the Tarchuarani?"

Carolina cleared her throat. "I know. I just... I can't think right now." She turned her head away from him. "What do you do? I mean, how are you here in Panama?"

Nick sighed. He wanted to force her to go over her story one more time. He hated that someone killed all those people and tried to kill his team, but he also understood if he pushed her too hard at this moment, he'd get nowhere.

"As I said, we're part of the Coast Guard. Specifically?" How the hell was he supposed to describe them? "We're a mishmash of guys from different parts of the special operations groups. Finn and I are from Maritime Safety and Security units which is sort of like a SWAT team you'd find in a major city or an FBI hostage rescue team."

"Is that what you were doing in Yemen? Some sort of hostage rescue?"

"Uh, I can't talk about Yemen but let's just say we also deal with pirates."

"Oh, I see. What about the rest of the guys?"

"Elias and Cain are MSRT." He glanced at Carolina. Her brow was furrowed. "It stands for Maritime Security Response Team. Think Navy SEALs. Same type of thing."

"And Axe?"

"He's from a TACLET team. Tactical Law Enforcement. Drug interdiction is actually part of his job along with a host of other things. He's sort of like a cop or a military policeman."

Carolina was still frowning. "So, are you guys normally together in a team like this?"

"No," Nick shook his head. "We've all been injured one way or another and our boss put us together down here in Panama sort of as an experiment. We're stationed here to keep a hand in—I guess you'd say—until we're a hundred percent again."

"So what does that mean exactly?"

"Panama is fairly quiet these days," said Nick, "at least in comparison to the eighties. We're here to keep an eye on things. You know, do jobs like I did initially with you and Dewey. Be José and stick a tracker on a shipment so the DEA can track it and get a bigger picture of how drugs are moved from country to country. Gather and analyze intel, that sort of thing. You and this whole vaccine business? It's straight out of left field for us."

"Tell me about it," she mumbled under her breath.

He laughed.

She glared at him but then started laughing as well. "Clearly, I'm not used to being hijacked by men with guns."

"Clearly," Nick agreed with a grin. Then the grin faded. "Now, we have to figure out why this is happening and who's behind it."

He glanced over, but Carolina had put her head back on the headrest and had her eyes closed. He had the urge to smooth back her hair. He clenched his jaw. He had to get his edge back and his focus. Having Carolina around was not helping that one bit.

Two hours later, as the sun was just peeking over the horizon, Nick pulled off the main road onto a dirt track. Carolina woke with a start when he hit a pothole. "Where are we?"

"At the rendezvous point." The dirt track wound through dense jungle for another few minutes until it ended suddenly in a clearing. On the far end of the open space was a beach. Nick let out a long breath. The rest of the team was already there. He hadn't lost anyone in the gunfight or the explosion. He parked the Jeep, and he and Carolina got out.

"You made it. Everyone good?" he asked as he rounded the front of the car.

"All in one piece," Axe replied. "Or at least in the same number of pieces as we were before the warehouse firefight." He came forward, and they bumped shoulders before he handed Nick a Styrofoam cup filled with black coffee. Liquid gold as far as Nick was concerned. Axe turned and handed a cup of some sort of fragrant tea to Carolina. She wrapped her fingers around it and mumbled her thanks.

Finn sat on the hood of the dark blue SUV, and Axe joined him. They had two Styrofoam cups next to them and a laptop. Cain and Elias were sitting with their coffee on the tailgate of a red late-model pickup truck. Elias had a laptop next to him, and Cain sat with an automatic weapon in his lap. At the ready as always.

Carolina sat down gingerly on the bumper of the Jeep while Nick leaned against the driver's side. "So, what do we know?" he asked.

"Not much," Axe responded grimly.

Nick agreed. "I think we can assume that the tracker was left to lure us there to find out who was tracking the vaccine. They followed us and tried to kill us."

Finn leaned over, resting his elbows on his knees. "Do you think they were after us, or her?" He nodded toward Carolina.

Nick scratched his chin. "Both, quite possibly. Anyone who seems to know anything about the Florevir ends up dead. Shit. Florez is still in a coma in NYU Hospital.

Considering the break-in at the doc's and what's gone on down here, he should probably have a guard."

"Break-in?" Elias asked.

"Yeah, a couple of guys broke into her apartment and stole the thumb drive Florez gave her with the plan for getting the vaccine to Ecuador." Nick didn't look at Carolina. He was still pissed she hadn't told them sooner about the USB drive.

Elias grunted. "So that's how they knew her plan."

Nick nodded.

"On the other hand"—Axe pulled himself back and leaned on the windshield—"if they are keeping an eye on Florez and police guards show up, they'll know we're on to them, or at least that someone is."

"Good point, Axe." Nick looked down at the sand for a minute and let the sound of the waves calm him. It could be a life-or-death call. If he made the wrong one, Florez might die, but it also might make their lives just that much more difficult.

Nick shrugged. "We'll let it ride for the next twenty-four hours. Florez is still comatose, so he's not currently a threat to anyone. If that changes, we'll have to reassess, but telling the world what's going on down here will just unnecessarily complicate the situation." An image of the dead bodies flashed into his mind. Things were already far beyond complicated.

Elias asked, "Who do we think is behind this? It doesn't seem like a cartel thing, and obviously the FARC wouldn't kill their own, so who does that leave us with?"

"Good question," Nick grunted. "And who would have the ability to take out all those members of FARC in their own compound?" He glanced at Axe. "See if you can track down anyone who's seen the shipment or anyone who knows anything about it. Actually, ask if anyone has seen any strangers in town flashing around money and asking about the shipment. See if the word 'vaccine' has come up. Check local hotels, et cetera. These guys will not want to attract too much attention, but maybe they won't be able to help it. There must be a fair number of people involved for them to be able to kill that many people at the FARC compound."

Whoever had the shipment had probably sent up red flags when they entered Panama if—and it was a big if—they had arrived legally. Somehow, Nick thought they did. Why take the risk of illegal entry if you didn't have to? "Who has the burner phones?"

Elias grabbed one of the bags in the back of the pickup and pulled out a phone. He threw it to Nick.

"Thanks. I'm gonna make a call." He walked down to the water's edge. The waves were small in the early morning light, and lapped rhythmically on the shore. He knew the sand would be soft and the water warm. He longed to go for a swim but he couldn't until this fucked up situation was unfucked. Sighing, he dialed a number.

After he heard the phone being picked up on the other end, he turned on the charm. "Angelia, how are you?"

"Nick Taggert. Do you know what time it is? What do you want?"

He put his hand over his chest, even though she couldn't see him. "Angelia, you wound me."

"Nick, you are so full of it. It's the middle of the night."

"The sun is almost up, Angelia."

She made a hissing sound. "We go out for drinks, and then I don't hear from you for weeks. Why should I even talk to you?"

"I had business out of town."

Angelia snorted. "You always say you have a business, and yet you won't tell me what it is you do."

"Angelia, you know I can't talk about it," he said in a husky voice. "It's classified."

"Classified. *Pfff.* I don't believe you."

He could picture her tossing her black glossy hair. He smiled. "Angelia, how about if we go out to dinner this weekend? Your favorite restaurant, the one on the square."

"*Riesen* is expensive. You must want something badly." Her voice had turned soft and seductive.

"I need you to do me a small favor."

She heaved an exaggerated sigh. "Of course, you do. What is it?"

Yes. He smiled. "I need to know if anyone has entered the country in the last week or so that set off any alarms."

"Alarms?"

"You know, anyone who triggered any red flags or grabbed customs' or any other department's attention. Probably ex-military types."

"Nick, this is Panama. There are all kinds of...interesting ex-military types here, including you."

He laughed. "You know what I mean. Can you get me a list?"

The sigh sounded over the phone line again. "I'll see what I can do. But dinner at *Riesen* in Panama City on Saturday night."

"Deal."

"I'll send you an email if I find anything." She made kissing noises and hung up.

It was Wednesday now, so there was little chance he was going to make Saturday night's dinner the way things were going. He made a mental note to send her a huge bouquet of flowers on Saturday to make up for the cancellation. She'd make him pay big time, but if his hunch was right, it'd be worth it.

CHAPTER FIFTEEN

Carolina's stomach growled. She glanced at her watch. It was only five twenty a.m., but her body wanted breakfast. "Does anyone have something to eat?" When all heads turned to her, heat climbed up her neck to her cheeks. "Sorry, but I'm hungry and I don't function well if I don't eat."

Axe grinned. "You're my kinda gal." He reached in a duffel bag and pulled out an apple. He tossed it to her.

"Thanks." She took a big bite. It was sweet and juicy and quite possibly the best thing she'd ever eaten. She munched happily as the guys relaxed in the clearing. All except for the guy with the large gun. Cain. She looked around at the men, reviewing their names in her head. It was all very surreal.

She glanced out at the water. It was beautiful, and so was the man standing next to it. Well, maybe not beautiful, but sexy as hell. He looked good standing there in his black T-shirt and cargo pants. Tall. Dark. Dangerous. Just the type of man she'd avoided all her life. She always went for the geeky guys. She liked intelligence. She found it sexy. How could someone who looked like Nick be so damned smart, too? It just wasn't fair.

She couldn't make out the words, but she could hear the tone of voice clear enough. He was flirting. Jealousy flared in her chest. He'd used that tone with her sometimes back in Yemen when they'd chatted. His teasing tone. She'd loved it. Other times, they'd been more serious. Like when he talked about his father and half-siblings. He had told her about feeling like he didn't belong within his own family, and she understood it to her core. They were peas in a pod in many ways. Too bad he seemed to hate her now.

As if he could feel the weight of her stare, he turned toward her. Their gazes locked. A rush of adrenaline shot through her and warmth pooled low in her belly. But then Nick looked away, and disappointment filled her. He ended his call and came back to the vehicles.

Carolina," Nick said, leaning against the Jeep again. "Can you think of anyone who would gain from the Tarchuarani dying? Anyone who doesn't want you to succeed?"

She shook her head.

"Did Javier mention anything else? Even the smallest thing could give us a lead."

She continued shaking her head but stopped suddenly.

"What?" Nick asked. "What did you remember?"

"Javier said he made a mistake. It didn't sink in when he said it. He had called the biotech company that's modifying the mosquitoes, Biodome Technologies, and told them the mosquitoes were making the Tarchuarani sick. He thought if he informed them, they'd do something about it. But they didn't know, or perhaps they didn't want to know. Weird things started happening after that."

"Weird like what?" Nick asked.

"Javier's research funding at NYU dried up, and he was dis-invited to speak at several conferences."

"Did that strike you as odd?"

"To be honest, the whole video was so strange I'm not sure I really thought about that aspect of it." She bit her lip. "I mean, funding does dry up, and sometimes event planners have to change things, so maybe there was scheduling problems with his lectures."

Nick frowned. "What does your gut tell you?"

She stared at Nick for a long beat. "Javier was telling the truth." She knew it in her bones.

Nick took a sip of coffee. "Why don't you tell us what you know about Biodome Technologies."

"They've been around for quite a while. I mean, they aren't one of the big guys like Bristol Myers Squib or Johnson and Johnson, but they've brought a few major products to the market. They've been successful in the vaccine game a couple of times for smaller vaccines. The head guy, Edward Langston, has a reputation for being aggressive and ruthless, but he gets results, and that's what his shareholders want."

"So they're well-funded," Nick said.

"I'd say so. With biotech firms, it's sometimes hard to tell. They play it close to the vest, but this mosquito project, if it works, would be a huge deal for them. It would put them at the forefront of the pharma industry. Their stock would go crazy."

Nick's eyes narrowed. "Can you explain what exactly Florez's vaccine is for and why it's so damned important? What exactly is Biodome Technologies doing? You need to enlighten us."

Her heart gave a thump. She'd promised Javier she wouldn't say anything, but given the current circumstances, well, they were beyond keeping anything a secret now. She took a last bite of her apple and threw the core into the jungle.

"Javier spent time with the Tarchuarani as a kid. His dad was an anthropologist. Javier has sort of kept an eye on them over the years. It was something he promised his father before the man died. Anyway, a while back—I'm not sure how long—Guillermo, a family friend of Javier, got in touch with Javier and said the Tarchuarani were getting sick and dying in record numbers." She stopped. "Do any of you know about the Tarchuarani?"

The men shook their heads except Nick. "Assume we don't know a thing and start from the beginning," he said.

"Okay, well, the Tarchuarani is a small tribe, just a few hundred people left, that lives in the Amazon in what is now Ecuador. They avoid any contact with the outside world. I can't remember when they were first discovered by outsiders, but it wasn't a pleasant experience for them, and they have no interest in connecting with anyone else. They live as they have always lived for hundreds of years.

"Javier's father established contact in 1962. He helped them with a tuberculosis outbreak by supplying them with some antibiotics to supplement their natural medicines, and a friendship developed. They granted him and his assistant— I'm guessing here, but I think it was Guillermo's father who was Javier's father's assistant—limited access. Both men brought their sons with them on healthcare checks, and so the Tarchuarani got to know Guillermo and Javier.

"Fast forward to Guillermo contacting Javier, saying the tribe was sick. Javier did some poking around and discovered that Biodome Technologies was doing a research study in the area using mosquitoes. Guillermo and Javier believe this is what is making the Tarchuarani sick and causing their deaths."

Nick ran a hand through his hair. "I don't understand.

What sort of insect study makes people sick? Are they spraying some sort of chemical?"

She shook her head. "It's the mosquitoes that Biodome has introduced into the Amazon."

"Does the Amazon need more mosquitoes?" Axe asked as he squished one on his arm. "I'm guessing they already have a shitload."

"Yes, there're many mosquitoes in the Amazon, and they can be carriers for diseases like Dengue fever, malaria, West Nile, Zika and typhoid. My guess—from the little that Javier said— is Biodome was developing a mosquito that could help stop the spread of diseases. I know research is being done on shortening their life cycles. Only the female mosquitoes bite humans and they do it when they hit a certain point in their life cycle; if you make their overall life cycle shorter by cross-breeding and changing their DNA, then they don't live long enough to bite, so they can't spread diseases."

"So what are they doing in the Amazon?" Nick asked. He shifted his weight again, now leaning against the Jeep with his right hip.

"I assume they released these new mosquitoes into the wild, and they're studying the results."

"And how is this affecting the Tarchuarani?" Nick asked.

Carolina shook her head. "The new mosquitoes would be genetically engineered mosquitoes, which will make them hardier, and they might carry different diseases. Javier thought one of these new diseases the mosquitoes are carrying are causing the Tarchuarani's organs to shut down until they die."

"Wait," Axe said as he plopped down in his chair. "I thought the mosquitoes weren't supposed to bite."

Carolina nodded. "They shouldn't."

"If they can shorten life spans and stuff like that, why

don't they get rid of pesky mosquitoes altogether?" Axe pointed at himself. "I, for one, wouldn't miss 'em at all."

"They're needed to maintain the proper balance of the ecosystem," Nick said as he straightened up.

"Exactly right," Carolina agreed. "Eventually over time the population of mosquitoes would dwindle using this approach, but it would take many years." She eyed Nick. His back was bothering him. She could tell by the way he kept moving around. No doubt it was aggravated by all the extra weight he'd been carrying. She would love to offer help, but there was no way he would accept it. Besides, now wasn't the moment.

Nick asked. "But why are these mosquitoes killing the Tarchuarani? Will they kill all humans?"

"Yeah," Axe said, his brow furrowed. "What's to stop them all from moving north and killing the rest of us?"

She smiled. "My guess is they won't kill you, Axe. Biodome wouldn't risk releasing these genetically modified mosquitoes into the wild if they thought they could kill the entire human race. It wouldn't make them money."

"But the Tarchuarani are dying," Cain stated as he watched the jungle for movement.

"Yes," Carolina agreed. "Living in total isolation, the Tarchuarani have a limited gene pool. Their homogeneity likely means the majority of them carry the same genetic abnormality that makes them susceptible to a new disease. They have no defense against it. It's like the First Nations and smallpox when white men first arrived in America. They had no way to save themselves."

She turned to Axe. "To your point, there will be other people in the world that will have the same reaction because they have the same mutation, but the percentage would likely be so small, it may be considered acceptable to Biodome. It wouldn't be enough to stop their project."

"Wait, what do you mean by acceptable? Like acceptable losses?" Elias asked.

She nodded. "Every new drug that's created has side effects. If you have ever watched one of the medicine commercials on television back in the U.S., you've heard them list the side effects. Headaches, nausea, or dry mouth are considered acceptable because they don't usually do any permanent damage and they are treatable with other drugs. Other side effects like cancer or permanent damage to organs are not acceptable if they occur in high numbers.

"The thing is…death is acceptable in the pharmaceutical world if the numbers are low enough. Knowing a drug may kill less than one percent of users is, although not ideal, at least tolerable if it cures or provides a good result to the other ninety-nine percent. It's an acceptable standard.

"So the idea is these new genetically modified mosquitoes will breed with regular mosquitoes, and their offspring will have short lifespans. If this experiment works, it could stop the spread of all these diseases. Think of how many lives would be saved. Think of the numbers globally. One percent is a tiny number in comparison. The needs of the many outweigh the needs of the few."

"Collateral damage," Nick said.

Carolina agreed. "Yes. It's not a perfect system, but it's what we have, and pharmaceutical companies have saved millions upon millions of lives using this principal."

"So then the Tarchuarani are collateral damage," Axe said.

Nick looked at Carolina. "You think it's no accident these mosquitoes are being tested next to this tribe?"

She shrugged. "All I know is that Javier pointed out they were dying, and suddenly he's in a coma."

"Why would someone want the tribe dead?" Axe asked.

Nick stood up. "I think it's time we found out."

Nick walked over and retrieved a laptop from Axe while the rest of the guys took turns scouting the area. The sun was crawling higher in the sky, and it was heating up. He set the laptop on the hood of the Jeep. Bertrand would go ballistic if he didn't call in soon. Nick and the boys had blown up HQ. It wasn't something he wouldn't find out about ASAP.

Nick sighed and caught Carolina's eye again. She sent him another sympathetic look like she knew he was in pain and wanted to help. He wanted her help all right, her hands on his body. He clenched his jaw. Focusing was hard around her, and it wasn't the only thing that was hard.

He needed Carolina out of his world. Even with a coating of dust all over her, she looked beautiful. Her dark hair had red highlights that looked like fire in the morning light. Her brown eyes were soft and sleepy. It was enough to make a man do something like grab her and kiss her.

No. This needed to be over with as soon as possible. Carolina caused too great a disturbance, and he didn't like it. Not one bit. She saved his life back in Yemen by giving him blood and sewing him up, but she took something from him as well. His trust that his body could function at peak ability when he needed it. His back was still numb in spots and his muscles just didn't feel fluid like they used to. His doctor in California confirmed that had his back been put together by a proper surgeon he probably wouldn't be experiencing these symptoms. He needed to remember that otherwise he might do something stupid, like fall for her. Hard.

He ran his hands over his face and looked up at his laptop screen. He checked his email. Angelia had been as good as her word. He opened an email with an attachment. She reminded him about dinner Saturday. He smiled and opened the accompanying file. He ran down a list of thirty-four names she'd pulled from Panamanian Customs and Immigration at the airport. Not so many considering that some weeks there were hundreds of shady characters arriving in-country.

None of the names popped out at him, but he cross-checked the list against several other lists the US government maintained of suspicious characters. Six names popped up. He did a deep dive on those names. With each one, the knots in his shoulders grew along with the acid level in his gut.

"We've got a major problem," he announced.

The guys all came back to the circle of vehicles. Finn and Axe climbed back up on the hood of the dark blue SUV. Cain and Elias hopped up on the tailgate of a red late-model pickup truck and Cain sat once again with an automatic weapon in his lap. At the ready as always. Carolina leaned on the passenger side of the Jeep.

Nick looked up from his screen. "Six men entered Panama three days ago. They are all ex-special forces. *U.S. Special Forces.* They all work for the Silverstone Group." The clearing went silent. Even the birds stopped chirping in the trees.

"Well, shit," Axe said. "Are you sure? All six?"

He nodded.

"Fuck," Cain mumbled while Elias shook his head and tossed a banana peel into the nearby bushes.

Finn leaned forward and rested his elbows on his knees again. "Do you think it was them who grabbed the vaccine and killed the men at the compound?"

"Them, with a few more friends. It makes sense. I'm guessing the Silverstone guys hired the FARC to grab the shipment and then killed them all once they got back to the compound. These men don't want any witnesses, and it's a powerful message to anyone they might have missed to keep their mouths shut. They aren't to be fucked with. No one around here would kill that many FARC members. It would upset the balance of power and start a war. No one wants a turf war. But the Silverstone guys wouldn't give a shit about the mayhem left in their wake. They have a job to do."

"Carolina, have you ever heard of the Silverstone Group?" Nick asked.

"I heard the name when I was in Yemen, but I don't know anything about them. Aren't they government contractors of some sort?"

Axe snorted. "Highly paid thugs is what they are."

"The Silverstone Group is a security company," said Nick. "They supply men and materials for black ops to those who have the money to pay their hefty fees. Mercenaries would be a polite term for them. Hired assassins and thugs would be a more accurate description. And you're right. They also get government contracts to 'help out' in some overseas countries, Yemen being one of them. They're controversial in political circles, but they get the job done when needed, so they also have friends in high places." Nick ran a hand through his hair.

"The Silverstone Group only hires ex-special forces guys," Axe said. "Moral code not required. To put it bluntly, they're a well-trained army for hire."

Carolina frowned. "Why would these nasty people want the vaccine? What on earth would they do with it?"

"We have to figure out who hired them if we want those answers," Axe said.

Carolina straightened and stretched. Then she walked around and leaned on the opposite side of the Jeep from Nick. "Do you think it was Silverstone who broke into my apartment, too?"

"That would make sense," Nick agreed.

Elias, who had been typing away on a laptop, looked up. "I took a look at the security footage from our HQ for last night. I managed to download just an hour or so before we blew the place. Take a look." He turned the screen around, and everyone wandered over to see the image.

It showed Axe, Elias, and Cain arriving back at the warehouse. They rolled through the gate, and it closed after them. About a minute later, two dark-colored SUVs pulled over to the curb across the street.

Elias froze the picture and zoomed in. "I VPNed into the system back in California and ran the faces through facial recognition. "Peter Louden is the driver of the first SUV. Ex-Army Ranger. The passenger is Daniel Hyatt. Also ex-Army. I can't get a clear enough shot of the guys in the second SUV, but both Louden, and Hyatt are Silverstone. Currently working on government contracts over in Yemen, according to their files."

"And yet here they are in Panama." Nick grimaced. "They weren't on my list, so you know what that means."

Carolina was standing next to him. She touched his sleeve. "I don't understand."

He looked down at her. She was standing so close that he could smell a hint of lavender, her favorite scent she had told him. Even after everything she'd been through, she still smelled good. It just wasn't fair. He cleared his throat. "It means that they're here illegally. And if there are two here illegally, who knows how many more there are. That means there are at least eight Silverstone guys here working to keep the vaccine from the Tarchuarani, but probably more."

Carolina turned pale. When she swayed slightly, Nick reached out to steady her. "Are you okay?" He did not like the way she looked. "Someone get her some water."

"Here you go." Elias handed Nick a bottle, and he opened it before handing it to Carolina. She took it and swayed again. Nick put his arm around her to steady her as she drank. As she leaned into him, he couldn't help but notice how nicely she fit against him. Any other time and place he would have explored that further.

She swallowed some water and took a breath. "Sorry, it's just been a long day, or couple of days, with little food and sleep. I think I just need to sit for a bit."

"Let's call it a day and regroup tomorrow. Do you guys want the safe house by the port or the one in downtown Colón?"

"Ah, Tag?" Axe said. "We've got a problem."

Nick turned and looked at his teammate. "What now?"

"The Silverstone guys. They aren't on this coast. They went across to Panama City already."

"Okay." Nick shrugged. "So we go to the safe houses there. We need to find the vaccine. Presumably these guys will have it close by." He was more concerned about Carolina. She still wasn't looking good, and she was leaning more and more of her weight on him. It was fine, he could take it, but he was worried he was going to have to pick her up and carry her soon, and he wasn't sure if his back would let him.

"No, that's not the problem. I called a source and asked if they'd seen anyone resembling me, possibly a group of them. My source said yes, and they are already at the port. They're currently loading a red container onto a ship.

"Well, fuck," Carolina groaned.

CHAPTER SIXTEEN

They'd arrived in Panama City a couple hours after leaving the north coast. Nick pulled the SUV into another underground garage and parked in a spot right next to the elevator. Turning off the Jeep's engine, he turned toward Carolina. The small lines around her eyes had become more pronounced. He once again had the urge to brush the hair from her face and tell her everything would work out, but he wouldn't make false promises.

"This is one of our safe houses. It's a nice plain two-bedroom apartment in an average building. Nothing to attract attention. We're going to grab the stuff from the trunk and take the stairs up to the apartment. Keep your head down and your hat on. I'm sure we weren't followed. I did a lot of doubling back and circles, but on the outside chance they know about this place, stay close."

Carolina nodded but remained silent. Her color was a bit better, but she still looked pale and drawn.

After grabbing their bags, they headed to the stairwell where Nick first did a quick check. He heard nothing but, more importantly, he sensed nothing. *Clear*. He made

Carolina go first but stayed close, urging her to move quickly. The stairwell was not the safest place, and the sooner they were in the apartment, the better.

Carolina reached for the door to exit the stairwell and he grabbed her wrist. "No, let me check first."

She nodded and moved back. Nick slowly cracked the door to the sixth floor. All clear. He moved quickly down the hallway, only stopping when he got to the door of the apartment. He checked for the thin wire he'd placed in the doorway the last time he was here. After finding it, he removed it and had the safe house door open by the time Carolina had caught up to him. Nick ushered her in, then closed and locked the door behind them. He gave the apartment a brief once-over even though the wire was still in place. No point in not being cautious.

He returned to the main living space to find Carolina standing frozen in the entryway.

"Are you okay?" he asked.

She blinked. "Um, yeah. I wasn't sure if it was okay to move around."

"You're fine in here. We'll only be here for one night so don't get too comfortable." He turned and pointed to her right. "What you see is what you get. Kitchen, living area." He indicated a door on the right side of the room with his chin. "That's a bedroom, and the door on the left side is its mirror image. You take the bedroom on your right. There are clean towels if you want to take a shower." He picked up all his gear. "I'll make us something to eat unless you would prefer to sleep first."

"A shower sounds like heaven. And food. I napped in the car so I'm good for a while." She gave him a slight smile. Carolina grabbed her duffel bag from the floor and went to her room, closing the door behind her. Nick sighed. What he really needed was to get the hell away from Carolina and then about twelve to fourteen hours of sleep. Since neither of those things were going to happen, he needed to take a shower and get his shit together. He couldn't be worrying about Carolina and still do his job.

And speaking of work, he had to call Bertrand. He'd put it off long enough. He should have done it back at the beach rendezvous point. It was time to face the music about Carolina and the whole exploding warehouse situation. None of it would go well. Bertrand was going to lose his shit. The team was down in Panama to lay low and recover, and they'd literally just blown that to smithereens.

He flipped the two deadbolts on the door and put the chain lock in place. His bedroom was spacious, if a bit generic, but it had a balcony overlooking the street, which made it great for spotting surveillance.

He had a burner phone in his hand but threw it on the bed. A quick shower wouldn't hurt. The hot spray worked magic on his back. It had stiffened up during the drive. He would have loved to linger there for an hour, getting his back massaged by the pulsating water but he needed to eat, and he needed to call Bertrand. He curled his hands into fists. This was his new normal, and he had little choice but to get used to it. Then the memory of Carolina's face floated to the surface of his mind. Her smile and laughter as she fed him the falafel she'd snuck in for him back in Yemen.

He grabbed the soap and started scrubbing, but his brain wouldn't let Carolina go. If circumstances were different, he wouldn't mind helping wash her back. He shook his head. Thoughts like that were not helpful. He had to focus on their goals and safety. Sex with Carolina—or even just thoughts about sex with Carolina—would unnecessarily confuse their situation, which was already at a critical point. He needed to keep his anger stoked. She'd screwed up his back. No matter how much he wanted to have her in his arms or how good it might be, he needed to maintain his distance. He turned the lever all the way over to cold. Icy spray hit his chest and lower down, cooling his ardor. He let out a string of curses, finished rinsing off in the icy water, and jumped out.

After getting dressed in jeans and a black T-shirt, he headed for the kitchen. The door to Carolina's room remained closed. He rinsed a thin layer of dust off the coffee pot and made a fresh pot. He also filled the teakettle. She didn't drink coffee, which made her a freak of nature as far as he was concerned.

He looked through the freezer. They didn't have much to choose from. He took out some chicken and frozen mixed veggies. In the pantry, he found a box of powdered mashed potatoes. Even the milk was the kind with a long shelf life. He grabbed a small box and put it in the fridge. At least the milk would be cold.

He spent the next hour cooking dinner. It might not be the best meal ever, but their options were few. He glanced at Carolina's door again. Maybe she was asleep. Should he wake her? Probably not. After the oven timer went off, Nick put on the mitts and bent over to pull out the chicken. When he stood up, he almost dropped the tray.

Carolina stood on the other side of the counter. Her long dark hair hung in big loose waves over her shoulders, almost to her elbows. She wore a black tank top that clung to her curves and a pair of tan shorts showing off toned legs.

The tray started to burn his hand through the oven mitt, and he swore as he dropped it onto the stove. "I made lunch. I hope you're hungry."

"Starving. I could eat a horse."

"Good. I also made tea if you want to pour yourself a cup. Lunch is baked chicken with veggies and potatoes. Sorry, no fresh vegetables. It's all frozen."

She smiled. "Thanks for cooking." She moved into the

kitchen and sat down on one of the bar stools by the counter. "I had a nice long bath. I was a bit sore after our run and everything..." Her voice petered out.

He glanced at her. Her color was coming back, but fear and shock were still in her eyes. "Carrying things on your back while running takes getting used to. You end up using different muscles." He grabbed plates from the shelf and put them next to the stove.

"I'm feeling that now." She shifted in her seat.

"I have some acetaminophen if you want."

She shook her head. "I'm okay, thanks."

"Carolina, I need you to be able to move at a moment's notice, and the stiffness will only get worse overnight." He gave her a look that he hoped she understood. Telling her they might have to drop everything and run from hired killers was not something he wanted to do.

She nodded. "I'll take some later." She looked down at her hands for a second and then said, "Is this one of the dishes your mom taught you to cook?"

Nick froze for a second. He'd forgotten that he'd shared stories about his mom with her. He cleared his throat. "Um...sort of. She loved roasted chicken and vegetables, but she added lots of spices and did a whole chicken. This is making do with what we have."

"Well, it smells great." She smiled. "How's your dad?"

Nick almost dropped the plate he was holding. She was just hitting all of his buttons. "He's fine. Excited that Kat is getting married next week."

He filled Carolina's plate and handed it across the island to her.

"That's great. Are you going to the wedding?" she asked as she took her plate to the table and sat down.

It was surreal being here with Carolina, discussing his

family. He needed to shut it down. "No." He came around with his plate. He handed her a knife and fork.

"Thanks." She grinned. "My mouth is watering."

"It's just 'cause you're hungry, but I'll take the compliment." He found himself smiling back. He sat down across from Carolina. "How are your parents?" *Let her answer questions about a touchy subject. See how she likes it.*

She shrugged. "The same. Honey disapproves of my career choices and Dad just goes along with her." She took a bit of chicken. "This really is tasty."

"Thanks."

She moved her food around her plate. "You know, when I think back, I get totally annoyed with myself for wasting all that time in research, trying to please them. I just wanted them to once say they were proud and that they loved me."

Nick's heart squeezed. She looked so sad. Her pale skin and the dark circles under her eyes just emphasized her sorrow. "I'm so sorry, Carolina." He reached out and touched her hand. She looked up and smiled the smile at him that always caused his heart to stutter in his chest. He pulled his hand back and tucked into his food. He needed some breathing room.

"You should go to the wedding, Nick. I'm sure Kat wants you there. You are her brother."

"She does." The words just slipped out. He hadn't meant to share, but that's the way it was with Carolina. He just told her things. "She found the rollerblades in my closet."

"The ones you got her for Christmas the year you left home?"

Leave it to Carolina to remember the story. "Yes. I had wrapped them and left them in the back of the closet with the hockey stick for Dave. He was big into hockey then. I had planned on putting them under the tree, but then I had that fight with Dad and just left. I assumed Dad, or my stepmonster Lauren, had gotten rid of everything years ago, but apparently, he insisted my room be left exactly as it was. Kat was finally cleaning out the room so some friends could stay for the wedding, and she found the gifts."

"What did she say?"

Nick put down his fork. "She called me in tears and said thank you. She'd always thought because I'd left without saying good-bye that I didn't care about her and Dave. Now that she found the gifts and the cards I'd written, she's sorry she never reached out. I told her it wasn't her fault, and I could have reached out at any time. It was just circumstances. That's when she invited me to the wedding."

"Oh, Nick." It was Carolina who reached out this time and put her hand over his. "You really need to go to the wedding. You have family that loves you and wants to see you. That's important. I know you said that you didn't get along with your father, but that was so long ago. It was a difficult time for both of you. You both lost a very important part of your lives. Just because your father moved on more quickly than you liked doesn't mean he didn't love you."

"You weren't there, Carolina. I couldn't do anything right. We fought constantly. He didn't want me around."

Carolina sighed. "Maybe it was because you reminded him too much of your mother. It was a big loss for both of you."

"Maybe." He couldn't think about all that now. Carolina's hand on his was giving him other ideas. He pulled his hand away and picked up his fork and ate the last mouthful of food. It was hard to chew and swallow. His awareness of Carolina was growing by the minute. So was something else.

"So, any ideas on why Biodome wants to kill the Tarchuarani?" Nick asked. He got up from the table and headed to the kitchen. Physical space was a necessity at that moment.

Carolina took the last bite of her food and cocked her head as she chewed. "I've been thinking about it. Biodome really has no reason I can see to want the Tarchuarani gone. There's no gain for them. None. If killing them was *accidental*, then I guess Biodome would want the Florevir for the Tarchuarani so they don't have any bad press should the truth get out. So that's a motive, but it's kind of farfetched."

"Explain what you mean," Nick called from the kitchen as he poured himself a cup of coffee.

"Well," Carolina said as she put down her fork on an empty plate, "if they did realize they were killing the Tarchuarani with their experiment, or Javier's call pointed it out to them, they—assuming they have a conscience—would have immediately stopped the trial and done everything in their power to help the tribe. At the same time, they would want to stop any of this from coming out in the press. Bad press on that level would sink their stock price and, more importantly, kill any ability to raise funds for ongoing projects. They'd probably go under."

"And if Biodome had less of a conscience?" Nick asked.

She shrugged. "If they weren't so aboveboard, they might want to steal the vaccine from me and treat the Tarchuarani themselves, thereby making them the heroes—not only creating a mosquito that helps stop the spread of viruses but also creating a vaccine for that tiny percentage of people on the earth that may have any issues with it. In order to claim it as theirs, they would have to kill anyone that knew it wasn't."

Nick came back and sat down again across from Carolina. "I'm sensing you're not buying this idea. Stacking those FARC bodies seems an unlikely part of a corporate PR scheme."

"Agreed." She shifted in her seat. "Most companies in this space would just buy the rights to the vaccine and be done with it. They'd still be heroes for saving a World Heritage tribe, and they would get to move along with their experiments. No one would have to die. Hiring Silverstone complicates things. It's not the way things work. Why would Biodome choose to do that? There's no real upside for them."

Nick studied her. "What? You look like there's something bothering you."

Carolina nodded. "Here's the thing. The mosquitoes should be dying before they bite. That's the whole point of this type of experiment. But these mosquitos keep living, so the experiment is a failure. They should have stopped before it got to this point. The experiment really never should have gotten outside of the lab. They would have known months ago that the mosquitoes would bite so the experiment wouldn't work."

"Huh. Do you think they are testing something else? Some other aspect of the mosquitoes?"

She shook her head. "No. I did some poking around before I left. I still have lots of friends in the research world, and they said they were pretty sure Biodome was working on shortening the lifespan of the mosquito." Lots of friends. That was an exaggeration. Many acquaintances for sure, but friends not so much. She sighed.

"Look Doc, I'm out of my wheelhouse here, so you have to help me navigate. What other ideas do you have about Biodome or who else might want this vaccine? Let your mind go and throw out any ideas that come to you."

Carolina looked around the room. "What if... Let's say Biodome Technologies is killing the Tarchuarani on purpose. They rigged this mosquito experiment to make them sick. They knew their engineered bugs would wipe out the tribe." She pressed her lips together for a moment as she thought. She shook her head. "But that doesn't make sense. What would Biodome gain?"

"What if someone else gains?" Nick asked.

She rubbed her face with both hands. "What do you mean?"

"What if they have a partner that gains something from the extermination of the Tarchuarani? I'm just throwing out ideas, but what if they partnered with another enterprise who profited?"

She tilted her head. "It's a possibility. Companies work together all the time. But still, who gains from the tribe's death?"

Carolina got up, went to the kitchen, and poured herself a cup of tea. "Do you want anything?"

Nick was already on his feet on the way to the kitchen. "I'll get it but thanks." He poured himself a second cup of coffee in the snug kitchen. Carolina took a quick sip of tea and started emptying the dishwasher.

"You don't have to do that. I guess I left when it was still running the last time I was here."

"No worries. Besides, you cooked. I don't mind cleaning. It's only fair." She turned to put a clean glass in the cupboard just as he reached for the milk she'd left on the counter, and he bumped into her. The cup went flying from her hand, but he snagged it mid-air.

"Sorry about that," Nick said. They were crushed together in the corner of the kitchen. "Here's your cup." He offered it to her.

"That was impressive." She gave him an appreciative nod. "Your reflexes are pretty quick."

He smiled. "A function of my job." They still stood close together. She smelled of her usual lavender but also a bit of citrus. The heat from her body radiated into his, causing a sensory overload. Her lips drew his attention, and he had the intense desire to kiss her. *Bad idea.*

But then he saw the same desire reflected in her own

eyes, and he gave in to his instincts, wrapping his arm around her waist, bringing her closer. He brushed his lips across hers as she put her hands on his chest. He waited a beat in case he'd read her signals wrong, but she tilted her head back and leaned into him.

He kissed her again, and this time lingered over her lips. She opened her mouth and kissed him back. Their tongues mingled, tentatively at first, but soon he deepened the kiss. She tasted like tea and honey, and he wanted more. She brought her arms up and wrapped them around his neck. Their tongues danced as his hands slid down to cup her ass. He pulled her hard against his length, the intensity of their kiss increasing.

Nick's cell phone went off and jolted him back to reality. He pulled back and dropped his arms. He grabbed his cell and, without looking at Carolina, announced, "I've got to take this." He walked into his bedroom and shut the door. What the fuck had he been thinking? *Stupid.*

He put the phone to his ear and heard Admiral George Bertrand's angry voice bellowing in his ear. "Goddammit, Taggert! You're supposed to be down there lying low and looking after that motley crew of yours. Why am I hearing about some huge explosion and a dead ex-marine who was dishonorably discharged?"

Fuck! Just what he needed now. "Sir. We were doing our job, sir."

"Why does it seem that Master Chief Nick Taggert just doing his job invariably leads to catastrophe? Fill me in. I've got a meeting in a few minutes where the top brass is going to chew my ass off, and I need to tell them a good story if I'm going to survive."

Nick paced his room as he filled in his boss about the shipment and all the pertinent details. Axe had told him earlier about the dead Silverstone guys. He hadn't told

Carolina. She seemed to be having a hard time as it was but leave it to Bertrand to be up on every detail.

"These men followed us back to the warehouse and tried to storm it. I guess they underestimated our ability to hold them off. Anyway, we got out and took Dr. Alvarez with us. We didn't have time to clean all the computers, sir, or pack everything, so I gave the order to blow the place. I didn't want to leave anything behind that could put us or the DEA agents we've been working with in any more danger.

"So you know, sir, we think Dr. Alvarez was the main target, but I think they want anyone who knows about the vaccine dead." He hesitated, and then, "And there's one more thing, the ex-marine that died? He's not the only one. They might find another three bodies. My guys are good, sir. You should also know all four most likely worked for Silverstone Group."

"Jesus Christ, Taggert! Why is it always a clusterfuck with you?" His commanding officer let out a string of curses. "Are you sure they were with Silverstone?"

"Ninety percent, sir. There're at least five guys here that were with him. There could be more."

"Any idea who hired them?"

"We're thinking it might be the biotech company Biodome Technologies, but can't be certain, sir."

"Silverstone has a lot of friends in Washington, Taggert. You need to be sure about this before we go forward and accuse them."

"I understand, sir. It seems outrageous to me that they would try to snatch Dr. Alvarez from us at HQ. That was a hell of a risk for them. They aren't stupid. They had to know we wouldn't hand her over."

"As you said earlier, many people underestimate us, Taggert. The Coast Guard isn't known for its military prowess, and usually that's a good thing."

"You think they didn't know how we would react, sir?"

"I think they didn't take the time to do their research. I wish you hadn't blown the guys up, but all of you did the right thing, Taggert. That's clear to me. Keep your head down and keep digging. I'll do what I can on this end to find out what the hell is going on with this vaccine. I don't have details on the dead man yet, but I will. Check in tomorrow after you meet with your people. Stay safe."

"Yes, sir," Nick said, but Bertrand was already gone. He let out a frustrated breath. Nick had been following a logical course of action but blowing the warehouse and killing the Silverstone guys was, nevertheless, a big damn deal.

He rolled his shoulders. Hopefully, they would have more to tell Bertrand tomorrow after they got a chance to scope out the ship with the vaccine on it. It wasn't scheduled to leave until tomorrow, so at least they had that going for them. He opened his bedroom door, and Carolina looked up from her spot on the couch. "Everything okay?" she asked.

She appeared perfectly normal, like they hadn't just been making out in the kitchen. Well, what did he expect? Just because their encounter had thrown him for a loop didn't mean she felt the same way. He cleared his throat. "It's the same, I guess. My boss is going to see if he can find anything out on his end about the vaccine."

She opened her mouth, but Nick put up his hands to forestall her comment. "Don't worry, he'll be discreet." He walked over and sat down on the other side of the couch.

"I've thought more about it, and I am convinced Biodome wouldn't hire Silverstone for their own purposes. They don't need to steal the vaccine. They could make their own if they had enough time or, if not, they could have purchased the Florevir, when Javier called them and started the dialogue about the Tarchuarani. They could save the

Tarchuarani people and stop the disease spread. It would have been a win-win."

He shook his head. "Then we're back to the partner theory."

"Yes." Carolina hesitated. "I could call my stepmom, give her a general picture of the situation and ask for her ideas. She's a world-renowned biologist at NYU, and she might see what we've been missing."

Nick got up and retrieved a new burner phone from one of the bags. Handing it to Carolina, he said, "I'm not sure I like this idea, but we have nothing else to go on right at this moment, so go for it. No details, just generalities. Tell her not to speak about this to anyone else. We don't want to put her life in danger. We'll toss the phone as soon as you're finished."

She paled. "You think they'll come after her?"

"Just keep the conversation general, and it should be okay."

"I'll give it a shot." She smiled slightly as she got up from the couch and went to her room with the phone in hand.

The bedroom door clicked shut. He wasn't keen on Carolina making the call, but any help would be welcome.

CHAPTER SEVENTEEN

"Hi, Honey." Carolina gritted her teeth as she swallowed her dislike for her stepmother.

"Carolina, the police have been calling. They said there was a break-in at your apartment, and they couldn't reach you." Her stepmother's voice had taken on a professorial tone.

The food Nick had prepared that had been so tasty was now a lump in Carolina's belly. "I know. It's fine. I will take care of it."

"Really, Carolina, I would have expected you to at least have the courtesy to let your father and me know you were traveling. It was horribly embarrassing for us to have no idea what was going on." And now she had progressed to a familiar cool tone that said, "We are terribly disappointed in you."

She took a deep breath and tried not to let the woman get under her skin. She was a grown-ass woman and Honey always treated her like she was a teenager. There had not been a "Are you okay?" or "We were so worried about you."

Instead, Honey's stepdaughter had once again been a source of embarrassment.

"I need information, and I'm wondering if, given your scientific expertise, you might be able to help me. It's about an experiment using a genetically altered mosquito. I know this isn't exactly your field, but I thought you might have some insight into this situation." There was a brief silence. She knew her stepmother was trying to maintain what she felt was a right-eous anger, but the idea of discussing a biological issue would be too great. Plus, she could never turn down an appeal to her ego.

"Go on." The cool professorial voice was back.

"There have been studies on genetically modifying mosquitoes in which their lifespan is shortened, thus not allowing them to mature to the point where they bite—this is in hopes of stopping the spread of diseases like malaria and Dengue Fever, yellow fever, West Nile and encephalitis."

"I am aware. This practice is reckless. It completely throws off the ecosystem. The natural predators of the mosquito—"

"Yes, I know," she cut in, risking her stepmother's ire, "but is there any reason a company would release genetically modified mosquitoes in the wild if they could still live long enough to bite? What data might be collected from that?"

"*Hmmm*. It's an interesting question." Her stepmother's voice warmed up considerably. "I can't see any real value in it. It defeats the purpose of their experiment. Perhaps... No, I cannot see any benefit to releasing mosquitoes that continue to bite."

Her stepmother was verifying her opinions, but Carolina wanted to make sure she covered all the bases. "Could such an experiment have to do with how long predators get to feed off the mosquitoes?"

"Doubtful. They could just as easily gather that type of

data in a lab and if, fundamentally, they wanted to shorten the lifespan, so the mosquitoes don't bite, why spend money on this type of experiment? No one wastes resources like that, as you know, or at least you used to know. Perhaps you've forgotten now that you've left the field."

The call wouldn't be complete without a jab or two at Carolina for practicing medicine instead of doing research. She bit the inside of her cheek for a second and then asked, "Could the mosquitoes behave one way in the lab but differently in the wild?" This sounded dubious to her, but she wanted to make sure.

"I suppose that behavior is a remote possibility but highly unlikely." Her stepmother's tone was dismissive. "The mosquitoes themselves certainly couldn't alter their own lifespan—not in a short timeframe. It would take centuries for that."

"Okay. Thank you for your help."

"What is this all about, Carolina? Is someone doing shoddy experiments? What are the environmental impacts? I would like to hear the details. You know we cannot let these companies get away with destroying ecosystems—"

"I have to go. Thank you for your help." Carolina clicked off the call and closed her eyes. That was the second time in recent days that she'd cut off her stepmother mid-stream during one of her lectures. Not even Carolina's father would attempt that. She'd pay for that little show of rebellion later. She opened her eyes.

Maybe it was because she was so far away or because she was in a life and death situation, but she was not in the least remorseful. As a matter of fact, there was a small bit of joy in her heart. She'd joined Doctors Without Borders to get away from Honey, but like a dutiful daughter, she kept in touch and always saw Honey and her father when she was back in town. Carolina was beginning to see the error of her ways.

Why put in the effort when Honey clearly didn't care? Because she wanted her father to care...

She caught a glimpse of her reflection in the mirror. The dark circles under her eyes stood out as a stark contrast to the paleness of her skin. The tiny lines on her face were more pronounced. Talking with Honey always left her feeling sad and alone. Speaking with her father wasn't much better. Long ago, Carolina had come to the conclusion that he was either afraid of his wife and too weak to intervene, or he just didn't understand how relationships worked. Either way, the effect on Carolina was the same. Sadness. Maybe it was time to stop waiting for that to change and just move on with her life in whatever way she wanted.

She touched her lips. At the moment she wanted to move on with Nick. A night in bed with him would help her forget. She had no doubts on that score.

CHAPTER EIGHTEEN

Nick pulled open the door to the rendezvous warehouse and came face-to-face with the barrel of a gun.

"Jesus, Tag, you could have warned us. We thought the Silverstone guys had found us again," Axe said, lowering his gun.

"Sorry. You didn't leave the signal you were here. I thought we were the first arrivals." Nick ushered Carolina inside the warehouse.

Axe pulled the big metal door closed behind them and then took the bags from Carolina. "I did leave the cloth," he said defensively. He hustled halfway down the length of the warehouse and dropped the bags. He hopped up on some boxes and peered out the windows just under the eaves to look for their signal. "Shit. The wind must have pulled it down. The cloth is on the ground by the pallets stacked on that other side of the wharf."

"Good to know. I was worried there for a second." Nick had walked to the base of the boxes.

"Yeah, me, too." Axe jumped down and landed next to him.

"Where are the others?" asked Nick.

"We're here, Tag."

Nick turned. He heard Elias's voice but couldn't locate him. He squinted. "What is that?" he asked Axe.

Axe grinned. "It's good, isn't it? We found the old black tarps on one of our scavenging runs last night. We hung them back there and realized pretty quick you can't tell it isn't the back wall because of the poor light in here. We've got everything behind there. It won't fool anyone for long, but it might withstand a cursory glance and buy us time if we need it."

Nick walked toward the back of the warehouse. "I like it." He glanced over his shoulder and realized Carolina was still standing next to the boxes. He motioned for her to follow. She'd been unusually quiet today. He'd kept telling himself there could be lots of reasons for that besides their kiss yesterday. It had been a stupid thing to do, but she'd looked so damn hot, and there was no denying they had chemistry.

Dumb. He needed to get his head back in the game. Worrying about her feelings wasn't going to get shit done.

"Hey," he said, rounding the corner of the tarp. The guys had arranged everything. Laptops were set up on empty pallets stacked one on top of another. There were makeshift tables made of boxes with guns and equipment laid out on top. There were a couple of old stools.

"Tag!" Finn was squatting by the equipment bags, re-organizing weaponry and the electronics.

Nick dumped his bags on the floor next to the others. "Looks good. You guys have been busy."

Cain squatted down and plugged cables into a power bar. "The outside CCTV cameras will be online shortly. The rats chewed through some wires, so repairs were necessary."

"Good." He walked over and stood in front of the pallets

so he could address everyone. The guys had all followed the protocol Nick had laid out and were wearing cargo pants with T-shirts. A couple even wore ball caps. They knew to blend in as much as they could. No point in drawing attention to themselves.

It felt good to see his team working so well together. Dumping a bunch of Coasties from different units in a foreign country to "heal" was a challenge. He was very pleased with how it was turning out. The guys were performing well and becoming a real team.

"I spoke with Bertrand yesterday. He'd already heard about the dead ex-Marine. I'm sure by now he's officially heard about the three others. I explained about the attack and how they obviously had orders to kill all of us. I'm not even sure they were going to bother to take Carolina and question her. Anyway, he's going to dig into things on his end. He doesn't like the involvement of Silverstone any more than we do." Axe caught his eye and flicked his head in Carolina's direction. Nick glanced her way.

She was leaning against one of the pallets. She'd gone completely white. "Those men died yesterday at the warehouse?"

Nick nodded. He wanted to comfort her, but he knew it was a slippery slope for him. He'd spent most of yesterday and what seemed like all of last night thinking about their kiss, and he'd decided he needed to be much colder toward her. It was for her safety as well as his. He couldn't keep her safe if he was distracted by the thought of being with her. And he couldn't focus on himself and his team if he allowed her into his world any further. She was already under his skin. Any more interaction like yesterday, and she'd be in his heart.

Axe grabbed one of the old stools, put it under her butt, and guided her down onto it. He crossed the room and returned with a bottle of whiskey and a paper cup. He poured a shot and handed it to her. She looked like she might refuse, but then tossed it back in one gulp. "Thanks." She gave Axe a small smile. "Sorry. It's just a bit shocking. I'm still coming to grips with the idea that someone wants me dead. The idea that other people are dying because of me is…just…hard."

"It's not your fault. Just remember that." Axe put the bottle back into the corner.

Nick fisted his hands. He wanted to go over and wrap his arms around Carolina and promise her it would all work out. He wanted to be the one on the receiving end of her smile, not Axe. A small flare of jealousy lit up in his chest. "So where are we?" he asked.

Elias spoke up. "We found the ship, and the vaccine is already loaded on board just like Axe's source said."

Carolina put the paper cup down on the pallet. "You did? Is it close by?"

Nick ground his teeth. "Way to bury the lead."

Elias smiled. "Sorry."

"Fill us in," Nick demanded as he positioned himself in front of one of the laptops. In just a few minutes, he was going to have to check in with Bertrand.

Elias stood and shifted his weight off his bad leg. "Last night, I did recon here on the docks. Panama City has been busy, and the docks are jammed with cargo ships. I think the whole unloading in Colón and loading again here on this side of the canal has become more popular because the line of trucks last night was more than I have ever seen before.

Anyway, the *Gilda Marie*, which is the ship that it's on, is at pier twenty-two, which is two over from here and heavily guarded by ex-military types. A lot of them. I'm assuming they're all Silverstone guys."

Nick frowned. "How many? More than were at the warehouse?"

"Way more. I counted ten guards on deck, and who knows how many below."

"Shit."

"That pretty much sums it up," Elias agreed.

Axe folded his arms across his chest. "We need a game plan for getting back Dr. Alvarez's vaccine. Since we're outmanned and outgunned, that's going to be tough. Any chance Bertrand will give us some backup?"

"Not likely." Nick clicked on the refresh button for his email. Nothing new had come in. "He was pissed we blew up the warehouse, but he understood the necessity of it." He held up a quieting hand since he knew complaints from his team were likely to follow. "There's a lot of CYA"—he glanced at Carolina—"cover your ass, Bertrand has to deal with since we blew it up, especially now that they found a dead ex-marine while putting out the fire. But enough about that. Anyone have ideas on how we approach the *Gilda Marie*?"

Carolina cleared her throat. "Where's she heading?"

"Good question." Nick turned to Elias and cocked an eyebrow.

"The main port in Ecuador, Guayaquil. They'll offload the vaccine there."

"So *we* don't have to get the vaccine off the ship," Carolina interjected, surprising everyone.

Nick blinked. "You're thinking that we just meet the ship down there and take the vaccine then?"

She fisted one hand on her thigh. "It gives us—you— more time to plan how to grab it, and it eliminates the problem of getting the vaccine there ourselves."

Axe smiled. "I like how you think, Doc."

Nick nodded slowly. "It's a possibility. Finn, what do we know about Guayaquil? Do we have any friendlies there we can ask for help?"

"Nope. All I know is that it's yet another port that's a bit...flexible in its regulation enforcement."

"You mean it's an ideal spot for the criminal element," Axe said.

Finn shrugged. "I don't know about ideal, but such a lax atmosphere makes it easier for bad elements to get things done."

"Okay, find out what you can and see if you can scare up some friendly connections there." Nick turned to Cain. "I want a look at the *Gilda Marie*. Give me ten minutes, and then you and I will go take a stroll in that direction."

Cain nodded and then went over to the equipment bags, squatted down, and started digging out binoculars and other items they might need.

"Elias, pull up whatever you can find about the ship," said Tag. "I want any internal diagrams or plans you can find, plus all of her specs."

"On it, Tag."

Nick pulled his phone out of his pocket and started out of the cordoned off area. "Axe," he called and jerked his head. Axe followed him around the barrier. "Talk to Alvarez and see how she's doing. She wasn't looking so good." That was the only concession he was going to give himself. He had to know how she was holding up even if sending another man made him grind his teeth.

Axe nodded and then turned and went back behind the tarp. Nick continued walking until he was two-thirds of the way toward the front of the building. He hit the redial button on his cell.

"Bertrand."

"Master Chief."

"Taggert. I just got off a call with Rear Admiral Duvall and his team. They want to know why there were four bodies left behind in your blown-up HQ."

"Those Silverstone guys were on a shoot-to-kill mission. As we discussed yesterday, they had no interest in disguising what was going on.

Bertrand grunted. "That's what I told them. What the hell is going on, Taggert?"

Nick ran a hand through his hair. "Honestly, sir, I have no fucking clue."

"The FBI is on the scene back at your HQ. They really want to talk to Dr. Alvarez now."

"Respectfully, sir, I don't think that's a good idea. These Silverstone guys are good, and they're here. If we bring in the FBI at this stage, I have no doubt they will find out. I'd rather we didn't have to have another firefight just yet. Plus, as you know, the former head of the FBI works at Silverstone now. That's a little too close for comfort in my book, respectfully speaking, sir."

"I don't like it either. I have always argued against groups like Silverstone, but no one cares what I think."

Nick heard the creak of the old man's chair through the phone. Nick hesitated before telling him the rest. "We found the vaccine, sir. Or at least we think we have. It's on a ship, destination Ecuador."

Bertrand was silent for a second. "Please don't tell me that you want to go after it."

"Yes, that's right, sir."

"Taggert, this has nothing to do with us anymore. You and your team are down there to work on drug interdiction. This vaccine is not coming into the US, and it's not an illegal substance. It doesn't fall under our purview. Besides, you and your team are supposed to be relaxing and healing. When I put you all together, it was so you could all regroup and get back into fighting shape. If you and the men are all good to go, then you need to go back to your individual jobs, and the team can be disbanded."

"The men are fine, sir, and so am I." They weren't on the top of their game, and he wasn't sure any of them ever would be, but that was a discussion for another day. "This op is much better for us than sitting on our asses. This gives us a chance to see just where we are in terms of our skills and our ability to function in the field. It's a chance to shake the rust off."

He took a breath. He had to wind it back. Pissing off Bertrand wouldn't help matters. "Sir, there are a lot of unanswered questions. Who wants the Tarchuarani people dead? Why hire Silverstone? Who—?"

"Enough! I'm with you. I can't stand an unsolved puzzle either. This is all so damn weird." There was a long pause. "Okay, keep at it and see what you can figure out. If anyone asks, you are escorting a dignitary. I'll back you up if need be. Take the opportunity to see how the men do, but I want a full report on their field readiness when all this is over. Make sure you keep Dr. Alvarez safe. And goddammit, don't blow anything else up!" Bertrand yelled and slammed down the phone.

Nick smiled as he tucked the phone into his pocket. It felt good to be doing real work again. Not to mention that any time he and his team could stick it to the Silverstone guys was a plus in his books. He returned to the work area.

"What did the old man say, Tag?" Elias asked.

Nick let a slow smile spread across his face.

Axe let out a whoop of joy.

"What's going on?" Carolina asked.

Nick turned to her. "We got involved in this because we thought you were smuggling drugs. It's our job to stop drugs from entering the States, or at least that's the main goal. Sometimes we tag it and track it to find out the distribution systems, which is what we did with your shipment. Once we learned it was a vaccine, we should have turned you over to the locals and let them figure out what to do with you. I strayed a bit out of our assigned duties when I went looking for your vaccine. However, my boss just gave me the go ahead to stay on this and figure it out. That's why we're happy. None of us want to stop now."

"I see. I'm glad you stuck it out." At her quick smile, his heart sped up for a beat or two. She was gorgeous when she smiled. He cursed himself for losing focus.

"Yeah, well...I'm going to go take a look at the ship. You stay here and..." What? He was drawing a blank.

"I noticed you have medical supplies," she said. "Mind if I take a look? I'll be interested to see what are considered basic supplies."

"Go for it. Axe will help."

Axe smiled. "Right this way, Doc." He gestured her toward the bags.

"Cain," Nick said, then turned and started walking toward the front of the warehouse.

Cain caught up to him and handed him a Glock. The two men tucked their guns into the waistband of their pants at the small of their backs and then put on their sunglasses as they approached the outside door. Nick called out to Elias to check the cameras. He got an all-clear, and he and Cain exited the building and started walking down the pier. They headed to the street that ran along the coast. Nick shot Cain a quick glance. "You okay?"

"Fine, Tag."

"Any thoughts on all this?"

Cain was the one on the team with the most experience. He was younger than Nick but had spent more time billeted out with special ops teams in the Navy and more years in the Maritime Security Response Team hunting terrorists. Nick trusted Cain's judgment. Maybe more than his own.

Cain grunted. "There's another player out there, one we don't know anything about."

"How can you be sure?" Nick asked, doing a quick check behind them. They were fine. No one was following them. Still, it was best not to relax.

Cain gestured with his chin to two men just down the block—definitely ex-military. Panama was full of these guys. It was the sort of country that attracted them. Lots of people here hired personal armies.

No need to alert the Silverstone guys, if indeed these were Silverstone operatives, that they were here. Nick tilted his head toward the shop on their right, and they entered. It was a small convenience store. They separated, and Nick stood at the back where he could see out a small bit of window that wasn't covered by fliers. Cain scouted the rest of the store and then took a post near the back door. No one else was in the store. The clerk gave each man a cursory once-over and then went back to reading a magazine. Apparently, he recognized the men were there for reasons other than buying a Snickers bar but was obviously smart enough not to ask questions or get involved.

Nick watched and waited. Patience was the name of the game in spec-ops work. Hurry up and wait. He glanced up and saw there was a mirror high on the wall behind the counter, facing out. It was tilted so he could see the street and down the block a bit. Someone had already stood in this spot to watch this block. No wonder the clerk had been so nonchalant.

Nick watched the two ex-military types approach and

made a small sound to alert Cain. The two men stopped and chatted on the sidewalk right outside the store. They were dressed in combat gear, and both were armed with handguns. They looked American, but it was hard to tell for sure. Nick was willing to bet these were the guys that Axe saw earlier, or at least part of that crew. The taller of the two, a guy with a square jaw and a blond buzzcut, put his hand on the door and had started to push it open when his cell went off. He stepped back and answered the call.

Nick glanced at Cain, who gave him a slight nod. He looked at the mirror. The shorter man on the sidewalk was looking around. *Keeping watch.* The first guy's voice got louder. He was speaking English. Yelling at someone for not getting the right supplies. Then the man on the phone turned away from the store and started moving rapidly down the sidewalk, back the way they'd come. The second man followed.

Nick stayed in place until they were out of mirror range. He signaled Cain, and they both went to the store entrance and did a quick check. Clear. They left the store and continued toward their destination.

"I'm not feeling good about what just happened," Cain said.

"Me either," Nick agreed. His senses were on high alert. They came to pier twenty-two and started walking down toward the end. There were a few ships docked on both sides. "Let's walk down the opposite side to the *Gilda Marie*. We'll go through the warehouse in the middle and see what we can see from there. I don't want to walk alongside her. No need to make our presence known just yet."

"Agreed."

They moved quickly down the pier, winding their way around cargo and forklifts. About halfway down, they cut into the warehouse through a loading bay door. They moved around stacked pallets until they had a good view of the *Gilda Marie* through an open doorway. Cain handed Nick binoculars. Taking them, he then hid most of his body behind the pallets.

The *Gilda Marie* was a midsize cargo ship. She rode low in the water, which meant the hold was full. There was only one container on deck that was bright red. Nick recognized the container as the one loaded on the back of his/ José's truck on the other coast. He couldn't see the whole ship through the doorway, but he didn't have to. He saw enough to confirm the worst. There were lots of well-equipped ex-military types guarding the vaccine. Probably Silverstone. He handed the binoculars to Cain.

Nick said, "You weren't joking about being outmanned and outgunned. That's Dr. Alvarez's container on the deck. Trying to get the vaccine off that ship would be suicide. The doc is right. We need to leave it on there."

Cain lowered the binoculars. "The thing is, what if they don't take it all the way to Ecuador?"

That thought hadn't occurred to Nick. "What are you getting at?"

"Well," Cain said as he put the binoculars in one of his pockets, "what's to stop them from pushing the container off the ship into the ocean once they leave port. If they don't want the Tarchuarani to have it, why keep it? Why take it to Ecuador in the first place?"

Nick frowned. They were damn good questions. "Shit."

Cain nudged him in the ribs and lifted his chin. Nick followed his lead and looked to the right. The two tough guys they'd spotted earlier on the street now stood on the pier with three other men. Two wore suits and the third was in full tactical gear. He was obviously the man in charge. Nick put his hand out, and Cain passed him the binoculars again. He took a look. He tightened his hands on the binoculars as the blood roared in his ears. A cold sweat broke out over his entire body. "Fuckin' son-of-a-bitch," he growled.

"What?" Cain asked.

"Roman fucking Vance, that's what." He handed the binoculars to Cain. "Fuck. He must be working for Silverstone now. By the looks of things, he's in charge of the operation. "

Cain took a look.

Vance had a long-standing reputation as a snake. He'd left the army a few years ago. Officially, he was discharged with no issue. Unofficially, he'd been kicked out for disobeying orders, but he had friends in high places, so nothing came of any investigation. Nick's hands had curled into fists. Roman Vance was the reason he had an ugly red scar that ran from shoulder to hip. He was the reason Nick had almost died.

Nick had been working a hostage situation along with the U.S. Navy. He'd been assigned to help them with the retrieval. The intel said the hostage was being held aboard a vessel off the coast of Yemen. Vance had left the army by then and was working as a private contractor. He was running the negotiations with the terrorist group that had the American prisoner. He was also the one who supplied the intel that the prisoner was on a specific ship. Except when the team boarded the ship, there was no hostage. Only a large group of well-trained militants lying in wait. The Navy lost several guys and Nick was attacked and thrown overboard. If those men hadn't found him on the beach and taken him to the pop-up hospital, he would have died. Cain lowered the binoculars. "Nick, I—"

"It's fine. We'll deal with it. He'd always known he would

come face-to-face with Vance again one day. He was going to make sure of it.

He felt the weight of Cain's eyes on him, and he waited for him to speak but Cain remained silent. Nick knew it with every fiber of his being. Roman Vance was a monster, and Nick was determined to be the monster slayer.

CHAPTER NINETEEN

"They're back," Axe said, looking up from the laptop's security feeds.

"About damn time," muttered Carolina. She was antsy and had been pacing behind the crates at the back of the warehouse. Any minute waiting was a minute wasted. She went over and hunkered down behind the crates, trying to remember all the reasons patience was said to be a virtue. She did her best not to tap her foot while she waited for the men to walk around the tarp in front of her.

"Well?" she asked as soon as they arrived behind the tarp.

Nick stopped at the opening and met her eyes. "It's not good." His face was blank, but there was something in his eyes. They were flat and filled with a coldness she'd never seen before. He hadn't looked like this yesterday when people were trying to kill them and they blew up a building, but now he looked…deadly. Goosebumps rose across her skin.

"Why?" Carolina didn't have to look around the room to know every man in there was wondering the same thing. She glanced at Cain. His face was blank. Whatever it was, he was giving nothing away. She found herself gripping the edge of the crates so hard the wood was cutting into her skin.

Nick's voice was like ice. "There are more guards there now than what you saw earlier, Axe. We'll leave the vaccine on the ship until it gets to Ecuador. We need to procure two boats to follow and make sure they don't dump it at sea."

Axe glanced at Nick and cocked an eyebrow. Cain shook his head slightly.

"There's more," Nick stated. "The men on the ship are under the command of Roman Vance."

It was like someone had sucked all the oxygen out of the room. Everyone froze. Carolina didn't know why, but she, too, held her breath.

Cain stood at the front of the area. "It's gonna be a tough one when we get to Ecuador. We are seriously outnumbered and outgunned."

Elias sighed. "Bertrand is not gonna send any more men. He's probably not—"

There was a crash. Carolina let out a small yelp and whirled around. Nick had just put his fist through several pallets. The sound of the wood breaking had been deafening. No one else appeared surprised or fazed by what just happened. A million questions ran through her head, but she kept her mouth shut.

Every man went back to what they'd been doing before Nick and Cain had returned. Carolina still remained next to the pallets, unsure of what to do. She looked at Nick and saw that his hand was bleeding. He may have broken some bones as well. She wanted to keep her distance, but the doctor in her propelled her forward. She went over to the side of the warehouse and rummaged in the first aid bags until she found what she wanted. She went into doctor mode and planted herself in front of Nick.

He glowered at her. Rage radiated out of his pores.

Instinctively, she wanted to step back, but after all those nights in makeshift hospitals in war zones, she'd learned to cope. This wasn't the first case of rage she'd had to cure. "Let me fix your hand."

"It's fine," he ground out. "You need to walk away."

She stood there, not moving.

"Carolina," Cain said. The warning in his voice was clear.

But she wasn't having it. She was tired of the bullshit and wasn't backing down. She would need Nick's help getting the vaccine. She needed every one of them, so having Nick drop dead because of an infection wasn't about to happen under her watch. Besides she'd already saved his life once. She wasn't about to let all her good work go to waste.

All the anger and frustration of the situation took root, and she let it fly. "It's not fine, Nick. If you don't take care of it, it could get infected, and you won't be able to use it. You could actually lose it or, worse, die. So now is the time to take care of it."

"I don't need—"

"Yeah, yeah. You're a big tough man, and small cuts aren't going to bring you down. *Blah blah blah.* Now stop being an asshole and focus. You just punched a bunch of wood that probably has traveled from God knows where and been exposed to God knows what but is currently sitting here, possibly starting to rot, in a warehouse in a hot and humid country. Do you have any idea of the germs and bacteria that live on wood in a warm place like this?"

She fisted her hands on her hips and took a step toward Nick. "Currently, people south of here are dying from mosquito bites. You don't think a bunch of cuts on your hand can bring you down? Think again. I hate to break it to you, but you're human, and humans die from this type of shit all the time. So stop being a macho asshat and give me your hand!"

The room was frozen again. No one moved. Nick gave her his death glare, and she returned it. Then, he slowly lifted his hand and put it in front of her.

She nodded and set the supplies down on the pallet beside them. "This is going to sting." She poured hydrogen peroxide over the cuts. Nick's hand jerked slightly, but he didn't say anything. She started cleaning all the little lacerations but quickly realized there were splinters inside many of the larger cuts. "Anyone have a light and some tweezers?" she called out.

Axe appeared next to her with both in hand. She looked up, and he gave her a quick smile and a wink. She smiled back. "Thanks." She pulled Nick over so his hand rested on the pallet and then positioned the light so she could see his cuts more clearly. She spent the next half hour digging bits of wood out of several cuts.

It was heaven, at least for her. The intricate procedure kept her focused on something that she could fix rather than worrying about everything else that she had so little control over. Nick grunted a few times, so she knew it hurt, but other than that, he'd stayed silent.

She wrapped his hand with a bandage. "There. All done." She looked up at Nick. "Now just don't punch anything else."

When she turned around, Cain tilted his head in a come-here gesture. He was sitting on a stool by the pallets with the laptops. She walked over and stood next to him. He gave her a look that she couldn't interpret.

"What?" she asked.

"That was a pretty foolhardy thing you did. You know Nick could have killed you in an instant, right? You would have been dead on the floor before we could have even gotten close."

She fisted her hands. His attitude pissed her off. "I face

worse than that every day in my current job. Nick needed someone to tell him to fuck off. He'd still be wound up and throwing things if I hadn't approached him. People sometimes need a reminder to keep their shit together.

Once you give them that, they usually calm down. Doesn't mean the problem has gone away, but it does mean they can consider their situation more rationally."

Nick wasn't the only one who needed a reminder. She needed it, too. She found it incredibly hard being that close to Nick and not being able to touch him other than to fix his hand. She was angry that he had stopped the kiss yesterday and showed no signs of wanting it to happen again. And she was frustrated that she appeared to be the only one suffering any ill effects. She hadn't slept a wink last night.

Nick walked over and sat heavily on a stool next to Carolina and Cain. He seemed to be back to his normal self but there was still a haunted look in his eye. "Dr. Alvarez, the vaccine, it doesn't require anything else to make it work, does it?"

"What do you mean? Like does it need another chemical or something?"

Nick nodded.

"No. Just the saline solution, but that was shipped with it. You would have seen it when you opened the container."

"No. I just opened the door and took a quick look. I didn't even get up into the container. So one palette is the vaccine and the other is the saline."

"Well, yes." She frowned. "Why are you asking?"

He spun on the stool. "Finn, there are two palettes, not one."

Finn nodded and started typing on his keyboard.

"What's going on?"

"We're going to need boats to follow the ship in, and one of them will need to be big enough to hold the cargo if they shove it overboard. The boats need to blend in so look for fishing boats or pleasure craft. Nothing that Vance and his men would pay attention to. Also, we're going to need transportation on the other end. It is still in the red container, so we used a big rig in Colón. I'm hoping we can use something smaller in Ecuador."

Finn chimed in, "But we'll still need access to a forklift or something on the other end to get it onto a truck."

"Yeah, and that's going to be a problem as well. How exactly do we do that inconspicuously?"

Elias leaned back in his chair. "We could continue the doc's strategy."

"My approach?" She raised her eyebrows. "What do you mean?"

"We let Vance's goons load it onto whatever they're transporting it with, then we steal it back. It will be set to go."

Nick tapped a pencil against his knee. "Less to deal with...but hijacking a truck from those armed thugs won't be easy. We can't set up an ambush once they get going because we don't know where they're taking it. Hard to plan with so many contingencies to consider."

"This is all assuming they don't just throw it over the side," Axe commented.

"They won't," said Cain. He had been leaning on a pallet but straightened to his full height and crossed his arms over his chest. "There's no way they hired Vance and his men to steal it if they didn't have plans for it. If they wanted it destroyed, they would have done that at the FARC compound."

"Agreed." Nick touched Carolina's arm. "Where do you think they're going with it?"

"Me?" She blinked in surprise. She had no fucking clue. "It depends on who hired the Silverstone goons. I mean, we're assuming it's Biodome, but what if it isn't?"

"Stick with the idea that it's Biodome Technologies for now," said Nick. "Why would they take the vaccine to Ecuador, and where would they put it?"

She thought a minute and said, "If for some reason the world started paying attention to the Tarchuarani's plight, Biodome could roll it out and, *ta-da,* they've saved as many as they could and they're heroes."

"So it could be part of their plan to have it as backup. If they didn't manage to kill everyone who knows about it and the story somehow got out, then Biodome could still save the day with the vaccine." Nick turned to Axe. "Do you still have that reporter friend at the *Times*?"

Axe looked sheepish. "I wouldn't say we're friendly exactly, but I know her, and she still works at the *Times*."

Finn grinned. "Pissed her off, did you, Axe?"

Nick grunted, "Call her up and see if we can drum up some press interest. It can't hurt the Tarchuarani, and it might help us."

"Will do, boss man." Axe pulled out his cell and got up off the stool. He went past the tarp toward the front of the warehouse to make the call.

"Tag, I got a line on a boat for us," Elias called out. "It's a fishing vessel with a rig on it to pull up nets. That should work if they dump it overboard. I thought we'd take the yacht as the second boat. I just checked—DEA didn't take it yet."

"I thought they were supposed to pick it up last month?"

"The guys didn't come," said Elias. "I just confirmed it with the marina."

"Okay, take Finn with you and check out the fishing boat. We'll get everything ready here. Do we know when the *Gilda Marie* is pulling out?"

"I spoke with the harbor master. Tonight, just after midnight," Axe said as he hustled back behind the tarp. "The trip normally takes between four and six days. I'm thinking it will be four not six."

"Agreed." Nick nodded. "So let's get to it. Axe, get food. You know the drill. Go to several different stores and buy differing amounts of groceries."

Axe gave a half-assed salute. "On my way. I spoke with Sloan, my friend at the *Times*. She was intrigued by the Tarchuarani and says she'll look into it and get back to me."

"Why would he do that, with the groceries, I mean?" Carolina asked.

Nick glanced over at her. "Because if anyone comes along asking about us, they'll find one store that can say Axe was there and bought enough food for a few people for a day or two. Then they won't look any further. It distorts our numbers and the length of our trip. Anything that can mislead is good."

She sank onto a stool. There was so much more to this whole operation-type lifestyle than she ever imagined. "Can't we do the same thing then?"

Nick looked over the top of his screen. "What do you mean?"

"Well, if someone would do that to find out about us, then can't we do the same to find out about them?"

Cain's voice came from behind her. "We don't have to. We know there are a shitload of Silverstone operatives on that ship."

"I mean in Ecuador. If we had someone down there discreetly asking around, we might be able to find out what their plans are and who else is involved."

"Who do you have in mind?" Nick asked. His face was blank, but his eyes were snapping. He had to suspect she was holding out on him. He was not wrong.

Guilt washed over her. She had mentioned Guillermo earlier, but she'd never specifically said she was still in touch with him. She was trying to protect him. Plus, there didn't seem to be a need until now. She licked her lips. "I have to call Guillermo and tell him the vaccine shipment isn't going to be on the other boat, anyway. He's a local. He can ask around and maybe find out something useful."

"Call him." His voice was harsh, and he slammed a phone down next to her.

Fair enough. Maybe she should have told them she could contact Guillermo before, but did it really matter? It wouldn't have changed anything.

Except she'd held out on him, and now he didn't trust her. *Well too bad.* Her goal was to get the Florevir to the Tarchuarani. Guillermo was the only person that the Tarchuarani trusted at this point. She hadn't wanted to put him in any kind of jeopardy. Look at what happened to Javier, and to her as well. It was bad enough that the Silverstone guys would know his name from the USB stick. She didn't want to draw any more attention to him in any way, shape, or form. She got up off the stool and went toward the front of the building. She wanted privacy for the call. She dialed the number from memory.

It was answered after it rang just once. "Hey," she said in a quiet voice.

"Carolina." The relief in Guillermo's voice was palpable. "Is the shipment here already?"

"No. The shipment isn't there, and I'm not on it."

"What? What happened?"

"The vaccine was stolen."

Guillermo let out a string of swear words in Spanish that didn't need translating.

"Guillermo, listen carefully. The vaccine is coming down on another ship, the *Gilda Marie,* but there's a large contingent of heavily armed men guarding it, men employed by the Silverstone Group. We need to know how the men who have the vaccine are going to move the cargo from the port and where they're moving it to. Do you think you can find that out?"

"Who's 'we'?"

"It's a long story, Guillermo. After the vaccine got heisted, some people have been helping me."

"I don't like this, Carolina."

"Neither do I, but we don't have a choice. Do you think you can check out the docks and maybe find something out? I know this wasn't our original plan, but we must do whatever we can to get the Tarchuarani their medicine."

There was a long pause. "Yes, of course. I will try."

"If these dangerous men find out you're asking around about them, they'll kill you. They aren't nice people."

"I will be discreet. I have friends who can help. Are you still coming?"

"Yes, I'll be there in a few days. Guillermo, one more thing. We think the drug company Biodome Technologies is involved in this somehow, and they're partnered with someone else, though who that is, we don't know. Can you nose around and see if they're meeting with anyone or talking to anyone on a regular basis?"

"*Sí*. There is a partner. Javier did not tell you? Carolina, it's—"

Guillermo's voice cut out. "Guillermo? Are you there? Hello?"

"Carolina, I have much to tell you, but I can't speak now. I will do what I can to find out these men's plan. How can I reach you?"

Good question. The cell wasn't going to work once they left port. She turned around and almost walked into Nick's chest. She jumped back, and he reached an arm out to steady her. The whole stealthy way he moved freaked her out. He should make more noise! It was only fair. He held up a phone number written on a small scrap of paper. She recited it to Guillermo. "Call me at this number if you discover anything of interest. I'll phone you with more details about our plan later."

"Okay. Good luck."

"You, too." She hung up and handed the phone back to Nick. "You know—"

He clamped a hand over her mouth as he looked toward the warehouse door. He moved her back into the corner of the building. It was dark there, with little light reaching them from the small windows that were up close to the ceiling. Nick removed his hand but put his finger to his lips, then pulled a gun from his waistband. He turned, and his back blocked her view. She peered over his shoulder.

A man pulled open the door and held it wide for another man who walked through into the warehouse. The first man followed closely at his heels. They were having a conversation in Spanish, one of them gesturing as he spoke. The other nodded, and they walked farther into the space, continuing their conversation. Carolina held her breath. These men seemed like they were discussing business, not looking for them. But it still wouldn't be good if they were seen.

As the men continued their conversation, Carolina released her breath slowly. The heat radiating from Nick was making her perspire. He remained stone still. It was amazing. She would have sworn he wasn't even breathing. The scent of the shampoo he'd used that morning filled the air around her. She had the urge to reach out and touch his back. It was stupid. She wanted to put her hands on him. Feel his scars. See how he was healing. Just touch him. She fisted her hands tightly and kept them at her sides.

The two visitors stopped and chatted some more. Finally, after what seemed an eternity, they retraced their steps and left.

The air hissed out of her lungs. That had been close, and Nick still didn't move. She was about to say something when he suddenly turned to her.

"If something like that happens again, I need you to stay perfectly still. If you find you have to move because you're scared, touch me. It will ground you and make you feel calmer."

"Um, okay. Thanks." *Fuck.* And here she thought she was being so cool. He *knew* she wanted to touch him. Of course, he thought it was about fear. *Yeah, we'll go with that.* They walked to the back of the warehouse behind the tarp, and she sat on a stool next to the laptops. Nick came to a stop beside her.

"What the fuck?" Nick stated in an icy voice. It was aimed at Cain who was crouched down in the corner.

Carolina blinked. He was really pissed off.

"You didn't see them coming or what?" he growled at Cain.

Cain didn't bat an eye at the tone. He just held up a wire that was obviously broken.

"Fuckin' rats," Nick said.

"Oh, my god!" Carolina immediately looked around her and pulled her feet off the floor. "That means they were *just here* eating the wires…because those worked earlier."

Nick grinned. "What's the matter with you? You don't like rats?"

It was good to see him smile. Much better than when he was pissed off. "Look, it's one thing, okay? Some people don't do well with spiders and snakes. For me, it's rats."

"Wait, didn't you work in medical research?" asked Nick. "I thought they used rats as test subjects."

"Why do you think I hate them so much? I've had nightmares about rats. You do not want to know what rats can do or what diseases rats in the wild carry. Did you know people still get the bubonic plague every year? Yeah, rats are no joke."

She shuddered and then glanced at Nick who was laughing at her.

She swatted at him. "It's not that funny."

"I know," he said, attempting a straight face. "Rats are no joke," he quoted her, laughing again. Even though she was annoyed, he looked sexy when he laughed. Of course, he looked sexy doing most things.

"You're willing to take on Cain over there but not a rat," said Nick. "Boy, is your sense of self-preservation warped."

Cain came back over to stand in front of one of the laptops. "I'm with her. I fuckin' hate rats."

"See?" Carolina smirked at him. "Normal people don't like rats."

"Normal?" Nick was still laughing when the phone rang. After answering, the smile fell off his face. "What the hell happened?"

CHAPTER TWENTY

"Are you sure, Elias?" Nick whirled around and looked at the laptop. The screen showed the area around the outside of the warehouse as being empty. How could it be empty if Elias was telling him the cops were outside?

The rats. It was a setup. The cops had cut their feed and tapped into it.

Elias confirmed. "Yes. It's definitely Captain Hernandez, and he's got his whole crew with him. They aren't preparing for a friendly chat either. They are loaded down and ready for war. Every single man is armed to the teeth. Automatic weapons. I knew Hernandez hated us, but this is over the top, even for him. He's not taking any chances on us getting away. It's definitely a shoot first scenario."

"Shit!"

"Do you want us to come in?" asked Elias.

"Stay where you are," Nick ordered over the phone. "We still have the advantage, assuming they don't know you're out there. Is Axe with you?"

"Yeah, and he's got all the food. We brought the fishing

boat to the marina where the yacht is anchored. So we're good to go."

"Okay. We'll meet you there." Nick hung up, put the phone back in his pocket, and slammed the laptop closed. He announced to Carolina and the rest of the crew, "The cops are outside. They know we're here, and they want to talk to us."

Cain hurriedly started packing gear. "So, we talk to Martinez. He's a reasonable guy. He'll understand our story."

Nick threw everything back in the duffel bags as quickly as possible. "Except it's not Martinez. He's back in Colón, I would imagine. It's Hernandez."

"Fuck," Cain muttered as he started zipping up bags.

"Will someone please tell me what's going on?" asked Carolina.

"The men that were just here were scouting. It was a setup. They must have needed to confirm we were here, or they wanted the layout of the building. Either way, the cops are outside. They are pissed at us about the warehouse explosion, probably because of the dead bodies. I'm sure they want to speak to us.

"The problem is Silverstone must have some kind of pull here because of the man they sent—Hernandez is one of the most corrupt cops in the country. He wants us dead because we confiscated a huge shipment of drugs that he was paid off to let through. He barely got out of being killed by his cartel contacts. He's going to shoot now and ask questions later."

Cain placed the duffel bags along the wall. "That man has a personal hatred for us. We made him look bad in front of a pile of higher-ups."

"Fantastic." Carolina walked over and slung a bag over each shoulder, then picked up one to carry in her hands.

Nick did a quick 360 to make sure they'd gotten everything. He called Elias back. "Okay. We're good to go. How long before they breach?"

"You got maybe five minutes tops."

"Is anyone at our back door?"

Elias said something muffled, then came back. "No, but it's going to be tight with the gear. The alley is very narrow, like maybe two feet wide. We'll leave a vehicle at the end. It's the dark blue SUV. Keys will be in the usual spot. Good luck."

"Okay. See you at the boats." He hung up again and turned to Cain. "We're going out the back way."

"Back way?" Carolina looked around. "I don't see a back door."

"We're going to make one." He set down the bags and dug through one until he retrieved a small torch, which he quickly lit. He started cutting through the old warehouse wall. It was slow going, but there was no other way out and no way to go faster. They wanted to be out of there before Hernandez realized they had left. "Cain, set up a small surprise for Sergeant Hernandez."

Cain dropped his bags, got to work and, a minute later, was done. "Where do you want it?"

"Put it among those crates by the window. It should slow them down."

Cain took off across the room. Carolina asked, "Did he just make a bomb?"'

"A small one."

"Oh, well, if it's only a small one." She shook her head.

Nick gave her a quick grin. Cain got back just as Nick finished and turned off the torch. "Grab the gear." He put everything away and pulled the bit of metal from the wall. "Okay, we're going out this hole, but it's tight between here and the next building. Carolina, you can't have the bags over your shoulders. They won't fit. You have to stack them and pull them behind you. Can you do that?"

Her fingers whitened on the straps. "I'll do my best."

He nodded. "Cain, you go first. Then you, Carolina. I'll bring up the rear."

Cain disappeared through the hole, then pulled his gear through. Carolina went next, and Nick pushed the bags she'd been carrying through after her. She stacked them like he'd said, then started pulling. He leaned through and pushed her bags from his end to help her out. He shoved the rest of his gear through, then followed. He climbed over the top of the gear and pulled the bags by the straps.

The building next door was maybe twenty inches from his face. He broke out in a sweat. If Hernandez found them, they were dead. It would be like shooting fish in a barrel, but they had no choice. There was no other way out that didn't involve getting shot by a pissed-off, crooked cop. In front of him, Carolina was slowing down. Nick gave her gear a push. They were nearly there. Cain was already outside.

From the end of the building to the SUV was about ten feet. Cain took a quick peek around the corner, then held up a hand and shook his head.

"Shit," Nick mumbled.

Carolina turned to look at him. "What does that mean?"

"It means we can't go yet."

Using hand signals, Cain indicated someone was coming. Nick glanced at Carolina, but she must have gotten the gist of it because she froze in place. A hulking man wearing all black came and stood just outside the mouth of the alley with his back to them. He turned and looked directly at them.

Nick tensed, ready to push Carolina down out of the way in case he had to shoot but the man turned back and started pacing while he smoked a cigarette and talked on the phone.

Why the hell didn't he see them? They were in the shade. That had to be it. They were about eight feet from the end of the ally and the man couldn't see that far. Nick let out the breath he'd been holding. For once he was grateful for the bright Panamanian sunshine.

"*Si, Señor.* They are in the warehouse. Hernandez wants to go in now. He wants Taggert dead." More silence. "*Si, Señor.* I will tell him five more minutes. That's all I can promise. You will have to hurry to get here in time. And Mr. Vance, you will pay me double for this."

The man hung up the phone. He took a couple more puffs and glanced at his watch.

The heat of the day was plastering Nick's clothing to his body. Being trapped between hot metal walls was not helping. He willed the man to leave. *Just walk away.*

A few puffs more, and the man dropped his cigarette. He ground it out with his foot and walked back out of view. Cain waited thirty seconds and took another brief glimpse. He turned to Nick and nodded. They were good to go.

When Nick nodded back, Cain sprinted to the SUV. He opened the back and threw in his gear. Carolina was still dragging hers across the sidewalk. Cain turned and picked all of it up and threw it in. Nick came up right behind her and dropped his stuff. He pulled her around and practically threw her in the back seat while running to the driver's side. Cain finished loading the gear and jumped into the passenger seat just as Nick started to roll.

"Stay low across the seat, Carolina, until we're clear," Nick instructed. He had his gun beside him. Cain did as well. They pulled on the baseball caps that had been left for them and pulled down the sun visors. It wasn't much of a disguise, but every little bit helped.

They rolled slowly down the street, keeping the same pace as the local traffic. It was moving at a snail's pace. All the drivers were looking at Hernandez and his men dressed in full riot gear and armed with automatic weapons standing on the sidewalk at the end of the pier. Nick gritted his teeth. They were going to have to drive right by them. *Fuck.*

Roman Vance, moving swiftly, arrived next to Hernandez, just as they were rolling by. About half a dozen Silverstone guys from the *Gilda Marie* came to a halt beside Vance. Nick took a deep steadying breath. He'd love to hop out and throttle Vance, but this wasn't the moment.

"I know you want to take him here, but we won't make it out alive," said Cain. "I don't so much care, but Dr. Alvarez needs to get through this so she can save those people. When this is over, I'll help you track him if you want."

Nick appreciated the support. Cain had been through his own hell, and he didn't need to volunteer for more. He nodded at Cain but said nothing. His anger was too raw at the moment. He needed to get his head back in the game.

They rolled silently past the rest of the men. No one even looked their way. All eyes were focused on the warehouse Nick's team had just vacated. When a cop directing traffic waved them on, Nick nodded and put his foot down on the accelerator. Within seconds, they were down the block and turning onto a different street. He let out a sigh of relief. He glanced in the rearview mirror and caught Carolina's eye. "How are you doing?" She looked pale but not nearly as bad as yesterday. Maybe she was getting used to these close calls. Not good.

"Um, fine, I guess." Her voice wavered.

That made Nick feel marginally better. Somehow, he didn't want her to become used to being in danger. He wanted her safe somewhere. This could be a story for her grandchildren. He glanced over at Cain who had his eyes closed and his head back on the headrest. If Nick had to guess, he'd bet Cain was just trying to will his body to calm down. God knew he needed to do the same thing. The need to go after Vance was almost impossible to deny. Twenty minutes later, they were miles down the coast and pulling up at a marina.

Axe was waiting for them as they parked the SUV. "Glad you guys made it out. Fuckin' Hernandez is an animal when it comes to us. We're all damn lucky we got out."

Nick nodded. "You're not wrong, there." Axe had summed it up perfectly.

"Anyway, I thought you might need help unloading the gear," he said, lifting the tailgate. Cain got out and helped.

"Where are the boats?" Nick asked as he picked up a couple of the bags.

Carolina reached down to pick one up, but Cain brushed her hand away. "I've got it. You did good back there." He reached down and picked up the rest of the gear and followed Axe across the walkway and down the dock.

Nick touched Carolina's arm and nodded toward Cain. "You've made a friend. That was high praise."

Carolina gave a slight smile. "I didn't do anything. Just pulled a bunch of bags and did what you told me to."

"You didn't freak out or lose your shit."

"My whole job requires me to keep my shit together under pressure."

"Then you must be good at your job."

She smiled up at him. "I am."

He laughed. He liked that she was sure of herself. They followed Cain along an aging dock. It swayed slightly under their weight. Nick was picturing a nice swim when he spotted a small oil slick on the water. The sun's reflection created a rainbow on the surface, but the oil made him reconsider the swim. He glanced at Carolina, but she was taking in her surroundings. They came to a stop beside an old fishing trawler that had definitely seen better days.

Carolina groaned. "Tell me it runs better than it looks."

Finn caught the bag Cain tossed and placed it on the deck. "She runs great," he said. "I got it from a friend of a friend of a friend. It hasn't been used for fishing in many a day."

Axe grinned. "At least, this time, we'll be putting it to good use."

Carolina cocked an eyebrow. "What am I missing?"

Elias jumped off the boat and came to a stop beside her. "He means that it was used as a drug boat. On the surface, it looks like a fishing boat that's going to sink at any moment. Underneath, it's got brand new engines that are twice the speed of what they'd usually have, and there's all kinds of extra storage areas to store our gear. Makes it ideal as a cover vessel."

"Oh, well that's handy." She nodded in approval.

They got the rest of the stuff on board and then went down below into the kitchen area.

Elias was squatting down, taping a gun underneath the counter. "We're all set. Everything is stored, and I've put the backup guns in various locations around the boat. We should be good to go. We gassed her up earlier." He finished securing the gun and stood up.

"Good. Where's the other boat?" Nick inquired as he crossed his arms over his chest.

"Axe is gassing her up on the other side of the marina. He already took food and gear over and got it unloaded and ready to go."

"So who is going in what boat?" Finn asked.

Nick shrugged. "Anyone have preferences?"

"I'll stay here with Elias and Axe," said Finn. "Why don't you and Cain and Dr. Alvarez take the other boat? It will be easier to sell if it's a couple on board with a captain. Too many of us, and people might want to take a second look."

Nick shrugged. "It's fine with me. Cain?"

Cain lifted his chin.

"Okay, we're good to go then. We'll go pick the boat up from Axe. Have your coms on until we're underway. Once we're all out of the harbor, we can start working in shifts. We'll wait out there for the *Gilda Marie* to pass by and then we'll follow her. It's a four-day trip to Ecuador. We have to stay close enough to keep an eye on the *Gilda Marie* but far enough away to not attract attention. Radio check in an hour."

Elias gave a quick salute.

"Aye, aye, Captain," Finn responded.

The three of them trouped off the boat and started back along the dock. Nick rolled his shoulders. A hint of unease washed over him. He looked around but didn't see anyone watching. When he made another sweep, he caught Cain doing the same, too.

Carolina was a step behind them. "We're being watched."

"Yeah," was Nick's only reply. Once again, he was impressed by how intuitive, as well as smart, Carolina was. Good combination in anyone, but sexy as hell in this woman. And dangerous for him. He swept the area once more.

"It's a guy over in the green boat at the end of the next dock," Carolina said calmly, as if she tracked surveillance every day.

Cain glanced at Nick, who gave a shrug. She'd found the man that neither of them had. That was more than a little concerning. She really was killing his focus, but what was Cain's excuse? He took a quick look in the direction Carolina had mentioned and spotted the guy. He was sitting on the deck under a tarp used to block out the sun and blended in with the shadows. She must have some damn good eyesight to have picked him out.

"What do we do?" she asked.

Nick kept facing forward. "*We* don't do anything."

Cain already had his phone out and was speaking quietly. He put it back in his pocket and gave Nick an almost imperceptible nod. "Axe will take care of it. He'll let us know if it's something we have to worry about long-term or not."

He turned right, and they walked down the dock until they came to a large yacht. Cain boarded first. Nick helped Carolina step across then followed.

"We're taking this?" she asked.

"Yes, this one is ours," Nick confirmed.

Carolina's eyes sparkled, and her smile went from ear to ear. "The guys are totally missing out. This is a floating palace."

"Not quite, but yeah, it's nice."

"What is it?" she asked as she kicked off her shoes and pulled open the door to the living area.

Nick turned to Cain who was heading up to the flybridge. "See what Axe says before we leave. I want to know what's going on. We might have to come up with alternate plans if Vance and his crew are already aware of our plans."

He followed Carolina inside. She was checking out the entertainment. "To answer your question," he said, "this is a Hatteras M90 Panacera."

"Pretty fancy for a government vehicle. Is it used for undercover stuff?"

"Well, the Coast Guard didn't exactly buy it. We confiscated it during a drug bust. Technically, it's been turned over to the DEA, but they haven't gotten around to picking it up. They won't care if we borrow it one last time." He grinned.

Actually, they'd go apeshit when they came to get it and

found it gone, but that was a problem for higher-ups like Bertrand. He would back Nick up on this one. He was always trying to stick it to the DEA. It was some sort of personal thing.

"This was a drug dealer's boat?" asked Carolina. "He had good taste."

Nick looked around. The rich brown floor tile was made to look like wood. The couch Carolina sat on was a sectional in a medium gray with navy throw pillows and a matching navy blanket. There was a navy rug on the floor underneath the chrome and glass coffee table. Beyond the living area was the kitchen. It had all the latest stainless-steel appliances and matching chrome fixtures on white cabinets. In the front was the dining table that had leather wrap-around seating in the same color as the living space. He nodded. "Yes, it's not bad, and now it's ours for the next few days."

Carolina ran her hand over the cushion. "Oh, my God, this is amazing. This is by far the best part of this trip."

He laughed. "You mean you didn't like the interrogation room at HQ?"

"Funny."

"You know there could be rats onboard." He couldn't resist teasing her.

Her eyes narrowed. "Well, if there are, they'd be upscale rats. No slumming about this boat will be accepted."

He grinned. "Want to go below and see your cabin?"

She was on her feet in seconds. "Absolutely!"

He led her down to the sleeping quarters. He turned right into the largest bedroom. "This is yours for the duration."

Carolina's eyes sparkled. "It's huge. Is that a king-size bed?"

It was great to see her smile. This morning had been tough. Hell, her entire trip had been rough. This would give her a nice break. She deserved it. There was a rumbling sound, and the boat swayed. Carolina fell into his chest. Nick automatically put his arms around her to steady her. "Cain must have gotten the all-clear from Axe. We're pulling away from the dock."

She nodded as their gazes locked. He had the urge to pull her closer against him and kiss her senseless. *Bad idea.* Instead, he set her back on her feet and turned away to continue the tour. He tried to concentrate on what he was saying, but the imprint of her body on his was playing havoc with his brain.

He pointed to the room across from hers. "That's Cain's room."

She peeked her head in. "It has twin beds. He's kind of big to be sleeping in a twin. Maybe we should switch."

Nick snorted. "No. You should not switch. Cain will be fine. He's slept in a lot worse. Trust me."

"Where's your room?" she asked.

He gestured sideways with his head. "Down there. It's a smaller version of yours."

"Does it have a twin?"

"Queen."

She nodded. "So only Cain is going to be uncomfortable."

He frowned. *Why was she so worried about Cain?* "He'll be fine," Nick growled. "I need to go up and find out what the story is on our friend, the watcher. Your stuff is beside your bed. Dinner will be in an hour or so. I'll cook tonight. You can do it tomorrow night. We all take turns."

"Aye, aye, Captain," she said, giving him a mock salute.

He turned and headed back up the stairs. Four days with this woman on board this boat might not be the best idea. Maybe it would have been less complicated if he had gone on the trawler. But then she would be over here with Cain and one of the other guys. Nick's gut clenched. He didn't want to consider that option.

He headed up to the flybridge. "Cain, I assume you called Axe. What did he say?" he asked as he sat in a matching captain's chair next to Cain's.

Cain kept his gaze forward as he spoke. "He said the guy was actually DEA. They're doing some sort of op here. The guy just happened to be at the marina as part of the op. Seeing us with all our gear made him a bit nervous, so he was paying attention. Axe got Finn to call his connections in the DEA, and they said the guy checks out. Axe told him to keep his mouth shut and tell no one about seeing us. He said it wasn't a problem."

"Did Axe believe him?" Nick pulled sunglasses out of his pocket. The sun was starting to set as they moved out of the harbor, but it still blazed on the water. The trawler was off to their port side and slightly ahead.

"Maybe." Cain turned the boat, adjusting their heading slightly.

"That doesn't sound too promising." He scouted the area around them. There were a few boats heading out like they were, but more heading in. Time for dinner after a nice day out on the ocean. Nothing set off any alarm bells for him.

"Axe said the guy said all the right things and knew the right people, but he had an off feeling about him."

"Shit. Maybe we should ditch the boats and find another way down." Unease settled between Nick's shoulder blades. What if they were heading into a trap? Vance was a crafty bastard, and he had no qualms about shooting every man, woman, and child on sight if it meant a bigger payday. No one was going down on Nick's watch if he had anything to say about it. Having a civilian with them was going to make it more difficult. He'd have to rethink the plan.

"Axe took care of it." Cain made another slight adjustment on the instrument panel.

"How exactly?"

"He knocked the guy's phone in the water 'accidentally.' He told him he felt badly about it so he bought him a beer at the marina bar area. He made sure he didn't leave the guy alone until the locals showed up."

"What locals?"

Cain grinned. "Axe got Finn to call Martinez and tell him that this guy knew something about the dead bodies at the compound. Martinez sent over some guys from the local precinct that he trusts to pick him up. He's on his way to question the guy now."

Nick laughed. "I'm so glad Axe is on our side. Under that easy smile lies a very devious mind. Any ideas on how long Martinez will hold him?"

"Axe doesn't know, but he said Finn laid it on pretty thick, said the guy wouldn't break under questioning and that he might even try to pass himself off as DEA. He warned Martinez not to fall for it. I'm thinking that buys us at least twenty-four hours before he gets access to a phone. After that, we should be far enough away that it will be hard to spot us. The GPS locators are already disabled on both vessels so we should be good at least for the ride down, but once we get to Ecuador, it might be a different story."

"If this guy actually does work for Vance, or at the very least, gets paid to keep an eye on things by Vance, then he'll know we're coming."

Cain nodded. "That's the thinking, yeah."

"We've got someone on the ground trying to get us the intel on how and where they're moving the vaccine once they dock. Hopefully, that will give us a better idea of how to proceed."

"When did that happen? Who do you know down in Ecuador?"

"Dr. Alvarez called *her* contact in Ecuador, someone she'd previously failed to mention she could still contact."

Cain's eyebrows went up. "The pretty doctor has hidden depths."

"Let's hope she has no more surprises. We're already way out on a limb. I don't want it to break under us."

CHAPTER TWENTY-ONE

In her own private bathroom, Carolina climbed out of the shower and toweled herself off. It seemed like forever since she'd been in a comfortable space for longer than a few hours. The apartment had been fine for one night, but this fancy boat was a whole other level. The towel was thick and soft against her skin. It even smelled good. It was almost like being on vacation. Well, except for the fact someone wanted to kill her.

She went to open the cupboard for another towel but caught her reflection in the mirror. It made her wince. Dark circles under her eyes were outdone only by dreadful wrinkles etched into her worried forehead. Maybe now was the time to swallow her pride and start Botox. Being on the run was bad for the skin. There was not enough available moisturizer. She smiled at her own jest. If only it were all a joke. But it wasn't. People were dead and more could die. All the moisturizer in the world wouldn't change that.

When she lifted out a smaller towel, a gun lay beneath. Her hand jerked and she stepped back automatically. *Had it been left by the drug dealer with exquisite taste?* No. Carolina bet Axe had put this here when he was readying the boats. There were probably guns all over the place. Should she leave it there? Or move it over closer to the bed? No point in her changing things. She positioned another towel over it and closed the cupboard.

She put her hair up in the towel and pulled on clean shorts and a tank top. She was kind of relieved to have a gun nearby. When she'd gotten the job with MSF, she'd gone to the gun range and taken lessons. She was a good shot. She didn't carry a gun and was not a fan of them, but she also wasn't naïve enough to believe that she would be safe at every moment. She'd decided that learning to use a gun was the prudent thing to do. The hairbrush felt good on her scalp as she brushed out her hair. Hair still damp, she went topside and found Nick in the kitchen.

The scent of chicken with garlic and simmering cream filled the air. "Smells good." Her stomach growled. She hadn't realized how hungry she was until just that moment.

"Thanks. It's ready, so if you want to grab a seat, we'll eat."

Carolina sat on a bench seat at the table. Cain arrived, and Nick handed him a plate along with cutlery. But then he turned around and left.

"He's not joining us?" she asked.

"Someone has to drive the boat and keep an eye out."

"Oh, I hadn't thought about that." She cocked her head. "Do you want me to take a turn? I've never driven a boat, but—"

"Thanks for the offer, but we're good." He smiled. "Cain and I will handle it in shifts."

"Is there something else I can do to help?"

"No, it's fine. Just relax." He plated the food and brought it over to the table. "Do you want something to drink?"

"What do you have?"

He looked in the fridge. "Wine or beer, along with soda and water."

"If it's okay, I would love a glass of wine. White, if you have it."

"Yes. Sauvignon Blanc, okay?" he asked as he pulled out the bottle.

She smiled. "That's great."

He uncorked the wine, poured her a glass, and brought it to the table.

"You're not going to join me?" she asked.

"I have to take over from Cain a bit later. Better if I don't drink. I'll get sleepy."

"Oh." Remorse hit her in the belly. Here she was treating this like some kind of vacation when these men were risking their lives to help her and the Tarchuarani.

Nick put his plate on the table and sat across from her. "Don't feel guilty, Carolina."

She blinked. Apparently, he knew her well enough he could read her thoughts. That was not necessarily a good thing. Then he'd know how much she wanted him to kiss her again. Heat crept up her cheeks and she looked down at her plate.

"You have a very expressive face when you aren't being careful." He smirked. "Enjoy the food and wine and yacht. You've had a hell of a couple of weeks."

Her shoulders sagged. "I guess. I'm sorry that I dragged all of you into this mess. And now you are all going so far out of your way to help me."

"Carolina." He reached out and covered her hand with his. "Helping you has brought the team together and probably healed all of us faster than sitting around doing scut work. There is not one man on our team that would rather be back sitting on their ass at HQ, talking on the phone and staring at a screen all day. This is where we live."

She understood. Being in these dangerous situations had a way of making her feel more alive. It was the same when she was working in a war zone with Doctors Without Borders. "Okay, Nick, though I appreciate your help, nonetheless. And please, if there's any way I can pitch in, tell me. Whatever you say, I still feel responsible for you all being here."

"Agreed. I'll let you know. Now dig in."

When he pulled his hand back, she immediately felt its absence. She liked the comforting feeling of his hand over hers. She sipped her wine. "So, what is this gourmet meal you've made?"

"It's called chicken mixed with whatever I could find in vegetables and a touch of cream sauce. Cream sauce makes anything taste good."

She laughed. "That's the secret, is it? Cream sauce, good to know. I'll remember that." She ate her first fork full of chicken dripping in sauce. It *was* tasty. "You're right. It's delicious."

"I have many secrets I'd be willing to share with you... for a price, of course." His grin was wicked.

Her stomach tensed even as a small thrill went through her. She flashed back to the kiss they'd shared at the apartment last night and took another sip of wine. "What's your fee?" she asked as their gazes locked.

"It's a barter system," he said. His voice was deeper than normal, and it made heat flare in her core. Suddenly, his cell went off.

He looked away as he pulled it out of his pocket and then frowned. "Keep eating. Don't wait for me." He left the galley and went through the living area onto the deck.

Carolina sipped her wine and waited, but when it didn't seem like Nick was coming back anytime soon, she began eating again. She finished her meal and took her plate to the counter. She cleaned up the kitchen but still no sign of Nick. She did find another gun, though. This one was in with the dish towels. Good to know. She finished up by wiping down the counter. Should she have another glass of wine? Probably not, but what the hell? She poured a glass and put the bottle back in the fridge.

She grabbed her wine and walked around the main cabin, examining nautical knickknacks and searching for more guns. She swallowed the last sip of wine and looked out to the deck. Should she go out there and find Nick? Probably not. She might do something crazy like start kissing him. That wouldn't be helpful.

Yawning brought on a wave of exhaustion. She grabbed a couple of bottles of water from the fridge and went down to her cabin. She threw on a large T-shirt and slipped between cool sheets. With the light hum of the engine and the sway of the boat, she was asleep in seconds.

The silence woke her. Carolina sat up and listened. The engines were off. It was still dark out. The boat rocked gently in the waves, but she felt no human movement on board. Her heart thudded in her chest. The harsh sound of her own breathing filled her ears. She got up, pulled on a pair of shorts, then quietly crept out of her cabin.

When her foot hit the bottom stair, she hesitated. Would it be better to be armed? There was that gun in the kitchen. That was closest. She slowly climbed the stairs. The light above the stove was off. Nick's plate of food, which she'd wrapped up and left there, was gone. She hesitated by the drawer with the gun. She couldn't bring herself to open it. She knew firsthand from her work just what kind of damage guns did.

She moved quietly through the main salon and slid open the door to the deck. The running lights were on and provided a bit of light. Waves lapped gently against the hull of the boat and salt hung in the air. Still no human sound. She stepped onto the deck, wiping her slick palms on her shorts. *Remain calm. Breathe deeply. One step at a time.* She'd used the same mantra in med school when feeling overwhelmed.

She moved quietly up the stairs to the fly deck and over to the bridge area, but it was empty. Her heart rate skyrocketed. Where was Cain? Where was Nick? Their doors had been closed downstairs. Nick had said someone would be up here at all times.

Her foot stepped in something wet. She moved her foot and looked down. It was hard to see, but it was dark and a bit sticky. She was pretty sure it was blood. Fear clawed its way up her chest and into her throat. She looked out at the pitch-black water.

Jesus, was she alone at sea? She heard a sound. Her mouth went dry. There was nowhere to hide if the Silverstone guys were aboard. She crouched down and moved over between the flybridge coffee table and sofa. A gun! There had to be one up here. She kicked herself for not grabbing the one in the kitchen. As quickly and quietly as possible, she searched under all the cushions. She checked the throw pillows and in every crevice. *There must be one!*

"What are you searching for?" Nick asked in a quiet voice.

Carolina screamed and fell over. "Oh, my God! You scared the hell out of me!" she yelled. Her chest heaved with her labored breathing. Her heart was crashing against her ribs. "Where the hell were you?"

"What were you searching for?" Nick was standing over her, his eyes narrowed.

"A gun! The engines stopped, and I couldn't see anyone around. I panicked." She blinked back tears. "There was no sound, so I came up here, and you said there would always be one of you up here, but there wasn't. And then I thought I should find a gun." Her words tumbled out one after another.

Nick's expression softened. He reached out and pulled her to her feet. Her knees buckled so he wrapped his arms around her and pulled her to his chest. "I'm so sorry. I didn't mean to scare you. We stopped because we are ahead of the *Gilda Marie*. We need to let her pass us so I dropped anchor."

Her heart still slammed against her ribs. She was mortified to admit that she needed Nick's help to stand, but her knees refused to hold her weight. She'd been terrified that the Silverstone men had found them, and she was alone. It was the stuff of nightmares.

Nick rubbed her back with his hands. "I'm really sorry, Carolina, to give you a fright."

"I thought I saw blood on the deck."

"Yeah, I scraped my arm on a loose screw. I just went downstairs to clean and bandage it. I didn't want to get yelled at later by any bossy doctors." He smiled at her.

She nodded. *Deep breaths.* Nick's scent swirled around her, more comforting and intoxicating than it should be. She swallowed. Her heart rate was slowing. Her breathing was evening out. Would her knees hold her? She was in no rush to find out. Nick still had her in his arms, and it felt good. Better than good. She should stand up, but she didn't want to. She was enjoying being tucked against his chest. She wanted to stay in the circle of his arms because she felt safe. Safer than she'd felt in a long time. A shiver went through her.

"Are you cold? You should go back down to bed." He started to pull away.

The shiver had nothing to do with the cold and everything to do with Nick being this close. She lifted her head from his chest and turned to face him. Their gazes locked before he bent down and brushed her lips with his. It started as a slow tentative kiss but built quickly. She wrapped her arms around his neck and pressed herself full against him while their tongues danced and explored. That set all her nerve endings on fire.

He pulled away from her and drew a ragged breath. "Carolina, you need to go to bed." His tone was harsh.

She blinked. *What just happened?* One minute, it was all systems go, and the next it was full stop. "But—"

"Now, Carolina. Go to bed now." He turned away and went back to the controls.

Heat rushed into her cheeks. She turned on her heel and stumbled across the deck. She made her way down the ladder and into the main salon. That was mortifying. She'd never been dismissed quite like that before. It made her feel like a kid again, being sent to her room.

She stopped dead in the middle of the salon. She'd spent most of her life doing what she was told and doing what others wanted. Why was she doing that now? She was an adult with her own mind, and she wanted an explanation.

She turned to go right back up there but stopped again. Because he was right. It was stupid. Them being together now was ridiculous. Heat moved back up her neck and into her cheeks. He was being the adult, and she had a bruised ego. She had wanted him in Yemen and had fantasized about them being together, seeing the world together. He was smart and funny and caring, but seeing the reality of the situation, of his work, his life, she knew he was right. This was untenable. She went down to her cabin.

She got back in bed and pulled the blankets up tight to her chin. Closing her eyes, she let the sound of the waves soothe her raw nerves. She was overtired and overwrought. Tears rolled down her cheeks into her hair. If she could go back in time and make different choices she would, which didn't make her a very nice person. She was trying to save the Tarchuarani. That should be the most important thing but, somehow, it wasn't at that moment.

She wanted to be well and truly loved. In her fantasies, it was Nick who had loved her. Since those four days they'd spent together in Yemen, she'd been in love with him, or the idea of him. The *him* that she had gotten to know by sitting beside him, tending to his wounds, talking through the night. It was a childish delusion that had been harmless until she'd run into him again. Now reality was clashing with her dreams, and it wasn't pretty.

The sun was high, and the cabin was hot when Carolina opened her eyes again. She sat up and rubbed her face. Groggy from oversleeping, it took a second for the events of last night to come flooding back, then it hit like a tidal wave. Her feet were made of lead as she swung them over the side of the bed. She took a deep breath and let it go. There was no point in lamenting about having her dreams crushed. They were stupid anyway.

She squared her shoulders. A shower was in order. She got out of bed, went to the bathroom, and turned on the water. After stripping down, she waited for it to warm. Seconds later, she was under the spray and trying to figure out how to put this mess with Nick behind her. *It was not a big deal.* It had been a non-event. *Yeah, right. Who the hell was she kidding?*

It had not been a non-event to Carolina. It had felt wonderful to be in Nick's arms. Last night's kiss had been even better than the one at the apartment. The first one had been tentative and questioning. This one had been driven more by a mutual understanding that everyone was game. At least that's what she'd thought. She shook her head. Nick had done the right thing. This was ridiculous. She needed to get over herself and focus on more important matters.

After she finished up in the shower and got out, anxiety swamped her, and she leaned her hip against the sink. The thought that someone wanted her dead had been lurking in her mind, but with everything that had been going on she hadn't had a chance to process any of it. But now having a moment to herself where she was feeling safe, fear was rearing its ugly head. Her palms broke out in a sweat. It wasn't that she hadn't been in danger before. She'd worked in war ravaged areas, but the violence was not directed at her personally. She was just one of the many people who were targets. Now, she, Carolina Alvarez, was very specifically a target. Her heart slammed in her chest. Her throat closed over.

No, she would not succumb to a panic attack. She took a breath and released it. She repeated the procedure a few more times. She had another couple of days on the boat, away from immediate danger. She needed to take some time and relax, come to grips with the events of the trip. The Tarchuarani were dependent on her success. Whether they knew it or not didn't matter. She was determined not to fail no matter how difficult facing Nick and spending time with him was going to be.

She brushed out her hair and put it up in a messy bun. It was a shame she didn't have clothing suited for a yacht, but that had definitely not been part of her plan when packing for the trip. But maybe...

Nick had said the yacht had been seized from a drug dealer. Carolina wrapped herself in a towel and returned to her room. She opened the drawers and closets one by one.

Nothing. *Oh well, it had been an idea.* She had bent down to get her shorts she'd left on the floor last night when she spotted a drawer in the base of the bed. It was hidden with no handle on it. Unless someone was eye level like she was, it couldn't be seen. She smiled. Maybe she would find some amazing jewelry or something cool left behind by some drug moll.

She tried but failed to pull the drawer out. But when she pushed on it, she heard a click. The door sprang open. Empty. Bummer. Well it had been a fun idea. She paused. Could there be a matching one on the other side of the bed?

She walked around the bed and got down on the floor. *Bingo.* Another drawer. She pushed on it and heard a click, but it refused to budge. She pulled on it, gently at first, but then gave it a hard yank. It flew open, and she fell backward, banging her head on a chair. She sat up, rubbed her head, then checked out the drawer.

Holy shit! There was a gun and several plastic-wrapped kilos of what she assumed was cocaine.

What the hell? She sat there, staring. Did it belong to Nick and his team? No. Had they missed this when they carried out the raid on the drug lord? That was possible, but it didn't feel right. Her belly tightened, and goosebumps appeared on her skin.

No time to waste. Nick and Cain needed to know about this. She pulled on her shorts and a clean red T-shirt and headed out of her room. She found Cain and Nick on the flybridge, sitting at the controls.

"Hey, guys," she huffed breathlessly as she approached. "I found something you should check out."

Nick turned her direction. He had on cargo shorts, but he was bare-chested. He wore dark sunglasses so she couldn't see his eyes, but her heart gave a little leap anyway. His chest was just as muscled as she remembered, only now it was tanned as well.

"What did you find?" he asked in a slightly bored voice.

She came to a stop between them. "Cocaine."

"Shit!" Nick jumped up off the chair.

Cain commented, "Well, that would explain their presence." He nodded toward an approaching ship. It looked like a military vessel.

Nick scowled. "Vance? You think he set us up?"

Cain nodded.

"Fuck. Where is it?" Nick demanded.

"In my cabin in a drawer. I left it open."

He nodded and then brushed past her. "Stay here with Cain." He turned back. "Remember we're Mr. Peter and Dr. Carolina James, and we're on a cruise. This is our captain, Paul Winters."

"Got it." She took Nick's vacated seat. She looked at Cain. "Does that mean the guy at the marina set us up? So maybe Roman Vance and his people know we're coming? Do you think they're watching us?"

Cain shrugged as he slowed the yacht down. "Distinct possibility."

"What is a distinct possibility? I asked three questions? You know, you could be a bit more forthcoming. I'd like to know if I'm going to be thrown in a Panamanian prison."

"Colombian prison. That's the Colombian Navy."

"Oh, fuck."

"Yep."

CHAPTER TWENTY-TWO

Nick grabbed the rails, slid down the stairs, then flew through the yacht at breakneck speed. How much coke was there, and how in the hell was he going to get rid of it? If Vance had set this up, then they were going to be taken by the Colombians for sure. Vance had way more connections and money than he did, which meant Nick had to move lightning fast. He didn't survive being slashed by a machete-wielding Somalian pirate to die in a Colombian prison. That was not how he was going out.

He entered Carolina's suite, went to the far side of the bed, and spotted the drugs. Five kilos of cocaine. *Shit.* Grabbing them, he slammed the drawer closed and headed back out. He didn't have time to check for more. If there was, he could only hope it was well hidden.

Throwing the cocaine over the side would be the best way to get rid of it. He looked out the window, but the navy patrol boat was floating not more than twenty feet away. No way they wouldn't see him. He went back to the suite and into the bathroom. Flushing it would take too long.

He went into the shower, pulled out a knife, and pried

off the drain cover. He slit the first package and poured it down the drain. He felt the yacht rock as the Colombians boarded. Time was running out.

Nick poured the second and third packages down the drain. Would he have enough time to do the rest? What choice did he have? He kept pouring, praying that Cain and Carolina could stall these guys long enough for him to finish. He poured the last package down the drain, put the drain cover back on, and turned on the shower.

The packaging. *Fuck.* Where could he put the packaging? The sound of voices reached him. He was out of time.

"My husband is sleeping. I'm sure he has no idea what you're talking about either. Really, the idea that we have drugs on board is ludicrous. You are clearly mistaken, Captain Rodriguez." Carolina's voice was getting clearer. They were already down the stairs.

"Seriously, I cannot believe you are doing this." Her voice was louder now, and Nick tensed but the voices continued down the hallway. *Good girl!* She was leading them away. Nick grabbed the gun that was in the cupboard and looked around. He quickly bent down and opened the vanity. He pulled out the first aid kit.

"Don't play games with me," A heavily accented voice said.

Nick worried that Carolina might do something stupid, but she'd handled things like a pro so far. He kept on task.

"Move aside, madam." The accented voice said.

"It's Doctor." *That's my girl.* Nick grinned as he pulled off his shirt.

"*Doctor*, move." Nick decided that must be the asshole in charge.

"My husband is sleeping." Carolina's voice was strong. "Ow!" Carolina yelled. "You're hurting me." This time the indignation was real.

Nick tensed but continued with his task. He wanted to kill whoever was hurting Carolina but if he didn't pull this off, they'd all be in a Colombian prison which would be a lot worse than whatever was happening in the hallway.

The door burst open and crashed against the wall.

"What the hell is going on?" Nick roared as he came out of the bathroom with shaving cream on half of his face, a razor in hand. He wore only a towel, and the shower was running behind him. Carolina was being manhandled by an officer and there were several men behind him. One stepped forward. He was a captain by the look of his uniform.

"Who are you?" he yelled at Rodriguez. "What are you doing? Carolina? Honey, are you okay?"

She nodded but glanced at the guy holding her. He was squeezing her arm so tightly that his knuckles were white.

"Mr. James, we have reason to believe there are drugs aboard this vessel. We must search it," Rodriguez announced.

"Who are you and what the fuck do you think you're doing?" Nick growled.

The man paused indignantly, then introduced himself. "Captain Rodriguez of the Colombian Navy."

Nick put his hands on his hips. "Why on earth would you think there are drugs onboard?"

"We received a tip."

"I see. Well, your tip is wrong. There are no drugs on this vessel."

The captain smirked at Nick. "We'll see." He nodded to his men, who started searching the drawers. Within seconds, one bent down and opened the drawer on the left side of the bed. It was empty. He went to the one that previously had held the drugs and gave it a yank. The drawer flew open, but it too was empty. He glanced up at his captain and gave a slight negative headshake.

The captain took a few more steps and peered over the bed to look for himself. "Check all the drawers again. Take everything out." His men dutifully researched all of the drawers in the cabin, throwing Carolina's clothing and belongings onto the floor. Nick leaned against the bathroom doorjamb.

The captain's posture became rigid. He turned to glare at Nick when it became obvious that the drugs weren't in the drawers. He gestured toward the bathroom with his head, and one of the men pushed by Nick. He pushed Nick's clothing out of the way with his boot, then opened all of the drawers in the bathroom and the linen closet.

Nick glanced at Carolina whose eyes shifted to the linen closet then back to Nick. There was a small crease between her brows. *She was worried about the gun.* He gave a quick nod. Hopefully she understood it was taken care of.

The officer checked all around the toilet as well as the vanity but finally shook his head at Rodriguez. The captain grimaced. "So, Mr. James, if we check the rest of the ship, will we find drugs?" He was studying Nick closely.

Nick shook his head. "No. There are no drugs on board this yacht." The captain was silent for a second, then gave a minor shrug. "Sorry to have disturbed you." He signaled his men and left the room.

Nick reached over and turned the shower off. He gestured for Carolina to stay put and followed the men from the room. He waited in the hallway until he heard the change in pitch of the other ship's engine. The Colombian ship was departing.

A minute later, Cain stomped down the stairs. He had the bug finder in his hand. They had to be sure their visitors had not left anything behind.

Carolina opened her mouth to say something, but Cain shook his head and held up the device. He swept the room.

Nick stood just inside the doorway, leaning against the wall with his arms crossed over his chest.

Cain went into the bathroom and came out again. He shook his head. "All clear. I'll do the rest of the ship, but I think we're clear. I'll talk to Axe. Let them know what's coming if it hasn't happened already. I tried to reach them earlier a couple of times, but they didn't respond."

"That's not good." Nick's gut knotted.

Not being able to contact the guys was alarming. They knew to be reachable at all times.

"Yeah." Cain agreed.

"Let me know if you can't raise them." He knew Cain well enough to see through what appeared to be his nonchalance. Cain was worried too. The set of his jaw was a dead giveaway.

"Will do," Cain said as he headed out the door.

Nick turned back to the bathroom. He needed to get dressed.

"What did you do with it?" Carolina asked, dropping onto the bed.

He glanced back over his shoulder. "I put it down the shower drain."

"Wow, you must be fast. What about the wrappers and where's the gun? Both guns for that matter?"

He leaned against the sink and grinned. "The guns are taped to the back of the TV with bandages from the first aid kit that was under the sink. The packaging for the coke is here." He lifted his clothing that he'd thrown on the floor.

"Seriously?" Her eyebrows were raised. "They could have found the guns and the wrappers pretty easily."

She looked so cute sitting there on the bed with her hair up and her feet tucked underneath her.

"True, but they knew what they were looking for, and the moment they didn't find it, Rodriguez knew that I knew what was going on. He had to assume we found the drugs and weren't stupid enough to keep them on board."

"Why didn't he search the whole ship?"

"At ninety feet, there's a lot of ground to cover and a ton of nooks and crannies where the drugs could be hidden. Not to mention, the former owner was a drug smuggler. If there are secret drawers under this bed, think about all the other spots that could have hidden compartments. It would take a good day to go over this boat, and Rodriguez wasn't going to waste the time. This was supposed to be an easy collar for him."

She sighed. "So Roman Vance set this up?"

"Yes. He knows we're coming. This was a long shot for him."

"What do you mean?"

He grimaced. "Vance knows us. At least he knows me and Cain. He had to know we had a good chance of figuring out there was a problem once we saw the Colombians heading in our direction. We're professionals just like he is—well, not just like. We're not for hire, but we're trained the same way and, ultimately, we think along similar lines. The chances of him catching us out on this were less than fifty percent, and he knew it, but it was worth a shot. It would tie us up for a while if we got arrested for drug trafficking in Columbia."

Carolina flipped her hair over one shoulder. "So Vance knows we're on to him.

Nick lifted one shoulder. "Now no one has the element of surprise. Can't do anything to change that."

As Carolina got up off the bed, the yacht surged forward, and she stumbled into the TV. She winced and rubbed her arm.

"Are you okay?" Nick came out of the bathroom to stand beside her.

"That soldier bruised my arm."

"Let's see it."

She held up her arm. There were large bruises in the shape of fingers on her arm where he'd held her. "Like I said, it's just a few bruises."

He drew in a breath, and her scent filled his nose. It caused a stirring in his chest. Memories of Yemen came up again. Her soft touch on his back. Her soothing voice keeping him calm as she treated his wounds. The scent of lavender that made him relax. She'd spent hours with him keeping him distracted so he wouldn't feel so vulnerable.

He cleared his throat as he examined the bruising. He wanted to throttle the creep who'd put those bruises on her arm. He reached up and gently touched them. "I'm sorry, Carolina."

She looked up at him. "Don't worry. If any of them tried anything, they would have been in for a rude awakening. I might not be a trained soldier, but I'm a doctor. I know how to cause major pain with minimal effort."

Nick grinned. "I'll remember that the next time I piss you off."

She laughed. "You'd better. I'm tougher than I look."

He could attest to that. She'd impressed him at every turn. Smart, funny, and hot as hell. He really needed to get out of the towel because, at this point, it was going to become too obvious what he was thinking. He dropped her arm. "Why don't you go up and see if Cain reached Axe? I'm going to take a quick shower and get on some clean clothes."

She smiled up at him. "Sure. Sounds good. Did you guys eat breakfast?"

"A long time ago. We're on to lunch now."

"Oh, my God, is it that late?" She turned and looked at the clock. "I'll go make us something." She left the room.

He leaned against the door jam and silently cursed. The

soft red T-shirt had clung to her curves, but her shorts emphasized the roundness of her ass. The view going was every bit as good as the view coming. He straightened up and went to turn on the shower, cold this time instead of hot. He was going to need every ounce of strength to keep his focus on the op and not on what he'd like to do with Carolina.

Twenty minutes later, freshly showered and back in control, Nick walked onto the flybridge. Carolina sat next to Cain, and they were laughing about something. A zing of anger flared in his gut, but he shook it off. It was stupid to be jealous of Cain. Nick knew Carolina didn't belong to him. *Yet,* a small voice in his head whispered. He ground his teeth and walked over to stand beside them.

"Hey." She smiled up at him. "Your sandwich is over there on the table along with a beer. Cain said he thought you probably needed to cool off."

"Did he?" He glanced at Cain, who was smirking.

Asshole. That was the trouble with working in a team like this. Everyone knew everyone else way too well. "Is everything okay on the trawler? Did you speak to Axe?"

"They're fine. They had the same issue. That's why he couldn't take my call. The Colombian Navy was already on board when I tried to reach him."

Nick grunted. "Where'd they find the drugs?"

Cain made a slight course correction. "Finn was taking a shower and noticed a panel cut into the wall above the shower stall. He found five kilos. He dumped it down the drain. So, they're fine, but the guys are definitely wondering what our plan is going forward."

Nick blew out a long sigh. "I wish I knew. Obviously, Vance knows we're coming." He turned and grabbed his sandwich. Carolina had added chips and a pickle. After sitting, he took a bite. Pastrami. It was delicious, or maybe he was hungrier than he thought. "He must have some serious pull to get the Colombians to search the two boats, not that I'm surprised. He's known for his contacts."

Cain grunted. "He has a lot of friends in low places."

Nick had no doubt Cain was right. "Still, the Colombians? Do you think he knew the captains, or even just one of them?"

Carolina frowned. "What do you mean?"

"Well, like we said before, Biodome probably has a partner, and it's the partner who benefits by the Tarchuarani's demise. Maybe this partner is the one with the pull with the Colombians."

Carolina brushed a stray hair out of her face. "Guillermo said there was a partner, but he had to go before we could discuss it. When we get closer to land and I can call him, I will ask who the partner is unless you want me to use the satellite phone."

"No. I don't want to use that to call anyone but the other boat at this point," Nick said. He stared out at the water while eating, avoiding looking at Carolina as she sat there chatting with Cain.

Since when did Cain chat with anyone?

He took another bite of the pastrami sandwich and chased it with a slug of beer. He wanted to regroup with the others on the trawler. He preferred having them all in the same space, bouncing ideas off one another. It wasn't the same over the phone or on comms especially if their frequency was being monitored. There was safety in numbers, but he wasn't sure it was worth the risk.

It would be easier for Vance to kill them all if they were in the same place. Then again, since Vance knew they were coming, why bother moving in on Nick and his team when Vance could just take them down when they came for the vaccine? But again, it would be much easier for Vance to get rid of them on the water. No muss, no fuss, no explanations required. Just two boats lost at sea.

He leaned back in the chair and faced the sun. Whether or not the team should reunite sooner rather than later was a tough call. The wrong choice could be fatal.

"What would you do if you were Vance?" asked Carolina. She sat beside him, arranging herself on the long end of the couch so she could lean on the cushions and still have the sun on her. He had to turn away or risk reaching out and touching her. He took a large gulp of beer.

"You said before you think like Vance," said Carolina. "So what would you do if you were in his shoes?"

Nick closed his eyes and rested his head on the back of the sofa. He willed himself not to think about how good Carolina looked or how she was just inches away. He folded his hands across his gut. If he were Vance, what would...

He bolted to his feet. "Cain!"

Cain was on his feet and moving toward Nick immediately. He had clearly recognized the urgency in his boss's voice. "What is it?"

"You checked for bugs, but did you check for bombs?"

Cain's teeth clicked together. "Fuck."

Nick's gaze met Carolina's. "I always have a back-up plan, so Vance likely did as well. If the coke scam didn't work, he also had an opportunity to place a bomb on board. Maybe the coke scam was just a smoke screen for the Colombians to plant the bomb."

"A bomb?" Carolina jumped to her feet.

Nick pointed at Cain. "Call Axe and tell him to search their boat as well. I'll start in the cabins and engine room. When you're done with Axe, find me." He turned to Carolina. "Cain was up here with the Colombian soldiers the whole time, so there's nothing here. I need you to steer the boat, keeping it headed in the same general direction. Can you do that?"

Her mouth gaped open and her lips formed the word *bomb*. Her face had gone pale.

Nick didn't have time to hold her hand. If he didn't get moving, there wouldn't be anything left of anyone to hold. He sped down the ladder, ran through the main salon, and flew down the stairs to the cabin level. He stopped. It wouldn't be in the main cabin. It would likely be lower, below the water line. They'd blow a big hole, killing everyone onboard and sinking the evidence.

He rushed to the engine room, stood in its middle, and scanned. The room was bright white and chock-full of equipment. Depending on the type of explosive, it could be jammed anywhere. It was hard to see around all of the pipes, gauges, and hoses. The noise of both engines going was intense. Cain touched his shoulder. Nick gave him a nod of acknowledgement.

Cain leaned closer to Nick and yelled to be heard over the engine noise. "I'm guessing it's on the extra fuel tanks the drug kingpin had installed."

Nick nodded again. He'd just come to the same conclusion. Each man took a side and started searching. The odor and sounds were making Nick nauseous. Fear unfurled in his gut. The Colombians left twenty minutes ago. They'd want to be far enough away so they wouldn't be affected by the blast and too far to help any survivors. He estimated that was about thirty to forty-five minutes. He and Cain had fifteen minutes, maybe, if they were lucky.

He stuck his head around the back of the tank. It was a tight fit since the tank was almost touching the hull. He didn't have a lot of maneuvering room, which was why it was the perfect hiding place.

He spotted the device on the floor next to the tanks. It

looked like C4 explosive. Cain's head came around the side of the other tank.

Nick yelled, "Can you disarm it?"

Cain squatted and looked at it a long moment. Nick moved opposite him and glanced at his watch. They had approximately thirteen minutes before it went boom. Suddenly, the engines cut out. "Carolina." Nick sent up a silent prayer of thanks. His head couldn't take much more.

Cain's voice was shockingly quiet after all that noise. "I can disarm it. It's not complicated."

Nick could manage in most circumstances with explosives, but Cain was the expert. "Go for it."

Nick didn't move. If Cain was doing this, he wasn't doing it alone. Cain gave him a quick frown, but Nick shook his head. Cain gave a shrug, then went back to staring at the bomb.

Nick sat on the floor and leaned against the hull. It's funny, people always said their life flashed before their eyes when they were about to die. He'd been in danger of dying more times than he could count, but not once did his life flash before him. Not even when he'd been sliced by the guy with the machete and was bleeding out.

His affairs were all in order, and those he left behind would be taken care of. He had no regrets, so he didn't have to wonder *what if.*

His mind turned to Carolina. These last months he'd blamed her for his back. For him not trusting himself to be able to perform properly, but it wasn't true. He wasn't really angry with her. It wasn't her fault. She'd done the best she could for him. All this time he'd been blaming the wrong person. Vance had caused his injury. Vance and the man who'd actually wielded the machete.

Nick swallowed hard. If Carolina died, it would be a big loss to society. She was in the lifesaving business. He could see why Dr. Florez thought she might be the one to help him discover the cure for cancer. She was certainly smart and caring enough, and she had dogged persistence. *She also has a restless soul. It takes one to know one.*

That was a regret. Instead of blaming her, he should have sought her out so he could take her out on a date like he'd planned. He would have liked to spend more time with Carolina. If they didn't blow up, that was going to top his list. The hell with the consequences. They were both adults. They could figure it out. Maybe then she'd stop being such a distraction.

Cain reached in and pulled a group of wires out of the C4. He looked up at Nick. "All good."

Nick cocked an eyebrow. "You stared at that thing for three minutes to do that?"

He grinned. "I had to be sure."

Nick shook his head. "Can you move it safely now?"

As an answer, Cain pulled it off the engine. They both got up and made their way topside to find Carolina piling all the furniture on the deck.

"Carolina," Nick called, "it's okay. Cain disarmed the bomb."

She dropped the chair she'd been carrying and sat on it. She was pale, and her hands were trembling.

Nick came to stand beside her. "Are you okay?"

She nodded. "I turned the engines off after a few minutes. I thought it might be better."

"It was helpful. Thanks." He smiled. "What's all this?"

Cain placed the bomb on an end table that was in the pile of stuff. "I asked her to gather this on the off chance I could disarm the bomb."

Nick cocked his head. "Why?"

"I thought if we throw all this stuff in the water, add fuel and the tracking device, set the timer and let it blow it up, it might fool Captain Rodriguez—and Vance— if there's enough debris. At least then they can't be sure if we're alive or dead."

Nick smiled. "I like it. Let's do it. We should tell—"

"I already called Finn. They're doing the same." Cain held up the sat phone. "Elias disarmed their bomb a few minutes ago."

"Let's get as much stuff as possible." Nick and Cain brought out all kinds of items including cushions and bedding. They added life jackets and clothing—anything that might float long enough to make it look like they sank. It wouldn't fool a professional, but Nick doubted the Colombians would get too close. Just close enough to see the debris.

"We good?" Cain asked.

Nick stood back from the pile. "As good as it gets. How are you thinking of doing the bomb? We only have maybe a minute or two before it will go off."

"I was thinking we throw all this stuff overboard and put the bomb in that Styrofoam cooler. It should float. If we time it right, it will give us about a minute to pull away."

"Works for me." Nick picked up a chair and threw it overboard. Cain and Carolina followed suit. In no time, all the stuff Carolina had gathered was in the water.

"Cain, you can swim faster. You push the Styrofoam cooler out into the middle of the debris and swim back. I'll go start the boat. Turn on your com and let me know when you're back on board. I'll give her everything, and we'll see how much distance we can put between us and the bomb before it goes boom."

Nick would have usually been the one to do the swimming but since the machete attack, his arm wasn't what it used to be. It was difficult to move fluidly sometimes. He just couldn't swim as fast as he used to, and time was of the essence in this instance. He pushed these depressing thoughts to the side and ran up the stairs to the flybridge. Carolina followed.

"It might be better to be inside where there's more cover," he commented as she sat next to him.

"I'm good here."

He let it go. She just didn't want to be alone, and he didn't blame her. He started the engine and put in his earbud. As soon as Cain gave the word, he'd hit the throttle. He glanced at Carolina. "You might want to brace yourself."

She put her feet up on the dash and clutched the armrests in a death grip. "I'm ready."

That makes one of us. Time ticked by. He wanted to go over to the rail and see how Cain was doing but he didn't want to waste a single second. They were going to need every advantage they could get to be far enough away when the bomb went off.

"Now!" Cain's voice vibrated in his ear.

Nick hit the throttle and the engines roared as the yacht lurched forward. It took precious seconds to build speed, but soon they were flying across the water.

The explosion was deafening. Nick ducked out of habit, but they were far enough away and there was no chance of debris hitting them. He kept the yacht at top speed.

Cain came up the stairs. "We're good."

When Cain's satellite phone rang, he handed it to Nick. "Taggert."

"Tag, how'd it go?" Axe asked.

"We're all alive. What about you guys?"

"Same. The bomb went boom, and the stuff we threw in the ocean got scattered. Let's hope they buy it. How's everything else on this beautiful day?"

He smiled. Axe had a way with words. "Fine." He took a breath and weighed the options. "Axe, I think with all the shit Vance has thrown at us, it's a safe bet they aren't going to dump the cargo at sea. We don't have to monitor the *Gilda Marie* anymore. Let's regroup and make the rest of the trip in close proximity. I think it might improve our odds."

"You think Vance might try something else?"

He ran a hand through his hair. "The fuck if I know, but either way, we have to be ready."

CHAPTER TWENTY-THREE

I n the salon, Carolina tried to calm down on the sofa, the only furniture left in the room other than the TV, but her nerves weren't cooperating. The bomb thing had really thrown her for a loop. It was so insidious, so sneaky.

She finally gave up trying to calm down and started dinner. Spaghetti with meatballs. It wasn't her favorite meal, but she couldn't concentrate long enough to make something complicated.

"Dinner is ready," she called downstairs. Cain had gone down a while ago. It was Nick's turn to steer the yacht. She made him a plate. Cain arrived just as she was about to bring Nick's up to him.

"I've got it." Cain took the plate and cutlery and headed up to the flybridge.

Carolina set the table then brought out a bottle of wine. Red this time.

Cain came back down and helped himself. "Thanks," he said, turning and going back downstairs to his cabin. She sat and sighed, staring at an empty wine glass. Her stepmother's voice rang in her ears. *Take this time to reflect on your goals and what you want to accomplish.* Carolina's current goal was survival. She reached over and poured herself a large glass of wine.

She sat staring off into space. She didn't care what her stepmother or her father thought. Like couldn't give a rat's ass level of not caring. Honey had gone so far over the line talking to Javier and trying to get Carolina's old job back for her that there was no coming back. It was just another example in a long line of acts that illustrated how little respect Honey and her father had for her. She'd kept trying because they were her family, and she craved their respect and, more importantly, their love.

But it was time to face facts. They were never going to change. Her father was never going to change. He wouldn't ever take Carolina's side and stand up to Honey. Whether it was because he was too weak or too disengaged, it didn't matter.

An old family friend, one who knew Carolina's mother, had suggested that her father was frozen. He'd loved Carolina's mother so much that he shut down at her death and just couldn't reopen. Maybe that was true, but it didn't matter to Carolina anymore. She'd spent too long waiting for him to open back up. If she learned anything from today, it was that tomorrow really wasn't guaranteed. Anything could happen. She was done wasting time on someone who couldn't or wouldn't be supportive of her.

It was freeing to admit it. She grinned. It was downright liberating. She ate her meal with gusto while contemplating other things she did or did not care about. Having a brush with death was leading her to all kinds of discoveries about herself. After Carolina finished eating, she cleaned up the kitchen, then went back down to her cabin and sat on the bed, leaning against the headboard.

She had to get the vaccine delivered—no easy task, but

she no longer knew what she wanted to do after that. Going back to Doctors Without Borders just seemed like more of the same. She was tired and needed to regroup. Amira's offer of a job in Morocco just might be the answer. She would still be on the ground, helping those in need, but she could do it with a comfortable home that had hot and cold running water in a place where she didn't have to wear water shoes in the shower.

It was time for her to figure out what she wanted her life to look like and give up trying to get the approval of her family. Relief washed over her, and a newfound sense of freedom hovered. This was what it felt like to not constantly worry about being a disappointment, to not care what people thought.

She glanced at the clock. It was late, and she'd given up any hope of sleeping. Even with the wine and her level of exhaustion, her brain didn't want to shut off.

There was a soft knock at her door. "Carolina?"

"Come in," she said.

Nick opened her door and then leaned on the doorjamb. "I saw the light on under the door. Can't sleep?"

She shook her head. "My brain is going a mile a minute."

He nodded. "It's been a long, stressful day. Sometimes it takes the brain a while to process that it's okay to relax."

"Yeah. How are you doing? You must be tired as well."

He shrugged. "I'm a bit more...used to this type of thing. My job is very much go full-tilt and then stop dead. It has less of an effect than it once did. Try a hot shower."

"What?"

"For sleeping. It helps."

"Right." She smiled, and there was a silent moment. He obviously wasn't going to leave. He looked worried. "Sounds like a good idea." She got off the bed and started to take down her hair. One of the hair ties got caught, and she struggled to get it out. She'd put in a few this morning, but it was just a mess now.

"Want some help?" He straightened and came up behind her.

She dropped her hands, and he slowly pulled out the hair ties. He handed her the first one, then the second. He then combed out her hair with his fingers. She was having a hard time concentrating. The heat from his body was penetrating her back, and it was all she could think about.

"There, all done."

His voice rumbled out of his chest, and made her skin tingle. She turned to face him and whispered, "Thanks." She tried to clear her throat, but it seemed to lock up. He leaned down and gently kissed her. He was giving her every opportunity to tell him to stop. He kissed her again with that same brushing of his lips across hers. She had no intention of stopping even if she should. She should be the adult this time and back away. This was stupid to pursue at the moment, but after the day she'd had, she was done with being cautious.

She deepened the kiss and wrapped her arms around his neck. Desperate to feel every inch of him, she pressed against his chest. She wanted to drink him in.

He pulled her closer, bringing her hips to his while cupping her ass. Leaving a trail of kisses across her jaw and down her neck, he found the soft hollow right behind her ear.

"Nick," she whispered while she fisted his hair.

Nick's name on her lips was enough to push him over the edge. A wave of fierce possession washed over him as he claimed her mouth again in a fiery kiss.

He rubbed her nipple through her red T-shirt and bra

with one hand as he continued to cup her ass with the other. He didn't want any space between them. He ran his hand down her ribs and then under her shirt. His fingers moved along her belly and then back up toward her breasts.

Carolina moved away slightly and yanked her T-shirt up over her head. She dropped it on the floor. Then she undid her bra. She moved back against him and pulled his head down to hers.

Nick broke off the kiss and dipped his head to suck her nipple. She moaned when he swirled his tongue around the hard bud. She stroked her hands from his hair down his chest, then wandered on to his shorts. When she touched the waistband, he took a quick breath. He was throbbing with need.

He moved his head to her other nipple, then stopped. He gazed into her now open eyes. "We've already talked about how this is not the smartest thing to do."

She touched his cheek. "Yup, and I don't care. Let's worry about that later, okay? Let's just be two people who want each other. No promises or thoughts about the future." She sunk her fingers into his hair again and brought his mouth back to hers.

He wasn't loving the idea of no future, but now wasn't the moment to discuss it. He wanted to take his time and explore her body. He tried to be gentle, but she wouldn't let him. Her mouth was demanding. Her hands ran down his back, pulling him closer. He tensed automatically. No woman had touched his back since the attack. Except Carolina. She didn't even pause or ask questions. He instantly relaxed. She already knew what his back looked like and she wanted him anyway.

When she touched him through the fabric of his shorts, he groaned. He couldn't help it and all thoughts of his injury fled. He wanted her touch badly, but he knew if she started, he wouldn't have the power to stop her. And he had so many things he wanted to do to her first.

"You need to wait," he said in between kisses and then grabbed her hands.

"But I want to touch you," she said, straining against his grip.

He dropped her hands and swept her up into his arms. He carried her over and laid her softly on the bed. He positioned himself over her and slowly lowered onto her. As he kissed her, he ran his fingers down over her hip. She was so incredibly beautiful. He lowered his mouth to one nipple, then the other. She arched beneath him, whispering his name again and again.

Slowly, he left a trail of kisses down her stomach to her shorts. He'd been dreaming of her, of this. Now with her in his arms, the dreams didn't come close to reality. Her skin was so soft. Her dark eyes turned black when she said his name. It was enough to drive a man mad. He ran his tongue over her hip and along the top of her shorts. When she moaned, he got harder still.

He ran his fingers over the skin his tongue had just traveled and then when he reached the middle of her belly, he dipped his fingers lower.

"Nick," she breathed.

The sound of his name on her lips touched something deep inside him. He undid the button and fly of her shorts, tugged them down over her hips, and dropped them to the floor.

He went back and ran his tongue over a nipple once again, then moved lower. As he hovered his mouth over her center, he blew softly. She whispered his name again, straining her hips to reach him. He dropped a kiss on her core.

"Oh, my God, Nick." Her fingers fisted in his hair as he

slid his hands under her hips to bring her to his mouth. He used his tongue to tease and suckle her.

He took her to the brink, then eased back. The sounds she made had him smiling all the while. She was under his spell, and he was hers to command.

"Nick," she breathed, "don't tease me."

He drove his fingers inside her in a steady rhythm, faster and faster until she crashed over the edge, yelling his name as she arched beneath him. He felt powerful and possessive of her. It made no sense, but he was beyond caring. She was amazing and incredible, and she was his.

Carolina lay panting on the sheets, Nick beside her. This man had taken her so far beyond anything she'd imagined, she couldn't process it. His caress was magnificent and his body hard and unyielding—she loved it. It didn't hurt that she also loved his laugh and his smile. She loved a lot of things about Nick, but now wasn't the time to think about those things.

She turned on her side and leaned against him as she ran her hand down over his chest. He was lying on his back. "Now it's my turn to play." She brought her mouth down to his and claimed it with a harshness she didn't know she possessed. She climbed on top of him. This man drove her to want him in ways she'd never before experienced. She wanted him. Inside her. Now.

She broke their kiss. Their gazes locked as she reached down to rub him through his shorts. He swore as her hand stroked him. He was hard as rock. Power surged through her. He was hard for *her*. She stuck her fingers inside the waistband as he kissed her neck. She undid the button, and he lifted his hips to help her pull them down.

She kissed him hard again, her tongue stroking his. She

broke off the kiss. "I want to feel you inside me," she purred. His eyes darkened, and he reached for her, but she batted his hands away. "Turnabout is fair play."

She rained kisses down his jaw and ran her hands across his chest. She sucked on his nipple, then blew on it. She did the same with the other. He groaned. She loved that she had the power to drive him crazy with her touch. It was intoxicating.

She shifted her weight until she was straddling his hips. As she slowly rubbed her core across his cock, he flexed against her. He reached for her, but she shook her head. "Not yet." She pushed his hands down onto the bed. "I'll let you know when you can touch me."

God, she was so ready for him. She raised her hips and moved over his cock. She lowered herself down onto him. First, she just let the tip enter her. Teasing him, she pulled back.

He swore.

Smiling, she started lowering herself again. This time, she took in more of him. She wanted to tease him longer but couldn't. She needed him now.

He reached out and grabbed her hips. She didn't deny him. Instead, she rode him, picking up the pace. The feel of him inside her, filling her up, was exquisite.

Her breath puffed out in small, sharp gasps. She was going to come. She said his name and urged him on, her hips rushing to meet his rhythm, her fingernails raking across his chest as he pounded into her. Nothing had ever felt this good, this right. She was teetering on the brink and had to bite her lip to keep from screaming.

He thrusted deep inside her, and she crashed over the edge, euphoria filling her every cell. Nick followed, and her body kept squeezing him as wave after wave washed over her.

She fell on top of his chest, sweaty and out of breath.

Neither of them could move. She wanted to stay there forever, or until the madness was over. If only that were a possibility.

Carolina slowly opened her eyes and glanced around. Nick wasn't there. She reached out and touched the bed. It was cold. He was probably long gone. She couldn't be sure if she was relieved or upset. The sex had been undeniably incredible. She closed her eyes again. Her body ached in all the right places.

Doubt filled her brain as Nick's words from last night rang in her ears. Sleeping with someone you were working with, especially in tension-filled situations, was not smart. Well, they'd blown it, and she was fresh out of fucks to give. The main thing was to not let it become weird between them. They needed to get the vaccine to the Tarchuarani, and then she'd be on the first plane out of there.

She grabbed a shower and then headed topside. Catching a glimpse of the fishing trawler out the kitchen window made her smile. Her shoulders dropped down a notch. Reinforcements were here. She went out on deck and waved hello. She got an answering wave from Finn. At least she thought it was Finn. It was a little hard to tell at this distance.

She made her way back to the kitchen and started rummaging for breakfast. She was craving pancakes. Surprisingly, she found the ingredients she needed to make them from scratch. *Thank you, Axe.* She also found bacon in the fridge, which was a damn good thing because after last night's activities, Carolina was ravenous.

She had the pancakes on the stove and the bacon in the oven in no time. Whether or not she was ready to face Nick, it was time to pull up her big girl pants and do it anyway.

She glanced at the clock. It was lunchtime, and if they didn't mind doing brunch, then she was happy to make more. She'd put the whole package of bacon on the pan anyway.

She grabbed the radio that was on the counter. "Hey, I'm making pancakes and bacon. Does anyone want some?"

Axe's voice crackled across the line. "I do! Can you send some over?"

She grinned. "Can't send them over, but if you want to swim for them, then I'll make you some."

"I'll have to take a rain check. Let me know how they turn out. I'll just be over here eating some stale crackers and cheese."

"I thought you bought groceries," she teased.

"I did, but these two eat a lot."

"I'm sure it's all their fault."

Cain cut in, "I'll be down. Let me know when they're ready. And Nick wants some, too."

Carolina's belly fluttered at the mention of his name. She really needed to pull it together. "Okay. Ten minutes." She put down the radio and checked the food. It smelled good. Her stomach growled again. The first round of pancakes were done. She plated them, covered them, and stuck them in the middle of the stovetop so they'd stay warm. The bacon was cooking in the oven.

Ten minutes later, as good as her word, the pancakes were on the counter along with the plate of bacon. She'd also made a fresh pot of coffee. Everyone could help themselves. She didn't bother to set the table. Cain and Nick would probably take their food and go. She filled her plate and went to the table. Sliding onto the bench seat, she got comfortable, then happily poured maple syrup onto her pancakes.

She'd just taken her first bite when Cain walked in. He nodded to her. "Thanks for the food."

"No problem."

He filled two plates then left. She watched him go. They'd arrive in Ecuador tomorrow. Her belly growled. She wasn't sure if it was because she was hungry or because she was tense. She looked down at her plate and lost her appetite at the thought of confronting the Silverstone people again. It was so much better when she was just a bystander trying to help people in dangerous areas than actually being the target of the fight.

She forced herself to eat a few more bites of food, then cleaned up the kitchen. She poured out her cold coffee, got some fresh, and went over and sat on the sofa. She didn't want to get a sunburn so she stayed in.

Sitting around with nothing to do felt wrong, so she ran down to her cabin and then came back up with a couple of medical journals and a notebook. She'd brought them to read on the voyage from New York but never got around to it. She might as well use the time wisely. Plus she didn't want to think about the events of yesterday or any of the happenings during this trip. She might have a panic attack. It was best to keep her brain busy.

She settled back on the sofa and dove in. The hours flew by, and soon her stomach was growling again. She glanced at her watch. It was well into the dinner hour. Since no one else had shown up to cook, she decided she might as well get it done.

When she opened the fridge, she saw they had leftovers from all the past meals they'd cooked. "The heck with it," she mumbled and got herself a plate. They could figure out their own dinner. She put a little bit of everything on her plate and then into the microwave. Two minutes later, she sat down and ate her dinner while reading another article in the last medical magazine.

"You've eaten," Nick said.

Carolina jumped. She'd been totally engrossed in the

article and hadn't heard him coming. "Um, yes. There's a lot of leftovers. Seemed a shame to waste it all by making something new."

He nodded. "In about ten minutes, we're going to stop, and the guys are coming over. We need to make plans. The *Gilda Marie* will be docking early in the morning. We want to be ready." He placed the sat phone on the table. "Please call your contact and see what he's found out."

"Okay." She got up, put her plate in the sink, then went out on the deck. There was no furniture left, so she went around to the bow where there was a sun pad. She laid on her belly and made the call.

"Guillermo?" she said hesitantly when the phone was answered.

"Carolina." The relief in his voice filled her with both joy and dread. Someone was happy she was still alive.

"How's everything? How are the Tarchuarani?" The article she'd been reading over dinner was about vaccines.

"Not good. Many are sick, and it's only a matter of time for the rest. Where are you?"

She bit her lip. She had no idea where they were. "Close." What else could she say?

"Good. The *Gilda Marie* arrives tomorrow, early in the morning. Their plan? It doesn't make sense."

"Whose plan? The Silverstone people?"

Guillermo's voice dropped. "Yes," he hissed. "It doesn't make sense. They are going to offload the vaccine to a truck and take it to a medical facility just outside of Quito. That's the capital city. I don't understand what they're going to do with it there."

"Me either," she admitted. "I don't understand why the drug company wouldn't want to give the Tarchuarani the drug in the first place."

"Javier didn't tell you? I guess he did not want to scare

you. Carolina, the drug company doesn't care one way or the other. It's the Ecuadorian government doesn't want the Tarchuarani to live. I think the President has made a deal with the drug company to get rid of them."

"What? Why?"

"It's too complicated to explain. I'll tell you when I see you. Right now we need to get the truck. I have a map of the route. I have a friend who is a waitress at the bar where the men drink. She took a picture with her cell phone."

"Wait, what men?" She tucked some stray hair behind her ear.

"They wait for their friends from the ship, and then they will all go to the facility near Quito."

"Can you email me the picture?" She gave him her email address. "I'll call you back as soon as we have an idea of the plan."

"Okay, Carolina, but hurry. We need to get the vaccine to the Tarchuarani as quickly as we can."

"Understood." She rang off. The boat was stopped now, and the other team members were onboard. She opened the door to the salon and looked up at Nick. He was frowning. She looked around the room. All the faces said the same thing. Something was very wrong.

CHAPTER TWENTY-FOUR

"Did you reach your contact?" Nick asked Carolina as she walked into the salon. He'd just gotten a call from Bertrand, and he'd filled everyone else in, but now he had to tell Carolina.

"Yes. Guillermo knows the truck route they're going to take tomorrow and where they're going. There's already Silverstone men onsite." She frowned as she leaned against the far wall next to the television. "He also said that Javier knew Biodome had a partner. He says it's the Ecuadorian government that wants the Tarchuarani dead."

"Jesus," Axe mumbled from his spot on the couch.

His gut tightened. "Why?" Nick demanded.

"He didn't explain," said Carolina. "He said he would fill us in when we got there."

"Well, that changes things." Elias, who was sitting on the other side of Axe, moved forward to sit on the edge of the couch.

"Yes, it does," Nick agreed. He blew out a long breath. Going up against the Ecuadorian government was not part of the plan. It was way outside of the lines, and Bertrand would have a fit. If the government said these people had to go, it wasn't up to them to say "no." This was a political hot potato. One he didn't want to touch. *Shit*. His guys were just getting back on their feet. He sat down hard on the arm of the couch next to Elias.

"What are we going to do, boss man?" Axe asked.

Nick rubbed his hands over his face. "We need to know more before we make any decisions." Like what the fuck was going on. "Why would the Ecuadorians want the Tarchuarani dead?" He couldn't wrap his brain around it.

"It makes sense." Cain leaned against the entryway to the kitchen with his arms folded across his chest.

"What do you mean?" Carolina asked.

"Well, it had to be somebody big who hired the Silverstone guys. Someone with pull and connections. Someone who gave them the license to kill a large number of people and stack them in a pile. When you stop and think about it, that has government op written all over it. Hell, even having the Colombians leave bombs on the boats. Someone had to have major pull to make that happen. A favor for a neighboring government would make sense."

Nick ran a hand through his hair. "Cain's right. The pieces fit. We just don't know why. I even had a call back at HQ from one of the aides to one of the President's top advisors. There was no way he should have been calling me. I originally called the health department. They should have gotten back to me, if anyone bothered to call at all. That should have been a signal. I just didn't put it together. Honestly, it never occurred to me that any government would want to kill off their own people."

Axe frowned. "So we're back to what do we do now?"

Nick hesitated. He looked at his men. They were happier. He knew it in his bones. This was what his men were trained to do. Sitting in Panama, playing at drug interdiction, was killing them. This mission had made all the difference. Not just for them, but for Nick, too, but this was serious shit. Taking on a government was a big fucking deal. They could easily be kicked out of the Coast Guard for moving forward with their mission. *Fuck it.* "We keep going. Until Bertrand tells us otherwise, our mission is to get the vaccine to the Tarchuarani people. But this could be a career ending move so if any of you don't want to do it, I'll understand."

"Fuck it. I'm in." Elias said. "I haven't had this much action in months."

"You never get much action." Axe grinned at his own joke. "But I'm in too."

Nick looked at Cain who just nodded his head. Good. They were all in. He'd give Finn the same out, but he was confident that Finn would want to keep going as well. If he didn't tell Bertrand what he knew, then they were all good. He'd just spoken to his boss, so he had at least twenty-four hours before he was required to check in again. Hopefully, he'd figure out something to say by then. In the meantime, they'd return to the task at hand.

Nick turned to Carolina. He'd avoided her all day because being involved with her jeopardized the mission. It already bothered him that he was going to hurt her with the news. And it wasn't like he could hold her to soften the blow.

"Carolina," he said, "maybe you should take a seat." On what, he had no idea since there was no furniture left.

He started to get up, but she waved him back down. "Just tell me. I know there's something wrong. I knew it when I walked in here. Where's Finn? Is everything okay?"

He braced himself. "Yes, Finn is watching the boats, making sure no one sneaks up on us" He took a breath. "Carolina, I'm sorry, but someone broke into your parents' place and attacked your stepmother. She was the only one home. She's in the hospital in serious condition."

She paused for a moment, then asked, "And you think it's related to this?"

Nick nodded. "She was threatened. They told her to keep her mouth shut about the vaccine or they would come back and kill her next time."

Carolina snorted. "Let me guess, it was the first thing out of her mouth the moment she was able to speak."

Of all the things he expected her to say, that was not one of them. He studied her. Everyone reacted to news like this differently, but Carolina seemed detached. Cold. And he knew firsthand she was a lot of things, but not detached and cold. She'd told him back in Yemen that her relationship with her stepmother was rocky, but she hadn't elaborated, and he hadn't pushed. Maybe he should've.

Carolina sighed. "You said she's in serious condition. What's wrong with her?"

"A couple of broken ribs, a partially collapsed lung, cuts and bruises."

She nodded.

"I think we should make landfall and get you a flight home. First thing. We can take it from here."

"Ah, no. Thanks. I will stay and see this through. Guillermo won't meet with you. Plus, you have no clue how to reconstitute the vaccine and administer it."

Nick frowned. "I'm sure we can figure it out. Carolina, I think—"

"Look, I care about my stepmother in that she's my step-mother, but we're not close. We're not friends. I can go home and see her, but her first words will be to blame me for this and then later she will criticize me for not finishing what I started." She mimicked her stepmother's voice, "'If you were going to go off and do something so incredibly stupid, you should have at least stayed to the end to make sure those people were helped. Leaving halfway through only illustrates your lack of commitment, Carolina. I am disappointed in you.'" Carolina returned to her normal voice. "Trust me when I say, I would rather be here. My stepmother will heal just fine without me by her side."

Nick tried to keep his face neutral, but it was hard. Axe didn't succeed. The shock and horror of that was written for Carolina to see. Cain's jaw pulsed. Carolina was part of the team, and none of them wanted to see or hear about her being hurt. He, himself, was horrified, but he also knew Carolina wasn't about to back down, so there was no point in pushing her. He cleared his throat. "Well, if you're good with staying, then we can certainly use your help. Now tell us again exactly what Guillermo said."

"He has a friend that's a waitress at the bar where the Silverstone guys hang out. She told Guillermo that they're taking the shipment to a facility outside the capital city. He thinks it's odd because what would they want to do with it there? He's going to send me a picture of the route they are supposed to take. Apparently, she managed to snap a cell phone pic."

"It's a setup," Cain announced.

"Yes," Nick agreed. "There's no way Silverstone guys would be that sloppy."

Carolina sighed. "So you think they knew she was paying attention? Does that mean they know about Guillermo?"

"Yes," said Nick. "They know about him. They'd have to since they know about the video Florez made for you. They probably tracked him down and are watching him."

"Which means they now are aware we're still alive. Shit." Axe rubbed the back of his neck.

"They knew we were alive," Nick stated flatly. "Don't kid yourself. It was worth a try, but I don't think they bought it no matter what the Colombians told them. Would you believe Vance was dead if you didn't witness it with your own eyes?"

Axe shrugged. "I guess you're right. We're screwed no matter what we do."

Nick stood. "Bertrand said he was working on something and would let me know more as soon as he heard back. I think we dock early at a marina and then find a way to the port. We stay hidden as best we can, lay low until we have a better idea of what's going on. It's hard to make concrete plans with no intel. We're just sitting blind here. It does mean that we can't contact your guy, Carolina. His phone could be tapped or, more likely, they're following him."

She frowned. "I don't want to leave Guillermo hanging."

Nick nodded. "I get it, but until we figure out what is going on, reaching out to him would just lead them to us. We will have to pick him up eventually, assuming we get the vaccine. He's the only outsider we know that the Tarchuarani trust. Let's plan to make landfall at zero five hundred. There's a yacht club in Salinas. We'll make our way to the port at Guayaquil and be there when the *Gilda Marie* docks. We'll make it up as we go along from there."

"What about transportation?" Cain asked.

"I have a friend who I can call. He'll get something ready. Axe, Elias, you two go back over to the trawler and fill Finn in on the plan, such as it is. Raise the anchor and get underway. We'll be right behind you. We will connect about a half hour before we dock and do the final check. Go over the equipment and make sure we're all ready to go."

Elias and Axe stood up. "Sure thing, Tag," Axe said. As he walked by Carolina, he reached out and squeezed her arm. "Sorry about your stepmom."

She gave him a brief smile. "Thanks, Axe." Elias nodded to her and offered her a small smile. She nodded back.

Nick turned to Cain. "Do you want the first shift, or do you want me to take it?"

"I got it, Tag." He nodded to Carolina and followed Axe and Elias out.

Nick faced Carolina. "I know you don't have the best relationship with Honey but you must be upset about what happened to her."

She shrugged. "I told her not to talk to anyone. She didn't listen, but it's my fault. I should have known Honey couldn't keep her mouth shut." She let out a long breath. "I think I'll head downstairs and pack up."

He wanted to reach out and bring her into his arms, but if he did, then he wouldn't let go. She was hurting, and he wanted to make that stop. He forced his hands into his pockets. "I think I'll grab some dinner and then do the same thing."

She walked by him. "Night, Nick," she murmured.

"Night, Carolina." He watched her disappear down the staircase. He forced himself to stay still, because the urge to go after her was strong. Finally, he put a couple of plates of food together. He took one up to Cain and then ate his in silence in the galley. Carolina had left her medical journals on the table. He couldn't make heads nor tails of what they were about. He stopped trying after reading three paragraphs of one article.

He gave up on his food and cleaned up. He went downstairs and hesitated outside Carolina's door. Last night had been amazing. And he wanted that again, but it would just complicate things. Hell, it already had. He didn't need to make it any worse. He needed all of his focus to be on this mission. The Ecuadorian government had a lot of resources. If he got distracted by Carolina, it could easily lead to her getting hurt. Or worse. Nick's body went cold. Nothing bad could happen to Carolina. He couldn't take it. If Vance hurt Carolina it would be his final, fatal mistake.

He went into his cabin and shut the door behind him. He threw his stuff in his duffel and then laid down on the bed. When he stretched his arms above his head, the muscles in his back resisted. He took a deep breath and worked on getting them to relax. His mother's voice popped into his head. *Everything happens for a reason.* She used to tell him that all the time when things didn't go the way he wanted them to. Was she trying to tell him that getting hacked with a machete had happened for a reason? What could that reason possibly be?

He wouldn't be on a yacht off South America if it hadn't happened, that was for sure. He wouldn't have this team either. He'd been working with a group of Navy SEALs when he'd gotten hurt. This was the first time he had his own team to lead and, in this case, look after. He was enjoying it. They were good men, and he understood them.

He also wouldn't have met Carolina. Was he supposed to meet her? The universe could've come up with some other way that was less painful and damaging. The reality was the only reason he and Carolina had spent any time together was that he was stuck flat on his…stomach. Otherwise, if he'd met her at a bar or a party, he probably wouldn't have gotten to know her. It would have been a one-night stand, and then he would have been gone. Before the attack, he'd been intent on his career, determined that nothing would stop him. Now it was different. He was seeing the positives in taking his time and getting to know people.

He thought about his bloodlust for Vance. He'd been doing his best to keep it under wraps, but he knew in his heart of hearts he hoped this was his chance to come face to face with Vance. What had happened to him, and his teammates was brutal, and Vance deserved to be hunted and killed like any other sick animal. But it posed a problem for this mission. This whole thing was a fiasco on many levels. Had his quest for a showdown influenced the decision to keep going on this mission? Probably.

He rolled over and closed his eyes. His sister's face popped into his brain. He'd searched her and their brother's profiles on social media after her phone call. He hadn't seen them in years. She'd grown into a beautiful woman, and Dave looked a lot like their father. They were strangers, but they were family. Maybe Carolina was right. Maybe he should go to the wedding.

He rolled onto his back again. He turned his mind to what he would do for vacation if he ever finally got to take one that didn't involve a family wedding. He'd take Carolina to the Caribbean. She would love it there. He took a deep breath and dropped off to sleep.

The alarm woke him several hours later. He quickly got up, had a shower, and was topside with the duffel bags full of guns and ammo in ten minutes. Cain was still at the controls.

"Hey, I've got it," said Nick. "Go get some shut-eye."

Cain stood and stretched. "I know you want Vance, and I don't blame you. He deserves everything you're thinking of doing to him, but just remember, there're a few hundred people whose entire existence depends on us making this work. If getting Vance jeopardizes that, we have to let him go."

Nick's teeth clicked together, and his jaw pulsed. "I'm aware. Do you think I won't do my job?"

Cain shook his head. "No but I know if it was me, I would be planning his death. Sometimes the reasons we do a mission can be easy to forget when we get into the thick of it."

"I won't forget," he ground out. "I know my job, and

I've always done my job. I won't stop now." Cain was right and that was the only reason Nick didn't tell him off. He'd somehow known exactly what Nick was worried about. Not surprising. As a MSRT operator with more missions than Nick, Cain was the top dog when it came to how to operate. Nick trusted and respected him. Still it rankled him that Cain felt he had to mention it.

Cain headed for the stairs and then turned back. "Nick."

"What?"

"If it doesn't happen now, I'll help you track him when you're ready."

Nick studied him for a moment, then gave Cain a curt nod. Cain disappeared down the stairs.

Nick turned back to the controls and took a seat. He was surprisingly calm for just admitting to wanting to track and kill a man in cold blood. But Roman Vance wasn't any regular man.

An hour and a half later, they docked at the yacht club and then used a motorboat to move farther down the coast to a small beach area. The team and Carolina were all standing in a dirt parking lot next to two old, battered SUVs provided by Nick's contact. The air was thick with moisture. The parking lot was dark, and the stars above offered little by way of ambient light.

Nick offered his hand to his buddy Ivan, who shook it. "Don't mention it." He held onto Nick's hand. "And I mean that. Seriously, do not tell a soul. It will be my ass if the world finds out I helped you." His thick accent made the words choppy.

"Don't worry about it, Ivan. It would be bad for both of

us if this got out." Nick smiled. "Take care and say hi to your beautiful wife and daughter for me."

Ivan nodded and then abruptly turned and took off at a good clip across the parking lot. He climbed into the passenger side of a waiting SUV, and it took off. Nick started loading bags into his SUV. "Hey, Finn, you guys use that one." He threw Finn the keys. "Load it up."

Axe grabbed a bag. "Do we ask how you know a former Russian intelligence guy and why he's helping us?"

"Nope." Nick loaded the last of the gear into the back of the SUV. "Carolina, do you have your stuff?"

She nodded. "Ready to go." She opened the door to the back seat of Nick's vehicle.

He'd been about to suggest she ride with Axe and the boys. He wasn't sure which would be better. She was a distraction, but at least he'd know she was okay if she rode with him. And she'd just made the decision for him. *Focus.*

"Okay, everyone load up. We'll rendezvous at the main port in Guayaquil. Keep your radios on. Stay in touch. Keep your eyes open. We have no idea what we're going up against."

CHAPTER TWENTY-FIVE

Carolina's belly churned. She tried to appear calm, but after everything that happened on the yacht, she was nervous about what would be awaiting them at the pier. She tried to look out the window, but it just added to her nausea. She was relieved to be sitting in the back seat behind Nick. At least she wouldn't puke on him.

She tried to rein in her agitation, but her nerves were shot. Not calling Guillermo was a mistake. It wasn't fair to make him sweat like that. He'd done everything Carolina had asked him to do. He'd even risked his life trying to get information, but Nick didn't want her to reach out. It made sense, but at the same time, she wanted to somehow warn Guillermo that he was almost certainly being followed.

And the idea that the Ecuadorian government wanted the Tarchuarani dead made her head throb. It was all so friggin' crazy. She just couldn't make her brain work to fit the pieces together. She rested her head on the headrest and tried to relax.

As they were pulling up to the port, she opened her eyes.

How had they made it there so quickly? She glanced at the clock on the dash. Jesus, had they flown?

Nick tapped his earbud. "Axe, we're parking here on this street. You guys go to the next block. Everyone spread out and blend in. Keep your eyes open." Nick parked the SUV. He turned in his seat and looked back at Carolina, giving her the once over. She'd put on a worn pair of cargo pants and an old gray tank top. Her hair was back in a tight bun. She had sunglasses on. It was the most incognito outfit she could manage.

He frowned. "I've got a ball cap you can wear. Tuck your hair under it. I'm going to give you a plaid button-down shirt to wear, too."

"Okay."

"I need you to stick close to me and do exactly as I say. This could get ugly."

She just nodded. "Are we waiting for Axe, Elias, and Finn?"

"No. They will enter on their own and spread out. If one of us gets caught, then the others still have a chance. We won't regroup until we have the vaccine."

Nick got out of the SUV and went around back. Cain joined him. Carolina turned and watched them over the rear seat. They pulled different bags open and took out various weapons: knives, guns, what looked like some sort of cans. Flash-bang grenades, they were called. At least that was what her teacher from the gun range had told her when they went to a gun show. She'd wanted to see what everything looked like so she would know if she saw them during her time overseas. Each man tucked the weapons in various locations, the waistband of their jeans, ankle holsters, and in backpacks.

Nick looked up and nodded.

She got out, walked around back, and took the hat Nick offered. She donned it and tucked her hair in as instructed.

Then she put on his plaid shirt. She buttoned it but left it untucked. She rolled up the sleeves, but it was too damn big, and it smelled of Nick Taggert, which was the last thing she needed. She needed to keep her mind clear.

He just shook his head. "Look, I wouldn't have brought you with us if there was anywhere I could leave you and know for sure you would be safe. Ivan was risking his neck just getting the SUVs. I couldn't ask him to look after you, and I don't know anyone else here. Vance and his people want all of us dead, including you, and they know we're coming. This could get very ugly. So here." He handed her a Glock handgun.

She took the gun and checked to see if it was loaded. Then she looked back at Nick, who appeared surprised. "I've spent time at the gun range and took some lessons. Working for Doctors Without Borders means going to a lot of war-torn countries that are not the safest of places. I wanted to make sure I could handle myself should the situation call for it. I don't have a holster so where do I put it?"

He stepped forward and took the weapon. He put his arms around her and tucked it in the waistband at the back of her cargo pants. Then he loosened the shirt a bit and pulled it down to cover the gun. "You need to be very careful. There's no safety, and it will go off if you pull the trigger. Be sure your finger is on the trigger guard as you are pulling it out. The only time you touch the actual trigger is when you are aiming it at what you want to shoot."

Carolina tried to focus on what he was saying, but it was hard. His closeness set off her senses, and electricity danced across her skin. *Don't shoot yourself in the ass* was essentially the gist of it. Good advice.

He stepped back when he was finished and then closed the SUV's tailgate. He and Cain started walking down the sidewalk toward the port. The clang of containers being moved filled the air along with the smell of salt water. The port itself seemed busy. Lots of machinery moving and trucks going in and out. Men were shouting at each other over the noise. How were they just going to walk in there?

Carolina kicked herself for reacting to Nick. She needed to keep her brain in the game. He didn't seem to have a problem doing that. He seemed to have put their night together behind him with no problem. She needed to do the same. *No more being stupid.* She took a deep breath and squared her shoulders. Time to focus on what they were doing. The Tarchuarani's lives depended on it.

They walked up to the gate. There was a guard in the booth and a wooden bar blocking the road in and out. A chain link fence surrounded the port side on the street but over to the side of the driveway was a barbed-wire-topped gate for people to move through. The guys walked right up to the gate and waited. She followed and waited with them.

Nick turned and waved at the guy in the booth. When he offered his hand, the guy frowned but took it. As they shook hands, the guard's face changed. He dropped Nick's hand, glanced at his own for a second, and then his arm moved. The gate buzzed, and Nick pushed it open. They all walked through.

How much had Nick paid the guy? He seemed awfully happy.

"Don't look back, Carolina."

She jumped a little bit. How had he known she was starting to look back? He was ahead of her. Did he have eyes in the back of his head? She gave herself a shake mentally. She'd been wondering how much Nick had paid the guy but, honestly, did it matter?

The group of them walked toward the containers as the sun came over the horizon.

They turned a corner and walked between two lines of

containers, making their way down the pier. Before they reached the end, Cain peeled off and disappeared down a different aisle. She moved closer to Nick. They came to the end of the row. It was just open pier between them and their target.

The *Gilda Marie* was just docking. Men were moving around the deck, getting everything in place for the freighter to be tied up properly. Carolina eased out a long breath. Her red container was on deck. Right next to a small blue one. Her heart gave a thump of joy. One hurdle down. Maybe they could do this. The Tarchuarani still had a chance.

Nick touched her arm. "We can't stay here. We're too exposed. We're going to go back one row and further in. Then we'll come out by the office over there." He nodded in the direction of a container used as an office. "It gives us more cover. Just be careful. There will be more people over there. Keep your head down."

"Sure."

Two minutes later, they were in their new position. He did a check-in, and everyone responded. They were all ready to go.

"What do we do now?" she asked.

"Wait." He leaned against a container.

She took up a position beside him. They had a good vantage point. The *Gilda Marie* was in full view, but it was hard for anyone onboard to see them. Lots of activity on the pier kept anyone from noticing them. "What are we waiting for?" she asked.

"For whatever is going to happen."

She bit her lip. Now that the sun was up, it was getting hot. "How long will that take?"

He glanced at her. "As long as it takes."

She ground her teeth. He was being abrupt on purpose. He wanted her to stop asking questions. *Fair enough.* She could be silent. It was the one thing her parents had taught her. How to be quiet for days on end. She ran through the periodic table in her head, each element and their atomic numbers. Then she moved on to how to treat different types of injuries.

As the sun moved higher in the sky, she reviewed emergency procedures. She went over treatments and options that were available if the patient didn't respond. She was reviewing the side effects of the most common medicines when Nick stirred.

He didn't move so much as just became more alert. She felt rather than saw the change in him. She looked around and tried to figure out what had triggered it.

There, on the pier at the bottom of the *Gilda Marie's* gangplank, were half a dozen Silverstone guys—at least that was what they looked like. A group of men all in great shape with muscles bulging, short hair, and dark sunglasses. They stood out like a sore thumb on the dock. The men here were well-muscled but from hard labor not working out at the gym, and they were dressed in stained work clothes not cargo pants and clean T-shirts.

Soon more joined them from the ship, and about fifteen men gathered at the foot of the gang plank. Carolina looked up at the ship and observed a man looking over the side. He yelled to the men below. Carolina was too far away to make out his words.

Nick touched his ear. "Go." There was silence and then, "What? Now?" He grabbed the sat phone out of his backpack. He turned it on and dialed a number. "Yes, sir."

Carolina waited. A shiver went down her spine. She glanced at Nick. His lips were in a thin line. She couldn't see his eyes behind his sunglasses, but they'd be the color of a stormy summer sky. He tensed his body as he straightened up. "But, sir, that doesn't make sense. The stack of bodies they left behind says that's a bullshit story." The pulse in his jaw was jumping, and the knuckles on his hand holding the phone had turned white.

Her mouth went dry. She hated that she couldn't hear what was going on because whatever it was, it couldn't be good for them or the Tarchuarani.

"But—" Nick's mouth clamped shut. Then he uttered a terse "Yes, sir" and ended the call. He touched his earbud. "We've got a problem. Come to my location," he said and then explained where they were.

She cocked an eyebrow, but he shook his head, then went back to watching the men on the pier. Two minutes later, the team jogged up to them.

Axe glanced at Nick and then at her, but Carolina gave him a small shrug. They stood silently, waiting for Nick to explain.

"Fuck," he spat. "There's a car."

The team all moved so they could see better. A long black limo pulled up next to the men. It had some sort of official plates, probably government. The driver got out and opened the door to let out the passenger. He was tall and wearing what appeared to be a very expensive suit, but it was hard to tell from this distance. There was no mistaking his importance, however. The men moved out of his way very quickly.

The man Carolina had seen standing at the ship rail came down the gangplank and shook hands with the well-dressed man from the car.

"Fucking Vance," Cain growled.

"Yeah. He's not the issue," said Nick. "The man in the suit is."

"Who is he?" she asked.

"Alejandro Garcia. A close advisor to the President of Ecuador."

"What the fuck is he doing here?" Axe asked.

"That's the right question, but all I've got are the wrong answers." Nick stared through binoculars that he'd just pulled out of his bag. "Garcia and Vance clearly know each other. This is not their first meeting."

"Is this what Guillermo was saying?" asked Carolina. "The Ecuadorian government hired the Silverstone guys? I'm lost. What does all this mean?"

Nick lowered his binoculars. "It means the Tarchuarani are screwed."

But then the two important men on the pier seemed to be yelling at one another. "Are they fighting?" Carolina asked.

"Looks that way," Nick responded. "The arrival of Garcia's soldiers has evened up the score. Vance isn't so smug anymore. He doesn't have the advantage. If those men open fire, they're all dead."

She frowned. "But wouldn't Mr. Garcia die, too?"

Elias shook his head. "He'd get into his bulletproof car and wait for the shooting to stop. Vance knows that. He's an asshole, but he's not stupid."

Nick sighed. "Look, Bertrand called. He did some digging on Silverstone and must have hit a nerve because, all of a sudden, the bigwigs at Homeland called him in. He had no choice but to tell them. They called the Ecuadorian government and were assured by one Alejandro Garcia, advisor to the President, that the government was aware of the problem, and they were working to help the Tarchuarani people.

"According to Bertrand, our side asked about the vaccine, and Garcia said he was personally working with Biodome Technologies to bring the vaccine to Ecuador. The vaccine would be delivered today and taken to a facility where it would be studied by the Ecuadorian scientists to confirm that it will do what Biodome says it will, and then they will happily use it to save their people. End of story. We have been ordered to be on the first plane back to D.C."

She frowned. "You don't really believe any of that, do you?"

"No. I asked Bertrand about the stack of bodies left behind, and he said it was not our concern. He knows it's all bullshit. He's told the higher-ups the truth, but they don't really care."

Finn piped up. "You have to understand Carolina, this is not our government's problem. We can't just butt in wherever we want. If Ecuador says it's all good and they have it under control, then the higher ups just have to say okay. A stack of bodies in Panama that aren't American citizens is of no interest."

"But does your boss know that if they study the vaccine, it will be too late? That the Tarchuarani will be dead by the time it gets to the human trials phase?"

Nick nodded. "It's out of his hands. This is a political thing now."

"So did Biodome steal the Florevir and bring it here for the Ecuadorian government to cover their tracks? Why would they release a mosquito into the wild that they knew would cause this problem? What does the government gain?"

Axe cocked his head. "Follow the money."

"What?" She looked up at him.

"This has to be about money. Figure out who gets rich, and we'll know who's behind this clusterfuck."

CHAPTER TWENTY-SIX

"Why are the Americans still alive? You were told to take care of them. I have been told they docked at a yacht club in Salinas," Garcia demanded.

Vance leaned forward. "I was told to handle the situation. It's been handled. We know they are coming, and we're ready for them."

Garcia fisted his hands. He wanted to reach out and snap the idiot's neck. No doubt Vance's men would kill in retaliation. If this had been left solely up to Garcia, Vance and his men would be dead like the pile they'd left behind in Panama. They had made a mess of things. They should have just taken the vaccine in Panama and gotten rid of it immediately and then killed all involved. Now, too many people knew about the damned vaccine. He'd even had to field calls from the US government.

"Langston made a mistake in recommending I hire you. I spent half of last night on the phone with your government. If you had been discreet, none of this would be happening. Instead, I had to call the Colombians for help, and your plan still didn't work."

He couldn't believe the audacity of this man, Vance. Standing here like he was king. He'd almost caused a major international incident. If it had not been for Garcia's quick thinking and even quicker tongue, the world would be watching Ecuador and the plan would be dead. The President would be overthrown.

Vance sneered. "The Coast Guard men are nothing to worry about."

Garcia ground his teeth. Americans were always so arrogant. It was always their downfall. Only this time, they were taking Garcia down with them. He was not going without a fight.

"Get rid of them!"

"I don't follow orders from you. Langston is my contact. He calls the shots."

"You will do as I say"—Garcia glared at Vance—"if you want to get out of my country alive."

Vance started to laugh, but then he glanced around. There were men with automatic weapons surrounding them. They were also above them on the ship, guns pointed down at him and his men. The smile fell off his face. "What do you want done?"

Garcia glared at Vance. "You need to dump the vaccine. I can't have it here. It's too dangerous. It could fall into the wrong hands, and all this effort will be wasted. And make sure you kill the Coast Guard team."

CHAPTER TWENTY-SEVEN

Nick looked at the team members. "If we do this, we're going against direct orders. I know you guys said before you were all game to keep going, but this is different. I won't force you guys to join me. You will get in a shitload of trouble, and it will likely end your careers."

Axe snorted. "We're already at the end of our careers. Why the hell do you think they sent us to Panama? They have no clue where to put us or what to do with us. We're damaged goods. I'd rather save a bunch of people or die trying than get on a flight home so I can be sent to some other version of Panama."

There were nods from the entire team. The knot in Nick's chest eased slightly. He would have continued on his own if he had to, but he was sure as shit glad his team had his back.

He glanced at Carolina. Her chances of living had just improved dramatically. "Okay then, let's do this."

The sat phone buzzed. He cursed and then answered it with a terse, "Taggert." There was silence, then he handed the phone to Carolina.

"Hello?" she responded in a quiet voice. She didn't hear anything on the other end. "Guillermo?" She hit the speaker button, and the guys gathered in a tight circle to hear.

"Where are you?" Guillermo asked in a hushed voice.

"Why? Where are you?"

It was quiet for a few beats. "What's going on, Carolina? Why didn't you call me?"

"Guillermo, the whole thing with the map—it was a trap. They knew you were trying to find out information. We think you're being followed. Your phone may be bugged."

"Yes, I realized I was being followed after we spoke. I took care of it, and this is a new phone. My brother-in-law is a policeman. I got him to slow them up enough for me to get away. I am sorry. Did they find you?"

"Not yet. Where are you, Guillermo?"

"I am not far from the port. I am not sure how long I can stay. The Tarchuarani are not doing so well. They have let a couple of doctors in to treat their people, but they need help. We need to get them the vaccine."

"There's a problem with that. The government has it. Someone named Garcia."

Guillermo let loose with a string of curses in Spanish. "Then the Tarchuarani are dead."

She bit her lip. "But I don't understand, Guillermo. Why does the government want the Tarchuarani dead?"

"They're behind all of this." Guillermo's voice crackled in the dense air.

"Explain what you mean by that."

"Alejandro Garcia is the President's henchman. He does all the dirty work. If he has the vaccine, it will not reach the Tarchuarani."

"Why?" Nick asked.

"Who is that?"

"It's okay, Guillermo. He's one of the people helping me. You can talk to him."

Guillermo continued. "The Tarchuarani live in a section of the rainforest owned by the Ecuadorian government, but it is their home, the only one they've ever known. They choose not to live a modern life. The government wants the land but can't remove them. A forced relocation would cause a great outcry both here and around the world."

"They can't move the Tarchuarani, but if they died of some strange disease," said Nick, "the government could control the land."

"Yes. I think they caused the illness on purpose." Guillermo's voice was almost a whisper.

Carolina's eyebrows shot up. "Why do you think that?"

"I asked around like you suggested. A female scientist was working on a mosquito project. I tracked her down and asked her questions. She said Biodome knew the mosquitos would make the Tarchuarani sick, but when she complained and said they needed to stop the experiment, her boss said it didn't matter because that's what the government wanted, and they couldn't do any other tests if they didn't do this one. The order came straight from the top of the company.

"Her name is Dr. Karina Cole. She quit her job. She is staying at a hotel near here. She just returned from a cruise to the Galapagos Islands. She is flying out the day after tomorrow."

"What hotel?" Nick asked.

When Guillermo supplied the name, Nick nodded at Finn. Finn hit Elias on the arm, and the two took off at a jog.

Carolina wiped her forehead with the back of her arm. "Thanks, Guillermo, for getting all that information."

"But it doesn't help. Garcia will not give up the vaccine. He wants the land too much."

Axe glanced back and nodded to her. She asked, "But what do they want the land for? Is it timber?"

"There is oil under the land the Tarchuarani live on. Enough to make Ecuador a wealthy country and the President and his rich friends."

Fuck. Everything suddenly made a whole lot more sense. Oil was big business. The vaccine was bad for the oil business in Ecuador.

"Guillermo," Nick said, "we're going to work on the problem from this end. You head to help with the Tarchuarani. We'll call you once we have the vaccine."

"Do you actually think you can get it?" he asked.

Nick looked at Carolina. "We're going to do our best," he promised, then hung up.

"Hey, I'm all for doing this, but if you have any ideas on how we're going to get that"—Axe pointed to the container being lifted off the ship—"to the Amazon, I think now's the time to share."

Nick stayed silent as they watched the red container being lowered onto the back of a truck. Silverstone guys swarmed the sides, securing it. Carolina wiped her forehead again and readjusted her hat. Axe handed her water from his backpack. She smiled her thanks, then drank half the bottle.

The container was secure, and the men grouped in a circle. Nick counted. There were ten of them divided between two vehicles. It would be damn near impossible to overpower ten of them to take the truck en route. He didn't have enough manpower. They were outgunned. Maybe at the facility, but more than likely, there'd be even more guards there. Nick looked at the men. Vance wasn't in the group. He smiled slightly.

As the trucks pulled away, a few of the group stayed behind on the pier.

"Are we just going to let them drive away?" Carolina demanded.

"Them?" Nick nodded at the truck with the container on it. "Yes."

Her eyes clouded over. Her lips went into a thin line. "But aren't we going to at least try to get the vaccine?"

"Yes." His gaze locked with hers. "The truck that just left didn't have your vaccine on it."

"What?"

Cain cleared his throat. "The blue container has your vaccine."

She looked over at the *Gilda Marie*. The smaller blue container was being offloaded and placed directly on the pier at the end of the next row over.

"How do you know that?"

Nick smiled. "Because Vance didn't go with the other shipment, and he didn't send his best men. Two of the five guys on the pier are his favorites. They always do his heavy lifting. If the other truck had the vaccine in it, they'd be on board."

"Why send the other truck then? What's the point?" she asked, her brow furrowed.

"Us. They want us to go for that convoy. It's a decoy. It also works to trick the satellites. Just in case Uncle Sam is watching, they have to make it look like the vaccine is headed to their facility. They're going to take the Florevir somewhere else."

"The question is, where are they taking it and what are they going to do with it when they get there?" Axe sipped from his water bottle.

"Vance is going to dump it," Cain stated.

Carolina whirled to face him. "Why do you say that?"

Cain shrugged. "The involvement of the US changed things. Garcia wouldn't come down here if things were going according to his plan. He'd meet them at the facility if that was the end goal. The fact that he came with his personal army to threaten Vance and his men means plans have changed."

Nick picked up the thread. "US involvement complicates their nasty scheme. There's pressure now to actually get the vaccine to the Tarchuarani. They can only stall so long before people start asking questions. If the vaccine is still around, someone could crack under the pressure and try to administer it. Garcia needs it to be gone so there's no possible way the Tarchuarani live. There's no going back. He's probably already getting everything in place to drill for oil."

"How can you be sure?" she asked. "Why wouldn't they keep it?"

He grimaced. "Because if the world comes asking and they have it in a warehouse somewhere there will be hell to pay. But if there's no vaccine left, then who's to say that it would work? Who's to say what the formula was? It's the government and Biodome as partners. They can say, 'So sorry, we tried. It just didn't work.' And then it's back to business as usual for the government, and Biodome can continue their real experiments with the mosquitoes here in the Amazon.

"Javier Florez is the one who created the vaccine, and he's in a coma. They've killed almost everyone else who knew about it. There's just us left, and we've been told to head home. If my guys or me open our mouths, we'll be thrown out of the Coast Guard or worse." He looked at Carolina. He wanted her full attention. "The only person left remaining that might make a fuss is you. And if you raise a ruckus, the Ecuadorian government and Biodome will kill you. They might kill you anyway. It depends on how quickly the Tarchuarani die."

There was a clang of metal on metal, and they watched as

the blue container was opened. A guy with a forklift picked up something and brought it out of the container. The object was covered in blue padded blankets that had been secured tightly around it. It looked like a large blue square.

"The Florevir," Nick stated.

Carolina rubbed her hands over her face. "You're sure?"

He nodded. "One hundred percent." The forklift driver took the blue square over to a silver box truck and placed it inside. Then he went back and brought a second pallet out of the container. He retraced his steps and deposited it in the box truck. Once the forklift backed away, one of Vance's men pulled down the rear door of the box truck and locked it.

Her heat-flushed cheeks lost color. "So what are we going to do?" she asked in a soft voice.

"We're going to steal the vaccine and get it to the Tarchuarani. It's the only way we can guarantee no one kills you."

"How are we going to do that?" Axe asked.

"I have a plan," he said with a grim smile. "It's not the best plan, but it might work. Who speaks the best Spanish?"

Axe pointed at Cain and said, "I can get by, but he actually speaks and understands the lingo."

"Okay then. Cain, see that guy with the clipboard? I need you to get him to go talk to Vance and his men. I need him to distract them for five to seven minutes. Tell him to demand paperwork from Vance but tell him to bring friends with him because Vance will definitely have his men." He pulled a wad of cash out of his bag. "This should be enough to make it happen. Remind him we need five minutes, but longer is better. When I give you the signal, have the clipboard guy go over to Vance."

"Got it." Cain took off his shirt, so he was just wearing an old T-shirt. He headed out toward the guy with the clipboard. On the way by the office, he grabbed a hard hat that was sitting on the steps. He swapped it for the ball cap he had on and tucked that hat in his back pocket. He adjusted his walk and kept his head down. He looked like every other worker on the pier.

"Axe"—Nick turned to him next—"I need a forklift. Ask to borrow one for a few minutes. You'll give it back shortly." He pulled out another wad of cash. "This should be enough incentive. Let me know when you're ready."

Axe gave a quick salute. "Aye, aye, Master Chief." He turned and disappeared around the end of the container.

Carolina looked up at him. Fear lined her whole face, and it hit him like a sucker punch to the gut. He hated that she was so scared, but there was nothing he could do about it except work for a good outcome.

"What's next?" she asked.

He smiled. "We're stealing a truck."

"Okay." She nodded like he'd just announced they were going out to eat. Nick loved that about her. She could land on her feet. It was the mark of a true survivor.

He grabbed her hand and pulled her along with him as they made for the end of the container. "Remind me after this is over to take you out for dinner. I have a favorite restaurant in Virginia where the chef is so good, even gluten-free food tastes amazing. You'll love it." He stopped at the end of the row. "Okay, I need you to wait here. If someone comes or you run into trouble, tap your earbud and let me know." He pulled a case out of the backpack and handed her an earbud. "Put this in your right ear. Do you know how to use it?"

"I'll figure it out, don't worry. Shouldn't I be helping you?"

He shook his head. "I'll be okay. I'll let you know when to come."

"Got it."

Leaving her behind, Nick walked swiftly along the pier until stopping next to a box truck parked to the side. It was for Maria's Doughnuts. He carefully approached. No one was around. After giving it a once over, he thought it looked perfect. He went to the back of it and lifted the door. It was empty. Again, perfect. Maybe their luck was changing. He bent down and removed the license plate.

He spotted another truck not too far away, its driver loudly arguing with a dockworker over cargo sitting on the pier. Nick crept up behind the loudmouth's truck and removed its plate. He switched it and screwed the other plate in its place. He stood up as his earbud crackled.

Carolina's voice filled his ear. "There's a guy coming up behind you, Nick."

He turned around. The guy was a local, but he was huge and well-muscled. Nick cursed under his breath. Why was it he never had to deal with the small skinny guys?

"Whatcha doin'?" the guy asked in Spanish.

Nick was going to spin him some song and dance but, honestly, he didn't have the time, nor did he want the attention a fight would bring. He glanced down the pier. Vance and his men looked like they were getting ready to leave.

"I need your truck," Nick responded in English.

The guy moved forward. "You can't have it."

"I'll pay you. It's not your truck, right? It's your company's truck. Tell them it was stolen at the pier."

"But it's not stolen. It's right here." The guy kept coming.

Nick pulled out his last wad of emergency funds. "You let me steal your truck. You wait maybe an hour and call it in. You get this money, and I get to borrow your truck. They'll get it back. I just need to borrow it for a few hours."

"That's why you did the thing with the plates."

"Yeah."

The guy lifted his chin. "What if I just beat you up and take the money and keep the truck?"

Nick didn't have time for finesse. "Then you die." He pulled a gun out of his backpack. "Your choice—money now and I borrow your truck, or I kill you and take the truck."

The guy gave Nick the once-over and smiled. "I like you. Take the truck. What the fuck do I care? My boss is an asshole."

Nick put his hand out, and the guy dropped the keys in it. He handed the guy the money. "Remember, give me at least an hour. If not—"

"Don't worry, man. Take all damn day. I've got plans. But just so you know, I'm gonna say there were...four of you, and you knocked me out."

"Fair enough." He grinned as he offered his hand, and the guy shook it.

He went around to the front of the box truck and got in. He hit his earbud and told Carolina to get ready. He drove the truck down to her, and she jumped in. They went down the pier until they were fairly close to Vance's truck loaded with the vaccine. Nick turned their truck around, so it was back-to-back with the vaccine truck, about one hundred yards apart. The five Silverstone guys glanced their way but did not appear alarmed. It was just another truck on the pier as far as they were concerned.

Nick tapped his earbud. "How are we doing?"

Cain responded first. "It's a go. Just waiting on you."

"Axe?"

"All good, Tag."

"Okay, drive the forklift over this way, Axe," Nick said as he glanced in his mirrors. Vance and his team were all doing a final check. They'd be on the road in minutes.

"On my way."

Thirty seconds later, Axe was coming toward him. "Okay,

Cain, set the guy loose. And see if you can get him to back up so the row of containers blocks Vance's view of the truck."

"Done. And will do my best."

Axe came to a stop next to Carolina's side of the truck. Nick had the window down and watched in his mirror as the man with the clipboard approached Roman Vance. He spoke in rapid-fire Spanish.

Vance shook his head.

The man started again in English. Nick couldn't hear them well, but it was obvious an argument was starting. The two men standing next to Vance moved a few steps closer when Vance started yelling at the guy.

The man with the clipboard yelled back. When Vance poked him, pushing him backward, several large men came to support the little guy with the clipboard. The Silverstone crew at the back of the vaccine truck moved toward its front. The guy with the clipboard turned and walked a few steps away and then turned back and yelled something. Then turned and kept walking until he was out of view. Vance followed, yelling at the guy. His men also followed until the containers blocked everyone's view of the trucks.

Nick hit his earbud. "Go, Axe." He put the truck in reverse, backing up until he was close to the vaccine truck. Cain approached from behind Nick's truck and opened the rear door, then did the same with the other truck.

Using the forklift, Axe lifted the pallet of vaccine out of one truck and put it in the other. Carolina's knuckles were white on the door handle.

"Don't worry," said Nick. "Axe's family is in construction. He was nine the first time he drove a forklift. He could do this blindfolded."

She shot him a quick smile but didn't say anything.

One of the Silverstone men came back around the corner of the containers. "Shit!" Nick touched his earbud, but Cain was already on it. Before the guy could do much more than raise his hand, Cain sucker punched him in the throat. He stumbled and made choking noises. Cain hit him again, and he went down. Cain pulled him over and propped him up against the stack of containers.

"All clear," Cain's voice came through the earbud. Axe drove by in the forklift, and Cain closed the other truck and their back door. He came around the side and climbed in with them. Carolina moved to the middle seat, pressed next to him just like when this whole thing had started in Panama. He grinned. At least he smelled better this time. Maybe his mom was right. Maybe some things actually *do* happen for a reason. Nick put the truck in gear, and they started down the pier.

"What about Axe?" she asked.

"He's getting the SUV." Nick drove to the gate and nodded at the guard. The guard waved. He turned on to the street and came to a rolling stop. Cain jumped out and jogged back to meet Axe at the SUV. As soon as Carolina moved back next to the door, he was aware of the loss of her body heat. *Focus on the current situation.* He shifted gears and started gaining speed. The faster they got out of Guayaquil, the better.

The sat phone rang. Nick answered on speaker.

"Hey." Finn's voice came down the line. "We spoke to Dr. Karina Cole. She said the scientists in charge of the study were forced to release mosquitoes in the area around the Tarchuarani even though they knew the insects would live long enough to bite. So that confirms Guillermo's story. She and the other members of the science team all knew it was pointless and not part of the experiment, but they were told if they wanted to release the real mosquitoes and study the results, then this was part of the deal.

"Once the Tarchuarani started getting sick, Cole

suspected it had to do with the mosquitoes. She talked to her boss about her fears, but he told her to keep her mouth shut. He said there were dangerous men involved and they were to do what they came there to do and nothing else. The orders came from the top of the company."

"Thanks, Finn. We're on the road, and we have the vaccine. You can pick us up on the highway just outside of town." He supplied directions and hung up. He glanced at Carolina. "What do you think?"

"I think the Ecuadorian government found a way to kill the Tarchuarani without the world even noticing. They made a deal with Biodome that worked for both of them. The President gets the oil and Biodome gets to test out their mosquitoes with no outside interference. If Guillermo hadn't called Javier and told him about the Tarchuarani being sick, no one in the world would have even known it had happened."

He could feel the weight of her gaze on him. He turned and glanced at her. "What is it?"

"If we don't get this vaccine to the Tarchuarani and live to tell the story, no one on earth will know the truth," said Carolina. "History will never know that evil men plotted a noble people's genocide."

Nick reached over and squeezed Carolina's hand. "Realizing the extent of human greed is always a profoundly disturbing thing. We like to believe that deep down humans are, in their essence, good and will do what's best for everyone given the opportunity. Sadly, that's not the truth. I wish it were."

He gave her hand another squeeze and let it go. He wasn't up for discussing it anymore. He'd seen tragic situations like this many times. Whether motivated by power or greed or both, humans were too often swayed from doing what was right to do what was right for them.

A few miles later, Finn pulled up behind them on the

highway. Now they had two SUVs and the truck in a convoy. Nick relaxed a bit. It was always better to have the team together. He looked over at Carolina. "It's a long drive. We're going to stop just ahead and get gas and supplies. Why don't you take a nap?"

"After the rest stop. If you want me to switch off driving with you, I can."

He cocked an eyebrow. "You think you can drive this truck?"

"I had a friend whose father drove a box truck and sold vegetables all over New York City. He taught us both how to drive it. I used to help out on his runs during the summer."

"I'm impressed."

She smiled at him. "You should be."

A few miles later, they pulled into a station and got gas. Carolina used the facilities, and Nick bought snacks using his cover ID credit card. He went over to Axe's SUV and pulled out a backpack.

"You feelin' antsy?" Axe asked.

Nick shrugged. "Just being cautious." He loaded up the backpack with a couple of handguns and some ammo. He also threw in a couple of flash-bangs.

Cain nodded. "Always good to be cautious where Vance is concerned. He's not done yet."

Cain switched to riding with Axe, and everyone was back on the road in short order. Carolina glanced at the backpack at her feet but said nothing. She removed the gun she'd been carrying and put it in the pocket on the door of the truck and then settled in for a nap.

Nick had Axe ahead and Finn behind him on the highway. It'd been smooth sailing so far, but he knew their troubles weren't over. Not by a long shot. Vance had to have realized the vaccine was moved out of his truck by now. Even if they hadn't done a check immediately, they would have checked on it before now. That had to mean Vance was regrouping. How would he attack? When would it happen? The only thing that was guaranteed is that it would happen. Vance didn't come this far to fail. Well, neither did Nick. If Vance wanted an all-out war, he'd get one. Carolina was right. This was genocide, and Nick was going to do everything in his power to make sure that didn't happen.

CHAPTER TWENTY-EIGHT

Carolina woke with a jolt. She blinked and looked around. Nick steered the SUV on a narrow road going up the side of a mountain. It was technically two-way, but there wasn't much space. She hoped they didn't meet a vehicle coming the other way because out the window to her right, it was a straight drop down. Nice. She swallowed. She looked over at Nick. His jaw was clenched.

"What's wrong?"

He glanced at her. "Sorry if that last bump woke you. This road isn't the best."

"I can see that." Looking out through the dusty windshield, it was obvious the road was in need of serious repair. It wasn't a popular route, and Guillermo had warned them that it wasn't an easy ride. She stretched and sat up straighter, then grabbed her water bottle and took a swig. She took the gun from the door pocket and replaced it at the small of her back.

"The pulse under your jaw is jumping," she said. "It only does that when you're worried or really angry. What's wrong?"

He rolled his jaw around a bit. "Good to know I have a tell."

"So, what's up?" She turned toward him. She didn't want to keep looking at the drop to her right.

He shrugged. "Nothing. It's all fine."

"I hate liars."

"I'm not lying." He hesitated. "Vance knows where we're headed and why."

She studied him. "You think he'll come for us?"

He remained silent, then gave a quick nod as he swerved slightly to avoid a large pothole. She hoped Nick was wrong. She was tired and wanted this to be over, but she also respected his instincts. He'd stayed alive this long doing dangerous Coast Guard work, and if this trip was at all indicative of his life, his mere survival was something of a miracle. The scar on his back was proof of at least one close call. She wanted to ask about it, how he was doing, but the other night hadn't been the right time. He'd tensed when she touched his back, so she didn't want to say anything, and he'd been long gone the next morning.

She glanced over at him. His jaw muscle jumped. This was his world, not hers. If Nick thought something was wrong, it probably was. Her shoulders tightened. "What do we do about it?"

"Nothing. We just have to be as prepared as we can—" He slammed on the brakes to avoid hitting Axe and Cain, who were sliding sideways in an effort to stop ahead of them. There was another SUV coming from the opposite direction that pulled across the road blocking both lanes.

Their truck was in a turn, so it snagged the guardrail and slid along it for a few feet before coming to a stop just beside the back of Axe's SUV. Behind them, Finn and Elias skidded to a stop as another SUV following them turned across both lanes, effectively blocking them from behind.

Carolina peered through the windshield. There were two more SUVs stopped behind the one pulled across the road. Men were coming out of them. "What the hell?"

The sound of gunfire ripped through the air.

Nick yelled, "Get down!" He pushed Carolina's head down on the seat. Glass from the windshield pelted her back.

She glanced up as he pulled out his gun and fired off a few shots. It sounded like a cannon next to her. She covered her ears. The response to Nick's gunfire was immediate. He flopped down on top of her as the back of their seat was torn apart by bullets.

After the shots stopped, Nick stayed down for a beat. Then he bolted up and fired a few more. He flopped down on top of her again. "I'm getting out. Get down on the floorboards. The engine block will protect you."

"Where are you going?" she yelled to be heard over the gunfire.

"I have to help Axe and Cain. They're pinned down." Nick slid out of the truck. The door was open, but all she could see was the side of the mountain about ten feet away on the opposite side of the road. She did what she was told and crawled onto the floor into the wheel well and pulled the backpack into her lap. Gunfire sounded all around her with some of it hitting the truck.

She stayed in a ball. Her heart was pounding in her ears, and her lungs felt like they were on fire. She was hyperventilating. *Get it together.* She worked on slowing her breathing. Losing her shit now was not an option. She'd been through so much in the last couple of weeks. She wasn't about to crack now. Her breathing regulated, and her heart rate evened out.

She opened the backpack. Guns. She took one out and made sure it was loaded. She still had the one at the small of her back, but it didn't hurt to have more. A shot ricocheted off the passenger side mirror. She reached into the backpack and felt around. She pulled out a cylindrical can. A flash-bang. She tucked it in the left side pocket of her cargo pants.

The gunfire was more sporadic, and then it seemed to stop altogether. *The vaccine!* Some of the bullets shot at their truck must have hit it. She prayed that at least some of the precious medicine remained undamaged. She reached in the backpack and pulled out one more flash-bang, putting it in her right pocket this time. Then she grabbed the Glock and pointed it toward the open door.

The sound of voices reached her ears. She couldn't tell who was yelling, but she thought it must be Vance and the Silverstone goons. She desperately wanted to stick her head up and see what was going on but didn't dare.

A man dressed in jeans and a camo-patterned shirt came to the open doorway. He pointed his automatic weapon at her. "Put the gun down and get out." He gestured with his gun for her to come toward him.

She stared at him for a moment. She hadn't been prepared for him to appear like that. Her reflexes were slow. If she shot him, chances were good he'd shoot her back or maybe even first. She didn't want to die tucked in the wheel well of a truck. She dropped the gun and lifted up her hands. She crawled up onto the seat, then slid toward him. He moved back, and Carolina hopped down from the truck.

All of the vehicles were full of bullet holes. Beside the front of her truck, Axe, Finn, Elias, Cain, and Nick were all kneeling on the pavement in the middle of the road, their hands zip tied in front of them.

Carolina stumbled and almost fell when she started to walk. Her legs wobbled, and she had a hard time staying upright. She couldn't seem to take it in. *Shock.* Her logical brain told her what had just happened, she and her friends were captured, and instinct told her to fight back, to break free. She straightened and glared at the gunman.

"Stay right there," said man with a deep voice. She turned and saw Roman Vance walking toward her. At least she assumed it was Vance. He was definitely the man in charge. "Your friends here are living on borrowed time. You might just have a little bit longer." Vance stood directly in front of Carolina now. He reached out and touched her hair.

She jerked her head back. "What do you want?"

"I want the vaccine." Vance's smile was pure evil. "And maybe a bit of fun with you."

Her belly churned and she was close to being ill. No fucking way was she going to let him touch her. She was going to vomit all over this man if he tried. She gagged. Vance's face clouded over. Without warning, he backhanded her.

She staggered but didn't fall. The last vestiges of fear receded. Instead, blood and adrenaline roared through her veins. She bit down on her tongue to stop herself from screaming and lunging at Vance. She wanted to tear him limb from limb. Her hands shook with the effort it was taking to keep herself in check.

Vance sneered. "Put her with the others."

The guy who'd gotten her out of the truck yanked her over and pushed her down onto the pavement. She yelped when her knees smacked the ground, and she fell over. The guy pulled her up, so she was on her knees again and put his gun in her face. She straightened up and laced her fingers together in front of her.

The guy reached into his pocket but came up empty. He was looking to one of the other men for a zip tie when Vance's cell phone went off.

He checked the screen and then answered it. Turning away from them, he walked around the SUV that was parked across the road and went behind it. The guy backed up to lean on the SUV by the passenger side front tire, his gun pointed at her the whole time.

Carolina took in the surroundings. There were five Silverstone guys as well as Vance. She did another sweep and spotted a pair of shoes sticking out from behind the truck in front of them. Another guy lay motionless on the side of the road. He appeared to be dead. That meant Vance had brought seven guys with him and two were dead. Were there more somewhere waiting for them if this hadn't worked?

She studied Vance's men. One of the Silverstone guys was on the other side of the SUV, guarding Vance. He had on full tactical gear and wore the ubiquitous sunglasses. His bulging muscles and close-cropped blond hair made him look like the stereotypical villain from the movies. He was more interested in what was going on with Vance than what the prisoners were doing.

Two other guys had the hood of Vance's SUV up and appeared to be working on it. They were also in tactical gear but weren't wearing sunglasses. One reached into the engine and tugged on something. The other nodded. Then there was the guy leaning against the SUV, the only one remotely paying attention to them. He looked like the first two with his bulging muscles, short hair, and sunglasses. Except he was chewing something, probably tobacco, and he spit off to his left now and again.

She glanced over her shoulder and saw one guy behind them. He was standing on the far side of the truck that had cut them off from the rear. He was a twin of the guy near Vance except his hair was dark.

"Are you okay?" Nick asked. His voice was soft, barely above a whisper.

It took everything she had not to look at him, but she

remained facing forward. "Fine. What about you and the guys?"

"We're good. For now."

He was right. Vance would kill them as soon as he was off the phone. There was no point in keeping them alive. The Ecuadorian government would make up a story to satisfy the US government, and that would be the end of it. Isn't that how things like this went?

Nick grunted. "We need an exit strategy."

"We need to get to the back of the SUV beside us," said a voice, probably Elias. "There's plenty of guns and other things in the trunk."

"Any ideas on how we get there without getting shot or falling off the side of this mountain?" Nick asked. "There's very little shoulder left and, it's a fucking long way down."

"How fast can you all move?" Carolina knew it was a stupid question. They could move a hell of a lot faster than she could but now they were ready to act.

"Carolina, whatever you're thinking, stop," said Nick. Even at a quiet level, she heard the concern and fear in his voice. "This is life or death."

"No shit."

Elias snorted. At least, she thought he did. He covered it with a cough. The gunman directly ahead of them gave them all a quick glance, then turned his head slightly so he could hear his boss arguing with someone on the phone.

"Okay," Carolina whispered. "I have a couple flash-bangs and a gun."

"Jesus, Carolina," Nick hissed. The muscle in his jaw was jumping again.

"On the count of three, move as fast as you can." She willed her heart rate down. She took a couple of deep breaths, then got her brain into work mode. Working with Doctors Without Borders had taught her that chaos in the makeshift tents leads to calmness in her head. She was ready.

"Carolina." Nick's voice came out as a warning.

"One…Two…"

"Wait! Pull the pin on two of the flash-bangs and give them to me and then shoot at the guy behind us." He shook his head. "You're going to get us all killed."

"You got a better plan?"

"Shit."

She checked out what the Silverstone guys were doing, but no one was looking their way. She quickly got the grenades out of her pocket and gave them to Nick.

"Three," she said as she pulled the gun from the back of her waistband and turned around. She squeezed the trigger once, twice, and then she was being dragged around behind the SUV by her team. Gunfire erupted around them. Nick pushed her behind the tire of the SUV and grabbed the gun from her. Elias and Finn were at the other tire. Axe and Cain were behind the truck that had the vaccine.

Elias grinned at her. "Nice shooting."

She smiled back, then the glass from the side window exploded. She closed her eyes, covered her head, and curled into a ball to hide behind the tire. When the glass stopped, she opened her eyes and realized the cliff was about three feet beyond the SUV. There was nowhere to go. They would either be shot or fall off the mountain into the jungle below. Her daring escape attempt hadn't gotten them very far.

Nick shot off a few rounds of cover fire while Finn scooted next to her. He waited until the next volley was over, then he popped up and reached through the broken window. He pulled out a huge bag and dropped it to the ground. After unzipping it, he handed Nick a large machine gun, then pulled out another for Finn.

"Nothing for me?" she asked.

Elias grinned and handed her another Glock. She got into a squat position as Nick ducked down beside her. "Don't even think about it," he said before standing and shooting again with the machine gun. Elias did the same.

She stayed crouched down but stood slightly at the sound of an engine turning over. Axe was at the wheel of the truck. Bullets were flying in his direction, but he kept his head down. He put the truck in reverse and hit the gas hard. The truck roared backward, and she heard the sound of metal crumpling and glass shattering. He must have smashed into the SUV that had been across the road. The Silverstone guys were all now hiding behind the SUV that had been ahead of them when they were kneeling on the road.

"Oh, my god! The vaccine!" she yelled.

"If we're all dead, it won't matter anyway," Nick pointed out as he reloaded. We're getting hammered. We're out-gunned." The sound of a helicopter came up behind them. "Shit!" Nick whirled around as they started taking fire from the hovering bird. "And out-manned!" he yelled as he pulled Carolina toward the back of the SUV. They were surrounded by gunfire. Finn and Elias ran around to the back as well. There wasn't much space, and they were all getting pelted with debris.

The vaccine truck roared forward and hit the SUV that was blocking the road in front of them, driving it into the one parked behind it. Cain managed to hit the two guys that had been working on the SUV and the one that had been guarding them. The last guy was with Vance by the third SUV.

The helicopter gunner was decimating the side of their SUV and there was nowhere left to hide. Cain opened the truck door and started firing rapidly at the helicopter. The rear rotor started smoking, and the helicopter started spinning away, but not before Cain was shot. He went down and hit the road hard. He managed to roll underneath the truck, but then he stopped moving.

Nick pushed her back behind what was left of their SUV. He, Elias, and Finn shot at Vance and the last guy, but they weren't having any luck. Vance and his goon got into the last SUV and reversed out of sight.

The sudden lack of gunfire was deafening. The men beside her stood up straight and started to move. *Nick.* She stood up quickly and looked at him with concern. He appeared fine with just a few cuts and scratches. She went around the SUV and headed for Cain.

She bent down and crawled under the truck next to him. "Cain."

He opened his eyes. "Good shooting, sister."

"Thanks," she said, moving his hand so she could examine his wound. He'd taken a bullet to the shoulder.

"You didn't kill him," said Cain.

"I didn't want to," Carolina replied." I hit him on the outer right side of his abdomen. It was enough to stop him. That was the goal." She probed his wound a bit.

"Jesus, is that necessary?" he growled. "And the goal, by the way, is always to kill."

Nick joined them. "How is he?"

She nodded. "He'll be fine. It was a through and through; missed all the major organs. Get me the first aid stuff out of the SUV, and I can fix him up well enough until we can get him to a hospital."

"Vance?" Cain asked.

Nick shook his head. "He and one of his guys got away."

Cain closed his eyes.

She finished poking and prodding just as Finn arrived with the bag. She turned to Cain. "When *you* shoot, it's to kill. When I do, I have to modify. Do no harm. I'm a doctor.

Killing goes against my whole profession but stopping an asshole seemed like an okay thing to do."

Cain gave a half laugh. "You are crazy."

"Quite possibly," she agreed. She smiled. "Now, this is going to hurt."

Twenty minutes later, Finn and Elias put Cain in the back of the box truck with the vaccine and all their gear. They pushed the SUVs off the road enough to get by and then climbed into the cargo area with Cain. Some of the vaccine packages had bullet holes but not as much as Carolina had feared. There was still some saline as well. Hopefully it would be enough to vaccinate the remaining Tarchuarani.

Nick, Carolina, and Axe got in the front of the box truck and Nick rolled the engine over. They started down the far side of the mountain.

As they descended, she asked, "Do you think Vance will try again?"

"I have no idea," Nick said as he rolled his shoulders, "but I hope like hell he's done. I'm not sure we can survive another encounter.

CHAPTER TWENTY-NINE

"What do you mean, you don't have it?" Garcia demanded. "Was it destroyed?" He was leaning back in his chair in his darkened office. The only light was the desk lamp. He'd had his assistant close the blinds and leave as soon as Vance called. He hit the speaker button on the phone, and Vance's voice filled the room.

"No, I don't have it... but it did take heavy gunfire." Vance admitted. "The vaccine has to be damaged."

Garcia growled, "Damaged is not destroyed, Mr. Vance. I was assured by Edward Langston that you were the best and you would take care of things. He said Biodome has used you before."

"Yeah, well, it didn't go as planned. Sometimes it doesn't."

Garcia leaned forward in his chair. His hands were interlaced, and his knuckles were white. Everything he'd worked for depended on the Tarchuarani dying. The oil was waiting to be pumped from the ground, and he had all of the pieces in place. Companies were ready to drill and give him a hefty fee for the honor. He was going to take Ecuador onto the world stage. Give himself a seat at the table. It was his destiny!

He took a deep breath. He still needed Vance, but once this was over, he would strangle the man with his bare hands. He would relish the feeling of squeezing the life out of this man that had disappointed and aggravated him so much.

"What do you need to finish the job, Mr. Vance?"

"Well I—" A finger pushed the disconnect button and Garcia looked up.

"*Señor Presidente*," he said as he started to rise. He hadn't heard the man enter.

The Ecuadorian President waved him back into his seat. "Sit, Alejandro, sit." Garcia sat. "I take it things did not go as planned?"

"No, *Señor Presidente.*"

"Alejandro, drop the formalities." He waved his hand again. "It's just us in here. We chat like old friends. So the medicine for the Tarchuarani has not been destroyed?" he asked as he walked over to the windows and looked out between the blinds.

Garcia cleared his throat. "No, but it has been damaged. The man I was speaking with can finish the job—"

The President shook his head. "No, I think it is over, Alejandro. This was all supposed to be taken care of quietly. I am afraid too many eyes are on this now. Too many nosy people are asking questions. No, it is time to let it go."

"But, *Señor*"—Garcia rocketed to his feet—"we have been working for this for a long time. It is a perfect opportunity and it's within our grasp to make it happen. Once the Tarchuarani situation has been taken care of, we can have people and companies in place quickly. We can have oil flowing within the year."

The President nodded. "You have been working for this for a long time, it is true." He smiled a sad little smile. "But sometimes, Alejandro, things don't work out as planned. Now the United States is asking questions about missing members of their Coast Guard. They are questioning what is going on with the Tarchuarani, and I have had reports of a gunfight—a gunfight! On one of my roads. There are dead bodies."

The President walked back to stand in front of Garcia's desk. "Alejandro, it is a sad day for our country. The dream has not been realized."

Garcia's gaze locked with the President's, and a very small ripple of fear ran through him. The hairs rose on the back of his neck. "As I was saying sir, I do think the situation can be rescued. We can create a narrative of events that will satisfy the United States."

"Agreed. I have already begun work on it." The sad smile was back. "We have come far, you and I, Alejandro."

Garcia's heart hammered. "Yes, we have sir. We have been friends since childhood."

"Yes. It is a sad day when that friendship has been taken advantage of and turned into something ugly."

"Sir? I assure you—"

"No Alejandro. You were right. You have been working on your dream for a long time. Fixing things behind the scenes and smoothing the way for genocide to happen all in the name of progress, but today it stops." The double office doors opened, and a group of six soldiers walked in and surrounded Garcia. "I have already informed the US government of your plot and issued an apology. I will be holding a press conference shortly to tell the world of your despicable crimes while I extol the virtue of the Tarchuarani. You will be held to account for your heinous crimes."

"But *Señor*—"

"Alejandro, I am sorry, but as you always say, there must be sacrifice to achieve success."

CHAPTER THIRTY

Two hours later, they pulled off on to a tiny dirt track. It took them thirty minutes of driving twenty miles an hour to reach their destination, but finally they rolled to a stop in a small clearing in the jungle. There were a few other vehicles parked, but it was quite literally the middle of nowhere. A short, thin man with a mustache walked across the makeshift parking lot to meet them.

"Guillermo?" she asked as she descended from the truck.

"Carolina!" He came over and enveloped her in a hug. "I am so happy to see you. I heard there were problems getting here. I had a friend stationed on the mountain, watching the road. He radioed us about a gunfight. Is everyone okay?"

Nick came over. "We have one man shot in the shoulder. Is there any medical facility nearby? I'm Master Chief Nick Taggert." He offered his hand.

Guillermo frowned as they shook. "My friend"—he opened his arms up wide—"there is nothing nearby. But when they are not sick, the Tarchuarani are good healers. They will help."

He gestured for them to follow him down a path. Carolina was initially reluctant but followed. The path darkened as the dense canopy of trees grew above them, cutting off the sky. The path itself wasn't very wide, and it felt as though the jungle was swallowing them up.

Two minutes later, they came to another smaller clearing. There were a few other people there dressed in jeans and T-shirts. "These are the people who brought the vaccine," Guillermo told them, pointing at Carolina and her crew.

Those gathered there cheered. Guillermo smiled. "Carolina, these men work with me. Because of the dire circumstances, the Tarchuarani will let them disseminate the vaccine."

"Do they know how to reconstitute it?"

"Yes. Yes. Is it okay if they get it?"

"Oh, yes, of course." She smiled.

Nick pointed them back in the direction they had just come. Finn and Elias showed up carrying a weak but grumpy Cain.

"Axe stayed back to monitor the unloading of the vaccine," Elias said.

Nick nodded. "Guillermo, you said they could help my man?"

"Ah, yes. Bring him over here." Guillermo showed them a makeshift wooden bench, and they put Cain down on it.

Then one of Guillermo's people came over. "I have a poultice that the Tarchuarani make. It should work. They won't come out here themselves. Too many *extranjeros,* foreigners.

"That looks good. Go ahead and apply it." Guillermo smiled at Nick. "It's smelly, but the medicine works wonders."

Two women took that moment to approach Nick. "Hi,

I'm Axe's friend Sloan Bishop from the *New York Times,* and this is Kyla Taylor from *Reuters*. We have questions for you. Would you mind chatting with us?"

Nick shook his head. "Sorry, we're busy right now. Can't help you."

"What about you?" the second woman asked Carolina.

She was torn. She didn't know if it was wise to speak to the press.

Nick leaned down and whispered, "Tell them everything, but ask them to keep your name out of it."

She nodded to the woman. "Sure. Let's find a seat. I'm exhausted."

The women led the way to a couple of tree stumps, and Carolina gratefully sat down. While they got organized with recording devices, Carolina took in her environment.

She'd traveled quite a bit, but this jungle was something else. It had a mossy, green smell that made her think of vegetables. She was surrounded by a wall of green which simultaneously made her feel like she was wrapped in a warm cocoon and being swallowed by a monster. The lack of bright sunlight did not help. It made everything seem dark, which made Carolina start thinking about the bugs that lurked in the jungle. With all the heat and moisture, those suckers would be huge. She glanced down at the stump she was sitting on. *Yeah, no.* She hopped up.

"You ready to start?" Sloan asked.

Carolina nodded as she glanced around, "But let's make it quick."

About forty minutes later, Sloan Bishop asked Nick, "Is Axe here?"

Nick nodded and smiled. After she reported this explo-

sive story, Axe was going to be in her good graces for a while
—at least until he messed it up which, for him, meant a
week tops. The sat phone in his pocket went off. He glanced
at the screen. Bertrand. *Fuck*.

"Yes, sir."

"I explicitly told you to leave and come home. What the
hell is the *New York Times* doing calling me up and asking
me questions about this vaccine?"

"Sir, I can explain."

"You're goddamn right you can, and you can do it while
standing right in front of me. I have a plane waiting for you
in Quito. I want you and your whole team on it—pronto."

"Sir, we're seven or more hours from there."

"Well, then you better start driving! And just so you
know, the President of Ecuador has acknowledged the whole
plot but said it was all orchestrated by his right-hand man,
Alejandro Garcia. He, of course, is blameless and had no
idea. Garcia was plotting a coup as well apparently."

"That's bullshit!" Nick protested.

"Agreed, but that's what he's selling, and since we have
boots on the ground in his country without his permission—
namely you—the US can't argue with them. So get your asses
back here now!" Bertrand yelled, then hung up.

Nick closed his eyes and cursed. He opened them again
and looked around the clearing. The vaccine was unloaded,
and Guillermo's people seemed ready to start the inoculation
process. Cain was resting on the bench with Elias, with Finn
standing guard. Axe was probably back at the truck with his
lady friend because she wasn't in the clearing anymore.
Carolina was sitting on a boulder, coordinating with
Guillermo. Nick walked over to her and touched her arm.
"Carolina, can I speak with you a second?"

She nodded and followed him to the edge of the clearing.
"I have to go."

"What? Now?" Her eyebrows went up.

"We're all being called back to Washington. I'm sure we're about to get our asses handed to us. I have to explain everything to my commanding officer. He's smoothing the way for us through customs but, " Nick frowned, "how are you going to get out of the country since we didn't exactly enter legally?"

"I…don't know but I am sure I can think of something," she said in her calm doctor voice. "I'll call the embassy and throw myself on their mercy if I have to. Don't worry, it will work out. I'm guessing no one wants to make this incident any bigger than it has to be."

Nick nodded. "Look I…that is… Ah hell, I like you, Carolina, and I would like a chance to take you out to dinner sometime." He wanted to say more, so much more, but this wasn't the time or the place.

She gave him a small smile. "It was…interesting getting to know you, Nick. I had always thought that, well after Yemen… Anyway, thanks for everything you and your team did for me and the Tarchuarani. These people would be dead if it weren't for you."

This wasn't how he thought it would end. He nodded. The rain that had been threatening to fall all day started coming down. Small droplets at first, then the heavens opened. He moved Carolina farther under the trees in a futile attempt to keep her dry. The rain poured off the leaves in torrents. "I'm sorry. I must leave."

"I understand. No worries. Thanks again for all your help." She offered him her hand. He hesitated for a second and then took it. After a quick shake, he dropped it. This was ridiculous. He'd blamed her for his injury, so he hadn't gone to find her after he got back from Yemen, and then fate put her in his path at the worst possible moment. Damn.

He turned and started walking away, then stopped and

came back. He pulled her close and kissed her hard. Rain pelted off both of them. He broke off the kiss and pulled her in for a tight hug. Letting her go at last, he walked back down the path to the truck. He couldn't look back. If he did, he might not leave.

CHAPTER THIRTY-ONE

Carolina turned off the rental car and sat quietly for a moment. It seemed like forever since she'd had a moment's peace. After getting back to NYC two weeks ago, she'd spent much of the intervening time answering questions from various agencies. The FBI wanted to know about Javier and the vaccine. Homeland wanted to know what the hell happened from the beginning, and then a man who said his name was John Smith came and asked her all kinds of questions about what they did, what she saw, who she spoke to, and anything that she noticed.

She spent days with him, going over things in a room with no windows at the FBI head office at the base of Manhattan. No one would tell her who he was, but she assumed with all the cloak and dagger stuff, he was with the CIA. Whoever he was, he was interested in Silverstone and their involvement.

She was exhausted and grumpy. Who knew all those agencies would be so interested? Why didn't they know more about everything on their own? Doesn't say much for their intelligence gathering skills. She'd said as much to the last guy, and he'd agreed.

The good news was that Javier had awoken from his coma. He'd also corroborated Carolina's story. The FBI and the mystery man didn't seem to believe her until they'd heard it from him. She wasn't sure if he carried more weight because he was a man or because he had a stellar reputation. Either way, it pissed her off royally. Why would they believe the woman that had just gone through the whole experience physically and emotionally when they could take a man's word for it? Asshats didn't quite cover it.

She took a deep breath and squared her shoulders. She'd been to see her stepmother at the hospital briefly, but with everything going on, she hadn't been back. Carolina braced herself to face the anger now. She got out of the car and moved along the brick walkway to the blue front door. She opened it and walked in. Her father was in the living room to her right. The door to Honey's study was on the left. It was closed, a sure sign she did not want to be interrupted.

"Hello, Dad."

"Carolina, where have you been? Your mother and I have been calling. She's terribly upset you haven't been here."

Not *"How are you?"* or *"Are you okay?"* No *"We were so worried."* Just *"Your mother is upset."* Some things never changed. But then, some did.

She smiled. "She's my stepmother, and it's good to see you, too. I'm doing okay. It's been a rough couple of weeks. Lots of questions to be answered, as you can imagine, but I think the authorities are finally finished with me. Thanks for being concerned."

Her father's face flushed. "Carolina, I didn't mean we weren't concerned. Of course, we were concerned—"

"Save it, Dad. I'm tired of the bullshit. There was a point

when I was getting shot at down in Ecuador, I realized that life was too short. I have spent years waiting for you to acknowledge me. To tell me you loved me, that you're proud of me, to offer your support, and you know what? It's never going to happen." She glanced away for a moment, and then turned back to him. "I was a fool to think it would. You're broken, Dad. I don't know why, but I do know I can't fix you or wait for you to fix yourself. I'm leaving Dad, and this time I'm not coming back. Take care of yourself." The look on her father's face was priceless. His eyes were wide, and his mouth had fallen open.

Carolina nodded toward the door across the hallway. "She's in her office I assume?" Carolina strode over and opened the door. She approached her stepmother's desk. "Hi, Honey. How are you feeling?"

Honey Alvarez sat behind the large desk, making notes on a printout she was reading. Her reading glasses were perched on the end of her nose. As usual, her short salt-and-pepper hair was perfect.

"Carolina." Her stepmother's eyes were snapping, and her lips were pressed together in a thin line. "You don't see me for weeks, and then you burst in and interrupt my work. Completely unacceptable. You are incredibly selfish. I'm disappointed in you."

Carolina smiled slightly. It was the exact response she expected. "The feeling is mutual."

Her mother blinked. "Pardon me?" Icicles dripped off each word.

"You heard me." She was undeterred. This had been a long time coming. "I spent ten terrifying days trying to save hundreds of lives, and your response to me when I come to the hospital is that it was my fault you were hurt."

"It is your—"

"No, it's yours. You spoke to Javier and brought me to the forefront of his mind. He would have found someone else to ask for help, but you interfered. So it's your own fault. I asked you a hypothetical question, and you couldn't let it go. You needed to be at the center of things, as always. The universe cannot be allowed to exist if it doesn't revolve around you. You couldn't help yourself and immediately went and blabbed to the world."

Her father had followed her into the room and gasped behind her.

"Carolina, I will not be spoken to in this manner."

"You will be spoken to in any manner I please. You are a horrible parent. You are mean, selfish, and uncaring. You are also a busybody, a control freak, and generally a bitch. The whole world thinks so. I used to get sympathetic looks from all your staff. They had no idea how I tolerated living with you." She turned to include her father. "Either one of you. You, the world's biggest bitch, and you, the doormat. Well, I'm done.

"You've both made your choice to barely tolerate me all of my life, and I've made my choice to not tolerate you any longer. And for the record, I know you take credit for any of my achievements behind my back while telling me I am not working hard enough and need to do better. The truth is, I am an amazing woman, not because of you, but in spite of you. So, fuck you, *stepmother*."

With that, Carolina turned and strode out of the house. Joy filled her soul at that moment. She knew that, later, doubt and worry would set in, but she also knew she'd done the right thing, and about bloody time, too.

Two days later Carolina took the last framed picture off the wall in her apartment and gazed at it. She and her parents on the day of her graduation from medical school. Her father looked perplexed, and her stepmother—well, she looked like she always looked, as if she wanted to be somewhere else doing anything but spending time with Carolina. Was Honey ever truly happy? Carolina put the picture in the box. She just didn't care anymore. She did feel for her father, but he'd made his choice.

She grabbed the tape roll and fastened the last box closed. The movers were coming tomorrow to put it all into storage for her. She looked around her apartment. It had been her home since she'd started working with Javier, yet she felt few emotions upon leaving it. It hadn't been a home; it had just been a place where she slept.

Carolina had never really had a home, a place where she felt safe and loved. But she was going to change all that. An image of Nick flashed in her mind, but she gave herself a mental shake and let it go.

She was learning to love who she was, and that was a good start to a new life. She'd come to realize that working for MSF was just a reaction to her parents. A type of rebellion. Honey had suggested the same, and as much as it galled Carolina, she had to admit Honey had been right. But she'd learned so much about herself and what she was capable of that, all in all, it had been an amazing experience. Now it was over, and Carolina felt truly content for the first time. She smiled as she walked back into the bedroom to get the black marker to label the boxes. She returned to the living room, marker in hand, and came to an abrupt halt.

Nick Taggert had made himself comfortable on one of her breakfast bar stools.

He wore a blue button-down with the sleeves rolled up to the elbow. The shirt matched his eyes perfectly. He was clean-shaven, but his hair was a bit longer and curling around his ears. His jeans were faded, but not by design, and he had on black dress shoes that matched his belt. It was a totally different look than she'd ever seen on him, and he was incredibly hot. Her heart picked up speed. This is what she'd dreamed of after Yemen, but since Ecuador, she never even let herself fantasize about their reunion. She thought Nick was gone from her life for good.

With one eyebrow cocked, he asked, "Going somewhere?"

Her belly rolled like she was on a ride at the fair. She smiled. "Yes, as a matter of fact, I am."

"Care to enlighten me?" He leaned back on the stool.

"Morocco. A friend has just started a medical clinic there, and she's been after me to come join her. I think it will be...interesting."

He grinned. "Interesting is a good word to describe Morocco."

"You don't like it?" she asked as she went over to the box she'd just taped up and labeled it *Family pictures*.

"I love it. It's one of my favorite places."

"Really?" She turned to meet his gaze.

He laughed. "Yes really. The food is amazing, and the people are friendly. There's lots to do, and they have great beaches."

"That all sounds good to me." She leaned over the stack of boxes. "What are you doing here?"

"I'm on...vacation for a few months. I decided to drop by and take you on that date I promised you."

She chuckled. "Just drop by for a date, huh?"

Nick's voice dropped. "Among other things."

It sent electricity skittering across her skin. "I guess you can buy me an early dinner." She pointed to her suitcases that were by the door. "My flight leaves late tonight."

"I see."

"How's your sister and brother doing? Did you end up

going to the wedding?" She noticed Nick's shoulders didn't tense and took it as a good sign.

"I did, and it was good to see them. I've been hanging out with them for the last couple of weeks. Getting to know them again. It's been…nice. Thanks for asking."

She dropped the marker on top of the box. "Well, I'm glad it worked out."

"How about you? How's your stepmother? I know she spent some time in the hospital."

She grinned. "Beyond the fact that she's home now, I have no idea, and I couldn't be happier. I've decided to do what I want from now on and not care what other people think. It's about time I grew up."

"Sounds like a plan. Have you heard from Guillermo? How are the Tarchuarani?"

"They're doing well. The vaccine worked, and life is getting back to normal for them, even though they lost a lot of people. The Ecuadorian government's investigation into Garcia is ongoing. In the end, Guillermo says Garcia will get a long prison sentence, but the President won't be touched. Typical politics, I guess."

"I saw on the news about Javier."

She grimaced. "Yes, that whole stupid story about how he had worked with Biodome to save the Tarchuarani and how Biodome was looking forward to funding many of his other projects. Javier always comes out on top. I should have known he would make a deal. He's got a huge ego and has always been desperate for the adoration of his colleagues. But I got to have my say at least."

"You went to see him?"

"Yeah. He tried to get me to come work with him for those assholes who helped to try to kill the Tarchuarani and us. Seriously. I couldn't believe he actually thought I'd consider it. I broke his nose. Flattened it like a pancake."

She grinned. "I heard he had to have surgery to have it fixed."

Nick threw his head back and laughed. "That's great. He deserved it for sending you down there on your own and not telling you the truth. Getting a payout from the company that tried to kill his beloved tribe from his childhood, the one that his dad cared for so much, shows you what an asshole he really is."

"Yup." She glanced at her watch. "How about that dinner?"

He slid off the stool and came over to stand directly in front of her. "Morocco, huh?"

She nodded. "Yes, Morocco."

"How would you like some company?"

The breath froze in her lungs. *Was he serious? Had she heard him correctly?* She swallowed hard and then found her voice. "Do you mean you want to come with me to Morocco?"

He smiled. "I could show you around a bit, help you get settled. How's your Arabic?"

"Nonexistent, really, " she murmured. She was still trying to get her head around the idea of Nick joining her in Morocco. *Wait. Had he said he was on vacation?*

"That's okay. They speak a tough dialect. Better to learn that first. It's hard to communicate in regular Arabic there. Do you speak French?"

She nodded.

"Then you'll be okay. Most people speak French."

As he stared into her eyes, a wave of desire started at her toes and raced its way up her body, leaving a tingling sensation in its wake.

"So how about it?" he said, a sparkle in his eyes. "Mind if I join you?"

She cocked her head. "I suppose that would be okay. I

don't start work for a couple of weeks. I wanted time to get settled." She smiled slowly up at him. "How long is your...vacation?"

Nick grinned as he pulled her into his arms. "A few months."

"Unpaid, is it?"

"Something like that." He tilted his head down and captured her lips in a scorching kiss. She was breathless when he finally lifted his head. "When's your flight? How do you feel about takeout on the way to the airport?"

She laughed. "That works for me. Actually, you can buy me dinner for the next few months in Morocco."

"Deal." He bent and kissed her again.

She wound her arms around his neck. Being in Nick's arms felt like home. That was Carolina's only coherent thought for the next few hours.

Keep reading for a peek into Lori Matthews
Break And Enter
Book 1 in the Callahan Security Series

SNEAK PEEK: INCINERATED
COAST GUARD RECON BOOK 2

From the bestselling author of the Callahan Security Series.

Meet Axel Cantor of the US Coast Guard's TEAM RECON. As in reconstructed. As in broken and needs fixing.

When a cargo ship gets stuck in the Suez Canal and an American journalist on board ends up dead, Axel is sent in to investigate. He didn't count on running into Sloan Bishop, another reporter, and the love of his life. Or maybe the hate of his life. Ever since he ended up in one of her articles.

Sloan is a driven reporter who fights to get the story at any cost, even if it means jeopardizing her personal safety. She's on board the *Sea Jewel,* to document the first-ever female pilot to navigate the canal. But it all goes sideways, literally, when the ship becomes mired in the narrowest part of the canal. As worldwide shipping backed up, the female pilot is blamed. But Sloan knows there's more to the story. When one of the other journalists covering the historic story is murdered, Sloan casts aside her misgivings to find out why.

As the body count rises on the stuck cargo ship both Axel

and Sloan must lower their defenses to work together to undercover the real motive. There is something much bigger at play here, so big that Axel has to call in reinforcements – his RECON teammates.

INCINERATED PROLOGUE
PROLOGUE

Omar Balik leaned back in his desk chair and stretched his long legs out in front of him, crossing them at the ankles. He looked out the window beside him at the Bosphorus strait in the distance. Istanbul was not only his home city but also his favorite. Usually he found the sight of it refreshing. Today it did nothing for him.

He ran his hand through his short black hair and closed his chocolate brown eyes. He was exhausted. His father had been riding his ass for months, years even. There was always something else to do. Some other crisis brewing. Omar had been working on the deal with the Germans for months. It was supposed to be all signed and sorted by next week. *I'll take a few days off then.* Surely, his father would agree that he'd earned the time off.

Hakan Balik had built the company from scratch, and they were one of the biggest textile suppliers in all of Turkey. The deal they were making with the Germans was massive. It would escalate them to the next level. It would put Omar's name on the map. He had put the deal together. He'd approached the Germans and got them to agree. This would establish him as a serious player in the textile game, and he would finally be out from under his father's shadow at last. His father would *have* to see him as worthy of inheriting the company *when* the deal came through.

It had been the longest fucking five years of Omar's life. His father had insisted Omar go to work for him immediately following his graduation from university. He'd taken no breaks other than a few long weekends, and he'd worked long hours, but it was never quite good enough for his father.

Well, this deal was good enough. It was better than that. It was the best deal to come to the company in a long time and he, Omar, had made it happen.

"I am the head of one of the biggest textile companies in the world," Hakan would say when Omar complained. "And you need to toughen up. Stop whining. If you want to take over the company someday, then you need to earn it."

Earn it. He'd been earning it since the day he'd been born. Always trying to live up to his father's dreams. It had been brutal.

Omar's gaze roamed over his office. He'd decorated it in the latest modern fashion. All white. White furniture, white walls, and white floors only broken up by splashes of color from the view over Istanbul and the Bosphorus and the artwork he'd purchased. It was perfect. "Divine" was what the designer had called it, and Omar agreed. One day he would be the god running the company. Best to look the part.

His cellphone vibrated, and Omar glanced at the screen. *Aysun.* He didn't feel like talking to her now. She was... boring. He only dated her because it made his father happy. He liked women who were more willing to party. That's what he needed right now. Some drinks and a good fuck. He was too tense about the deal with the Germans. He needed some stress relief.

There was a quiet knock on and the door before it

opened. His assistant, Fatma, walked in. She was carrying some papers. "You need to take a look at these." She walked over and placed them on the desk in front of Omar.

He nodded his thanks and then watched her walk out. She had her long black hair up in a bun. Her white blouse and navy skirt emphasized her generous curves. Fatma was someone he'd like to party with. She had a great ass and those big dark eyes. He'd love to hear her scream his name as she came. But she was off limits.

"You never fuck at the office," his father reminded him time and again. "It's bad for business."

When this deal came through, that was going to change. A lot of things were going to change around here. He sorted through the papers Fatma had dropped off. At the bottom of the stack was a magazine. As soon as Omar saw the picture on the cover, he froze. A familiar face smiled up at him. The face from his nightmares. The face of the man that his father had held up as the one to beat. And he never could.

Omar grabbed the magazine as he ground his teeth. It was one of those "top thirty under thirty" lists. *Tristan St. Claire, The Man to Watch*, the headline screamed. He was the best of the best because he not only tripled the size of his family's textile business, but he was also helping the environment and trying to help the less fortunate in Australia where he was from.

"Fuck!" Omar spat.

St. Claire had been his nemesis at Lassard Alpine Academy, the boarding school they'd both attended. They'd hated each other on sight. That had never changed. At least not from Omar's end. St. Claire was everything he was not, tall, blond, athletically gifted, and smart. Very smart. He'd come first in everything. Now here he was first again. He flipped to the article and started scanning. St. Claire was nothing short of a god, according to the magazine. And Omar? Where was he on the list? He flipped the pages until he found himself. Number twenty-three. Twenty-three. Not good enough. Not even close. That's what his father would tell him.

Heat crawled up Omar's neck to his cheeks. He swallowed hard. Even St. Claire's picture was mocking him. Where Omar's picture was taken at his favorite restaurant, St. Claire's was taken while he was working in a field. In a fucking field, for fuck's sake!

Omar crushed the magazine in his hands. Then he froze. His father would see this. He would call Omar into his office and ask in a deceptively quiet voice if he'd seen the article and what was Omar going to do about it? How was he going to stop coming in second to this man?

Last time Hakan had brought up St. Claire, it was at Omar's college graduation. He and St. Claire had, of course, ended up at Oxford together. St. Claire had taken extra classes and finished early with a double major. Omar had taken the standard amount of time and only studied one thing: business.

"This man is wiping the floor with you," Hakan had said. "You, you're known for your parties. What's he known for? Saving the fucking world! Developing some machine that will clean the oceans. Now he wants to revolutionize the textile industry so the materials are organic and produce less waste. What are you going to do? How will you beat him?" His father had been livid.

Omar had partied at university, and he'd thrown the best ones. No one wanted to miss any of Omar's parties. He'd been proud of that, but it wasn't good enough for Hakan. Why wasn't Omar out saving the world like St. Claire?

Omar released the magazine from his fists. He would have to face his father but, this time, *this time* he had an answer. The deal with the Germans. It would catapult them to number one. Their revenue would be the largest. His father would be the top man in the number one textile company in the world, and Omar had been the one to make it happen. His father would *have* to be proud of him then. He was ready this time. Ready for when his father called.

The phone on his desk beeped. He hit the intercom button. "Yes?"

Fatma's silky voice came through the phone. "Your father wants to see you."

Omar smiled as he stood. He straightened his tie and put on his light grey suit jacket. Things were definitely going to change, and it was all due to him.

INCINERATED CHAPTER ONE

CHAPTER ONE

Sloan Bishop wiped sweat off her forehead with the back of her arm as she lay on the single bed. It had to be a hundred degrees in the small cabin she'd been assigned. As the only woman reporter on board the *Sea Jewel*, she got her own room, but it was the size of a broom closet with just enough space for a bed and a small table with a lamp. There was a tiny mirror over the table. Probably for the best since she was sure she looked like shit.

The size of the room didn't bother her. Neither did the beige walls with their peeling paint or the ultra-thin mattress with its thread-bare blankets that she was now lying on. Even the smell, a mix of metal, salt water, and years of wear and tear didn't really get to her. This was actually a step up from some of the other places she'd stayed, and wasn't that a sad statement? What kind of life was she leading that a cell-like room was a step up?

No, the thing that bothered her the most was the fact that the air conditioning was non-existent. Oh, there was a vent, but the limp flow of air coming from it was more like a hot breath than a cool breeze. Being in a metal box in the middle of the Suez Canal in spring was not her idea of fun. Normally, it would be in the eighties, but they'd been having abnormally hot days with temperatures in the high nineties, and it wasn't getting much cooler at night. She imagined this was what being slow roasted in an oven would feel like. At least, it wasn't summer. She'd be well cooked by now.

She checked her watch. Just after two a.m. local time. Her navy T-shirt was sticking to her, and her khaki cargo pants were making her legs sweat like crazy, but she didn't feel comfortable sleeping in anything less. If something happened, she wanted to be fully dressed and ready to go. Plus, the lock on her door was flimsy. She wasn't taking any chances.

Sloan rolled off the bed and slid her feet into her sneakers. It was too damn hot to sleep. Maybe if she went up on deck, she could at least get a breeze. The Suez Canal is an engineering miracle. The man-made shipping channel connects the Red Sea and the Mediterranean but it's also a pathway through the desert. She hadn't paid enough attention to *that* fact in her research. She would have packed more deodorant. The desert was supposed to be colder at night and it was, just not enough to cool down her room before the sun rose again.

She piled her shoulder-length dark brown curly hair on top of her head and pinned it there. A few tendrils escaped but Sloan didn't bother redoing it. It was the middle of the night and too damn hot to care what she looked like. Having it off her neck made her slightly cooler. She glanced in the mirror and wished she hadn't. Her big blue eyes had large dark circles around them. The lack of sleep was definitely getting to her.

This had seemed like a dream assignment when she was picked to be on board when the first Egyptian female canal pilot took her first ship on its voyage through the Suez

Canal. Canal pilots work for the port authority. Sloan composed the introduction to the article in her head: the pilot's job is to guide and advise the ships on how to proceed through the canal. It's a big deal for a woman to succeed in this traditionally male-dominated field.

Perhaps dream job was a bit strong, but it was a hell of a lot better than running around, trying to scrape together scraps of other people's interviews to write a story. Charlie Philips, a good friend of her father's before he passed away, had pulled strings to get her the assignment, and she was truly grateful.

Being a newspaper reporter was damn hard in this day and age. She wasn't a full-time employee, and she had to shop around everything she wrote. She'd been lucky enough to break the story about the Tarchuarani, and *The New York Times* had run that and all of the follow-ups she'd written, but she needed to come up with something good if she was going to keep getting picked up by the Times. Sloan liked to win, and she was ambitious, but even she had to admit that a lot of being a reporter was luck, and hers seemed to have turned sour lately.

Sloan opened her door and slid quietly into the hallway. She moved as silently as possible through the freighter. Being one of the few women on a ship filled with men meant keeping her head down and staying out of the way.

Most of the crew was nice enough, but a few of them looked more like mercenaries than crew and they made the hair on the back of her neck stand up. She had no intention of running into one of them at this hour. Extra security for the ship and cargo, the captain had explained when she'd asked him about the abnormally large number of security guys on the ship. Security for something to be sure but what remained to be seen.

After breaking the story for *The New York Times* about

the Tarchuarani, she'd thought she might get an actual job offer from them, graduate to being a salaried employee, but after a couple of weeks, that bubble had burst and she was back trying to dig up something of interest. When the Egyptian government had announced they had their first female Suez Canal pilot, she'd jumped at the chance to interview the woman. Zahra Nabil would be the name on people's lips for at least a news cycle or two. She would be held up as an example of how things were changing in North Africa and the Middle East, albeit much more slowly than women would like.

Or she would have been if catastrophe hadn't struck, and the ship hadn't gotten wedged sideways in a narrow part of the canal. The bow was stuck in the left bank and the stern was beached on the right bank. There was even some talk that the stern might be stuck on the bottom of the canal as well. The ships that had been ahead of it made it through but now the *Sea Jewel* was blocking all the canal traffic from both directions, and Zahra Nabil was famous for all the wrong reasons.

Some people, the hardline religious groups were pointing to her and saying she was why women shouldn't have jobs that were traditionally male. They'd given a woman a chance, and she'd screwed up. Now everyone could see why women shouldn't have certain jobs.

Stupid.

And Sloan was pretty damn sure Zahra hadn't screwed up. Sloan had been on the navigation bridge when Zahra was advising Captain Svensson on entering the canal. She heard the argument between the two about the wind and how it might not be the best time to take the ship through. They'd started in English, but then Zahra had switched to Arabic and got the interpreter to translate to Norwegian. Sloan thought she switched languages because the captain wasn't listening, and Zahra was probably worried she wasn't communicating well enough for him to understand. Or, at least, that was Sloan's theory. Who the hell knew what really happened? She spoke neither Arabic nor Norwegian.

Then the second in command, Rohan Patel, had pushed her and all the other reporters out of the bridge onto the bridge wing, saying it was dangerous to have them in there. They were distracting the captain. With a strong wind pelting sand at them, the rest of the reporters left except for her and Eddie. He'd stayed right along with her like she knew he would. Eddie had a nose for a story just like she did.

Sloan was about to leave when she felt something, a shuddering of sorts. Zahra and several other people on the bridge looked around in alarm. Then the whole ship rocked slightly. Patel saw her standing outside and signaled to one of the other officers. The officer chased her and Eddie out of the area. That had been two days ago and it was the last time she'd been able to speak with the canal pilot about anything.

Sloan quietly moved through the doorway out onto the walkway on the left side of the ship. *Port.* She needed to use the proper terms so she didn't forget them. She'd had to look them up continuously when she'd written the first story about the ship getting stuck.

There was a slight breeze, and it felt like heaven. The air was dry, and she knew from experience that she would end up with sand in her hair and her mouth—the fine flecks that were carried on the breeze stuck to everything—but the cool air of the desert night was worth getting sandblasted.

She walked along the rail toward the bow. The outside lights were dim, but a bright waxing moon provided enough light to cast shadows. She made her way to a set of steps up to the main deck. There, she picked a container to lean on. She was about a third of the way down the ship toward the bow. The spot gave her a nice view of the canal as well as a cool breeze. It also meant she could see anyone coming from either direction. Of course, they could also see her, but she didn't imagine too many people would be around at this hour.

She sat down, stretching her legs out in front of her and crossing them at the ankles. What could she write about? Being on a massive container ship was interesting for her, but she wasn't sure it would be something people wanted to read. It was daunting being a small speck next to all the containers. The sheer volume of them was intense. She'd filed her story about the ship being stuck as soon as the incident happened and filed several more updates, but there was nothing new to report. Well, nothing she was allowed to report.

She'd tried to ask Zahra about the shudder that she'd felt, but the captain had cut her off. He said Ms. Nabil couldn't talk about it because the incident was under investigation. Sloan had tried to approach the woman twice more, once during lunch and once when she bumped into her in a hallway, but each time Zahra had refused to speak to her. Her entourage, two of the "security" men, was determined to keep anyone from having any meaningful exchange with her anyway.

Sloan might have let it go if the woman's eyes weren't so filled with terror. There was more to this story, but how to dig it out was the question. How could she get access to Zahra without those goons around?

She closed her eyes and let the breeze roll over her skin. They weren't allowed to leave the ship yet. As far as the world knew, everyone was staying on board because they would be free any minute now and the historic journey would continue, but the reality was different.

She'd asked to get off but was told by the captain it wasn't possible at the moment. He hadn't given her a reason, and when she'd pointed out the interpreter got to leave immediately, the captain just told her to leave his office. Her reporter instincts were screaming at her but so was her well-developed sense of self-preservation. There was something major going on. She just had to figure it out before anyone else did, or at the very least, at the same time so she could get credit for breaking the story.

Off in the distance, a door clanged loudly, metal hitting metal. She heard footsteps and then the murmur of voices. The voices were getting louder so they must be coming closer. It sounded to her like people were arguing in English. She could catch the occasional odd word.

She peeked around the edge of the equipment and looked up at the flying bridge. Two men stood arguing in the middle of the deck, but at this distance, she couldn't tell who they were. There were too many shadows.

Then one took a step back, and the light hit his hat. Eddie. Who else would wear a fedora? He was the only guy she knew who could get away with the hat and the swagger. He was a damn good reporter, and it didn't hurt that he was charming as hell. He claimed his dimpled smile and his charm were his secret weapons. Sloan didn't doubt it.

Eddie was definitely arguing with the other man. He had his hands up in front of him like he was trying to calm the other guy down, but the other guy wasn't having it. He took a step closer to Eddie. He was taller than Eddie, and the moon shone off his hair, but she couldn't tell the color. They were too far away. A good chunk of the men on board, including the scary security guys, were taller than Eddie. The man moved closer still, and Eddie backed up another step.

Should she go help him out? There was a sound off to the right, and a man came into view. Sloan watched as he headed in her direction. He was one of the normal crew, but she still did not want to be discovered. She had mentally divided the crew into the "normal" category, those who were usually thin and strong with deep tans and calloused hands and the "secu-rity" group, those who were bigger, very muscular, less tan, and meaner.

They scared the crap out of her.

Her heart pounded, and her palms broke out in a fine sweat. Why was she panicking? She wasn't doing anything wrong, but this whole situation had her spooked. Being stuck on the ship and knowing no one was telling the truth made her nerves raw. The crew member stopped about twenty feet away, checked something on his hand-held device, and then turned and left again.

She tried to calm down. She took a deep breath and then another. Her heart rate was returning to normal. She was turning to look at the two men once more when she heard a sickening thud. Her stomach rolled. She instinctively knew the sound. Her hands started shaking. She slowly leaned out a bit and looked back up at the flying bridge. Eddie's body was lying on the deck about fifty feet away. He wasn't moving. She wanted to move, to go to him, but her limbs refused to move. Her mouth was open in a silent scream.

The sound of boots on the deck cut through her paraly-sis. The light that had illuminated Eddie went out and then a man appeared from the shadows. She got up and scooted around the corner of a shipping container so they couldn't see her. She leaned out just so she could see Eddie with one eye and then quickly held up her phone. She snapped several pictures of Eddie before a man with a flashlight came to a halt next to him.

It was too dark to make out the man's features, but it was probably the man who had been arguing with Eddie moments earlier. She couldn't tell anything about him except he was tall. Two more men joined him on the deck. They all looked down at the body while they were talking. They were still too far away for her to hear exactly what they were saying. She wasn't even sure they were speaking English. A lot of the crew didn't and the security guys appeared to be from all over the world so they spoke in various languages at different times depending on who they were speaking to. Sloan snapped another few pictures, but she knew it was too dark to make any of them out. She wanted to turn on the flash, but then they would know she was there, and who knew what they would do to her. When her stomach rolled, she tried not to retch.

The three men all bent down and picked up Eddie's body. Sloan whirled around and leaned back against the container. She swallowed hard, fighting to keep the lamb kofta she'd eaten for dinner down in her belly. Eddie's head had lolled at an odd angle and his eyes had stared sightlessly at her. He was dead, no question.

She closed her eyes and then opened them again. She needed to get up to the flying bridge to see how the incident had happened. Her friend was dead, and she needed answers. But her limbs wouldn't move. She got up and tried to take a step, but her knees wouldn't cooperate. They wouldn't move. Nausea rolled through her. Maybe just another couple of minutes. Eddie was dead. There was no rush now.

She sat on the cool steel decking and tried to gather herself. Her hands shook so she balled them into fists. Eddie's voice rang out in her head. *Get it together, doll. You've seen dead bodies before.* Which was true, but it had never been someone she knew and never under those kinds of circumstances.

She heard voices again and another sound like water being sprayed. *Come on, doll, you have to go after the story. Snapping the pictures was quick thinking. Don't stop now. Follow it wherever it takes you. Get to the truth.* She could see his goofy grin in her mind's eye.

"I will Eddie. I promise," she murmured as she wiped

away a few tears that had escaped and rolled down her cheeks.

A few minutes later, after more tears than she would ever admit to, the sound of multiple voices reached her ears. The smattering of multiple languages seemed more excited somehow. They were also much closer. She got to her feet and walked out from behind the container. The captain and several crew members, both regular and security, were standing on the deck closer to the cabin area. They were looking over the side.

Sloan bit her lip. She didn't want anyone to know she'd been on deck when Eddie fell. *Or was pushed*. At least not yet. She needed to find out what people were saying before she said anything herself. Moving quickly, she stepped out from her spot and crossed to where the others were standing. With any luck at all, they would think she came from somewhere in the midst of the containers tied down on deck, *if* anyone noticed her at all. They were all engrossed in something that was happening over the side of the ship. Maybe they were finally getting freed from the deep sands of the canal.

Sloan hesitated as she passed the spot on the deck where Eddie had fallen. There was nothing but a wet spot now. No blood. Nothing to mark where he fell. Certainly nothing the police could use as evidence of a crime. That was the sound she'd heard. A hose spraying down the metal decking. All signs of Eddie's demise had disappeared.

Her heart rate increased again. How dare they? How dare they erase him like that? He deserved better. Sloan marched over to where the captain and crew had gathered at the rail. "Captain Svensson, I need to speak with you," she demanded.

He glanced over his shoulder at her. "It will have to wait, Ms. Bishop." He gestured over toward the railing. "I am dealing with a serious situation at the moment." His accent was thick, so it was hard to understand him.

"I'm afraid I must insist," Sloan said. The other men glanced at her but returned their gazes over the railing. She put her hands on her hips. Was he seriously going to ignore her?

The captain turned to her. "Ms. Bishop, we lost a person overboard. They are pulling him out now. You'll have to wait." He turned back to look over the side again.

Sloan frowned. Someone overboard? She moved closer to the railing and the gathered crew made room. With all the lights shining on the water from the side of the freighter, it was bright as day out there. The water looked black but calm. There were people out on the decks of all the other boats that were waiting to enter the canal, watching what was going on.

Sloan leaned over the railing slightly and gasped. On the deck of a smaller boat was Eddie's body.

READ THESE OTHER EXCITING TITLES BY
LORI MATTHEWS

Callahan Security

Break and Enter

Smash And Grab

Hit And Run

Evade and Capture

Catch and Release

Cease and Desist (Coming Soon)

Coast Guard Recon

Diverted

Incinerated

Conflicted

Subverted

Terminated

Brotherhood Protectors World

Justified Misfortune

Justified Burden

Justified Vengeance

Free with Newsletter Sign Up

Falling For The Witness

Risk Assessment

Visit my website to sign up for my newsletter

ABOUT THE AUTHOR

About Lori Matthews

I grew up in a house filled with books and readers. Some of my fondest memories are of reading in the same room with my mother and sisters, arguing about whose turn it was to make tea. No one wanted to put their book down!

I was introduced to romance because of my mom's habit of leaving books all over the house. One day I picked one up. I still remember the cover. It was a Harlequin by Janet Daily. Little did I know at the time that it would set the stage for my future. I went on to discover mystery novels. Agatha Christie was my favorite. And then suspense with Wilber Smith and Ian Fleming.

I loved the thought of combining my favorite genres, and during high school, I attempted to write my first romantic suspense novel. I wrote the first four chapters and then exams happened and that was the end of that. I desperately hope that book died a quiet death somewhere in a computer recycling facility.

A few years later, (okay, quite a few) after two degrees, a husband and two kids, I attended a workshop in Tuscany that lit that spark for writing again. I have been pounding the keyboard ever since here in New Jersey, where I live with my children—who are thrilled with my writing as it means they get to eat more pizza—and my very supportive husband.

Please visit my webpage at https://lorimatthewsbook s.com to keep up on my news.

Made in the USA
Las Vegas, NV
17 November 2023

81036264R00203